On *Wearing the Cape*.

"This is such a solid book that I have difficulty believing it is Mr. Harmon's first novel. The story is polished, well edited, tightly plotted, and stocked with interesting characters. Like Peter Clines' debut novel, Ex-Humans, this sets the bar so high for follow-up work that I'm sure Mr. Harmon is feeling the pressure."

Michael of Dover, Delaware

On *Villains Inc.*

"A riveting follow-up to Wearing the Cape, Harmon's sophomore novel continues to satisfy those of us who need a fix of well-written superhero fiction. Fans of the first book will not find its sequel lacking, and while it might be more of an adjustment to readers who haven't picked up the first book, it stands well enough on its own."

Avander Promontory

On the *Wearing the Cape* series.

"The Wearing the Cape *series is the gold standard that all other superhero novels should aspire to.*"

Hero Sandwich

<u>Books by M.G.Harmon</u>
Wearing the Cape
Villains Inc.
Bite Me: Big Easy Nights
Young Sentinels

<u>Short Stories by M.G.Harmon</u>
Omega Night

Young Sentinels

A *Wearing the Cape* Story

by

Marion G. Harmon

For Kaitlyn
We all wear masks.

DEDICATION

To Stan Lee, L. Frank Baum, and all purveyors of modern myths.

ACKNOWLEDGMENTS

Becoming too many to count, now including a lot of fans who are only too happy to point out editing and even *continuity* errors (someday I'm going to go online and find a *Wearing the Cape* wiki). Thank you.

Episode One

Chapter One: Astra

We got a breather after taking down Villains Inc., sort of, or a chance to change to a slow dance anyway. I missed Jacky, but the new members fit in nicely, even if sometimes I thought Watchman was trying to kill me. While peace didn't exactly descend on our great metropolis, we didn't see all-out supervillain battles slaughtering civilians and wrecking real estate. Except for the one Omega operation — and the public never found out how close that one came to ending the party — nothing came along to bust up the good time.

But Charlie was about to dance the foxtrot and we didn't have enough partners to fill her card.

Astra, Notes from a Life.

We were just lucky I was flying morning patrol instead of sitting in class when Potowatomi Woods decided to destroy the Chicago Executive Airport.

"Shelly? Are you seeing this?"

My patrol circuit had taken me over the greenbelt that ran through the suburbs and communities of North Chicago. From my height, the wave of green erupting out from tiny Potowatomi Lake looked like a surging carpet of leaves — at ground level, the edge of waving trees had to be moving faster than the panicked early-morning joggers using the forest park's running trails could run. And they *were* running.

"*Jeepers creepers!*" Shelly whistled in my ear. Now that she was Galatea, she couldn't tap our old neural link to see with my eyes anymore, but she remained my Dispatch wingman and had full access to the microcam they'd built into my mask. I'd have head-smacked her if she'd actually been with me, but her joke nailed the scene below perfectly.

"Get more eyes on it, Shell!" I yelled. "I'm going in!"

I dropped, counting on her to bring the rest of the team into the loop — even to light up the whole Crisis Aid and Intervention dispatch tree; we were *so* going to need the help. Watching morning joggers flee along the trails under trees suddenly whipping like they were being beaten by hurricane winds, I wondered if every hero in town would be enough.

There was no wind, and the trees were *growing*.

"*The spread is stopping at the Des Plaines River,*" Shelly reported as I landed hard on the running path, leaping up to shatter an oak branch as it curled down to sweep a crowd of stumbling joggers.

"Stay on the trail! Cross the river!" I yelled to them.

"Thanks!" one of the men gasped. He and a buddy pulled a hobbling, pink-suited fitness granny into a two-man shoulder carry, and they all broke for the turn and the bridge. Popping up above the trees again, I could hear panicked cries on surrounding trails and wanted to swear. There was only one of me! I saw my joggers hit the wider trail and left them to drop back down and pull a middle-aged jogger out from under a tree root that looked like it had thrown itself over him. I lifted him into a fireman's carry as the forest groaned around us.

"Any help would be nice, Shell!" I shrilled.

"*Speed-evac commencing, sheesh! Rush, Crash, Sprints, and Sifu are on it!*" Further down the trail, a jogger disappeared in a blur. *Yes!*

Lei Zi broke in. "*Astra, I want you to get back upstairs, stay available for any extraction assistance our speedsters may require. Copy?*"

"Get high, assist evac where necessary, got it."

With Sprints from the South Side Guardians *and* Sifu helping our own, Dispatch had fielded all four of the city's fastest speedsters. Dropping my shaken but unhurt jogger across the river, I got back in the air — high enough that I could see the leading edge of the whipping green tide. Yeah, like I was going to stop any of that with my little maul. *Ajax's* maul. What would *he* have said? Use a bigger hammer? There was no hammer *big* enough.

"*Astraneedalittlehelphere!*" Crash's run-together call for help reached me through Dispatch, and Shelly obligingly threw a red bracketing box up on my new contact lens display. I dropped again, breaking through swirling tree limbs to find the narrow forest path beneath. Crash struggled to pull another twisted root off of a trapped morning hiker's legs. Around us the path *shrank* and suddenly I was in the middle of a childhood flashback of *Babes in Toyland* and The Forest of No Return.

"Go!" I ripped the exposed root out of the ground with more force than I needed to — I'd lived in fear of the old, gnarly trees on our street for *months* after seeing that show. Crash pulled the hiker up into an assisting carry and disappeared in a red blur, and I launched up through the thickening canopy of branches. Back up in the open air, I spun around slowly, trying to put a frame on what I was seeing.

The trees weren't walking, they were *growing*; seeding, springing up, the spreading edge of the growth made it look like they were on the march. But the growth wasn't in a neat circle — it had started at Potowatomi Lake and was moving south, expanding to fill the entire greenbelt between the Des Plaines River and the Tri-State Tollway as it went. *Why* —

The sharp *crack* of snapping roadway cut off my thought. The south edge had reached Dundee Road, the four-lane road that ran through the wide greenbelt to connect Wheeling to Northbrook. Arching roots buckled the pavement while new saplings burst up and out, trapping morning commuters.

"Evacuating Dundee Road! Get here now!" Choking down rising panic, I dove again to snatch up a minivan full of screaming carpoolers and drop them gently on the other side of the river, flew back for more. How many could we get out before growing green started grinding people under?

"*Watchman and Variforce on station!*" Lei Zi returned as Watchman dropped out of the sky above me, Variforce in tow. "*Continue vehicle evac!*"

Watchman joined me in picking up and airlifting cars while Variforce configured his golden aura of variable-property forcefields into whirling blades, decapitating climbing saplings before they could thicken and crush trapped cars.

"It's worst on the edges!" Watchman shouted. Coming down, he'd had a wider perspective, and he was right; as the edge swept south of Dundee, the frantic, twisting forest growth left behind slowed. He smashed a tree aside as it tried to anchor itself across a sporty convertible, extracted the terrified driver. I lifted a delivery truck up and out of the danger zone and returned for more, listening for more intervention calls.

"*The next road south of Dundee is a ways down, Willow Road,*" Shelly informed us. "*But then there's the Northbrook Hilton on the wrong side of the river, businesses south of that. The Northside Guardians are assisting evac there, we've got other teams moving up, and here we come to save the day!*"

The Sentinels floater came diving out of the morning sun, Shelly-Galatea hitching a ride outside the canopy. Variforce swept a landing zone clear and Lei Zi, The Harlequin, Riptide, and Seven piled out. Rush appeared in a red blur.

"Dam Number One is still out from the spring flooding," he reported to Lei Zi. "So Dam Woods Road is clear and there aren't many civilians in the woods south of Dundee. We're ahead of it, boss."

Galatea settled next to me. Her newest silver-and-blue chrome body was almost completely covered in weapons and magazines, but she'd had a strong hand in designing it. Underneath, it looked even more like her old Robotica sketches than the first model. She leaned in as close as her shoulder-mounted missile racks would allow.

"Wow — so *Babes in Toyland*, isn't it?"

I snorted before I could stop myself, turning it into a sneeze that wouldn't have fooled any of my old schoolteachers. Coach Gorski would have asked me to share the joke with the team — and then do laps around the field.

Lei Zi considered the scene, expressionless as if she was looking at a traffic accident that needed unstacking, as if we weren't *standing in the middle of a walking forest*. I tried to ignore the crunch of roots, the groaning wood, the crashing beat of branch against branch as they fought for room. And the weird smell — churned earth and tree sap.

She nodded. "All right, then. We move south, follow the edge, leaving no one inside the live zone. Watchman, finish clearing Dundee, then catch up. Astra, stay on backup with the speedsters. The rest of us will follow the edge. Everyone?"

There were salutes, nods, *got it bosses*, and other affirmatives, and we got to it. I flew through the creepy trees answering Dispatch calls, but like Rush said, there weren't many left to pull out. I rescued an older couple — she'd gotten trapped between two new oaks and he wouldn't leave her behind, so I carried them both out — then there was the early morning birdwatcher who'd started snapping pictures instead of, oh, *running for his life*. He'd gotten knocked down and concussed by a fleeing white-tailed deer smarter than he was.

Everyone got dropped at the designated evacuation stations across the river, and Galatea's drone video showed the rate of expansion was slowing, short of Willow Road. Maybe —

"The woods just jumped the river!" Shelly-Galatea sang out. *"It's headed for the Chicago Executive Airport!"*

And that was just *wrong*. Sure, Dundee hadn't stopped it, barely slowed it down, but for a forest, even one growing fast as a wildfire, to take a *right turn*?

An airport — a place where things happened at high speeds and lots of flammable fuel lay around just waiting for Bad Stuff to Happen — comes equipped for disaster and able to let the whole wide field know to Head For Cover; sirens began wailing as the forest threw itself over the road and across the parking lot at the main terminal buildings in a cacophony of ruptured pavement and breaking glass. Explosively erupting trees thrust cars aside and smashed into the glass-sided buildings, and the screams inside told us not everybody had seen it coming soon enough to get out.

Despite being further away when the alarms sounded, Watchman and I hit the airport before anybody but the speedsters. Watchman simply battered trees down or uprooted them in the loose soil and torn paving while I swung my short-handled maul with both hands, shattering reaching trees as they tried to thicken and dig into the buildings.

"They'll tear the terminal apart!" I shouted.

He pulled another tree. "Rush's team is on it! All we've got to do is slow it down!"

Thunder shook the air as Lei Zi arrived to make her contribution; lightning split trees from crown to roots, throwing chunks of tree and boiling sap with each strike. Riptide splashed down, changing from flying spray to pissed-off man in an eye blink. Trees went down, sliced away at their bases as he called water from the air and forced the flow into pressure and velocity high enough to make a water-saw that could cut rock. Variforce arrived to add his whirling forcefield blades, edges only microns thick. Smoke-trails in the sky ended in erupting craters as Galatea emptied her missile racks into the trees on both ends as they tried to outflank our zone of destruction to get at the buildings to the north and south.

"*Mainbuildingemptied!*" Rush reported over the general channel, voice ragged.

Lei Zi's orders came sharp and fast. "*Let it have the building! Speed-evac the neighbors! Everyone work the sides, let the forest have the field!*" Good plan — beyond the terminal lay wide open space, acres of runway and parked private and small commercial planes for us to channel the growth into. But how long could we keep it up?

Just another twenty minutes, as it turned out, even with the help of another dozen heavies from the Guardian teams. The new spur of forest made it more than halfway across the airfield, grinding under hundreds of millions of dollars worth of private and company planes, and then just ran out of steam. Growth slowed, trees shivered, reaching branches turned skyward, and there was nothing to fight; just a dense wild of primeval trees where a commercial airfield had been.

Which was good, because my arms were on fire from wrists to shoulders and I was gasping for air. I could barely feel my hands, and had to force them to release their grip on Ajax's maul. Everyone tends to think that, just because you have superhuman strength, you don't get tired. Don't I just *wish*.

Everyone was covered in bits of oak, hickory, and other tree species that should have known better than to mess with us; my hair was sticky with maple sap, and the tiny splinters of wood that had worked their way under my mask made my face itch.

"Is — is that it?" I gasped.

"*The greenbelt is quiet,*" Shelly confirmed. "*The south edge stopped growing when the woods took its turn.*"

"Look sharp, everyone." Lei Zi landed, the shimmer of air made by her electrostatic field barely visible. "They're evacuating the surrounding neighborhoods, and the DSA is sending an environmental team. We don't know who started this, and until we know it won't *restart*, we're on station."

Seven handed me a water bottle, looking disgustingly fresh; he and The Harlequin had stayed with the floater for this one, ready to drop in with reloads for Galatea or make a quick evac.

"Thanks." Trying to ignore the fluttering stomach he inspired in me ever since our "kiss" the night of the Omega operation, I took a long draw, hand shaking, stopped. "Do you hear that?"

"What?"

My super-duper senses would drown me if I couldn't ignore uninteresting sounds and Seven might be distracting me, but I *always* heard explosions in my range. I looked west as the distant boom turned into a roar, pointed.

Seven squinted. "Is that what I think it is?"

"Yep." I could see details he couldn't, and the boy climbing into the sky on top of a brilliant column of explosive flashes was wearing a red varsity jacket.

"Breakthrough?"

"Probably."

"Does he know what he's doing?"

I sighed, handed him the bottle. "Probably not. He's screaming. Tell Lei Zi I've got him."

Chapter Two: Megaton

Everybody wants to be a superhero, because nobody knows what a shit job it really is.

Malcolm Scott, aka Megaton

"Mal! Dude! *Look* at this!" Tony nudged me hard for the third time, eyes glued to his epad.

"Malcolm Scott!" Mr. Winfield called, going down his list.

Ignoring Tony, I raised my hand. "Here." Winfield didn't even raise his eyes to look; he'd stopped looking at anybody years ago, which made it easy to ditch his class — just get a "friend" to answer to your name, he didn't even have to disguise his voice. Sophomore year, I'd been as many as three kids a day in his class, until I got onto the wrestling team and was able to shrug off those kinds of friends.

"Tina Halls! Rachel Kerry!"

Even out here, standing in the middle of the soccer field in our designated "homeroom station" for what had to be the third Emergency Evacuation Drill since school started, Winfield acted like he talked to disembodied voices. At least here, the Emergency Class Monitors — Doug Lee and Tiffany Bright this fall, poor guys — were checking the same lists. Tiffany held one of the class's two emergency phones, the ones they were supposed to call us on to tell us where to go or if the drill was over, in a death-grip. I wanted to tell her to lighten up.

"Bradley Card!"

I pushed my fists deeper into my pockets. A varsity jacket was good for two things: putting you out of range of the bullies and keeping you warm, and fall was coming early this year. The field hadn't had time to warm up yet, and I wondered how long they'd keep us out here chilling until they decided the drill was over.

"Tiffany Bright!"

Dude, she's standing right beside you.

"Mal, will you freaking *look* at this?" Tony shoved the epad in my face, almost dancing. "Not. A. Drill!" I pulled my hands out and managed to grab the pad before he dropped it. It would have been okay in the grass, but he was enough of a spazz he'd probably have stepped on it.

He had it set to *Powernet*; not a shock — he wasn't a supergeek, but only because they were the worst kind of geeks and he wasn't interested in getting beat on or hazed every other school day. The pad showed a streaming video identified as news helicopter footage.

The Sentinels and every Guardian team in Chicagoland were fighting a bunch of *trees*.

Holy *crap*.

The information bar scrolled team stats and facts, going on about how Riptide had obviously leveled up — he'd never shown the ability to use his water jets to *cut* before.

"Dude, it's at the municipal airport! No wonder they've got us out here!" Tony took the pad back, keeping it tilted so I could see, and we watched mutant trees waste a bunch of connected buildings the infobar said was the Chicago Executive Airport terminal, the place rich guys kept their jets. The capes kept working the edges, like they were trying to trim a hedge growing faster than you could cut. They blasted trees, smashed them, sliced them, and the bar kept referring back to Riptide's new attack style. *Trees are eating the airport and* that's *their priority?*

"That is one bad-ass Crip," Tony said admiringly. He had more than just my attention now, and we became the center of a crowd as half the class tried to look or asked what we were watching;

nothing like this ever happened out in the burbs. I smelled lavender, turned, and had to grab Tiffany before she hit the grass.

"Sorry!" she said as if my bumping her was her fault. She got herself straight and flashed me a smile when I let go of her arm. "What's going on?"

I shrugged, not sure what to do with my hands. "It's not a drill."

"Oh, no!" She dropped her clipboard and spun around, looking up like she expected the capes to airdrop right into the soccer field. I bent and scooped the board up from the wet grass, reattached the emergency phone she'd clipped to it, but kept hold of it all as some of the guys laughed. She flushed. Skinny and awkward, Tiff was probably the girl who would bloom into a supermodel after graduating, but guys are dicks and right now it sucked to be her.

"I've got to take that to the flagpole," she explained, ignoring the guys. "Now that everyone's been counted."

"So let's go." I started off and she skipped to catch up.

"You don't — Thanks. For back there."

I shrugged, still walking. "Not a problem."

"So, do you think they're going to evacuate us?"

Coming around the side of the school, we watched school buses pulling into the half-circle drive that separated the front parking and the flagpole lawn from the main doors.

"I think that's a strong maybe." We crossed between two buses already in line, engines idling while they waited to move up and load, and joined the crowd of students and adults at the flagpole.

Vice Principal Blevins stood at the center of the group, looking at his own clipboard and talking into his phone. He nodded and said something as a packed bus pulled away. The sound of the engines made it impossible for us to hear him, but after all the drills he was probably totally into finally *doing* it. Tiffany pulled herself up straighter and reached for the clipboard.

"Thanks Mal, I — Wait! The phone!"

Shit. It had come unclipped somewhere. I looked around behind us, spotted it back in the drive. One of the buses we'd passed between had moved up but the other just sat there, and of course the phone lay on the pavement in front of it.

"I'll get it!" I darted back across the drive.

"No, wait!" Tiffany cried, but I crouched and grabbed it. I turned back to her, heard the engine throttle down, and the lurching bus smacked me to the ground.

Shit. The pain of my head hitting the drive blinded me, but I felt the scrape of the pavement as the bus fender caught my jacket. Blinking my eyes clear as the rolling bus twisted my body into line with it, I saw the right wheel coming at my legs, *knew* it was going to roll right over me. Panicking, I kicked, the wheel caught my shoe, twisted my foot. My scream went higher than Tiffany's at the wrenching pain, sharper than any wrestling hold and hot pressure erupted beneath my skin, flared out as I *pushed.*

The concussive explosion hammered my ears and I barely heard the shriek of wrenched metal, couldn't see through the blinding flash. I blinked, blinked again, desperately scrubbed my eyes and tried to hear through the ringing. *What —*

The bus, what was left of it, lay twisted on its side twenty feet away from me — the entire front window buckled and craze-cracked and pushed deep into the cabin with the rest of the front of the bus. Blood painted the webbed glass, dripping onto the drive. Tiffany wouldn't stop screaming.

The crowd around Blevins added its noise, mute in my ringing ears, and my stomach rolled with a way too familiar nauseating panic. I tried to stand but couldn't make my legs work. Blevins yelled something, pointing, and two of the campus-cops headed for me, pulling the guns we always teased them about — like they'd shoot kids. I scrambled uselessly backward as heat and pressure flashed through me. I exploded again, and kept exploding.

"*Aaaaaaaaaaaaah!*"

I rocketed into the air, acceleration squishing me like a thrill ride. Hersey High dropped away under my feet and my ears popped hard as the buildings shrank and the clouds got more personal.

"*Aaaaaah stop!*"

It did. The burning thrust bursting from my bones vanished — and with it the roaring flaring column pushing me up. Now my stomach decided we were falling. *Nope*, the buried science-geek in me said. *We're just decelerating, coasting to apogee. We'll be falling in a few seconds.*

Awesome — I'd burned through all my adrenaline and my brain had decided that sixty seconds of non-stop terror were enough, so I was going to die calm and sarcastic. *I should have been nicer to Tiff—*

"Are you done?"

I flailed about my center of gravity. A tiny, blonde sticky mess, lightly swinging a bell-shaped chunk of metal that probably weighed more than I did, hung in the air beside me.

"Because I can give you a lift."

Chapter Three: Astra

"Life is unfair. I know that. I may have been born with a silver spoon in my mouth, but I have a dead older sister I was too young to remember, childhood cancer I remember too well — seventh grade was **not** *fun — lost my BFF to terminal stupidity ... But my breakthrough was a* **good** *thing. I was able to use it to save people. I got cool, helpful powers. The public loved me, mostly. Lots of breakthroughs aren't so lucky."*

Astra, Notes From A Life.

"It happens more often than you think."

Blackstone looked old — well, *older*. Thanks to iron discipline and Chakra's help (a regimen of aerobic exercise and tantric magic, *don't* ask) the white-haired magician and ex-Marine could run a marathon and hold his own in mixed martial arts, but his age showed when he was tired. Or sad. Like the night in the chapel when he'd held me while I cried like a child.

I'd dropped Malcolm Scott off in the infirmary for the Dr. Beth Treatment; just a look at his head and foot and a physical — our team doctor wasn't asking for any power demonstrations yet. Now Blackstone, Chakra, and I sat in Blackstone's office and watched Dr. Beth run Mal through his tests. Early news footage of the accident scene — the smashed bus and the ring of emergency vehicles —

filled a second screen and showed glimpses of Watchman and Seven, who Lei Zi had sent over to the school. Hersey High. The rest of the field team remained out at the airport.

On Dr. Beth's table, the kid had taken off his scraped and soiled varsity jacket. Average looks, brown hair, brown eyes. He was pretty big, overweight but in a fit way, decent muscles under the fat. I guessed linebacker or wrestler.

Chakra looked up from the screens, brow furrowed. "What happens more often?"

"Deadly breakthroughs." Blackstone sat back and closed his eyes, pinching the bridge of his nose. "Many breakthroughs come from trauma inflicted by other people, and the reaction is often extreme. Look at Safire — a nice enough stripper going to business school until her abusive boyfriend nearly beat her to death and she broke through as a B-Class Atlas-type. She killed him with one punch before she knew what she could do."

"Jamal — " I said before I could stop myself. I'd stripped off my filthy mask and wig and washed my face, but hadn't changed before quietly joining them.

He nodded. "Crash, indeed. Fortunately, you and Rush stopped him from doing anything unforgivably permanent to the young hoodlums who attacked him."

Chakra watched Dr. Beth poke and prod our new problem. "Poor kid," she said, echoing my own not happy inside-voice. "What will happen to him now?"

"Legally? Nothing. Sometimes it's hard to prove whether a breakthrough-related death was intentional or not, but in this case the death of the bus driver was clearly accidental." He sighed. "But mentally?"

Oh, yeah. This was going to mess up the kid's head in so many ways. I must have given something away; ever-alert, Blackstone looked up at me, a bit of the twinkle back in his eyes.

"Could you take this one, my dear? Young Mr. Scott's parents are on their way, but Dr. Beth will be done with his poking and prodding soon, and we don't want the boy left alone too long.

Heaven knows, he could work himself back up and start blowing holes in the Dome. And Chakra and I are rather...fragile."

I opened my mouth to protest, closed it as Blackstone's point sank in. How sensitive was the kid's trigger? Would any normal person who upset him now end up drippy paste on pieces of wall? Dr. Beth was *insane* just being in the same room with the unexploded boy without knowing what could set him off.

Jeez, calm down, he hasn't blown anyone else up yet. Shelly wasn't in my head anymore, but I could still hear her sarcastic response.

I nodded, wishing Seven were here. "Okay. How long have I got?"

Blackstone focused on the screen, where Doctor Beth had the boy's shirt off. "I would guess you have perhaps ten more minutes before the good doctor is finished."

And Dr. Beth's friendly talk could calm anybody down, giving me just enough time to change. I ran.

"*Want to hear all about him?*" Shelly whispered in my ear as soon as the door closed behind me. I didn't answer until I was safe in the elevator.

"*Tell* me you didn't hack the school's student files."

"*Hey, it's a good cause.*"

"No, it's *not*. It's curiosity and we'll know soon enough the legal way. We've *talked* about this." Boy, had we *ever*, and she wasn't *listening* and one of these days...

I wanted to bang my head against the wall, but even Dome elevators could be fragile. Hindsight is always perfect; you've had time to think about the decisions you made, maybe more information than you had then, enough time for horrible realizations.

The night of the Omega operation, I'd asked Shell to hack a military system, to redirect a missile, and now the U.S. military knew that someone could dance through their most vital defense systems and play with their hardware — which made her a Threat To National Security. To make it worse, she wasn't a *person*, not legally. If she kept exposing herself, if they traced the hack to her ...

even if the ACLU had three cases of Verne-science augmented animals and one unique car working their ways through the federal courts, Shell had no rights.

Some nights, I woke up in cold sweats from a nightmare that they'd come to take her away and there was nothing I could do about it but go full supervillain. It was my fault, and I had to fix it.

One problem at a time.

"Later, Shell. Right now, I have to go poke a boy and see if he explodes."

Megaton

The doc gave me a lollypop and an epad displaying directions, and nudged me out the door. Which was really *weird*, cutting me loose in the middle of Sentinels central. I just followed the map, trying not to think too much; the parentals would be here soon and Mom would be freaking out. No idea what Dad would be doing — he'd hated the wrestling thing since it "distracted" from my studying to make something of myself. What he'd think about *this*... I ran fingers through my hair, winced at the goose-egg the doc had promised wasn't a concussion.

Testing the ankle brace the doc had fitted me with, I limped back past Laconic Bob in the lobby. He'd said four words when Astra introduced us, two were my name, and he didn't add to them now. Turning a corner, I went through a door and walked onto a movie set.

Okay, not a movie set — but I'd seen it in *The Sentinels I, II, III, IV,* and *V*. I'd been directed to the Assembly Room. Huge oak table, check. Sentinels "S" engraved above their motto — "We stand ready" in fancy Latin — check. Huge screens, ceiling-mounted projectors, check. The I Love Me wall full of pictures and news clippings was new, or at least not in the shows. Looking closer, they even had a black-framed cover of Time Magazine's special Funeral Edition. *Right...*

"Morbid, isn't it?"

I spun around and nearly tripped as my ankle screamed and heat and pressure shot through me, leaving me lightheaded. The tiny blonde standing behind me smiled.

"You didn't blow anything up, so that's good."

She wore dark blue cargo pants and a tight white athletic shirt with Astra's star symbol on it in sparkly silver. Platinum blonde hair pulled back in a short ponytail framed a freshly scrubbed face. I went cold, like I'd fallen in ice water.

"Are you freaking *crazy*? I could have — "

"Gone off? I know." She hopped up to dangle her legs off the edge of the conference table. "That's why I'm here — I'm tougher than a bus. How's the bump?"

"You're tougher — wait — you're *Astra*?" Her smile widened while I tried to make it work in my head. I hadn't believed the tabloids, but she couldn't be *legal*, let alone a full-on superhero; *Tiffany* had more going on under her shirt than she did, and... *Sure, stare at her chest, moron* — great *way to make an impression.*

She actually laughed, and my face burned.

"My bust is mostly in my costumes," she said with an easy shrug. "For superheroes there's a certain look that's expected...and wow is this conversation familiar." *Huh?* She smiled at something, shook her head. "FYI, I turned nineteen last spring, which makes me totally the opposite of jailbait."

The burn deepened. "Shit — I mean, sorry..."

She actually looked sympathetic, not disgusted like she smelled dog crap on my shoe or something, and that just made it worse. She wasn't supermodel-stunning or anything, but she was cute and confident, the kind of girl who wouldn't have given me a second look last year.

When I didn't add to my stupid, she waved it away. "Moving on, may I call you Mal?" Her easy smile disappeared and she looked older, all the teasing gone. "We need to talk. About your accident."

Five minutes later, I wanted to kill myself.

She'd sat me down and sunk into a chair beside me, tucked her sneakered feet up, and walked me back through the steps that led to my launching screaming into the sky. The smashed bus. The blood.

"The driver, he's..."

"Dead." She watched me carefully, eyes wet but steady. "He probably didn't even have time to realize what happened."

The hot pressure was back, swelling beneath my skin. I couldn't breathe. "I think, I think I'm going to be sick." Instead of recoiling, she scooted forward and put a hand on my knee.

"Nothing — Nothing I say right now is going to help," she said earnestly. "But your breakthrough saved you, protected you, and you didn't mean to hurt him. It was a thing, it's awful, it *happens* sometimes, and it's absolutely not your fault."

"The hell it's not!" I was on fire.

Her grip tightened, a soft vise. "*No*, it's *not*. But it's a debt. You owe a life, so save a life. It won't make up for it, but we all have debts we can't repay."

"Save *who*?"

"Start with yourself and work outward." Letting go, she sat back but kept her eyes on me. "So, are you going to..." She mimed an explosion.

I realized what she'd done and almost hurled for real. "You just tried to, to — "

"Twice," she agreed. "I meant to sneak up on you, too. Did you know your body temperature spiked both times?" Her smile came back, tentatively. "So I'm pretty sure you're safe to stand next to, at least while you're here. And we'll help you figure it out so what happened today won't happen again. Promise."

Chapter Four: Astra

Today, Representative Mallory Shankman spoke out in favor of the hotly debated Public Safety Bill, which would require the certification of dangerous breakthroughs and establish a public database of the names and addresses of all known superhumans. In the representative's words, the recently passed School *Safety Bill is "no more than a symbolic Band-Aid." Representative Shankman also responded to this morning's tragic breakthrough-related death with a call for more research to "detect these unstable breakthroughs before they kill more innocent people."*

Chicago News.

That nobody had died in the woods was an absolute miracle. After handing off Mal to Willis (the Dome's majordomo's lunch creations were better than therapy), I went and lit a candle in the chapel and thanked the white jade statue of Quan Yin, Mary of the Pagans, while waiting for the team to come home.

My lucky early spotting had helped, but also the wet chilly morning had meant the greenbelt paths were lightly used, Chicago now had *four* A Class Minuteman-types able to evacuate in between seconds, and the wave of growth started at the lake and didn't jump the river until we'd had time to gather most of

Chicago's heavies. Mal's bus driver was the only related fatality and I lit a candle for him too, and one for Mal.

The FBI and the Department of Superhuman Affairs got permission from the mayor and landed a field team to examine the site before noon. Once they determined that there was nothing remaining of whatever had driven the explosively guided growth, the rest of the team came home. Blackstone gave them time to shower and change into fresh costumes before summoning us all to the Assembly Room to give us the bad news.

"Humanity is destroying itself with its gasses and wastes. It breeds to fill every remotely habitable ecological niche, destroying biodiversity throughout the world. It wrecks the equilibrium of ancient ecosystems. It is a plague upon the Earth. Humanity is now served notice: it will voluntarily clean its house and reduce its numbers, or it will be removed as a threat to the continuation of life on this planet — "

Blackstone froze the Viewtube file and left the symbol of the Green Man on the screen. The leering face of twined leaves, it was the only visual the file had shown. He looked around the table. We were a much nicer looking bunch than we'd been an hour ago, and we filled the table in our by-now completely predictable order.

It had really started happening without our paying attention to it, the way cliques form and freeze in school, and now the way we sat said everything about the team. Seven and Riptide and Rush tended to hang together off-duty. Chakra and Blackstone were an item of course, but with Blackstone doing research so much, Chakra and The Harlequin formed the Girl's Club. Lei Zi didn't mix much, Vulcan rarely came out of The Pit, Watchman and Variforce trained as obsessively as I did, and Variforce had family (so did Riptide, but he had a nanny for little Carlos). I was younger than the Seven-Riptide-Rush and Chakra-Harlequin sets and had a civilian social life I was trying to keep alive, so I sort of floated outside all the circles and Shelly and Jamal usually grabbed seats by me.

"This video-file appeared online two hours ago," Blackstone said. "The DSA assigns a high probability that this 'Green Man' is indeed the individual responsible for this morning's events."

"He doesn't see any need to be original," Watchman observed. My fellow Atlas-type *sat* at attention, fresh Army-green jumpsuit and black uniform beret pressed and set with military precision.

"Yes," Blackstone agreed. "He lifted his manifesto almost verbatim from Deep Green's official declaration." Groans rose around the table.

Riptide sneered. "Those the *pajeros* that think the world would be a nicer place with less of us in it?"

"Indeed. Deep Green is one of the FBI's top-list domestic terrorist groups. Among other things, they call for the abandonment of industrialism and urbanism and the reduction of humanity to no more than 100 million souls. So far, they have demonstrated their resolve only through extreme vandalism — destruction of infrastructure of construction companies, energy companies, buildings, equipment. Millions of dollars of damage but, as yet, no one has been hurt."

"Yet." Watchman didn't raise his voice, but looking over I could see that his fists were clenched on the table. "If the Green Man is with them, they weren't careful today." Watchman had been in no more personal danger than I had, but this morning was a special kind of nightmare for breakthroughs like us; as fast, tough, and strong as we were, we hadn't been that much help and if we'd been fighting alone, the disaster would have just rolled right around us.

Blackstone nodded, acknowledging the point. "The DSA team has provisionally ruled the new forest safe, and City Dispatch has thrown every drone it has into the sky to monitor the rest of the greenbelt and city parks. All Crisis Aid and Intervention capes with applicable powers remain on alert, and for now that is all we can do. So now let's talk about the elephant in the room."

The screen changed to an aerial view of the new woodland. It sprawled across roadway and field, a wild green growth thrown across the orderly lines of the metropolis.

"There have been florakinetics, plant-controllers, before, but never on this scale. The strongest previously has been Vitaceae, an Italian hero. He can control an acre of heavy-growth plants at one time. *This*," Blackstone pointed at the screen, "is far beyond A Class. In the same way that the terrakinetic who triggered the Big One last January was beyond A Class."

I felt like someone had dropped an icicle down my throat to grow in my stomach — by everyone's faces, a feeling shared around the table.

"Didn't the DSA investigation decide that Temblor's powers had been boosted by his psychosis?" The Harlequin asked.

"Yes, and they labeled the new power level Ultra Class and concluded that it had been a one-off event. Now, I'm not so certain. Both events were acts of terrorism. Both are beyond what anybody thought possible. I believe it may be possible we're facing something new, breakthroughs whose psychosis or fanaticism boosts their powers to unwitnessed heights. We know nothing about the Green Man yet, but I will be digging into Temblor's history; perhaps the DSA investigation missed something."

He looked at me when he said it. Or Shelly. We both knew what he meant; the three of us knew that Temblor had been used by the Dark Anarchist — that the time traveler had somehow *triggered* the exponential boost to the psychotic villain's powers.

"I'm going to assume the worst-case scenario," he concluded. "If someone out there has found a way to reliably boost breakthrough powers, we need to know. We could be facing a lot more than explosively growing forestlands, so stay ready everyone. Astra, would you remain behind?"

I'd expected Lei Zi and Quin to stay, too, maybe talk to me about my scheduled testimony in court tomorrow, but they left with everyone else. Shelly looked questions at me, and Chakra gave me an encouraging smile in passing. The ice in my stomach thickened. What was going on?

Not Shelly, please, not Shelly.

Blackstone sighed and stood. He *really* didn't look good — even with Chakra's help, he had to be burning his candle at both ends. Normally, he moved as if he stood on an intimate stage, but now his fingers played with his epad without direction.

"Hope." Another slip — he always called me *Astra* when I wore the mask. "We're going to launch a cadet team, and I want you to lead it."

Not Shelly, and nothing I'd dreamed of. "But — *why?*"

He smiled at that.

"Why, when I've always resisted fielding minors even where it's legal?"

I nodded. Different states had different laws; in Illinois, so long as they didn't deploy them directly into "combat situations," CAI teams could field minors sixteen years and older if they had emergency-appropriate powers. Still, Blackstone had brought Crash on only provisionally; he trained with Sifu, sidekicked with Rush, and wasn't part of the regular field team. Shelly...was a special case, but I was pretty sure he'd brought her on the team just to keep an eye on her.

He sighed again. "The Green Man is not in the Big Book of Contingent Prophecy."

Oh. That explained the private talk. Blackstone now belonged to a secret society of *three*.

Shelly and I had taken to calling the huge database of future histories the Teatime Anarchist had left me the Big Book of Contingent Prophecy, and we really hadn't known what to do with it. What kind of person left that kind of thing in the hands of an *eighteen year old*? Even if he'd seen lots of potential Future Hopes and been totally impressed — which I didn't *know* since he'd also blocked all direct historical references to me and my potential lives.

After our fight with Villains Inc., I finally asked Shell to sort and classify the thing. She ignored stuff that *might* have happened but definitely wouldn't now because of the Big One, pulled together all the stuff that might *still* happen, and we gave the whole thing to Blackstone — who promptly freaked over the fact that someone had entrusted the contingent future histories of mankind to an *eighteen year old*.

Well, *yeah*.

Seeing I was following his track, Blackstone nodded.

"In the futures the Teatime Anarchist left us to see, Ultra Class superhumans do not begin appearing until much later — and their existence is one of the things that nearly brings future society to collapse. Temblor was an obvious insertion by the Anarchist's twin."

He ran fingers through his hair, disordering gray locks. "We can spend a great deal of time debating the altered chains of cause-and-effect that are leading to the accelerated appearance of threats like the godzillas and the Green Man. What we can't ignore is that a bad situation is getting worse, and in some ways we are the victims of our own success."

Now, I blinked. "I don't understand."

"Today is a perfect example. The Green Man made his debut *here.* Not New York. Not L.A. Atlas and the Sentinels created the template for the post-Event superhero and superhero team, and since then Chicago has been *the* place for breakthroughs to come and make a name for themselves — the reason we have so many CAI teams. Culturally, we're the superhero center of the world, the focus of superhero fandom.

"But the Guardian teams are mostly street-heroes, my dear. Today, all the added effectives from the other CAIs only doubled our weight where it mattered, and when a new supervillain wants to make a big statement, he comes here. Last spring we were the only freshwater port to get a godzilla. The Green Man started here for the same reason. And although the future files are far from a sure guide, in all previous contingent trends, once begun, the proliferation of Ultra Class threats continues."

He looked away. "And in those previous futures, we still had Atlas."

I swallowed past the block in my throat, nodded. Reading the Sentinels' pre-Big One future files still wasn't easy for me, as useful as they might be; I was blocked from reading the ones involving me and in most of the older ones Atlas, John, died hard. Sometimes sooner, sometimes later, but always hard.

"So — So, we need a bigger team. More heavies."

"Indeed. More like young Mr. Scott, if he proves able to control his power. But we can't simply expand. People identify with a smaller team, and if we just bulk up on more big guns, we'll start looking like an army."

That I understood. I'd spent too much time with Mom and now with Quin to miss his point. It was all about *optics*, public perception.

Blackstone tapped the table. "You and Shelly and Jamal have helped to counter that impression, which has been a very good thing. And Hillwood Academy has been trying to convince us to take part in their internship program for many years now. As much as a third of their graduating students go on to wear the cape, and their program allows chosen seniors to finish their education while imbedded in a sponsoring team. We can start our new members in their senior year, keep them until twenty-one, bring new members in as they come of age. If they do well with us, they'll be able to find positions in any CAI in the country.

"And me?" The ice in my stomach was gone — replaced by mutant butterflies. *I'm only just nineteen! The media still thinks I'm underage! I'm Girl Friday!*

He smiled warmly. "The junior team would of course include Shelly and Jamal, and you did very well in our fight with Villains Inc. last spring. It would look very odd if you *didn't* lead it, don't you think?"

"But—" I shut my mouth. Under the screaming panic, my inside-voice was trying to get my attention.

Hillwood.

I'd spent sleepless hours searching through the future files for a solution to Shelly's dangerous situation. In all the previous contingent histories, legal protections for Artificial Persons had been years away, and Legal Eagle didn't see anything on the near horizon. But there might be a *superhuman* solution, and one of them was at Hillwood now. Maybe. If *that* hadn't changed.

Blackstone had no idea, but he was waving an opportunity so golden I hardly dared look at it for fear it would disappear.

"I want my own picks," I blurted, dread and hope leaving me dizzy.

"Agreed. Anything else, my dear?"

Everything. I wanted to run screaming — instead I took a breath.

"No. No, I'll do it."

"Excellent. I believe that we can bring on three more, giving you a team of seven." He handed me an epad. "Let's talk for a moment about power-sets and team balance."

Shelly bounced on my bed, reached over, and poked me.

"Admit it, Hope, you were wigged."

She'd ducked into my rooms on her way to somewhere else and caught me reading. Blackstone thought it unlikely, but for all we knew the Green Man might pop up any time, and we all had to stay ready to suit up as long as the Sentinels remained first in the response queue. I was back to wearing everything but my mask and wig, cape, and the breastplate armor I could buckle on in a second. Shelly needed the assembly rack upstairs in the launch bay to bolt her into her blue and silver "Fighting Galatea" gear and loadouts, so she dressed civilian.

I swatted her hand away, resisting the urge to hide my epad — she'd just hack it if she thought there was something I didn't want her to see — and sighed. "No."

"Really? The tree outside your window made you cry for *weeks* after that silly movie."

Raising the pad higher, I ignored her smirk. "It kept scraping the window when the wind blew. I was *seven*, Shell — I was scared of a lot of things."

"Doctors, trees, frogs..."

"Hey, they jump at you!" Eventually Dad had cut back the tree branch, but until then I'd slept with the parentals when Shelly couldn't stay over. Mom and Dad never understood it; I'd get scared and cry, then Shell would tease me until I cried about *being* scared. "Mom expects you for dinner Friday night."

She nodded absently, rolling over to lie on her stomach and pick blanket-fluff. "So..."

I switched off the pad and laid it on the bed, stretched. My eyes burned from hours of browsing the Hillwood Academy files and preparing my arguments, trying not to think about court tomorrow or about Seven (he wasn't becoming an obsession, *really*), and I was glad to see Shelly for guilty reasons.

She was still Shell, my BFF, but we weren't joined at the hip anymore. I wasn't the girl who'd followed her everywhere. When I wasn't training or studying or patrolling I was at school or trying to absorb all the procedures and manuals and action-histories Blackstone was dumping on me (in bigger and bigger piles, recently), and she liked to hang with Crash. She didn't try and take my time with the Bees — didn't even ask about them — and only went out with me now when I went home.

We were a team again, *different*, but I could still read her; I couldn't tell her about Hillwood and my new plans, not yet, but I'd been expecting this conversation anyway.

"Mal isn't in the Book either, is he?"

Shell rolled back over and kicked her bare feet. Only her too-smooth skin hinted that she wore a body fabricated in Vulcan's labs.

"No, he's not." Which made sense and echoed Blackstone's observations. It was statistically *un*likely that many post-January 1st superhumans from the old future, the one without the Big One in it, would be appearing now. Instead we'd be getting more and more new and different superheroes and supervillains that the Teatime Anarchist had never seen or read about. Like the Green Man. One change led to another in a domino cascade; alter one tiny detail and change could propagate pretty fast.

Like how I would have never have become Astra if TA's evil twin hadn't changed my future by dropping a freeway overpass on me.

Like how I would have *died* in Washington fighting The Ring, if TA hadn't asked Atlas to bring me onto the team and keep me in

Chicago. Like how The Ring would have attacked Washington later, instead of hitting us early in Los Angeles because of the opportunity created when DA triggered the Big One and pretty much derailed the future.

Like how Atlas wouldn't have died instead of me.

"Hope?" Shelly tipped her head back, looking at me upside down. "You've got that look."

"Sorry." I rubbed my eyes with fisted hands. "M'okay, seriously. I just..." I looked for a distraction she'd accept, found it and realized my face was heating up. Knowing she could tell just deepened the flush.

"Do you think it's okay for me to be — to like someone now?"

I realized I should have known better than to give her that kind of ammunition when her eyes lit up. They didn't look artificial at *all*.

"Eeeeee! Ohmygodwho?" She'd never stop now.

"Seven," I whispered. "He kissed me the night of the Omega operation, but it wasn't like..." It wasn't like for luck, or like the time he'd playfully kissed me at Metrocon last year. It was different, like he hadn't been sure I was coming back and wanted to get it in *just in case*.

Did I *want* it to be different? I'd finished the mission, gone back to pizza with the Bees, and Seven hadn't said anything about it. Not a word, which was just *wrong*. Who does that? And I didn't dare ask, but The Kiss kept getting bigger and bigger in my head and the current security situation meant Blackstone was sending us out together *all the time*. My dreams were getting interesting again, and his blond mop and chin dimple were getting *way* too fascinating. Nope, not obsessed.

I dropped back against the headboard, and Shelly rolled to her knees so she could get a better look. I closed my eyes but she'd seen enough.

"OMG," she breathed, whatever else she'd come in here for forgotten. "I'd been wondering — you used to crush at least once a year and it's been almost that long. But you never had one of them *die* before."

I groaned and grabbed a pillow to hide behind. "Don't *say* that. What do I *do*?"

"Kiss him back!"

The pillow turned my scream into a muffled protest. She grabbed it and pulled. Since she was as strong as Vulcan could make her and I didn't want feathers everywhere, I let her tug it down.

"Seriously Hope, you are *such* a chickenshit. You *never* make the first move. Or even the second unless they're stupefyingly obvious. We could pass him a note: 'Check *yes* if you want to go out with me.'"

"Don't you dare!"

She rolled her eyes. "Duh — we're not in middle school anymore. But I'm not letting you do this again, so *one* of us is going to pin him to a wall and ask what his intentions are." She slid off the bed.

"Wait!"

"One week," she agreed with a laugh and a wink. "Then if you haven't, I will. Study if you can..." She was out the door and on her way to her next scene of mischief before I could think of *anything* that didn't involve threats of dismemberment. My head hit the headboard again. *Thunk, thunk, thunk.*

Vulcan could always put her back together, anyway.

Geez, what had I done?

C'mon Hope. You fight godzillas, intercept nuclear missiles, give safety lectures to six year-olds. You literally threw yourself at Atlas. How can you be so scared?

It didn't even occur to me to wonder where she was off to.

Megaton

Seven showed me my rooms, like he was staff and not *Seven*. He hadn't talked much while my parents were here and we listened to Legal Eagle explain everything. Astra hadn't been lying — nobody was saying what happened had been my fault, thanks to school security cameras that caught the whole thing. But the superhero-lawyer explained what had to happen, now that I was a "known risk." I had to get trained, and if I couldn't control my *gift*, I had to cooperate in finding ways to mitigate it or "go where I wasn't a danger to anybody."

I was all for that; Mom couldn't stop crying and Dad would barely look at me. They signed a bunch of papers turning me over to the state, then they were *gone*.

"Mal," Seven repeated.

"What? Sorry." The guy had been freakishly cool about me all day; everyone else except Astra — who hadn't come back — had been *careful* around me. Not that I blamed them. Now he leaned against "my" computer desk, watching me look at my room. Rooms.

He grinned. "Astra told me it's the nicest jail she's ever seen."

It took me a moment to catch what he was getting at. "This happened to her?"

An easy shrug. "In a way. Ask her about the downside of super strength some time." Tapping the narrow brim of his fedora, he straightened up and headed for the door. "Night, sport. Big day tomorrow."

"Say hi to Sammy and Dean for me." I didn't know why I said it — sure he'd been watching me like entertainment the whole time, but he'd been friendly about it. He just laughed.

"I will." And he was gone.

"Don't rob any casinos," I said to the door. Yeah, that would secure my geek-cred.

I looked around. Damn but Seven wasn't lying, either. Entertainment room and kitchen combo, bedroom, bathroom and walk-in closet. The place was a five-star hotel suite, *not* what the wrestling team got when we traveled for matches. The bag Mom had packed sat on the bed with my plastic-wrapped varsity jacket. Somebody'd stitched and dry cleaned it.

Kill somebody and you got *service*.

I was getting warm. Shit.

Someone "knocked" on the door, which meant they touched the screen outside and the door gave a musical two-note bell chime. Seven? Astra? That Willis guy? The main room was big as our living room back home, and they had chimed twice by the time I got there.

Not Astra. "Hey there!" A redheaded girl pushed her way in, followed by a black kid less certain of his welcome. They looked close to my age, and I tried to guess who they were in costume. The black kid had to be Crash, but the girl I had no idea.

"'Sup?" He bumped my fist while the girl claimed the center of the room and spun around to check everything out. She wore a baggy off-the-shoulder t-shirt that said *I died origin chasing and all I got was an extended warranty.*

What?

"It needs posters, but it'll do," she said. "And we've *got* to upgrade the game system."

What?

Crash put his hoodie down to look around, shrugged. "Go with it, dude. It's easier if you don't fight her." He stuck out his hand. "Guess we ought to, you know, introduce. Jamal. This one's Shelly, or as I like to call her, The Ghost in the Machine."

"Hey!"

Jamal ignored her.

Okay... We shook. "Mal," I said. "Where's the machine?"

He grinned like I'd passed a test. "You're looking at her. Cutting-edge autonomous transformable gynoid unit — the best Vulcan can make. I've got a bet with Astra over how long it takes her to break this one."

It just kept getting weirder. She stuck out her tongue at him. "Says someone named *Crash*. In public I'm Galatea, and lots shinier. Did they stock your fridge? Woohoo!" She double-fisted some soda bottles by their necks, tossed a Dew to Jamal, a Coke to me, and hopped onto the couch to land cross-legged.

"So." She popped the top of her Coke. "Do we get to keep you?"

Jamal dropped to the floor. The kid was track-and-field lean, even his tight cornrows streamlined front to back, but compared to the hyper redhead he moved like he had all day to get anywhere.

"What the girl is trying to say is, are you going to train here? Or are you going to the Academy?" He said it like there was only one.

And there really was, at least for me now. Legal Eagle had dropped the news on me; the Illinois Legislature had just passed the School Safety Bill, which meant that known breakthroughs couldn't stay in the public school system — they were too scared someone like me might go nuts and start popping bully's heads off or something. Even if I hadn't blown up a bus driver, for me it was Hillwood Academy, the boarding school that took in the juvenile breakthroughs for half the Midwestern states.

After all that work to get on the wrestling team...

I thought about how weird it had been to walk into the Sentinels' Assembly Room today. How would it feel to go to Hillwood? *Hillwood* the show was in its fifth season, the student council had saved the world twice, and a secret society of student-villains was plotting to take over the school.

And then there were the news exposés that said it was really half boarding school and half military academy, that *really* half the student body had serious breakthrough-related trauma and mental problems.

I couldn't taste my Coke. "Maybe I belong there. I kill people."

Shelly blew a raspberry. "You killed *one* person, by accident. Sucks, but that's like... I don't know what that's like, but you make it sound like a lifestyle choice! Do you want to run out and kill everyone now?"

"No!"

"There you go. Besides if you'd, you know, really had it in for that bus driver, you wouldn't go to Hillwood — you'd go straight to the juvie breakthrough wing of Detroit Supermax."

Suddenly I was burning inside-out.

"Hey! Breathe! Breathe!" Shelly gasped, wide-eyed and flapping her hands like she was trying to put out a fire. Jamal rose into a crouch. I stared at the carpet, focused on the bottle in my hand, and the heat dropped until I didn't feel like I was shining through my skin.

Okay, okay, no bang, all good. "How could you tell?" I asked finally. It wasn't like it *showed.*

"Vulcan made my eyes to spec, duh." She dropped her hands. "Might as well get them in infrared, match Ho — Astra on something."

I gripped the bottle, put it to my forehead for the chill. "Are you guys *testing* me again?"

She looked away. "No. Well, giving you practice, really. We think you need to, you know, learn how not to sneeze. Crash could have got us both out of here before you went off, and we can always repaint."

"You're all freaking *crazy.*"

The insane robot girl actually looked hurt. Jamal put his bottle down and stood up. "Hey, you walk by falling."

"And what is *that?*"

"Sifu stuff. Like, if a mighty pine falls in the forest we can't see for the trees, does it hit the bear crapping in the woods? Later. C'mon Shell."

She shot me a look promising this was *so* not over, and marched out with what she probably thought was dignity. Crash gave me a shrug that could have meant anything and closed the door behind them. I resisted the urge to kick the half-empty Dew he'd left. I'd probably blow it up.

Shit.

Chapter Five: Astra

"Traffic remains blocked along Dundee Road between South Milwaukee Avenue and the Tri-State Tollway. Despite protests from the Sierra Club, which is attempting to get the new old-growth forest declared a national park, the city has directed The Crew to clear the growth from the connecting roads so that repairs may begin.

"The Green Man has released a second Internet video, demanding the city close its nuclear power stations and tax private vehicles to build a larger public transportation system. The Office of Emergency Management recommends citizens keep evacuation packs handy and be ready to relocate to a temporary living situation; for most Chicagoans, such arrangements are typically reciprocal guest-agreements with family or acquaintances living in different parts of the city."

Chicago City News

Blackstone looked up from his desk when I knocked on his open door. Blackstone's office door was always open; anyone getting past Bob had a right to be there, and an open door said "No secrets in here."

"I have my choices."

"Do you, my dear?" No *are you sure?* or *That was quick.* His smiling eyes weren't a mask, really, just the surface of something deeper.

"May I see them?" he invited. He still hadn't finished his morning coffee. The way I felt, I needed the stuff administered intravenously.

I had stayed up until it was pointless to go to bed, but I was ready with my facts and my arguments, and one tap on my epad sent the file to his mailbox. He opened it to read while I sat and looked around to keep from watching and fidgeting. There was always plenty to look at. *Atlas* had kept his office nearly featureless (he'd spent as little time there as possible) but bookcases covered Blackstone's walls. The few open spaces were covered by framed vintage show posters of Blackstone the Magician, his inspiration and namesake. The one exception — obviously Chakra's touch — was a framed lotus sand-mandala behind his desk. Bright trophies looked back at me from the book-filled shelves, awards from Blackstone's years as an actual stage magician. A crystal goblet with gold engraving, *Best Sleight of Hand Performer, World Magic Awards 1998*, held pride of place.

I twitched my cape, settled deeper in my chair, and read the rest of the awards without getting up — super-duper vision was socially useful — then started counting the books whose names I recognized.

Blackstone looked up. "Well, my dear, you have not failed to surprise me." A touch to his keyboard closed his office door, and he leaned back to stroke his beard. Again, no *Are you sure?* "Will you explain your choices?"

Okay. Deep breaths.

I opened the first page on my epad, back straight like I was presenting a Foundation event report. The school files didn't tell everything, of course — only the power descriptions, grades, rankings and psych-profiles available to potential recruiters. Personal information, even legal names in the cases of students who'd managed to keep their breakthroughs secret, had been redacted. The first profile picture showed a boy, fair-skinned and hair black as coal, thick eyebrows over a scowl; he hadn't been happy getting his picture taken.

"All of my choices are from the senior class, close to their official eighteenth birthdays, and qualified for the internship program. The first is Reese Lasila. He's an A Class aerokinetic from Saint Paul. His dad is Jetstream, the aerokinetic hero on Saint Paul's only CAI team, the Saint Paul Protectors. He had his breakthrough three years ago, making him one of the rare family breakthroughs — even rarer since he actually 'inherited' his father's power-set. His aerokinetic power-set is well rounded, giving mobility, offense, *non*lethal offense, and of course it's great for fires and storm rescue. He's spent the last year at Hillwood, after an incident that got him expelled from public school. Nobody was badly hurt. His chosen codename is 'Tsuris.'"

"And?"

I looked up from my pad. "The Big Book of Contingent Prophecy has him going full supervillain in eight years as his powers grow. He'll pull together a team of midflight hijackers and rob a string of planes of their high-value cargo. He gets caught and sent to Detroit Supermax, and the psychiatrists there diagnose him with severe father issues. I think if we give him an early chance to shine at least as bright as his dad, give him mentors, there's a good chance he'll stay on the side of the angels."

Blackstone nodded. "Next?"

A breath and a page-flip brought up Brian, poor kid. "Brian Lucas. A transformed and limited Darwin-type, A Class, he chose the name 'Grendel.'" He came from a background nearly as privileged as mine, but his picture showed a monster; grey skin, *big*, low-slung jaw and a mouth full of short, sharp fangs, almost tusks, a nose so flat and broad it practically disappeared into his face, long black hair in dreadlocks he'd tied back.

"In his baseline form, what you see here, Brian is rated as an A Class Ajax-type. His metamorph power allows him to 'stack' towards greater strength — then he's stronger than me — or towards greater toughness. At his toughest, he appears invulnerable to anything short of depleted uranium anti-tank rounds. He may be tougher than that. He can lose nearly a third of his baseline mass, trade some of his strength and toughness for speed — then he's one of the fastest non-speedsters alive. He can also evolve claws and more exotic 'natural' weapons depending on what he's facing."

"And?"

"The Big Book has him turning mercenary a few years after graduation. In his worst contingent future, he's implicated in several warzone massacres and dies before he can be captured and brought to trial. A speculative post-mortem psych evaluation suggests he 'snapped' under the stress of not being able to save the civilian communities he was hired to protect from ethnic cleansing."

"And your final pick?"

I cleared my throat, flipped to the last page, and mentally crossed every finger and toe.

"Ozma. No known legal name." The girl in the school picture had alabaster skin, eyes that sparkled like diamonds, and unsmiling tourmaline-pink lips. Gold hair tumbled about her shoulders and down her back, and her features were so regular she could have been any age from fourteen to twenty-four — just the way L. Frank Baum described her, aside from age and attitude.

There are moments that make me wonder if the world isn't what I think it is. Like the time Mr. Swenson, my high school physics teacher, explained that light was both a particle and a wave. Particle: a discrete object of measurable dimension and position, like a marble. Wave: a disturbance propagated through a medium, like water. And whether light acts like a particle or a wave depends on *how we observe it*. Like it knows we're looking. It's moments like that that make me feel like I'm standing on the edge of something dizzyingly deep and fathomless.

Learning the truth about Detective Fisher last spring had been another one of those wobbly moments — after the fighting, anyway, when I had time to think about it. Fisher was *real*. And he was...fictional? The guy *donated blood*, but was pretty sure he was the creation of an unsuccessful and now deceased author. Even for the post-Event world, that was messed up, and just thinking about it made me want to look for the Fourth Wall. Madness.

So I didn't think about it; Fisher was Fisher. But Ozma? She was a whole new bucket of wrong.

When Blackstone didn't say anything, I pushed on. "Ozma has been at Hillwood for two years, since appearing in the Lucas Oil Stadium Attack, the same incident that generated Brian Lucas' breakthrough and killed his family."

"Did any source in your Big Book ever confirm that the attack created her?" Blackstone asked mildly.

I shook my head. Neither of us needed to discuss the particulars — the LO Stadium Attack, the worst tragedy in the history of Indianapolis, was also the worst supervillain attack in post-Event U.S. history until the Big One topped it. "The Ascendant" had never been identified or caught — he thoughtfully provided the media with his name when he claimed credit by doctored audio-file (lots of them did that). But everyone guessed him to be a Verne-type; he gassed the competitors and crowd in the stadium — there for the Drum Corps International World Championships — with a synthesized psychotropic that turned the attendees into a raving, hallucinating mob.

Nearly eight hundred dead out of a crowd of more than ten thousand, another hundred catatonic or insane, dozens missing, and twenty-four *breakthroughs*, only eight of them sane and stable. The "missing" died in ways that made identification impossible, and for all the breakthrough survivors, *sane* was a relative term. The body-count would have been a lot higher if Ozma hadn't appeared and, among other things, turned several newly transformed and rampaging monsters into *hats*.

Brian took down five tripped-out monstrous breakthroughs himself — the only upside to his transformation (drug-induced breakthroughs could get really, really *weird*).

"Ozma is a reality-shaper," I finished, "rated as an A Class Supernatural breakthrough. Her powers are growing." In the face of Blackstone's silence, I stepped on the urge to babble more details. He sighed.

"Astra, she believes she really *is* Ozma of Oz."

"She's perfectly sane otherwise." And she might really *be* Ozma, the same way Fisher was Fisher.

"Yes." He smiled without humor. "And ten years from now she'll sanely conquer Kansas."

"Only temporarily!"

"Because she disappears with every living resident of the state and their pets."

I didn't have to point out that it might have been — might be — a *good* thing; when Kansas "disappeared," the SB Virus would be — would have been? — sweeping through the country and Blackstone knew that as well as I did from his copy of the future files. The removal from production of that much farmland (it took a few years to re-settle) wouldn't help the situation, but how many Kansans would have died from the virus?

Thinking about future-ifs made my head hurt, but I was suddenly, burningly curious.

"Does the DSA know about them now? Their possible destinies, I mean?"

Blackstone sighed again. "No. After many drinks and more sleep, I segregated the potential future records of any breakthroughs who didn't start their villain careers before last January. If they still go supervillain, the files will become available."

"Oh." That was...good. A neat solution to an ethical dilemma I hadn't been able to unravel.

He read my thoughts (sometimes I'd swear he was telepathic, but no), and smiled. "On the other hand, I did flag them 'watch carefully.' There is principle — they haven't done anything yet and shouldn't be punished for what they *might* do — and then there is blind optimism. Which brings us to you, my dear. Which one are you being?"

I didn't flinch, but I gripped my epad too hard and felt the screen crack under my thumbs. "There's precedent. Riptide. And their Hillwood councilors all give them good marks for 'adjusted,' even Ozma. If we give them a path now — "

"You can't save the world, Hope," he said gently, and I flushed.

"And, I approve."

He chuckled at my confusion. "It's good strategy. We're looking at multiplying threat-sources; every potential threat we can turn into an asset is weight to our side. This isn't going to be a *second-chance* program, but even Ozma will be acceptable to our public — all truly powerful breakthroughs of her type are delusional in some way, so it's even normal."

His smile turned serious. "Hope, I wouldn't have made these choices, but they're good choices. *Very* good. Four flyers, three lift-capable; three ranged force projectors, two heavy close fighters, one evac-specialist, one outstanding support generalist. And picking your team is a leadership function. So is making it work. Are you ready for this?"

No, no I'm not. "Yes, I am."

"Well then, let's see if your draft picks are open to our proposition. You realize, my dear, that Quin is going to want to strangle you?"

I sighed. "Yeah..."

Quin had been on all of us to keep our publicity *positive* since Katy Barnes' exposé, *Watching the Watchmen,* came out and hit the New York Times Bestseller list. The investigative journalist sold it as "the shocking dark side of superhero celebrity," but it was really just a collection of anecdotes and speculation. Rush's well-known sexcapades and Chakra's whole Sacred Sex philosophy had given her a lot to work with, but so had Atlas with his old Atlas-girl hookups.

And she'd devoted a whole chapter to me and Atlas and our January "getaway," managing to make it sound like he'd taken advantage of my innocence *and* like I'd gone after him. Insinuation and innuendo made what had been so beautiful seem so wrong and just thinking about Katy's smarmy speculative "account" made me feel dirty. It also made me feel guilty, like I was responsible for dirtying Atlas's reputation, when it hadn't been that way at *all.*

It wasn't fair. John had died saving the President of the United States, his *friend,* and the city had dedicated the Atlas Memorial just last month, but the book practically insinuated he'd been a sexual predator. Quin was *still* doing damage control, grabbing every item of news she could for positive spin and a bright, shiny, *clean* junior team would have helped. The future teammates I'd chosen — a juvenile delinquent, a crazy, and a monster — weren't going to go over real well with the skeptics, even with a lot of our fans. And if any of them blew up on us...

When I didn't add anything, Blackstone nodded.

"Well then, don't you need to be in court? Dan called to ensure you wore your formal uniform. Good luck, my dear."

I got out of his office before he noticed I'd wrecked my epad. Once safe in the hall, I leaned against the wall and just *breathed* for a moment. I was actually shaking. *Please God, don't let this be my biggest mistake ever.* Did Blackstone understand what I was doing? What I was trying to do?

Maybe. Probably. Meanwhile, I had to go see a judge and jury. It was going to be *so* much fun.

Chapter Six: Grendel

Teenage superheroes are huge — in comics and on TV. In real life? Not so much. Forget child-endangerment laws; want to know why kids with superhuman powers make adults twitchy? Just imagine the daily life of any high school. Remember the angst, the drama, the hazing, the pranks, the insecurity and attitude, rivalries and one-upmanship? Remember what it was like for you? *Got it? Now add superpowers.*

Yeah, now you've got it. Hillwood Academy.

Brian Lucas, aka Grendel.

"Brian Lucas, Her Royal Highness requests your presence!"

I rolled over and up off the bed, nearly stomping Nox before I'd woken enough to realize I didn't need to maim somebody. Two years of Hillwood Academy pranks had turned me into a light sleeper. I growled at the doll and he sneered back — neat trick for a foot-tall ball-jointed toy made in Japan.

"When shall you attend her?"

Sitting back on the bed, I retracted my claws to push dreads out of my eyes. I held one up and squinted at it. I needed to dread-ball and wax soon.

"Did someone break into the lab again?"

Now he just looked insulted. "No one would dare, and we wouldn't need *you.*"

"Right." On both counts; the last student who'd tried to raid the lab on a dare had disappeared for three days while Ozma wore a new hat. Todd never remembered those three days, and she promised to burn her next hat.

When it came to psychological warfare, the princess took no prisoners.

"Then you can tell Her Highness that I'll see her after breakfast and before first period."

"She — "

"Tell her, Nox."

"As you wish, monster." He dodged my kick, not that I'd been trying, and disappeared back into the vent he'd come through. With two students on campus who could *shrink*, forgetting about Nox and Nix, you'd think the school would invest in more secure air conditioning.

Nox's wake-up had put me a few minutes ahead of the alarm, and I used it to work on my dreads before heading down to the dining room. Latisha had convinced me to style them back from my face, almost like cornrows so they stayed off my forehead and hung down my shoulders and back. The locks were so long they hung almost to my pecs now, nearly a mane, and she considered that progress.

"Nice." She grabbed one and sniffed when I sat down with a full breakfast tray beside her, smiled back at the stares she got. *Nobody touches the hair* was one of the best-known laws of Hillwood. She'd made it *Nobody touches the hair except Latisha*. It worked for her; most Hillwood kids at least talked about wearing the cape after graduation — she talked about hairstyling, and since her mom was a world-famous celebrity stylist, she'd do better than anybody here.

She eyed my stack of bleeding steaks. "Plan on doing a lot of morphing today?"

"Nope. But Her Highness calls, so you never know." I grinned around fast-growing fangs.

She sighed and reached across the table to snag a double handful of napkins. "Then I'm gone, sugar. Tuck your tie in your shirt and use some of these." Planting a kiss on my cheek, she rose and sashayed away, paused at the door to toss a final finger wave.

It was my turn to grin back at stares. I even put a little Nox-sneer into it.

Yeah guys, you just wonder and weep.

Nobody else tried to talk to me, not that I could talk back with a mouthful of serious fang. I finished fast and flexed my jaw to dial my pearly whites down from their breakfast time shark-like size. Pushing Nox's buttons was always fun, but if Ozma had sent him to get me then something was up; with still half an hour until class, Stanniger Hall was empty, echoing as I took the stairs up to her lab three at a time.

"Normal" students don't rate their own labs, and lots of us would rather be anywhere but Hillwood; two years ago, Ozma had demonstrated that she *could* be anywhere but here, and the school had given her the lab to get her to stick around. She had plans, they had plans, and the relationship was a friendly one. Probably.

I knocked politely and the door swung open; it wouldn't have if I hadn't been someone she'd introduced to it as "on the list."

"Good morning," her Royal Majesty Princess Ozma of Oz said without looking up. Already in her school uniform, she wore a surgical mask over her face as she measured something gram by gram onto a set of apothecary scales. Without asking, I grabbed a mask from the box by the door.

"More Powder of Life?"

"Crystallized Water of Oblivion."

"No freaking way." I'd read all the Oz books, even though most of them, canon and non, made me want to stick nails in my brain. I edged for the door and she laughed, a bright, sparkly sound.

"Don't worry. In crystallized form, the effects are determined by dosage — if you accidentally inhaled a speck, you would forget a few minutes, not your whole life." She put another gram on the scales. "Nox says you tried to kill him. Did he deserve it?"

"He was rude."

She gave a regal nod. "Nix says he's been bullying students. There wasn't much point in making Nix so he could have a girlfriend if she can't stand him."

"I wouldn't call it bullying, but the little Goth maniac has some of the nastier guys convinced if they don't toe the line they'll wake up with a fork in their eye."

"Well." No more needed to be said; Ozma was a big believer in applying the Golden Rule, which to her meant "you got what you gave." For some, that might be a fork. I edged closer to the bench.

"So, Your Highness summoned me?"

"Her Highness did." She finished her measure and carefully tipped the grains into a glass vial. When she sealed it I breathed easier. "We need you to look in the Question Box."

"The last time I did, it told me to go away."

"That's because you were asking it for football spreads. Naughty." She carefully wiped her hands and dropped the wipe in a hazmat burn can. She'd explained once that while Oz magic was fairy magic underneath it all, it looked a lot like chemistry and computer programming; all powerful sorcerers and sorceresses, witches and wizards, were *careful*. Or they were careless and a potted plant. A confused potted plant.

She raised an eyebrow. "So, the box? We both need to get to class."

"Right. Okay, fine. Where is it?"

She pointed to an oak cabinet, which opened to reveal Glegg's Box of Mixed Magic. She'd managed to find it last year, and she was still looking for most of the other Royal Treasures. It didn't worry me anymore that she was actually *finding* them, and the school didn't complain as long as she kept most of it in the lab.

Most schools might object to a student keeping the magical equivalent of high-grade explosives on campus; at Hillwood, a lot of the students *counted* as high explosives — or at least military ordnance — and Ozma's security measures were better than the school's.

Even the Magic Belt, which she wore all the time and used for her famous hat trick, didn't freak me out like the GBMM. The chest was an "empty" casket of gold filigree studded with gems. You knew it was empty because you could see right through its wire-thin sides. If you held it up in a sunbeam, the light shining through made cool patterns on the wall that were almost letters (you could never quite read them because they *changed* when you blinked). You could tell which side was up because the Great Sorcerer Glegg had considerately spelled out *Gleggs's Box of Mixed Magic* in gemstones on a plaque on top, the modest bastard. To open the lid, you said the magic words, which Ozma changed as often as she changed her locker combination.

I went over it in my head, already feeling stupid.

"Ras rats rax rast rascal."

The lid popped open to reveal the red velvet-lined interior that *still wasn't there from the outside*. Carefully removing the top tray with its four gold flasks, I pulled out the miniature tea set with its pack of Triple Trick Tea to get to the bottom and the acid-etched silver box labeled *Glegg's Question Box: Shake three times after each question.*

The guy had *no* imagination. The other box read *Re-animating Rays, guaranteed to re-awaken any person who has lost the power of life through sorcery, witchcraft, or enchantment.* If the rays didn't work, did you get your money back?

I held the Question Box up. "So? What do I ask?"

"That was a question."

"Crap!" I shook the stupid thing three times, opened the sliding lid and carefully pulled out the slip of paper inside. Putting the box down, I unfolded the note. It read *Ask what you're doing today.*

"Seriously?"

She laughed. "Go on."

I growled, asked, shook the damned box. This time the piece of paper read *When all you got to keep is strong, move along, move along like I know you do! And even when your hope is gone move along, move along just to make it through!*

"The All-American Rejects? Really?"

Her laugh was crystal bells. "Well that's a relief. The Question Box started rattling this morning, and I got a haiku about autumn and moving court. Pack your things, oh mighty Army of Oz — we are going somewhere."

Chapter Seven: Astra

These days more and more people are heard saying (and often shouting, cursing, or screaming inarticulately) "We need to know who they are!" Do we really?

New York is a No Privacy State, and the only breakthroughs allowed to use their powers as first-responders there are cops. They wear supercop uniforms and take codenames on the side, but their identities are public and masks are verboten. *Illinois is a Privacy State: any breakthrough here can shield his identity with a mask and a legal codename. If he wants to work with the police or emergency services, then the state needs to know who he is, but no one else. A third of all CAI heroes are masked mystery men. Guess which state has more superheroes and less superhuman crime?*

Terry Reinhold, *Citywatch.*

"Your honor, I would like to call Astra, of the Chicago Sentinels, to the stand."

I took a deep breath and stepped past the oak rail. The courtroom was packed, and Judge Sanderson had threatened to clear the gallery if he saw another camera flash; it wasn't often that a "mystery man" testified in court, and the newsies, wild and domesticated, smelled blood. Or hoped they did.

I smiled briefly at the judge and jury, switched Malleus to my left hand so I could take the oath on the Bible, and sat at the judge's invitation. Putting Malleus down with an audible thud, I adjusted my fringe of a skirt. Both Legal Eagle and Dan Raffles, the fresh young assistant DA prosecuting the case, had insisted I wear the velvet sapphire blue one-piece I thought of as my "skating costume." *I* insisted on the maul and convinced them it was a good idea.

Dan smiled at me. I smiled at him. We both smiled. I'd been *coached*.

"Can you state your legal name for the court?" Dan opened.

Smile. "My legal codename is Astra."

"Objection, your honor." The defense attorney stood behind his table.

"Grounds?" Judge Sanderson asked. He didn't smile.

"My client has a constitutional right to confront his accuser, your honor. Not someone hiding behind a mask and a fake name."

"Your honor, if I may approach the bench?" Dan had already stepped back, and when Sanderson nodded he returned with a page his assistant had ready. The judge accepted it without looking at it.

"This point has been addressed before, your honor. *Stacy v. Illinois.* The Supreme Court of Illinois has ruled that state-granted aliases are fully legal identities so long as the state knows the person's private identity and can hold that person liable for any perjury or malfeasance for actions committed under his state-sanctioned public alias.

"As to whether or not the young lady under the mask is indeed the person legally known as Astra ... Miss, will you please stand?"

I picked up Malleus and stood.

"Did anyone here see you arrive?"

I nodded, waved. "Hi, Terry." He waved back; the exchange got a ripple of laughter out of the jury and observers. Judge Sanderson tapped his gavel lightly.

"Order. Your point, councilor?"

"Just this, your honor. A show of hands, please? From everyone who saw her fly in?" A scattering of hands. "And if your honor and the jury will observe, the person in question is carrying a weapon formerly wielded by Ajax, one of our city's fallen heroes. Miss, would you care to describe it?"

I nodded again. "It's cast titanium, about one hundred pounds." I flipped it like a baton and gently set it on the front corner rail of the witness box, handle up.

"Your honor?" Dan invited.

Sanderson waved a bailiff forward. The beefy court officer looked appropriately serious, but he gave me a friendly smile before he braced himself, wrapped both hands around Malleus, lifted with a soft grunt, and carefully put it back down. Dan looked at the defense attorney. "Would you like to give it a try?" Another laughter-wave. The man shook his head as the guard returned to his post.

"Lastly, your honor," Dan said, "we have requested the presence of someone acquainted with our witness. The Sentinels have provided Doctor Jonathan Beth, the team physician. Doctor Beth is also a noted research scientist, but in his medical capacity he examines each of the Sentinels after any physical altercation. Doctor? Could you please stand?"

Doctor Beth stood from where he sat behind the rail, smiling and looking totally at home. Was he hiding as many butterflies as I was?

"Doctor, please consider yourself under oath. I saw you speaking with the witness before this session began. Is she, to your satisfaction, Astra?"

He smiled at me, faced the jury. "Yes, she is."

"Thank you, doctor." Dan turned back to the bench. "Of course, our witness may in fact be a shapeshifter, or a duplicate of some sort. But then, who isn't these days?" Another ripple and a light tap of the judge's mallet. The latest round of tabloid revelations claimed President Touches Clouds had been replaced with a mind-controlled clone. By Martians.

"You have made your point, councilor," Sanderson ruled. "The court finds that it can, in good faith, accept the witness as Astra, legally recognized by the State of Illinois. The defendant will be able to confront his accuser in cross. Objection denied."

I let out a breath I hadn't realized I was holding. It had mostly been a mime show for the benefit of the jury and media, but not completely. The legal principle had been firmly established, but still wasn't universally accepted. Other state courts had ruled differently, appeals were still winding upward to the U.S. Supreme Court, and Judge Sanderson had never ruled on it in trial.

"Thank you, your honor." Dan turned to me. "Astra, can you state for the record your whereabouts on the night of May twenty-fifth?"

When court adjourned, I found Seven in the private hallway outside the courtroom, talking to a pretty young woman in a pencil skirt. Seeing me, he broke off. She brushed his lapel and gave him her card before turning away. My escort these days, Seven had been in the crowd when I landed on the courthouse steps. He was really there to protect everyone around me from collateral damage if I got attacked in public.

The Paladins had taken a shot at me last spring, but nobody had been able to prove Conspiracy to Commit against the organization. So now wherever I was publically scheduled to go, outside of patrols, Seven went ahead unobtrusively. Even to my "good" stops, which this wasn't.

He misread my look and smiled, showing his cheek-dimple. The man had too many dimples. "Thinking the goons will try something?"

The accused, Benny Larkin, was a *goon* (over-muscled, shaved head, steel-capped boots, a tattoo somewhere that said "Kill them all"). Goons had started showing up in Chicago after our takedown of the Brotherhood and Sanguinary Boys last year; organized, they'd gotten busy thinning out the villainless minions. Now, with Benny, they'd moved up to taking on the few street-villains we'd left free and the new ones creeping in to fill the void.

Goons vs. minions, now goons vs. supervillains. Did they just want to fill Chicago's vacated ecological niche? And did we care? *I* just wanted to get back to the Dome to see how Shelly was doing on her lunch-date with Mal and find out when we got to make our pitch to Hillwood.

Dan joined us in the hall. We'd both left by the judge's door to avoid the gallery and the newsie flock in the public hall. He shook my hand.

"Thanks, Astra. I'd have rather gotten Judge Halder, but we took it. The jury loved you. Great testimony, you've put Benny away."

I squeezed back carefully and let go, just glad my part in the trial process was over.

Last May, Benny had walked up to Taipan — a D Class generic strong/fast muscle-type — on the street and shot him three times in the face (heavy caliber, armor-piercing rounds), dropped the gun, and ducked into a crowded theater-club complex. Taipan had been without minion backup that night. Drunk and surprised, he hadn't had time to use his speed and strength at all, and Benny had been able to disappear. The only reason he hadn't gotten away free was the single witness: me.

With villain violence way up (Blackstone said a power vacuum encouraged the survivors to take a proactive and competitive approach to filling the spots at the top), the CPD had asked us to stage random and targeted night patrols in high-violence areas. I'd been taking a break on top of a tenement building across the street.

I hadn't been close enough, couldn't move fast enough to stay with him, and I *couldn't* chase suspects once contact had been lost unless they were in the process of committing a crime. But my description had led to a CPD BOLO and Benny's arrest, and today my reading five random names — scribbled in tiny letters on an index card and flashed from across the courtroom — convinced the judge that I'd been able to read the tattoo on the back of his head from across the street and ten stories up.

Dan straightened his autumn-orange tie, cleared his throat. "Going out the back?"

I shook my head. "With all my fans out front? Never." Much as I wished they'd all disappear. Seven laughed and Dan nodded reluctantly.

"Well then. I — my office will call you if we need you, but you were perfect in the cross. No chance Benny's attorney is going to put you back on the stand. Good luck out there." He juggled his briefcase, offered his hand again to both of us, and departed for his next engagement. Seven watched him go with his usual quirky smile, then crooked his arm.

"Shall we?"

I held up my hands. "You first — even your luck won't let you blend in if we step out together." He waved my excuse away but followed Dan, leaving me to give him a head start. I bit my lip, watching him disappear around the corner, and almost went the other way. *Coward.*

Past the guard securing the hallway's privacy, the public hallway echoed with feet and conversation as attorneys, court officers, defendants, litigants, and court-watchers negotiated the space with the Brownian motion of busy crowds. I kept a good pace and probably some of Seven's luck rubbed off on me, because I made my way downstairs and out of the Daley Center before anyone paid attention to me. Then, of course, the crowd got noisy.

Citizens for Constitutional Rights protesters covered half of Daley Plaza, only a police line keeping them away from the doors. I could tell it was the CCR by the placards saying things like "Uphold the Sixth Amendment!" and "What do you have to hide?" I *liked* the CCR; they weren't politically extreme, mostly, and even had a point. But then there were the rest; Humanity First extremists were the loudest part of the crowd, the pro-registration advocates holding up slogans like "Don't live in fear!", "Do you know what your neighbors are?" and "We register guns, why not superpowers?" Lots of registration advocates discovered their vocations the day of the Event, and the Domestic Security Act had only been their latest try.

"*Wow,*" Shelly whispered in my ear. "*Did you know Jamal's getting a new last name? Gee, I wonder why?*"

"Don't." I managed to keep my face straight. "And hush — there's Shankman."

Mallory Shankman stood behind the police line a few steps from the Picasso — the ugly, metal, monumental cubist sculpture Picasso gave the city (Was it a baboon? An aardvark? Picasso's pet dog?). He perched on a box, flanked by three of his bodyguards, to work up the crowd with a megaphone. *Representative* Shankman now; he'd won election to the Illinois General Assembly in April, mainly on a law-and-order and anti-cape platform. Word that Judge Sanderson had accepted my testimony had obviously gotten outside a while ago; he had the crowd doing a call and response.

"Let them hear you!" "NO MASKS!" "Let them hear you!" "NO MASKS!" It turned into a general roar when they saw me, and the cops stood even straighter, trying to stare down the crowd. Maybe the front door hadn't been the best idea...

Then the guy in white popped out of nowhere between Shankman and the crowd with something in his hand. Adrenaline shot through me. Used to the way Rush and Crash could just appear from nowhere out of hypertime, I leaped forward before Shankman or his men even twitched. Not fast enough. *No, no, no...*

The man's arm went back, came forward hard enough to deliver whatever weapon he held in a straight shot into Shankman's face. Shankman staggered back, and I was there to get splashed as I pulled him down, came up between him and the thrower — who'd vanished again. Turning back to grab Shankman, fly him to the closest emergency room, I stopped. It wasn't blood — his face was covered in...cherry filling? What?

Then the idiot bodyguard on his left *shot* me. It went downhill from there.

Chapter Eight: Megaton

The Sentinels are masters of the superhero image. Blackstone is the elder statesman and mentor, dignified and mysterious. Lei Zi is appropriately professional and dangerous — a storm that's on your side. Astra is their golden girl, noble and natural and wholesome despite sensationalist smear campaigns. The Watchman exudes patient ... watchfulness, and so on. The public forgets that Blackstone is an ex-Marine intelligence officer, Lei Zi and Watchman are ex-Army, decorated combat veterans, and Astra, mentored and trained by Atlas and Ajax, killed enemies of this country in the first attack on American soil since Pearl Harbor.

We forget because Astra gets cats out of trees.

Geraldine Roche, *Public Opinion.*

My day started out surreal.

First, I was on Powernet. Sure, trees ate an airport, but they hadn't killed anybody so I came in a close second; the news page already had pictures of the bus and witness interviews. The only student they talked to who didn't say something like "We should have seen it coming" was Tiffany, and she was barely coherent. There were no interviews with the driver's family, but they had my freshman-year Fat Picture and last year's wrestling team shots. They were building a story and had me halfway to supervillain.

Well, screw them.

When I finally came out of my rooms, The Harlequin cornered me over my corn flakes in the dining room that did not, in any way, resemble a school cafeteria. She grilled me about color preferences, but the first thing she said when she sat down was "Leather. Definitely." Then Chakra joined us and got in an eye-rolling argument with The Harlequin over the merits of duster coats while I tried not to dribble into my cereal bowl. Both of them were *seriously* hot, even if "Call me Quin" looked like she was molded out of latex. Chakra knew they were shaking my couth, and obviously thought it was funny. I ate fast and excused myself for my morning appointment with Dr. Beth.

The Sentinels' doctor reminded me of my childhood dentist: always happy to see me, and so cheerful it almost didn't matter that visits were *painful*. He asked me to take off my shirt again. Even after years of high school gym I hated undressing in front of anybody, but he'd already figured that out and made it easier by not looking until he was ready to poke me with something.

He patted the examination table. "Sore anywhere this morning?"

"Not really." After smacking the concrete yesterday, I'd expected to hurt all over. Instead, even the bump on my head barely felt tender. I'd put on the ankle brace this morning, but hardly needed it.

He "hmm'd" to himself, poking and prodding my back with latex-gloved hands. Nodding, he turned to a cabinet to retrieve a white metal box, opening it behind me.

"Tell me if this feels uncomfortable," he said cheerfully and pressed something against my back, below my ribs. A click, and a little tap from the...rod? Tube? I shook my head. *Click*. A slightly stronger tap. *Click*. Tap. *Click*. Tap. *Click*. Tap. "Now?"

"I'm good."

"Excellent." More rummaging in the box. *Click*. TAP.

"Ouch!"

"And what did that feel like?"

I reached back and rubbed the spot. "Like someone poked me with a stick! What is that?" He held up what looked like a plastic gun. A tube ran from it to the box and it had an extended ring on the end — the part he must have been holding against my back.

"An air gun." He checked its setting, made a note. "It fires bursts of compressed air at set pressures. At higher settings it can drive nails, and the last shot you felt would have driven the nail through steel sheeting. Congratulations."

"For *what*?"

"You now possess D Class toughness. You had to, really, but it's always good to confirm."

"Huh?"

Leaning back against a counter, he regarded me with bright eyes. Something was seriously wrong with the man.

He boxed the air gun as he talked. "Yesterday, your first eruption threw a bus off of you. Your second, more sustained burst, threw you into the air. You obey at least one of the basic laws of physics: for every action, there is an equal and opposite reaction. So your first eruption should have flattened you into the ground, but you didn't describe that at all."

Letting me put my shirt back on, he led me over to one of his banks of screens. Tapping a couple of keys, he brought up a picture of a spray-painted "X" on a scorched and shattered concrete drive. "Also, judging from your elevation and velocity when your thrust cut out, you should have blacked out from the g-force involved."

I stared at the picture. "That's where I was?"

"Oh, yes." He nodded happily, tapping the screen. "See. You struck the bus with several tons of explosive thrust, and the opposite 'kick' cracked the pavement. If your body had not also changed to withstand that force, it would have been like a paper gun firing a high-caliber bullet." He slapped his hands together unnecessarily — I got the idea: *squish*.

"So, I'm stronger now, too?"

"Not stronger. Tougher. More resilient and resistant to damage. And you'll find you heal faster too." He made a wavy motion with his hand. "Perhaps a little stronger. Let's find out."

A series of scans and muscle-hammering sets later, he let me go with another lollypop. I *was* stronger. Not superhuman, rip-the-door-off strong, but I could rack more than I'd ever seen anyone do at school. Probably the only thing that stopped Dr. Beth from continuing his tests was a court appointment, but before pushing me out into the hall, he promised to drop a file in my Dome mailbox giving me the numbers.

The warm glow from realizing I was never going to be humiliated by some steroid gulping turf-head ever again lasted for all of a minute.

"You going to eat?"

"Shit! Don't *do* that!"

Shelly — Galatea — tried to look innocent, like she hadn't just snuck up behind me in the empty hallway and nearly scared the *bang* out of me. Giving it up, she closed her mouth on whatever she'd been about to say, sighed loudly.

"Sorry. It's a habit — Astra's super jumpy. And ticklish, not that it's safe to do *that* anymore. Really, I was coming to apologize for last night."

"And how 'bout now?"

The laugh was back. "Don't push your luck. Are you going to eat?"

She's going to kill me. Never kissed a girl, and I'm going to stroke out.

"Great!" she said, because obviously I'd agreed somehow while imagining my death. "Let's get out of here." *Out of here* meant escaping the Dome. She collected a blue hoodie from Bob at the lobby desk and tossed it to me. We were in the elevator before I remembered I was *news* and said so.

"So what?" She turned on me, exasperation rolling off her. "You going to hide in here for the rest of your life? First, you look nothing like your yearbook pictures; you were shaved *bald* in that team group shot. Plus you...had more padding. So put up the hood — you'll be *fine*."

She pulled me through the crowded atrium lobby and out the doors, and it seemed to work; at least nobody stopped us or even looked twice. Not that they'd recognize *her*, anyway, and she wasn't wearing the same attention-grabbing t-shirt as last night. How many obsessive cape-watchers could be here?

How many gambling addicts do you find at the track?

"C'mon!" she urged, tugging. Her hand felt warm, real, and *cut it out — she's a robot.*

"Where's Jamal?"

"Probably studying or washing cars or something."

"Huh?"

She dodged us around a flock of tourists. "He's getting homeschooled while learning to kick much ass — Sifu makes him do that whole 'wax on, wax off' thing to build character or something when he's not out with Rush. C'mon, we want to beat the lunch crowd!"

Her choice was the Artist's Café, in the Fine Arts Building across Michigan Avenue from the new Atlas Memorial. Starving art students made good hamburgers, and we did beat the midday crowd. She explained all about Crash's foster situation (living in a martial arts school sounded pretty cool). I had to ask why a robot would want a burger with an egg on it.

"Because I'm not a robot. Well — I *am*, but that's not all I am."

"So Jamal was serious? You're really a ghost?"

She picked at her fries. "Sort of. I'm a 'quantum-mirror mind emulation.'" A shrug. "I really did die origin-chasing. Nearly four years ago now, though for me it's been less than a year and I only got my first prosthetic body last spring. I was Astra's BFF 'til I... Which makes the irony of her breakthrough just ginormous, you know?" She gave a huge sigh, bit a fry.

I didn't follow any of that. "How did you..."

Her smile flashed. "I'd tell you, but then I'd have to kill you. Seriously, no-kidding top secret stuff. What it *means* is that it's all me in here now — I don't even have an active or updated backup anymore, the platform tech isn't compatible. But I didn't drag you here to talk about *me*." She looked at me sideways. "How are you, you know, doing?"

Suddenly, I wasn't hungry.

"Besides ki — Besides my accident yesterday and all the cape-watchers deciding I'm the new twisty breakthrough? I'm great."

"No — well yeah, that stuff too. But I meant, you know, *family.* Your parents will come around you know."

And now I wanted to return what I'd eaten. "They just *sat* there."

She shook her head emphatically. "You weren't listening, yesterday. They didn't *abandon* you — they gave the team provisional power of attorney, the right to act as your legal guardian. You'll get a state caseworker, but *we're* here to help you get what you need."

"But — "

She bounced a fry off my head and leaned in, voice low and intense. "Just don't give up on them, okay? You just jumped out of their make-him-do-his-homework-and-keep-him-out-of-trouble box. So they're not handling it well. Big freaking deal, most parentals don't, even if — "

Even if their kid doesn't kill somebody. I could feel the burn coming on, pushed it down. Like it was her business, like she knew *anything.*

"And why do you give a flying — "

"Because I'm *dead*, duh. My mom *buried* me, and I would give anything to — You know what? Forget it, screw up your own family, I am so out of here — "

The girl dropped her burger, but whatever she'd planned to do changed when the waitress serving the next table over screamed. I looked up to stare into the barrel of a *gun* as the waitress threw her tray at the hooded guy holding it. The gun blast hammered my ears, Shelly spun up and away from her chair — I'd never seen *anyone* move that fast. Lines split in her skin as she turned to shiny chrome, all silver and blue, and she nailed the hooded shooter behind her with a stiff open-palm thrust that sent him crashing through tables, gun flying away.

"Get the gun! Everybody down!"

She leaped after the guy, who made the mistake of trying to get up. He pulled a big knife but Galatea just slapped it out of her way and grabbed the throat of his hoodie twisting it into a chokehold. Pulling him off his feet, she flopped him onto his stomach and zip-cuffed him while everyone else was ducking or screaming.

I just sat there, frozen, but the waitress who'd screamed found the gun on a customer's plate, picked it up and safetied it before dropping to the floor with everyone else. Galatea grabbed my arm and pulled me out of my seat but not to the floor. "Move!" She wasn't being gentle now, and her blue chrome robot hand was a vise as I stumbled along. Stopping at the doors, she stood between me and the street, a frozen statue, while my heart thundered and my skin burned.

Then she was alive again.

"Street and building cameras have nothing," she said, voice flat. "Our guy was alone, and the CPD is coming." Her words became a meaningless buzz. I leaned against the doorway while she ducked back in and reassured everyone inside the café. The shooter had only gotten the one shot off, and nobody was hurt. *Nobody*.

The first of the police arrived while I stood there like a lump. Galatea handed the shooter off to the pair of officers fast, then steered me away.

"Don't we need to make statements?" I wasn't thinking very well, but I knew *that* much.

"Hey, you talk!" She negotiated us back across Michigan Avenue. "The café's security tapes will show everything, really, but we will. But we need to get back to the Dome, *now*. Somebody shot Astra at the courthouse. What is going *on* today?"

Chapter Nine: Astra

I figured it out a long time ago. When you shoot someone in a video game, they fall down — unless they're zombies, and then you have to blow them apart. When you shoot someone in real life, they fall down — unless they're zombies (don't ask). So the human brain knows that if you shoot people they tend to fall down, and when it panics, it forgets that there are exceptions. It can't help itself, especially when the exception looks like me — so the opposite of tough and bulletproof.

Astra, Notes From A Life.

I was a bad, bad person. If I took a breath, I was going to burst into insane giggles.

Of course news crews had been covering the courthouse and protest, so we got to watch the catastrophe from multiple angles and freeze-frames. Blackstone froze the newsfeed at the moment of the hit: Shankman rocking back, spreading pastry and filling, the masked guy in the white chef's uniform stretched out at the end of a throw so graceful it was balletic, arm extended forward at the end of the perfect delivery.

It was beautiful. Shankman had been *pied*.

The Pieman was one of those thrill-villains the public loved and public figures dreaded. Some kind of teleporter, he'd racked up an impressive "victim" count around the world. He always delivered *two* pies — the first nicely boxed and by courier, the second in person, in public, and in the face. Shankman had kept the first delivery secret (I could understand that; the usual response to someone revealing he'd gotten a delivery from the Pieman was late night comedy skits and a bet-making frenzy).

Rush wasn't holding back his laughter and Blackstone's chosen moment was spreading smiles around the Assembly Room table, even to Mal. It would have been a *perfect* moment, too, if that had been the end of it. But when the Pieman made his delivery, a perfect pitch to Shankman's face, I'd thought it was a real attack — and so did his bodyguards, who thought I was part of it. The one who shot me just moved faster than the rest.

Seven took the idiot down before he got his third shot off, coming out of nowhere to plant him face down on the pavement in a hard armlock. Despite the *Hollywood Knights* movie franchise, with the way that Seven acts it's hard to remember that he's a kick-butt martial artist and marksman. The bodyguard drawing on *him* took a kick to the hand that flipped his gun into the air in a beautiful arc that ended on the third guard's head, *knocking him out cold* — all before I'd had time to realize there was no real threat.

But the damage had been done; one of the two shots bouncing off me hit Shankman in the chest. The second hit nobody, but the shots and the action turned the worked-up crowd into a fleeing mob. Nobody dead, but five trampling victims — *luckily* minor injuries — taken to the hospital with Shankman. All caught on camera for the evening news.

"So." Blackstone smiled, shook his head. "Let's all get the humor out. The Honorable Mr. Shankman will recover, and no one else was badly hurt. It's always good to have Seven at the scene of a riot." Seven tipped his fedora and Blackstone waited for the laughter to die down. "Also, the two of you are to be commended. You both reacted swiftly and appropriately — had it been a deadly attack, you would have saved Mr. Shankman from any second assault. However."

He nodded to Quin.

"Shankman's PR machine is already spinning this," she said apologetically. "They're trying to make it look like you jumped into a situation that was obviously not dangerous, concussed Shankman by throwing him to the ground, and scared his bodyguards into opening fire."

I didn't want to laugh anymore.

"We're issuing our own statement, but it looks like he's going to sue us to keep this alive and in the news cycles. So if anyone is asked, remember 'swiftly and appropriately,' and move on. If pushed, you 'cannot speak about a lawsuit under litigation.'" Her gaze focused on Rush, the one of us most likely to be caught by the newsies on the street during a response-call.

He laughed. "If the asker is hot, can I still get her number?"

Quin winced. Rush had gotten a lot more serious since last year — he surprised everybody by being a solid mentor for Crash — but he still lived life like a rock star; he didn't do drugs or drink until he got faded, but he made up for it by chasing the wild sex. I was pretty sure Quin saw him as a walking, talking, sexual harassment lawsuit waiting to happen.

"*No*," she said. "Lois Lanes are off limits — "

He held up his hands, still laughing. "Don't get your — Don't get hot. Joking."

"Moving on," Lei Zi interjected, actually smiling. At least, her lips curved up a little. "Today's other shooting is more alarming." She looked across the table at Shelly, still in her sleek silver-and-blue Galatea form. Now I wasn't feeling at all funny.

"We have discussed being in public casually and openly since the Paladin attack last spring, and while Mr. Scott is not a Sentinel he is now recognizable to anyone motivated to find him. The police have only begun their investigation, but the café's security tapes clearly show that our guest was the shooter's target."

Shelly sat stiff and rebellious, but I'd seen the tapes; we owed Kristen Cho, the waitress, art student, and *policeman's daughter* who screamed, big-time. The shooter had come loaded with armor-piercing rounds. If Kristen hadn't seen the gun and thrown her tray at him, his first and only shot would have put Mal in the hospital or the morgue instead of killing an innocent cookies-and-cream malt and slicing a few customers with flying glass. She didn't know it yet, but she was about to get an anonymously funded full-ride scholarship. Quin knew how to do it.

Mal didn't look rebellious — he looked *green*. Not that anyone blamed him, or Shelly for that matter; *I* wouldn't have guessed he might be a target. Not before he even had a mask on.

"Mr. Scott," Lei Zi continued, "I'm afraid that, while you remain in the Dome, you will be covered by our protocols. And we will all be cutting back on showing recognizable faces, in or out of costume, outside the Dome when not on mission."

"Yes, ma'am," he said, and that was it. Lei Zi's mouth softened a little, an almost-smile of sympathy, but she left it there.

"The same applies to everyone here without a secret identity," Blackstone said gently. "We had two incidents today that could have resulted in civilian fatalities, one that targeted us. We cannot afford the bad press if a second attempt leaves innocents dead. Those of us who maintain true secret identities must also be doubly careful. The police have identified the shooter, and while they have barely begun their investigation they have informed us that his name appears on the Paladins' membership rolls."

That killed any leftover levity, but nobody looked surprised.

The Paladins *called* themselves patriots "preparing against the day that superhumans attempt to take over the country, steal America from its freedom-loving citizens, etc.," but there was a deeply racist streak to their worldview. Mal had killed someone, and not another SPB (Super Powered Being). It didn't matter that it was an accident, he deserved to die; it was like something out of the Jim Crow South.

Blackstone reviewed our security procedures, and Quin warned everyone again about loose talk online; she'd already updated our team webpage with today's events.

"Stay sharp, everyone," Blackstone concluded. "Bright side, cutting back on our scheduled public appearances will give us all some much-appreciated downtime. Astra? Would you stay behind again?"

"Totes awesome!" Shelly laughed in my earbug as I swung wide around the Lake Point Tower and turned south on my patrol circuit. Chicago always looked amazing from above and, with the sun setting, my wider-spectrum sight painted the streets between the towers as ribbons of light in shadow. Yesterday's private after-briefing meeting had slipped past her radar (probably because of Mal), but this last one hadn't and naturally she'd *hounded* me until I spilled the beans. Now, great as the view was, it wasn't what she was excited about.

"Totes?"

"Totally, duh. New slang — got to keep up on the wordage."

"No, no, I don't. And are you out of your quantum mind? In what evil mirror-universe is this awesome?"

"It's awesome right here 'cause it'll be 'Astra and the Young Sentinels!' Eeeee!"

"We haven't chosen a team name yet, and if you squeal like a fangirl one more time, I'm going to find you and hurt you."

"Spoilsport. Seriously — this is the next rung in your climb to total awesomeness. Before we're done, you'll be legendary."

I waved to some lingering office-bodies in the Aon Center. Blackstone had informed me that Hillwood's headmaster had rejoiced at our offer, then dug in his heels at one of our choices — I could guess which one — until Blackstone had suggested he might get better cooperation from another school. The headmaster caved and Blackstone and Quin were negotiating with our picks and their legal guardians now.

"So, who did you choose?"

"Grendel, Tsuris, and Ozma."

Only one of those three names publicly belonged to their owners yet, and I imagined I could *hear* her switch over to The Book for the others.

"You picked future supervillains?"

Yeah, that was predictable. "They don't have scarlet 'V's stamped on their foreheads, Shell."

She giggled. *"Blackstone must have* freaked."

"He never freaks."

"No, he doesn't. Ozma? Wow, that's just wrong. *Like tagging Mussolini for your team."*

"She never killed — never *will* kill — anyone, Shell. Okay, she wiped memories. And turned enough people into hats to open a haberdashery franchise, but not permanently."

"Kansas — "

"We don't know what happened in Kansas."

"Okay ... and we can certainly use some magic muscle. Grendel? You read his future war crimes file, right?"

I sighed. Shelly was the least *uncertain* person I knew in any situation — no matter how something turned out, she could never imagine herself deciding differently. Which was probably why, even with all TA's contingent futures in her head, she couldn't imagine someone *else* taking a different path. Change of plans? Yes. Change of direction? Not so much.

So how would she take it if she knew I'd used Blackstone's offer to get her a chance at her own change of direction?

Grendel

I closed my door and dropped on the bed.

Latisha hadn't been understanding. She'd never had a problem with Ozma; as beautiful as the princess was, she was also a 100–year-old virgin and therefore not competition, and Latisha had initiated our relationship in the first place — a wicked-smart, smoking hot D Class, she'd made up for her lack of serious power by accessorizing herself with one of Hillwood's current alpha-supers, me. But she'd assumed somewhere that it would last until graduation.

My telling her that I was leaving because the princess had crooked her finger told her everything she'd needed to know about where she ranked. She was cool and fun, and we'd been good with each other, but she'd never asked for more, I'd never offered, and

I'd leave with Ozma because two years ago she'd promised me justice. Latisha knew that now; she just didn't care.

"Brian?" Nix called softly from the vent.

"Come in, Nix." She fluttered up to perch on my lamp. Ozma had humored the little doll's wish to be a fairy by making her a pair of attachable butterfly wings that, against all laws of nature, *worked*. She adjusted her gauzy lace skirts.

"Are you ready to go?"

I gave her the kind of toothy grin that reminded most people of my willingness to rip arms off. She sighed, not exactly the reaction I'd been aiming at.

"My aunt and uncle have signed off on it," I said, wondering what she was looking for.

That had been an intense conversation but they were just glad I knew what I wanted to do, and it was normal enough even if it was all happening pretty fast. CAI teams creating spots for Academy seniors with valuable power sets was pretty routine, and we'd finish our classes by computer correspondence and return for graduation.

She tucked her legs up, rested her chin on her ball-joint knees, and her next sigh turned into a sniff. I put down the six-pack I'd pulled out of my closet for the common hall party downstairs. Since we weren't sure when we were leaving, Gilmore House was throwing us a farewell party tonight. Carlton House was probably doing the same for Reese.

"What's the matter, Nix?"

"I don't — I don't..." She put her head down. "I don't want us to go."

Dammit. Ozma was serenely confident that her yellow-brick road home was opening at last, even if it took years to walk it. Nox was ready to wade in the blood of his princess' enemies, or at least make them hurt a lot. But Nix — Nix's home had always been Ozma's room and the lab, and the fairy garden she'd made of boxes and soil and the flowers and tea-plant vines she'd collected and raised.

Dammit. I could find a shipping pallet behind the groundskeeper's sheds, rig something, but moving the boxes would tear the vines ... It wouldn't work. I patted my shoulder and Nix fluttered over to tuck herself in by my ear. She loved the spicy smell of my dreads.

"We'll find you space for another garden." It was lame, but I wasn't about to give her a line like *It'll be all right*. I felt her nod, but she heaved a sob. Dammit, I wasn't equipped to help a heartbroken doll. And she wasn't going to have another real home until it was the Emerald Palace.

I was going to have to talk to Latisha again. *Great*.

Chapter Ten: Astra

Superheroing is rescue and aid work, and sometimes police-assist and fighting. But mostly it's studying and training and trying to have a life outside of the job. Most of the time, that's not too hard; there are enough of us that we all have downtime, and months can go by between serious action.

But then, there are the other days.

Astra, Notes From a Life.

"Shelly says he's good at swallowing the mad," I said.

Chakra smiled at me over her tea and toast. "Is that her professional assessment?" It was easy to forget she held a doctorate in behavioral science; she dressed like a gypsy, practiced pranayama and kundalini manipulation, and talked like a sex therapist (which made our conversations all *sorts* of fun). Her breakthrough-powered tantric magic was just *bonus*.

Last night, Blackstone had insisted Chakra and I watch the tape of Mal's meeting with Quin, Seven, Legal Eagle, and his parents from the day of the Green Man's attack. I'd felt like a complete voyeur. Mal had got *intense*, his dad got cold, his mom wouldn't stop the quiet hysteria. Nobody fought, but at least twice I'd thought he was going to redecorate the whole Assembly Room.

Sitting beside Mal, Seven hadn't so much as twitched.

And this morning over breakfast, Shelly had fessed up about where she'd gone that first night and how it had ended. Shelly shouldn't happen to unsuspecting people and it had been *so* Shelly — I couldn't believe she'd managed to drag him to lunch after that, and now she was scoring 0 for 2 with the boy. Chakra had listened to the story, too, and had looked quietly thoughtful after Shelly left. Then she'd started the questions.

"So, you think he's safe?" she prodded. I squirmed.

"Not *safe*, just...on top of it?"

"I agree," she surprised me, thoughtfully nibbling on her jammed toast. "Our Mr. Scott has a great deal of experience with 'swallowing the mad.' Have you given much thought to what shapes breakthroughs? His experience would seem to parallel yours, wouldn't it? Little direct physical trauma, a disproportionate response to the danger..."

"Well, we were both afraid — "

"Bullshit."

"Excuse me?"

She laughed. "Did I stutter? I remember the report, and you didn't break through when the overpass pinned your car. You weren't badly injured, and several minutes went by before you changed. Did you get *more* afraid? Panic?"

I tried to remember my state of mind back when it happened. "I wanted to..." What?

"May I offer a working hypothesis?" She sat back. "You'd seen lots of disaster-scene news footage where Atlas flew in for the rescue. You *needed* a rescue, but couldn't wait for it because others were in danger too. So, you did what you'd seen him do."

"You think I was a copycat obsessing on him?"

"No, but you did idealize him. Understandable — there was a lot to idealize. My point is that your breakthrough was triggered by the need to *help*, so it gave you a very helpful and familiar power set. Our boy's breakthrough the other day was triggered by pain and perfectly natural fear. It gave him the means to strike back hard at the cause, even using something he was familiar with — did you see his school records? Ace chemistry student until last year, did a science fair project on high-energy reactions and lift; he's a rocket scientist in the making. But the bottom line is his trigger was fear, and fear and anger have similar physiological responses."

"So, you're saying Mal can already control his power."

She frowned thoughtfully, tapping her cup. "Suppress, maybe. When you grow up in an emotionally stressful environment, you learn to keep things in early, and his family obviously has issues. But let's get back to you and your impulsive promise to help." I could swear her eyes twinkled. "I know a technique..."

Seven laughed.

"It's not *funny!*" My ears were burning again. I'd fled the breakfast table and Seven found me in the gym ringing the gong, the massive strike-plate I used for a punching bag. All I'd had to say was "Chakra talked to me" for him to go off, which didn't help. Shelly's "Seven days to move on Seven" ultimatum wasn't helping me, either.

"I swear — " *bong* "she does it to — " *bong* "traumatize me!" *bong*. Kinetic-to-thermal energy transfer was actually starting to heat the plate. "She makes me want to wave my Saint Agnes medal like a cross for vampires!" Seven just laughed harder, and my worked-up gasping turned into giggles. "Not — " *bong* "funny!"

I gave up and leaned against the plate, slid to the floor.

"It's a little funny," Seven admitted. He sat down and took the spot beside me.

"What does he *want?*" I asked, trying to ignore the way our shoulders touched. Since we were off the top of the response queue, I wore spandex spanky pants and an athletic shirt I'd thrown on this morning to sweat in, and I could feel the brush of his Egyptian cotton suit when my bare arm twitched.

Of course, he didn't notice. "Who?"

"Blackstone. He's up to something." I understood Blackstone's rationale — if we were going to start a new team, *someone* had to be its familiar face. But putting me in *charge?* Letting me pick my team? He'd given in on my picks way too easy and was pushing to make it work. Not that I wasn't grateful, but...

"So, what's going on?"

He whistled when I told him, then just sat there thinking. Finally he skimmed his hat, took it off, put it back with a little hat-flip and gave me a guileless smile. "Thinking five steps ahead is his job, and I'm pretty sure he's always up to something. Mind like a snake."

"You say that like it's a *good* thing."

"Since he's on the side of the angels, yep." He climbed to his feet and pulled me up. The stomach-butterflies were back and I sternly ignored them. I didn't have *time* for it, and right there, I realized what I had to do about it.

Letting go, he gave me his patented grin. "So, I'm spotting Rush at a neighborhood safety conference this morning. What are you doing?"

"We're still on alert, so I'm not going to classes, and I'm pretty sure Watchman is going to take advantage. Not like *that*," I laughed at his playful look. "But Dr. Beth will probably be checking me out by the time you get back."

His smile-dimple appeared. "Maybe I shouldn't *leave*."

"That's sweet. And cheating. Go. I'll live." He left, whistling, and I gave myself a moment after the doors closed before going back to the gong.

Megaton

I had no idea what they wanted from me, which sucked because I was finally starting to care.

My second morning started with a text from *Tiffany*. Just an RUOK?, with a link attached. The link led to a Chicago News story on yesterday's café shooting. I texted back that it was no big deal, but it was cool that she cared — nobody, and I mean *nobody*, had bothered until now, and some of the posted responses to the story suggested it would have been better if the shooter hadn't missed.

Police were still "questioning" the shooter and "pursuing inquiries."

After breakfast, The Harlequin took me upstairs and introduced me to my case worker, a guy named Allen Nenbauer who gave me his card. He came armed with a briefcase and an agenda that began with a monster questionnaire, and he thought smiling like he'd snorted nitrous oxide was part of the process. It was like watching a grinning ventriloquist's dummy, but after hours of inane or insane questions and warnings, he let me go with instructions to call him any time "should issues develop."

All part of being a minor the state wanted to "protect."

After he finished, The Harlequin returned and took me back down to the living levels to drop me at a door across from the infirmary. When it opened, she gave me a wink and a push before turning and leaving me there. Okay...

The doors closed behind me, making me jump; I still wasn't used to the way all the doors came from the USS *Enterprise*.

"You made it." Across the big room, Watchman broke away from Variforce to step my way. They'd been working out against each other in the center of a red-painted circle on the bare floor.

He shook my hand. "So, are you ready?" He was actually breathing hard. Behind him, Variforce let his origami aura of gold force fields fade and drift until they blended with his black-and-gold spandex bodysuit.

"For *what*?"

"For us to see what you do."

My skin tingled and my throat went dry, but I nodded.

"Good." He slapped my shoulder, waved Variforce over. The other guy, built like a dancer, practically steamed. Breathing deep but not hard, he combed fingers through his short and kinky hair and flipped sweat away.

"Relax, kid," he said. "We're not going to blow anything up. Check this." He held up his arms and waves of gold flowed off him, building layer by layer into a long translucent column stretching away from us along the floor. Spreading his hands widened the column, thickening its rim without hollowing it out.

"Right here." He pointed to a spot beside him for me to stand. A pushing motion indented the end in front of us until it was deeply concave. Watchman joined us on my other side, and Variforce pulled a few layers of glowing field around himself.

"Okay." He studied his creation and nodded. "This is just like a shooting-chamber for firing rounds for ballistic tests. The fields aren't hardened — they'll absorb the blast through their combined volume, and the room's sensors are going to measure field density and deformation; that'll give us an idea of your power's energy density. Got it? Just point and fire."

"Got it." I wiped my hands on my jeans, looked at Watchman, and lifted my arms. Just thinking about it, I felt the heat coming, the pressure building. I braced, leaned in.

Nothing.

"Any time, now," Variforce said. Watchman shook his head.

Nothing. Embarrassment added to the heat until my skin felt on fire and I thought I'd pop from the pressure in my bones, and *nothing*. Watchman studied me. "Think about the bus."

That busted it — the heat and pressure dropped away like someone had stuck a tap in me and turned it wide. It all went back wherever it came from, leaving me light-headed and shaking.

He sighed, patting my shoulder. "Sit. Breathe. We'll try again in a moment, without the bus." He didn't have to tell me twice. I dropped to the steel shock-plated floor and he squatted beside me.

"How did it feel?"

I told him. He rubbed his chin, shook his head again. "Well, we'll try some more."

Fifteen minutes later, Variforce was getting tired of holding his "shooting chamber" together and I was no closer to anything. Watchman called it a day.

"I almost had it!"

"No, you didn't — your peak temperature has been dropping for at least five minutes." An Atlas-type hero, he could watch me in infrared as easily as Astra. "Let's get a sandwich — you've got to be burning calories and I need my strength to go beat somebody up."

Chapter Eleven: Astra

Sure, superhero costumes are flamboyant acts of self-expression, but they're useful, too. The PR benefits aside, everyone knows you on sight — important if you need instant trust in a crisis. And recognizing friendlies is deadly important on the fast-moving superhuman battlefield.

The Harlequin, *Citywatch Interviews*.

Shelly ignored the red Occupied light, and nearly got decapitated when Watchman cannoned off the wall by the door.

"Bystander handicap!" she announced after ducking. The designated "villain" in this after-lunch fight, Watchman didn't waste a second — he spun around to go for the grab and I dropped hard to deny him the hostage, but that was the inevitable move so he was ready, turning into my drop with a raised palm-strike that narrowly missed my chin as I twisted aside. Kicking off of the floor at the bottom of the drop, I grabbed his extended arm, spun to put my back to his chest, and curled to throw him hard at the far wall. *Yes!*

"Go!" Shell gave a fangirl-cheer as I leaped after him. He got control and curved around without meeting the opposite wall, and we smacked together in the center of the Hard Room to wrap up into a clenching, punching, digging midair ball of nasty moves. Too close for fists, I got a knee into his kidney but he rang my head with an elbow under my ear, our hits echoing off the plated walls. Rocked by the elbow-strike, I let him get around me and he took full advantage with a groin-and-neck hold that pointed us in opposite directions and dropped us *hard*, hammering me face first into the floor. It rang like a gong as my world lit up.

I tried to push off, but my vision refused to clear, I'd lost track of down, and I could barely feel the grinding hold he put me in. Then the pressure went away and the floor rang again as he tapped out for me, calling it.

Enough situation-awareness came back that I could roll over, and a fuzzy blob above me resolved into his face.

He held out his hand, breathing hard. "You okay?"

The vertigo warned me against shaking my head or taking his hand. If I moved, I was going to vomit.

"Nuts," I finally gasped. He laughed, winced.

Drat. Darn. Nuts. Phooey. My language was ridiculously sanitary — growing up emulating a mom who was Ms. Manners (the truly *nice* kind, not the stuck-up kind) meant I felt bad about even a mild "dammit," because "Good manners create respect and are a courtesy to those around you." It was hard to be taken seriously when "darn it!" popped out under pressure, and when I really *needed* a colorful word, I had nothing. Thanks, Mom.

When everything steadied, I accepted his hand up.

"You almost had me until Shelly stepped in," he fibbed politely. "I asked her to, but you made the right move and nearly carried it through."

"She'd have won if she had her maul," Shelly defended me.

"Maybe," he nodded. "But she doesn't carry it everywhere."

He'd caught me still in my workout clothes, which had kind of been the point. Blackstone had asked Watchman to focus my training on situations when I didn't have all the advantages I'd figured out, so I hard-sparred with my personal nemesis in full gear and without.

And he *was* my nemesis. He'd been recruited to add more muscle and mobility to the team, but also to continue my regular beatings. They *called* it training, but what Blackstone hadn't told me was that Watchman's last assignment had been as a fight instructor at Fort Hood in Texas — where he'd trained supersoldiers for special Army, Air Force, Navy, and Marine units.

That's right; he'd trained superSEALs, superRangers, and other insanely lethal gods of war. His motto was "Training should be tougher than combat"; he'd gotten the scar that ran from his eye to his jaw in a *training exercise*, and now he got to focus on *me*. Oh, joyous day.

I wanted to score a real win off of him so bad I could taste it like the blood in my mouth (Somewhere in the fight, I'd bitten my cheek.). I grabbed a towel to mop the sweat.

"You're really getting better," Shelly said loyally, handing us the bottles she'd brought with her. "At least you're lasting longer..."

"And I feel it. Ghah!" I stretched, flexed my neck, and felt something pop back into place. Watchman politely accepted his and took a drink, then reset the room's function. The variable-mass weight machines Vulcan had designed and fabricated for us rose from the floor and he began doing shoulder presses.

I considered joining him, but I'd had enough. Finishing the stretch, I started doing yoga postures while Shelly watched; Chakra had started me on yoga when she introduced us to the mental tricks that *might* help us detect telepathic manipulation, and training against my own body's resistance made sense and was even fun. I lingered a bit five moves into the routine, poised on my left foot, right leg straight out parallel to the floor and toes pointed at the ceiling, bent forward with arms extended along my leg, fingers interlaced as a saddle for my right foot, forehead resting on my knee.

"Now you're just showing off. What is that even *called*?"

"Dandanayama-janushirasana."

"Bless you." She fidgeted, and I smiled against my leg where she couldn't see. Should I ask Watchman how his session with Mal had gone?

"So, Seven?"

Okay, maybe Mal wasn't the one on her mind.

"To quote Jacky, 'Bite me.'" Cutting the routine short, I dropped into toe-stand position, balanced on the toes of my right foot so my butt rested on my heel instead of the floor, left leg folded over so my left foot rested on my right thigh in lotus position, hands in prayer position above my heart, eyes closed and breathing controlled. Since I hardly felt my own weight, I could keep it up as long as I maintained my balance (but staying up by "flying" was cheating).

"So, how long are you going to do that?"

"Shhh."

"Seriously."

"Waiting is all."

"You know Chakra was quoting a science fiction character, don't you?"

I kept my eyes closed, but couldn't hide the grin. "Wisdom is where you find it, Sifu says. You gave me a week, Shell, now leave it alone." I wasn't about to tell her my Seven resolution; waiting would drive her *crazy*.

Not that she'd have to wait long; enough was enough. Last night, I'd woken from a courtroom dream that started with Dan Raffles asking me to describe the events of May 25th and ended with the defense attorney asking my opinion of Seven's hazel eyes. *And may I remind the witness that she is under oath?* Judge Sanderson overruled Dan's objection — that my opinion of the defendant's eyes would be prejudicial to the jury — and my horror as my mouth started to open rocketed me out of bed. Literally.

I wasn't twelve anymore, I had things to do, and it was time to get proactive; the next time Blackstone sent Seven and me out in the field together...

Shelly huffed. "So then — " The lights dimmed, came back up shaded Emergency Red, and her eyes unfocused. "Crap. Blackstone's calling. Something's going down at the Daley Center."

I fell out of position.

Megaton

Failure tastes like acid, the bile at the back of your throat when you think you're going to toss your cookies. So lunch sucked. After Watchman and Variforce left me in the dining room with some encouraging words, I tried to slouch back to my rooms.

This ride blows. I want my money back.

Instead Willis found me — The Harlequin had summoned me back upstairs, this time to her office.

The idea of superheroes having offices was just ... wrong. Headquarters and briefing rooms and high-tech workout and training rooms? Yeah. But, offices? Rooms where you read reports and sign stuff? It turned out that hers was on a balcony level open to the City Room, so she could step out and watch Dispatch as it coordinated the patrols and responses of all the CAI teams in Chicago.

I'd seen the City Room before on a grade-school tour, part of the Dome Experience not available since Villains Inc.'s attack on the place last spring; now, visitors had to stick to the atrium, museum, theater and gift-shop. I took the stairs up to her office two steps at a time, wondering what she could want with me.

The Harlequin's office was as colorful as her costumes, walls covered by Cirque du Soleil show posters. She looked up and smiled when I knocked on her open door, and the big guy with her stood up when I came in. He was taller than me, wide shoulders and all lean muscle.

He looked me over and nodded. "I can work with this."

I looked back, feeling myself heat up. "Work with *what*?"

The Harlequin rolled her eyes. "Andrew, play nice. Sit, both of you."

He laughed and handed me a large epad — the kind that could display whole magazine or comic-book pages in bright color. It showed *me*, front and back in ink and color, wearing a short, zipped-up red leather jacket with black shoulders and trim over a black high-necked shirt and cargo pants. I also wore combat boots, gloves, and a utility belt with the Sentinels "S"-logo. An asymmetrical explosive starburst decorated the back of the jacket. He gave me a moment to absorb the picture, then leaned forward and tapped the screen to drop a dark visored half-helmet on the figure. He'd written *Megaton* under the costume sketches.

Whoa. That's just —

"The shoulders are padded to de-emphasize your waist," he said. "But you'll probably work off your leftover child fat if you stay."

That brought me down. "I can't — I haven't been able to control it yet."

"Are you going to give up?"

"No!" I caught The Harlequin smiling. Andrew made a forget-about-it gesture and winked at her.

"They'll get you straight, then. Might hurt. Might not. So, the design?"

I couldn't stop staring at it. *"Yeah. That's just..."*

"Amazing," he finished for me.

"Yeah. But I don't know what's going to happen to me, yet."

The Harlequin coughed, making me look up.

"Assuming we fix your trigger — and there are *plans* for that — we're going to make you an offer you can't refuse. No details, just assume it's an apprenticeship like Jamal got. The question is, do you want to be a hero?" I looked at the epad again, but couldn't stop seeing the wrecked bus, crazed and bloody glass. *Megaton.* The name was as much as warning as anything.

"I — I don't know. I don't want to — you've seen what they're saying online."

She nodded.

"I don't want that being what everybody remembers, but I don't know if I can — I don't want to hurt anybody else." I hadn't thought about it in those words, but it became true as I said it.

I couldn't read the look she gave me. "Then we'll leave it here for now," she said after a moment. "If you decide to wear the cape, Andrew will help. The right look and name is important, not that

Andrew can do the impossible. He tries, but without that huge mallet she carries, Astra can't do threatening *at all*."

Andrew smiled like it was an old joke, and I wondered who he was fooling. Designer, right — the guy was the total alpha-male without even trying. He was a *cape*. Had to be. And he and The Harlequin looked at each other like Mr. Brian and Ms. Steward, the two voted most likely by secret student poll to be doing it in the faculty restrooms.

He started to say something, but the lights dimmed and came back with a red tinge. The Harlequin held up her hand, listening to the earbug they all seemed to wear. She stood, all humor gone. "Possible situation developing. Move, people. Outside."

Astra

As Watchman headed out and I scrambled to get into uniform, all we knew was that the Daley Center had dropped completely off the Dispatch grid. Something had cut the building's landlines without triggering an alert, which shouldn't have been possible. Shelly confirmed that the building also had zero cell reception before I'd even made it to my rooms.

"Who are they sending?" I asked Shell as I buckled up.

"Just Watchman and Safire so far — she's close by on her own Guardian patrol — and they won't be diving out of the sun, either. After all, it might be nothing, and even if it *is* something, Lei Zi says one stampeding mob is enough for Daley Plaza this week."

However serious the situation, Shelly's grin said what she thought of a Watchman-Safire teamup. Mr. Military and Ms. Party Girl; just the mental image of his military styled one-piece uniform and her purple-and-pink flame latex bodysuit in the same picture made me smile, and Shell's grin widened off of mine.

"Rush and Seven are right behind them on Rush's bike — she says we're the reserve." She actually sounded put out, making me laugh as she transformed into blue-and-silver Galatea and we headed up to the City Room to watch the screens and listen to the chatter.

Blackstone was already there, out on the Dispatch floor with Chakra and Lei Zi to watch the screens. Quin, Andrew, and Mal watched from the office balcony. The big screens showed street-camera shots from Daley Plaza, and everything looked normal — just the usual midday business and public-servant crowd. The protesting crowd was gone since nobody in a mask was testifying today and Shankman wasn't there to bring his people, but Protest Man stood in his usual spot in the northwest corner of the plaza, dressed in his business suit and domino mask and holding one of his usual obscure protest signs (today, it said "Stop the black cars!"). Safire, Watchman, Rush, and Seven had already gone inside — and dropped off the Dispatch net.

I stopped at David's station. The senior dayshift supervisor surrounded his workspace with Sentinels and Guardians bobbleheads; when we were in the field, he'd perch our figures on top of his station's dividing wall. He'd held his post for five years and had dozens of little superstitions like that, but he knew the feel of a situation like nobody else. (Atlas had introduced us on my first patrol day and asked him to look after me, and when Villains Inc. attacked the Dome last spring, he'd stayed at his station and directed the citywide Dispatch response.)

"What do you think?" I asked softly. He looked up, played with his loose tie.

"The whole building's a dead zone — no electronic penetration. Something's happening in there and somebody doesn't want us to see it. Dammit!"

The street cameras didn't give us sound, but the flashing lights announced the arrival of the first squad cars and I relaxed a little; the CPD was good at clearing an area fast. *Chakra* didn't relax. If anything she wound tighter, and she looked across the room at me. What —

"Doors!" David shouted; on the screens, the first of the silently screaming mob fleeing the building hit the glass doors and pushed through them into the plaza at the head of the flood — lawyers, bailiffs, businessmen, journalists, judges, the denizens of the halls and lower-floor courts and offices. Above them, Safire came through the windows in an explosion of glass, flying like she'd been shot from a cannon, to crash into the base of the Picasso.

"Astra, Galatea, go!" Lei Zi snapped. "No loads!"

"But — " Shell started to protest as I grabbed her and flew us up the emergency shaft to the launch bay. The bay doors barely had time to make a crack for us before we were up and out. In the open air, I torqued us around in a g-pulling turn and threw us up Congress Parkway at just above streetlight level, pulled us up and over Chase Tower in a steep rollercoaster arc to drop into Daley Plaza.

"*Drop Galatea outside,*" Lei Zi instructed through Dispatch; when I let her go, she stuck an indignant three-point landing beside Safire and the twisted wreck of the Picasso. It made sense; she could remain outside the dead zone and follow the action inside by auditory analysis (she could even analyze *ground vibrations*) and let Lei Zi know what was going on inside. Did she like it? No.

Atlas Rule # Something: Never make a hole when you can find a hole. I flew in through the hole Safire made on her way out.

Safire had gone through a couple of inner-office walls, but nobody had been in her way. Outside the office and across the hall was, yes, the courtroom hosting Mr. Larkin's trial, and it looked like her involuntary flight had started inside, where the fight continued. The floor shook as something hit the other side of the wall beside the wrecked doors.

"Dispatch?" I whispered, just to see. Nobody came back. *Okay, onward.* No one needed assistance in the hallway — I saw that much before I felt and heard the crash and the power cut out. The emergency lights came on, and I stared at the hole where the courtroom doors had been.

Someone had thrown Safire through those doors and three walls, was still fighting Watchman, and at least *Rush* should have come out and reported the sitch so we'd know what we faced — that was *procedure*. The floor shook again and wall-dust puffed out through the broken doors. Anything could be in there. I'd met anythings before and didn't want to meet them again without backup, but we were already mixed into it.

Once more into the breach, dear friends, once more. College Literature was good for *something*.

You never go in at head-height — it's a natural zone of attention; gripping Malleus, I went in fast and high, through the hole and brushing the ceiling as I aimed at the back of the courtroom, taking in the scene as I flew.

Rush was *down*, sprawled across the center aisle, and the bystanders who couldn't get out crouched between the benches on either side for cover. No Seven, and my heart clenched. *Please God, let him be all right.* Watchman stood mixed in with a big, armored brawler by the shattered judge's bench and a big hole in the wall, along with another armored guy twisting him up in...steel tentacles? A third armored villain stood back from the fight, at the center of an orbiting cloud of softball-sized spheres.

Spheres that spun towards me.

If they were effective against Watchman, they'd be on him, so I ignored sphere-guy and went for the one tangling him up.

Wrong move; the spheres went for *me*.

I barely had time to flinch before the first one hit my leg and *exploded*, a shaped-charge punch that threw me off course to crash through the jury box rail. I twisted, swung to crush one, sent another flying, and they swarmed me. *FLASH!* Blind, I desperately rolled through the chairs, blinking while all my eyes' photoreceptors tried to reset from the flashbang blast and my ears came back from the high-decibel attack. *Bangbangbangbangbang.* Muffled gunshots — whose?

Bangbangbangbangbang. Seven's grouping, yes! I could see again, sort of — like looking through a tissue blindfold — and caught another sphere flying at my face, crushing it before it could suicide. *And where is sphere-guy?*

He flung his guardian spheres across the room at Seven, who'd stood up from behind the back row of benches, the swarm of balls disintegrating as Seven's dead-eye target shooting blew them apart. I shook off the last of the vertigo and leaped again for Tentacle Guy, to get him away from Watchman. A thick steel cable snaked from each of his arms and he'd wrapped one around Watchman's neck, pulling him off of Big Guy. The other whipped out at me.

I ducked, realized he hadn't been aiming at me as the cable buried itself in the wall and wrapped around a support beam. He heaved on the other, and suddenly *Watchman* was flying. *Oh* — We went through the wall together in an explosion of plaster dust and snapped conduits and I lost Malleus.

This time the whole world wandered away for a moment. Maybe I wasn't quite recovered from my earlier sparring head-smash? *Must have Dr. Beth check me out.* When the world came back, Watchman had his hand out. He spat drywall dust. "You okay?"

"Gee, don't know, somebody threw the *Dome* at me?"

He actually laughed as he pulled me up. "Bright side, nobody's shooting at us. Use the courtroom door, get Rush out." And he was gone back through the new hole. We'd gone through a couple of walls and I oriented myself fast, missing Shelly like crazy. Out into the hall, around a corner, and through the broken doors, grabbing one on the fly.

Seven ducked as I flew over him where he stood at the back of the courtroom, and I swung the door at the thinning cloud of spheres harassing him. He continued to methodically pot them. *Bang. Bang. Bang.*

He popped a new clip. "Cavalry coming?"

"Me?" I tried to count spheres, and why weren't they just burying us? "Cover me?"

He laughed. "Always." I dropped to the floor, holding my piece of door, and flew low down the aisle to where Rush lay exposed while bits of spheres that got too close sprinkled down. *Had* lain — where was he now?

"Astra!"

I twisted around. Dan Raffles hadn't made it out of the courtroom, and he'd risked dragging Rush out of the aisle and between two benches while I'd been getting knocked through walls.

The man was totally freaked; he stared at me, eyes wide, and flinched at each gunshot.

"I think — I think he's stunned. He hit his head on a bench when he fell."

"Thank you." I couldn't believe he'd done it. "Are you hurt?"

When he shook his head, I quickly examined Rush. *Bad* bump on his head, but no obvious spine trauma, breathing and pulse regular. How had he lost his helmet? Was he safe to move again? Then I *knew*, feeling the warm certainty of Chakra's mental presence like a wind of blossoms. *Okay.*

"Stay down," I said. "Crawl to the back, you'll be all right. Seven is there."

Raffles nodded spastically, started crawling. I slid Rush out and onto the door in one smooth heave, grabbed the edges on either side of his body, and *flew*, low and fast and holding him so close between me and the door that, if he were awake, he'd be making improper suggestions. Out of the courtroom, through Safire's exit, and down onto the plaza by Shelly and Crash, who'd obviously arrived while I was busy.

"*Astra*," Lei Zi spoke in my ear, confirming I'd cleared the dead zone. "*Chakra reports severe injuries inside. We're inbound, but we need you to get it done as quickly as you can.*" I laid Rush down and the two equipment-laden paramedics with Crash got to work. Safire was already gone.

I nodded automatically. "On it. Galatea?"

"*Stays on post. Go.*"

I launched, not looking at Shelly — this time I knew the route, and used it. *Get it done.* The walls and broken doors blew by at blurring speed as I went in hard.

The spheres might have been able to knock me down, but they had to be directed; I blew through the wrecked courtroom without slowing and into Big Guy, going for the clinch. We crashed past Watchman and through the remains of the judge's bench. Wrapping my legs around his armored waist, I hammer-punched him with the base of my fist. His battered helmet crumpled with a tin-can *crunch*, tore away on my second hit — and I stared, paralyzed.

No. It wasn't — It couldn't *possibly* be —

"Nobody move or the hostage gets it!" Tentacle-Guy had dragged a business-suited victim from the benches. Spheres surrounded the poor man as he hung wrapped in the animated cable, loafers kicking uselessly. Watchman froze, stood back, and I didn't — I couldn't —

Tentacle Guy shook his victim. "Back up! I mean it!"

I let go of Mr. Ludlow and the three armored villains moved in together, Tentacle Guy dangling his hostage between him and us. "Look," he said, sounding calmer through his voice-distorting helmet. "We did what we came to do, no need to wreck the building. We're leaving now."

"Put the hostage down, and nobody else dies." Watchman said it like he was talking about the weather. *It's raining; you should wear a coat.* The depleted sphere-swarm gathered in around the three.

"You're right," Tentacle Guy said just as reasonably, and the hostage's loafers touched the floor. *FLASH!* I threw up my arms as at least five spheres exploded, blinked, blinked again to clear tearing eyes. Horribly abused, my ears barely registered the panicked bystander screams and the rain of thumps as the remaining spheres hit the floor. When my ocular and aural nerves unfroze — lots faster than any normal person's would — I wanted to swear. Or cry.

They were gone.

Episode Two

Chapter Twelve: Megaton

One thing you get used to fast, is going into situations that are "developing," when you have only half an idea what's going on — and that's if you're lucky. Which makes it nice that you usually get to bring friends, lots of them. In shows and movies, superheroes go one-on-one with supervillains all the time; in real life, there's no such thing as too much backup.

Astra, *Notes from A Life.*

Back out on the balcony with The Harlequin and Andrew, the City Room was totally different than it had been when I'd passed through on my way upstairs. They'd dimmed the lights, and the atmosphere on the Dispatch floor felt tight, intense. The big screens showed the Daley Center, flanked by rows of icons I guessed represented different heroes. Lei Zi arrived quickly, followed by Blackstone and Chakra. Lei Zi and Blackstone conferred and studied the screens.

"Roster check," The Harlequin explained quietly. Leaning against the railing beside me, she pointed to two bright icons as they came up: a circle in an inverted triangle and a pink "S" in purple flames. Both were crossed by diagonal yellow bars. "Watchman and Safire are heading for the scene. The steady icons show who's on-site. The flashing icons show who's available, relative brightness indicating who can respond most quickly. The yellow bars mean they're out of contact. Someone's made the Daley Center an electronic dead zone."

Rush's angled "R" and Seven's "7" started flashing before she finished explaining. Then their icons yellow-barred too.

The City Room doors opened and Astra and Galatea came through them. Galatea almost skipped, obviously impatient, but Astra moved through the dispatch stations like — I wasn't sure *what*, but in armor and absently holding Ajax's maul, I couldn't see the peppy and earnest kid who'd swung her legs from the Assembly Room table and then practically cried for me. She stopped at a colorfully decorated station to talk to the guy there, not taking her eyes off the screens. He answered back, shrugged, obviously frustrated.

Lei Zi started giving instructions.

"Doors!" the guy with Astra shouted as a mob erupted from the Daley Center's glass doors, pushing and shoving to escape the building. Suits, mostly, but nobody looked businesslike now. Then Safire burst through the windows, practically destroying the ugly Picasso sculpture in front of the building.

"Astra, Galatea, go!" Lei Zi snapped. "No loads!"

Galatea started to say something, but Astra grabbed her by what looked like a *handle* that popped up between her shoulder blades and they were gone, through a hatch I hadn't seen. One of the screens switched to a dizzying picture marked with Galatea's symbol, gears and a lightning bolt. A mounted camera? It took us down a street, up and over a high building too fast for me to catch which one it was, and down to the plaza.

"Drop Galatea outside," Lei Zi instructed. The view dropped, then steadied as we watched Astra fly through the hole Safire had made. Astra's icon yellow-barred, but Lei Zi was already calling out more orders. "Riptide, Variforce, Quin to the bay, now. Blackstone, Dispatch is yours." Then she was gone, too, through the same hatch taken by Astra and Galatea, and The Harlequin went over the railing to bounce after her.

The tension didn't die when they left — if anything it ratcheted higher. Chakra said something to Blackstone, then stepped away and headed for the stairs. Taking them quickly, she brushed by us to turn into the next office over, closing the door.

"I don't get it." I wasn't really asking a question, but Andrew answered anyway, not taking his eyes off the icons on the main screen..

"They don't know what's in there, but if the fight's inside then there are hundreds of trapped civilians on the floors above it. They're going in blind with everything they've got. It's what they do." He looked at the closed office door. "And in a minute they won't be *totally* blind."

What? Oh. Chakra. The hero news sites speculated endlessly about what the psychic hottie did for the team.

Crash's icon lit up, joined by another one — a yin-yang symbol I didn't recognize.

"Crash does civilian evac and delivers paramedics and other first-responders to the scene," Andrew explained. "It looks like Sifu is helping him." Wow. The kid was, what, sixteen? How did they get away with that? Whatever I thought about fielding kids younger than I was, he and a paramedic were waiting by the ugly sculpture when Astra flew out carrying Rush on what looked like part of a *door*. Rush's icon lit up, with a bright red bar across it.

"Red bars mean a hero's down, red X's mean dead." Andrew whispered.

So he was alive. I let out a relieved breath. Astra only stayed for a couple of words before flying up and back through the hole. The room wound tighter, Blackstone conferring and watching the screens while everyone else did whatever they did. A second screen came up, showing a zooming scene — the team floater? — following Astra's original route. I looked over at Andrew, but he stayed focused on the screens. Watching The Harlequin's status icon?

"*Zone in sight,*" Lei Zi's voice came over a room-wide broadcast. "*Galatea reports sounds of at least two physical altercations in-zone, stood down. Preparing to shake out and enter.*"

Then all the yellow bars vanished and the main screen view split into multiple pictures, info-bars scrolling across their bottoms. Watchman's voice filled the room. *"Dispatch, hostilities have ended, repeat, ended. Rush is down, civilian fatalities and casualties. Request all available medical assistance."*

Sighs of relief, scattered cheers, even cut-off applause ran through the stations.

"Hostilities ended, Watchman," Blackstone acknowledged. "The Harlequin, all other field Sentinels incoming. Secure the situation until the CPD relieves you, expedite civilian aid."

"Secure, aid, understood. Watchman out." The lights came back up to normal office brightness, and that was it. Blackstone looked up, gave us a nod. Andrew returned it, clapped me on the shoulder.

"That's the show, sport. They'll be out there awhile, until everyone hurt is helped and in the ER and the cops have yellow-taped the scene. Give it an hour, they'll be back for after-action debriefings — analysis and evaluation to follow when Blackstone and Lei Zi have had a chance to go over everything."

"That's... What the hell *was* that?"

"The glamorous life of a superhero. See you around the Dome." He went down to the floor, said a few words to Blackstone, and left at a trot. I stayed on the balcony, trying to figure out what I'd just seen, until the office door behind me opened. Chakra stepped out, drooping but eyes bright.

"Uh," I stuttered. "You okay?"

She looked me over from head to toe, drew in a deep breath, smiled wide, and reached up to pat my cheek. Heat flashed through me, and her eyes got bigger. She laughed.

"Yes. Yes, I am. And you're adorable. Come see me after dinner. Doctor's orders." A final stroke and she turned, leaving me frozen. Gathering her skirts, she turned and proceeded down the stairs.

What the hell was that?

Astra

Dispatch came online the instant the wrecking crew disappeared, my frantic call for medical assistance got a "Can do," from Lei Zi before I'd finished making it, and less than a *minute* later Variforce floated himself and The Harlequin, wrapped in a rolling cocoon of glowing fields, through the courtroom doors. Lei Zi really had mobilized the team behind us — another minute and every Sentinel would have come down on the bad guys like the wrath of God.

Shaken court attendees trapped by the fight climbed out of their refuges, coughing in the drywall dust that floated in the air and covered everything. In the beams of the emergency lights, the courtroom looked like contractors had started an unscheduled demolition without getting everyone out first. Already under Chakra's remote guidance, The Harlequin went to work on an unconscious bailiff while I stood there. My cheek was bleeding again, copper on my tongue, and I needed to *move*.

So why did I feel like the whole scene was far, far away?

"Shelly?" I whispered. "Get Blackstone, please? Private?"

"*Yes, my dear?*" he answered.

"Sir? I unmasked one of the attackers. It was Eric Ludlow. And he was standing up to *Watchman*." I didn't know which was worse.

"*You're certain?*"

"Yes, sir. But he's only a *B Class* — I pinned him *easy* last year — *Dad* works with him and the rest of The Crew on cleanup emergencies. He cried, he's cleaned up — I mean — "

"*I understand.*"

"I can't believe he'd — "

"*Of course not. I'll alert the proper people, and we will find out what has happened to our Mr. Ludlow. It may be that he is being used, even controlled. Are you all right, my dear?*"

I heard his subtext: *Can you do your job?* Taking a deep breath, I let it out. "Yes."

"*Then we will speak more of this at the Dome. Try not to be concerned.*"

I got busy, flying paramedics and their equipment up from the plaza as Chakra directed them by psychic triage, then flying their strapped-down patients out. Benny Larkin was dead, along with one of the bailiffs — the nice one who'd tested Malleus' heft just yesterday. I read the name above his badge: Officer Travis Delcort. It looked like he'd just been in the wrong place when they came through the wall. I dusted him off, closed his eyes, straightened his blood-matted hair — a useless gesture, he was just going to go into a bag — and whispered his name so I could retrieve it from Dispatch if I forgot. The luckier bailiff looked like he'd been thrown, and nobody else who'd been trapped in here was more than battered and shaken, in shock or suffering transient tinnitus from the repeated flash-bangs of the stun spheres. Even Safire would be fine, according to Dispatch.

Our part of the cleanup didn't take long and, before we finished, we got word that Rush would be fine, too; he'd been shocked and concussed, but he'd been lots worse.

Getting back to the Dome meant writing up a report and going through a quick one-on-one debriefing while my memories were still fresh. The report was for the action review board and I was getting pretty good at those, but the debriefing was for our own benefit — Lei Zi and Watchman used them to analyze our encounters and tactical responses and to shape our ongoing drills and training. Also, dumping my experience and impressions onto those paid to think about them left me free to remember my earlier, happy resolution this morning.

I caught Seven after his debriefing and invited him home for Friday Night Dinner. He accepted as casually as he did everything else, which gave me a beautiful opening for carrying out my fiendish plan.

I had other motives, too. I'd invited Julie, Annabeth and Megan out of desperation — I hadn't seen them in weeks outside of the classes I'd managed to scramble to (my professors were beginning to think I was a rumor) — and with all us girls, including Shelly, Dad really needed more testosterone at the dinner table. Toby had a *date* (I seriously questioned the intelligence of anyone willing to put up with Toby, but the IQ curve meant there had to be someone who'd date my troll of a brother), and Dane was in New Jersey having one of the most impressive rookie years in professional soccer.

Being in a fight meant we were all completely off the watch roster for twenty-four hours, so I threw on a Bees-coordinated skirt outfit — Friday nights were *not* casual, even when it was just family — and drove Shelly and me home. Seven followed in his sporty Maserati, but nobody would notice him if he didn't want them to.

The trees of Oak Park had started to turn, lining Chicago Avenue with oranges and yellows. There'd be weekends raking the front and back yards soon, with sandwiches and lemonade and pie; Mom wasn't big on homemaking (we had a cleaning service), but she made us celebrate certain calendar events in a way that would make Norman Rockwell proud. As I pulled up to the curb, Shelly made a weird strangling sound and all my instincts went into overdrive.

"What?" I whispered, parking but not turning off the engine, scanning the shadows between the trees and houses for threats as Seven pulled in behind us — he hadn't missed a single traffic light on our tail. The Bees weren't here yet. Earbug out but not yet on, I reached for my cell. Home had *security*, darn it,. It was invisible and courtesy of the Sentinels and probably as good as anyone's who wasn't the leader of a country, so what could be wrong? Shelly grabbed my wrist before I could hit "0" — our personal 911 if not canceled once punched.

She pointed to the faded green Volkswagen Beetle in the driveway. Okay... With my eyes, I could see the light pattern of old curb rash on its left bumper, but I didn't see — A blue and white bumper sticker clung to its back bumper, seriously faded but I could read it, and it said *My daughter is an Oak Park honor student.* I spun in my seat, nearly destroying the steering wheel. Shelly wasn't moving, and her eyes had gone huge.

It was *Mrs. Boyar's* car. I hadn't seen her in four years, since a little after the funeral. She'd moved away where everything wouldn't remind her of Shelly.

Breathe, Hope. You can breathe, and WHAT IS SHE DOING IN OUR HOME? Parked behind us, Seven didn't get out of his car but my cell started singing *Luck, Be A Lady.* The Frank Sinatra rendition, of course.

Shell let me go so I could answer it.

"Is everything okay?"

I twisted to look back at his car. "Yeah. Just unexpected company."

"Should I go?" His Lucky Cloak of Anonymity would never last through a whole dinner.

"I don't — could you wait — " I tried to think. Shelly desperately shaking her head decided me. "Could Shell wait in your car? I need to go in." Mom hadn't called. She hadn't called after I'd texted her to get late approval for Seven, so she didn't want us *not* coming home. Whatever was happening, I could be sure of at least that.

Shelly finally moved enough to do more than nod, and then she was scrambling out her door and around to Seven's car. Ducking in, she slumped down below the level of his dash. Okay.

For a moment, I considered putting my earbug on so she could listen in, dropped it as a *bad* idea. During my required therapy sessions, I'd talked to Doctor Mendel about the idea of bringing Shelly and her mom together; she'd categorically dismissed it — any move before Shell was ready to do it herself was a huge risk, and she obviously wasn't ready now. Letting her listen in, when I didn't know the sitch or what I'd be hearing, seemed to fit the same category.

I turned off the engine, checked my hair, swore off procrastinating, got out and resisted the urge to *sneak* up to the front door and eavesdrop with my super-duper hearing. *"Once*

more into the breach, dear friends..." Pull on your big-girl panties,
Hope.

Flying blind into the Daley Center had been easier.

"I'm home!" I called, closing the door behind me. "Hi, Mrs. B.
Saw your car, you're still driving it?" *Ack. Dumb — no, stupid, she*
pushed *it here because that's what people can do in your world.*
Mrs. Boyar sat beside Mom on the living room couch, on its edge
like she'd almost jumped off of it when I opened the door.

Mrs. Boyar had never been comfortable in our house. *Mr.*
Boyar had only ever been Shelly's dad in the sense that he'd
donated chromosomes, but by the time Shelly and I had met in
grade school, her mom had worked her way up to practice manager
for Larkin & Carosi, corporate attorneys — or as she'd affectionately
called them, inveterate shysters — while raising Shelly on her own.
I'd never understood why she hadn't liked to come over; Shelly had
practically lived here with her blessing. Like my family, hers had
deep roots in Oak Park even if she'd grown up on the poorer side,
and she'd liked me; a kid can tell when parentals are faking, just
being polite to offspring's friends, and she hadn't been. Now...

Now, I had serious dry mouth. I knew what she saw; I'd grown
maybe two inches since she'd last seen me, but the tomboy was
gone. The evil, evil Bees had turned me into a fashionista, and if I
couldn't be beautiful, I could manage stylish. Tonight, I wore a
sleeveless silk blouse with a loose cravat collar, calf-high leather
boots, and a belted and triple-layered seriously mini skirt saved
from immodesty only by the opaque white tights I wore under
them.

Mrs. B smiled, but didn't look surprised. It helped, but she was
still wound tighter than a cello. If she was the A-string, I was the D.

"Hello, Hope. You've turned out wonderfully."

"And you look great." She did, but I was running out of words. I
searched Mom's face for a clue, but she'd gone completely Zen and
sat there at one with the universe. *Thanks, Mom.* "Are you staying
for dinner?" *Beeeep — wrong question! Easily misinterpreted as a*

hint to go away. I longingly contemplated making a cowardly break for my room, or at least the kitchen and a glass of water; I didn't have enough spit left to sound natural.

Mom *still* didn't say anything, and Mrs. B wouldn't stop staring. Dropping my gaze I finally saw the leather executive folder she held neatly on her lap, the kind you might take documents into a boardroom meeting in. Mrs. B started, looked down at the folder like she'd forgotten it was there, and drew a breath.

"I came to see you, Hope." Her hands stroked the leather. "I needed to ask you something."

"Okay. Sure." What else could I say? *Still* no clue from Mom, and we were *so* going to have words later. Mrs. B opened the folder, held it out, and I accepted it automatically.

And almost dropped it. The top page was a character study in colored pencil. A sleek, anime-style figure, blue and white, seams and rivets suggesting a retro automaton. I helplessly flipped the pages. More Robotica sketches. Shell had actually been very good, but a corner of my brain wondered how Mrs. B even *had* these. Shell had kept all her superhero sketches at our place; her mom hadn't approved and hadn't let her work on them at home. And I'd *burned* everything — hadn't I?

"Your mother gave me those," Mrs. B said, like she was reading my mind. "She brought them to me when I left for the position she found me."

And I'd explore *that* later, too. Now, I just nodded. She held out her hands and I returned the folder. It went back in her lap, her hands sliding over it until she folded them together. Her eyes were bright.

"Hope, I — I've known that you were Astra for some time." Her face was a tight, controlled mask. "I saw you at the power station ribbon-cutting last year, and nobody who really knows you can miss it."

Maybe I could faint; I was pretty sure all the blood had left my head. "You must absolutely hate me," I managed. Her eyes widened.

"No! No, never." Her hands tightened over the folder. "It was my daughter's obsession, always, not — You enjoyed playing in the world she made."

My cold cheeks were wet. "She didn't want to go."

Mrs. B didn't ask what I meant by that. Instead she gave me a look that was pure Shell in an adult face, and took another deep breath.

"I came tonight to ask if you used her designs. I saw the news today."

Oh, God. Shelly, standing sentinel on Daley Plaza, no gear, all sleek chrome lines. "I'd never — " I blurted, stopped, horrified. What could I possibly ...

Now Mom nodded. It was over.

"I'd never do that, Mrs. B. But — " *Deep breath, Hope.* "But Shelly did."

I couldn't bring Shelly in — not before I told her mom everything about the Teatime Anarchist and quantum-ghosts, made sure she understood what Shelly was now, that she was our Shelly's Siamese twin, joined at the brain. Finished, I prayed to every saint, promised a million Hail Marys, while my BFF's mom wrestled with the mystery that was Shell.

In the end, I'd been afraid for nothing; Mrs. B's face was a study in wonder.

"Can I see her?"

"She's hiding in the car."

Seven was great, giving us space and staying quiet while I tried to talk Shelly out of his ride, but I felt like I was negotiating for hostages (not that I've ever done that *myself*).

"She *knows,* Shell."

"She can't!"

"She knows *everything.* Well, not *why* the Anarchist backed you up — I told her he thought I needed a sidekick."

"How can she — "

"*Please*, Shell. You've *wanted* this."

"I *can't!*" Seven shrugged, no help there. I closed my eyes, counting, and wondered if Vulcan had thought of the need for off-switches in hysterical robots.

"Shell, please," I tried again. "I know you're scared, but your mom — I swear to God that I will drag you inside if I have to." Then I followed Dad's ever-valuable negotiating advice and shut up while my BFF worked it through.

"Okay." I barely heard her. "I'll come in. But — Stay with me?"

"Always." If it wasn't so serious I'd be laughing at the freaky role-reversal. *Shelly* was always the one pushing, daring me. "C'mon." She took my hand, let me pull her out of the car, and didn't let go till we were through the front door. At least she had the presence of mind to set her strength parameters to "teenage normal" before Mrs. B pulled her into her arms. Otherwise, her return hug would have crushed her mom's spine.

More hysteria, but of a nicer kind. "Mom" and "I'm sorry" were the only words in her vocabulary for a while.

Dinner was late, with an extra setting, but Mom always planned for surprises. The Bees arrived after the drama, and though only Julie had known Mrs. B at all — our families had all shared the same parish — they didn't miss a beat.

With only eyes for Shelly, Mrs. B didn't blink at the gorgeousness that was Seven, and he seemed to know exactly what *I* wanted to know — drawing her out in the smoothest friendly interrogation I'd ever seen. Shelly sat by her mom and kept touching her, and Mrs. B's eyes got bright a lot, but the dinner conversation stayed inside social protocol; I found out that Mom had tried to talk Mrs. B into staying in Oak Park after Shelly died, found her the job she took with a lobbying firm in Springfield, even saw her a couple of times a year when she went to the capitol to do her own lobbying for state funds (and now I knew, to my shame, why Mom had never taken me with her on those lobbying trips).

One call to Mom after she'd seen the news, and Mrs. B had driven straight up Highway 55, nonstop, to get here.

The one thing nobody asked was *What now?* Mrs. B would want Shelly back, and worrying that I might lose her to Springfield made me feel small — I was *happy* for her, really, and I was an awful, awful person. We left with more hugs, tears, and promises to see Mrs. B at the Dome tomorrow (Mrs. H now — she'd finally remarried), and I hid behind the thought that Blackstone might be able to figure it all out.

I hugged the Bees at the curb — they'd been great and Megan had even laid off the snark — but then darted over before Seven could climb in his car. Door open, he turned with a smile. Even with all the drama, I hadn't forgotten my original plan for tonight.

He looked down at me, hand on his door. "Yes?"

"Thank you," I said. "But that's not what this is about." Ignoring the audience, I put my hands on his shoulders, floated up a few inches, leaned in, and kissed him. Not a peck, either; full, soft lip contact, held long enough to settle in and with a little hum on the end. Surprised, he still dropped his hands lightly to my waist, reciprocated nicely, and didn't protest when I drew back and then leaned in closer, lips to his ear, to whisper.

"Your turn."

Then I was back down on my feet and into my car, face burning as the Bees clapped and whistled. Shelly scrambled in beside me, laughing uncontrollably, and I managed to start the engine and drive away without hitting anything as I watched Seven in the mirror.

He didn't follow.

Chapter Thirteen: Megaton

Perhaps the most disturbing conclusion by researchers into breakthrough phenomena is that reality appears to be multiple-choice. Pre-Event, we could say with confidence that God exists or he doesn't. The same could be said about mind-waves, phlogiston, the luminiferous aether, and the Laws of Magic. Magical lands only existed in the imagination, but the Event has done more than merely make the laws of nature open to exceptions. Today, we live in a world where Alice can fall down the rabbit hole and come back with the Jabberwocky's head, and sooner or later someone is going to raise Atlantis from its watery grave. Superheroes are the modern world's least odd oddity.

Dr. Jonathan Beth, addressing the Eleventh Annual Conference on Breakthrough Science.

Standing in front of Chakra's door, I almost turned around. If I were back at school, Tony would be fist-bumping me and trying to get my promise to feed him all the hot details later. *Chakra! Score!*

Last fall, after I'd spent the year seriously muscling up and losing most of my extra weight, Ms. Truman across the street had invited me inside after a job for lemonade. A seriously hot mom, she was divorced and had been paying me to do her yard since middle school, and she made it real clear once she had me inside that Billy had gone next door to play and she had something *very* recreational in mind for me. I never told any of my "friends" — they'd have laughed themselves sick at how fast I got out of there.

"A hot cougar mom offered me some afternoon delight and I ran like hell" doesn't make a good story.

This felt way too close to then, and I was remembering the queasy excitement and full-on mind-blowing *panic* I'd felt when Ms. Truman, who I'd had more than a few fantasies about, had dropped her robe. I wasn't *stupid* — Chakra couldn't be planning on jumping me — but what could she possibly want?

I finally touched the door screen, expecting an answering "Who is it?" Instead it opened before the chime faded. I hesitated in the doorway, heard her laugh.

"Come in!"

I had no idea what I'd expected, maybe a tacky fake-eastern Bollywood love nest, but this wasn't it. The air smelled of frankincense and sandalwood. I knew the scent from my mom's New Agey decorating, but here it was a hint and not an eye-stinging cloud. Candles floating in glass bowls added to the indirect ceiling lighting, and curtains hid the corners of the room. The dominant colors were yellow, white, and gold, and backless couches framed an open space wide enough for two people to sit on the floor with plenty of room. I knew it was wide enough because Chakra already occupied half of it.

She wore flowing white harem pants and a sleeveless midriff-baring white and gold stitched vest that showed off the henna patterns decorating her arms and stomach. Her dark hair framed warm brown eyes and a warmer smile as she looked up from where she sat, and I almost chickened out.

Her smile widened, but she didn't laugh again. "Sit."

There was a space by the door for shoes; I hesitated before toeing mine off, and the door closed behind me. Feeling big and clumsy, I lowered myself to the floor to sit cross-legged facing her. Our knees almost touched. No way could I put my feet on top of my thighs the way she did. What did Mom call that? Lotus position?

"Was that so hard, Mal? I won't eat you. Or — " she actually winked " — *compromise* you in any way. Disappointed?"

I couldn't tell if the rising heat was my power or just a full-body flush. She sighed and shook her head sadly without losing the smile.

"My *reputation*. Well. I'm not *all* about sex. I'd better explain at least a little — it's important to your decision and we can't have you jumping out of your skin. Is that all right?"

Her lips twitched when I nodded spastically, but she didn't continue. Instead, she rested her hands on her legs, palms up, and watched me. The silence stretched.

"What — "

"Shhh."

It was getting too weird, and I started counting just for something to do. Thirty beats later, I realized our breathing had matched. Another thirty, and we'd synced pulses too.

And how do I know that?

She opened her mouth, and this time there were deep, deep undertones beneath her words.

"Tantrism starts with the belief that the world we experience is reality, not an illusion, which makes it different from other Eastern and esoteric belief systems." She laid out her words with almost no emphasis, in time with my breathing. "It also rejects dualism, the division between physical and spiritual, and understands that everything is sacred. 'Nothing exists which is not divine.' So the tantric practitioner doesn't seek a mystery behind the world, outside of it; she seeks the transcendent and immanent in the truth of the world of her senses. She seeks the power inside herself, himself, through disciplines that include tantric meditation, yoga, and sex, which won't happen here."

I've been hypnotized. The thought wound its way through my head as she talked. Did I care? Not really. I felt the opposite of drugged, hyper-aware of everything but not reacting to any of it, not even the last bit that confirmed every hormonally charged fantasy.

"Getting down to mechanics," she continued in the same even pace, "the Tantric practitioner seeks to awaken her Kundalini power, drawing it from its base in the Root Chakra, the Muladhara, at the base of the spine. The Muladhara is the lowest of the seven major chakras; you may think of them as nodes in your auric body. By raising Kundalini power from the Root Chakra upward through the Swadhisthana, the Manipura, the Anahata, the Vishuddha, the Ajna, and finally the Sahasrara, the Crown Chakra, the Tantric can regulate her body and mind, see the world for what it is, even work her will externally in it. My breakthrough allows me to see, understand, and act to a degree unachievable even by Tantric masters, but the principles are the same. So, I can see *you*."

She said *"you"* with a beat, and I felt my heart jump, once, then settle again. I had to be hallucinating, because everything was glowing, Chakra brightest of all. Leaning forward over her knees, she reached out and lightly touched me, beneath my heart, right below my sternum.

"You are blocked, and by your own will. Here." Under her fingers, my chest glowed and pulsed a deep golden yellow and I *still* didn't freak. "You feel your power rise, but you trap it here. It gathers in your Manipura, the seat of both action and fear. You will not release it, because if you cannot use it then you cannot hurt anyone again."

Sitting back, she deliberately broke her breathing and I blinked. The *snap* as everything returned to normal was almost audible, and I realized I was practically burning up — she'd called *it* up, but it wasn't *going* anywhere. She raised an eyebrow.

"I can release it," she said in a completely normal voice.

I almost bolted. Except for the brief touch, she hadn't changed her position since she started talking, but she'd let me go as easily as she'd pulled me in. She kept her eyes on me as I sorted through a dozen flashing thoughts — from *Run, run now*, to *How the hell did she do that?* Her next words didn't help.

"I can cage it, too. Tighter than it already is, if you want. Everyone will be safe."

I was on my feet without even thinking about moving, at the door. "Stop." The depth was back in her voice, and I stopped. I couldn't move, couldn't touch the door screen, could barely hear over the roar in my head.

"What I can't let you do is leave without choosing," she said behind me.

I made myself turn around. She'd risen to her feet, and stood as gracefully and naturally as she'd sat.

Why? I didn't have to ask. I knew; I couldn't go home as an unexploded bomb. She could see I understood, and her lip-twitch was back.

"This is a traumatic day for everybody, it seems."

Huh? I shook it away, swallowed, finally found the words. "If all you're going to do is fix me, then why am I so scared?"

She closed the distance and reached out again, this time spreading her hand over my heart.

"Because you have to make a decision *here*. I can make you safe, but that will take away your power to help. You should feel lucky. Most breakthroughs don't get a chance to refuse their gift — all they can do is deal with it, find a blessing in it." Her eyebrow went up, daring me. "I," she laughed softly, "am merely a facilitator."

I could barely breathe. "Why do you want someone as dangerous as me around?"

"Remember Nimbus? Able to fly at the speed of light? Burn through ten-inch hardened steel? Think about the trees. We could barely slow them down, but *you* could level a forest if you had to. Blackstone says that sometimes saving people requires a really big gun. Sadly, he is right."

"Can you turn me off again if it doesn't work out?"

"No. I can tip the balance inside you right now only because you've already done half the job, but your decision will be final. Do you need time to think about it?"

The red and black costume Andrew and The Harlequin had shown me earlier leaped into my mind. And the City Room screens where I saw Astra and the rest throw themselves into a fight they didn't know anything about, because there were *people* in there. They called them civilians, bystanders, but they meant *innocent victims*.

You owe a life, so save a life.

"No, I don't. Not really."

She nodded, and I knew she was still seeing me with the same vision she'd shown me. She didn't ask if I was sure — just reached out again to touch me there, where she had before. I didn't explode but the world did, like the worst hit to the solar plexus I'd ever taken. I didn't feel my knees hit the floor, couldn't feel anything beyond the bursting star that linked my head and my core. I was pretty sure I shouted, and I didn't lose it completely; when everything came back, I was crouched on knees and elbows, head down, feeling channels inside me flood with slow heat radiating out from the spot where she'd laid her hand. The heat faded, steadied.

"Here," she said. While I'd been doing whatever, she'd retrieved a teacup from a sideboard I hadn't noticed. She put the small china cup on the floor in front of me. "Push it." I stared up at her. I felt like I'd run a mile — and could run a hundred more.

"Just push it."

Okay ... I touched it with my index finger, felt the heat waiting inside, *pushed*, as soft as a breath.

A dim flash, like a match-flare, and the tiny cup skidded across the floor to fetch up against the leg of the farthest couch. Upright and whole, unharmed.

"Yes!" I couldn't stop looking at it. She smiled enigmatically and slid down the wall to sit beside me. When I sat back, she patted my knee.

"Welcome to the game, hero."

Grendel

"I can't believe I'm doing this for a *doll*," Latisha groused.

I managed to keep the laugh in. Nix had solemnly informed me that her fairy garden, in the best tradition of fairy gardens, was *secret* — which meant that it was utterly hidden to mortals. This being Hillwood, "hidden" was a stretch; she'd located it in the shadow of one of the old main hall's chimneys where a joint in the roof created a deep nook, far back enough nobody could see even the climbing vines from the ground.

Flyers passed over it all the time, but Ozma had contributed a nothing-to-see-here charm; if Nix or someone else in on the secret didn't tell you where it was, you just didn't find it. Of course Latisha wasn't a flyer; she'd wrapped her arms around my neck and her legs around my waist and held on as I scaled the building wall to pull us up on the roof.

The roof-garden was completely against school rules, of course.

"Hurry, hurry, hurry!" Nix called from the shadows. I carefully leaned out and began pulling up the load from the ground. Getting everything over the edge of the roof without scraping the wall and gutter was the trickiest part — I had to throw the rope up over the peak of the roof where Latisha could anchor it; sure I could lift lots heavier stuff easy, but *leverage* was a problem if I didn't want to tip back over the edge. Finally, slinging it over my shoulder like a huge Santa-sack, I climbed over the peak to join them.

The night-poppies were open in the moonlight, drinking in starlight and moonbeams with their white petals. Half of the plants in Nix's garden were *different*. Environmentalists who got nervous over genetically modified organisms like transgenic corn or cotton would shit bricks if they ever found out where Ozma got a lot of her magical ingredients.

"Come on! Come on!" Nix flew around my head, and even Latisha smiled. Sliding down to the "valley" made by the U of joined roofs, I unpacked the box frames. Half the plant boxes went in easy, and Latisha went to work on the trellis-linked ones.

She touched a tea vine out on its reaching tip, and it began to unwind, curling around her finger like a friendly snake. Vine by vine, she coaxed them off the trellises, then the lower creepers wound in with them.

She really was going to make a fortune someday; her power was over *hair*, but by some weird quirk, she could extend it to anything from clinging plants to shoelaces and she could braid anything into her styles. The trellises cleared, I pulled them out and replaced them with separate climbing frames for her to wind the vines up in while Nix fussed over each box.

"Thanks," I whispered as she tied up the last climbing vine. She rolled her eyes.

"I'm not doing it for *you*. I'll miss Nix."

"Everybody will." I hefted the first boxes and walked them back over the roof. Down in the shadows, half of Gilmore Hall's residents were risking curfew to take them away and finish the packing job.

It was probably the biggest secret rebellion the Headmaster would never know about. We hoped. A perilous night for the temporarily expanded Army of Oz.

Chapter Fourteen: Astra

These children are dangerous! They are weapons pointed at your children! We do not allow children to own guns or to carry them to school; who knows how many "normal" students carry dangerous powers to school every day? And when they see superheroes, glorified vigilantes, acting outside the law, how many are inspired to take "justice" into their own hands?

Hiding the possession of superhuman powers should be a crime, must be made a crime, for their protection and ours!

Representative Mal Shankman

Shelly and I ended the night with a sleepover in my rooms. Robots don't snore, but they do like to cuddle. They also rise early and leave strange Post-It notes on your forehead. The one that stuck to my hand when I stretched and rubbed my eyes said *Soylent Green is people!* If I asked, she'd probably reference some obscure dystopian or post-apocalyptic sci-fi movie.

The morning meeting started with a group review on yesterday's fight. Blackstone and Lei Zi had spent the night breaking down our mask-cam recordings and witness accounts, and we got to watch a real time replay of the encounter. Which didn't tell us much, since even Watchman and Safire arrived late to the scene.

Blackstone froze the action at the moment when the villains disappeared under cover of the last wave of flash-bangs.

"The media has already named the three unknowns Balz, Twist, and Dozer — short for Bulldozer, and collectively dubbed them the Wreckers." A touch switched the picture for a close-up of "Dozer" — Eric Ludlow, Gantry, helmet ripped away, face pale and shocked. "We have not released any Sentinels footage for public consumption. Yes, Astra?"

I lowered my hand. "Do we know anything yet?"

"No, but based on your testimony, Detective Fisher has obtained a warrant for Mr. Ludlow's home, and they have placed it under discreet observation. If it was Eric at the Daley Center, he hasn't been home since. You are tasked to serve the warrant with the detective's team after the meeting."

I nodded unhappily.

"We also hypothesize at least one, possibly two more members of the team, a Verne-type and almost certainly a teleporter. They may be the same person, but we've named the hypothetical unknowns Phreak and Drop. This is based on the complete signals blackout, and, of course, their entrance and exit. Any reconstruction is speculative, but there is no evidence in the building's security footage of their presence before its system was hacked and shut down along with the phones. There is less than a three-minute gap between the time everything shut down and they made their appearance through the back wall beside the judge's bench. Since no witnesses place them anywhere else in the building, we believe they teleported into the private hall behind the courtroom.

"According to bystander accounts, the court bailiff was an unintentional death when the wall collapsed inward under Dozer; the three went straight for Mr. Larkin. Twist snapped his neck with one of his cables while Balz' spheres covered the scene. At that point they, might simply have been prepared to exit the way they came — witnesses generally agree that they weren't threatening anyone else. However, Watchman and Safire entered the action before they could withdraw."

He reset the scene to the beginning of the fight and we watched it again. Watchman's first move had been to fly through the doors opened by the fleeing audience and smack into Dozer, separating him from the other two and throwing him back from the bystanders and against the half-collapsed wall. Then things got busy. Blackstone froze the scene when the first flash-bang sphere went off in Safire's face.

"Debris analysis shows that the spheres wielded by Balz were not self-motivating or remotely directed. We hypothesize Balz to be a B or C Class telekinetic, unusually capable of multiple simultaneous levitations and manipulations. He fielded several types of spheres. Beyond the many flash-bang spheres, there were at least a dozen motion-triggered, short-ranged 'taser spheres' — which is how they neutralized Rush." Skipping forward to a slowed shot of Rush appearing out of hypertime and getting zapped from three sides illustrated the point.

Across the table, Rush actually *laughed*. He shrugged painfully. "They got me good, guys. Too bad I dropped Seven at the doors."

"Indeed. And considering the number of civilians within the combat zone, we are fortunate that no others became involved until Twist took his hostage." The next skip took us to the moment when Twist wrapped one of his two arm-cables around the poor guy and hauled him into the middle of the fight. "We have yet to identify the hostage. Of course, there was no police cordon on the building after the fight, and not everyone remained on the scene to give their account of events to the police."

I tried to remember if I'd seen him after the last flash. On the floor? Watchman saw my face and shook his head; he'd have checked first thing to make sure the guy was all right. *Wait.* Turning back I caught Blackstone giving me the eye as well — and he wasn't showing footage *after* the flash. He gave me a bland smile and moved on.

"Your epads will have full stats for the spheres' projected abilities once Vulcan has finished reconstruction of the bits that Watchman, Seven, and Astra left us, as well as an estimate of Dozer's and Twist's capabilities. Quin?"

Blackstone yielded Quin the screen. She moved slower today, and I wondered if she'd gotten any sleep at all last night; if not for her rubberized body, she'd probably have bags under her eyes. She brought up a frame from a news clip showing Daley Plaza, focusing on the shattered Picasso sculpture and the hole in the Daley Center.

"There has been no Internet download from the Wreckers declaring their intentions, but we are constructing a threat profile. Media reaction to our part has been mostly positive, although we are seeing the expected 'why didn't they respond sooner?' buzz from anti-hero groups. The usual conspiracy theorists are claiming we arrived late and let them escape to cover our part in the 'assassination.'

"The fact that there was only one bystander death helps. The second, injured bailiff is expected to make a full recovery. This will sound cynical, but bystander death in this case has had the positive effect of suppressing media commentators sympathetic to vigilante actions like these. Our assessment of the Wreckers, leaving out a few things such as Dozer's suspected identity, and our respects to Officer Johansen's and Officer Pratt's families, will be on our public webpage by noon."

That was it for Quin, and she didn't try to end her comments with anything upbeat. Yesterday's fight had sucked, and the only good thing to say was it hadn't been worse. Blackstone ended the meeting by announcing Mal's assisted success last night, and we all gave the boy a round of applause. He looked conflicted. Or constipated. Beside him, Shelly was almost as hard to read in her silver-and-blue form, but she'd spent most of the meeting in her own world. Now she dashed off without even giving me the wink she usually dropped whenever she knew I was going to meet Detective Fisher. Blackstone broke off his conversation with Lei Zi when he saw I stayed behind.

"Walk with me, Hope?" He steered us down the hall to his office.

"About Shelly — " I started as soon as his door closed. He held up his hand.

"I'm aware of her family reunion, my dear, and I hope it turns out well. Indeed, this is what I wished to speak with you about."

Sitting, he took a moment to collect his thoughts. What was going on?

"Our need for secrecy presents us with a problem, my dear. Presently, outside of us two and Vulcan, everyone believes that Galatea is a remote platform — essentially a telepresence-piloted drone. It is easy enough to let everyone believe that you and the 'pilot' share a past — which is of course true — but I also suspect she has let Jamal, at least, in on her secret."

He stopped again, which didn't help my tightening nerves.

"I have spoken to Legal Eagle, and he tells me that creating a cover civilian identity for Shelly will not be as easy as we might have thought. Legal cover identities of the kind used by Variforce and even Seven require a real, legal identity beneath them; the person must already legally exist, the applicable agencies must know both his cover and his true identity. Creating a complete and unsubstantiated identity out of whole cloth is legal fraud."

"Couldn't we tell them...oh." My stomach sank.

"You understand. To tell the appropriate authorities — the DSA in this case — exactly what Shelly is and why she needs a new identity would require full disclosure of her status, which is that of an artifact, not a person in the legally recognized sense."

He watched me carefully. "Which would also mean revealing that she's something that doesn't exist yet — a true artificial intelligence. And if they trace her back to the systems breach the military experienced during the Omega operation..."

I covered my mouth and clamped down babbling panic. Sure, they were on our side, but government paranoia knew no bounds. And yes, any paranoid government agency that tried to seize her as a threat to national security or to take her apart to see how her quantum-mind ticked would have to go through me to get to her. But if they had the *law* on their side... How could we fight?

"We could create a cover identity ourselves — indeed, Shelly could do it with a snap of her fingers by hacking the necessary databases and falsifying records. But it would be thin, and itself illegal." His face told me that was not an option he would support.

So Mrs. B — Mrs. H — couldn't just reclaim Shelly. Because she wasn't *real*. How was I going to tell her?

Blackstone just looked sad. "We will continue to pursue avenues of inquiry, my dear, but Shelly will not be leaving us any time soon and I thought that you should know. Perhaps now might be the time to broach another topic? Indeed, it is an observation Shelly brought me."

That got my attention back. He nodded when he saw I was focused.

"If this new Dozer is, in fact, our Eric Ludlow, it is a post-quake development. One of the first things Shelly did after the action was to look in the Big Book of Contingent Prophecy. There is no previous record of his going supervillain. To be frank, before he met you, all of his contingent futures ended in ... well, in a more personal downward spiral."

"I don't understand."

"You do remember that he is a veteran of the China War? It is my belief he was self-medicating his PTSD-related depression with alcohol. In his previous futures, he went in and out of rehab several times before, one way or another, ending in prison or merely ending it. When even a B Class Ajax-type goes on a rampage or commits suicide, it is rather spectacularly newsworthy. But his contingent futures changed the night he met *you*."

"Me?" I tried to remember the details of our "fight." It had been my *first* fight, but not much of one.

"You. Previously, it was Atlas who brought him down for the police that night; his encounter with you, instead, was yet one more change in events begun the day you became Astra."

He cleared his throat.

"I reviewed the recording of that fight. You understand that rehab only cleans the body of drugs? Certainly there is counseling, and it gives the patient space to review his choices and build new habits and resolutions with a clear head. However, afterwards, only a true commitment to change will keep him from going back into the same choices and patterns that took him there in the first place. That is why court-ordered rehab is rarely a permanent fix. So, something changed Eric's attitude regarding going into rehab, something that opened up new contingent outcomes that night. I believe that something was you."

"Now that's just — I took him down! Put him in an armlock and *sat* on him! How could I have changed anything?"

"I watched the police recording. You were quite comforting with him."

"I — " *Shhhh. It's going to be all right, Eric. You're going to be all right.* My first fight, and the memory was so strong I could smell the damp grass and cracked concrete we'd lain across.

"Atlas put you in front on that incident because he hoped that Eric would see you as less of a threat, be less confrontational. I believe your sympathy had more of an impact than we knew."

I shook my head. "You think I changed his life? Just by being *nice*?"

"No, and yes. Doctor Mendel could explain it to you better, but the psychology of decision-making is complex. The initial motivators of any path we take don't have to be especially strong; once momentum is imparted, each decision, each action, adds to it until it takes a great deal of force to derail it."

He tapped his forehead.

"Memory is a funny thing, so we may even look back at a particular moment, relatively inconsequential by itself, and assign it great retroactive significance. I believe you had a significant impact on his attitude the night he was arrested, which made a difference in the attitude he took with him into rehab. Ultimately, he rebuilt himself through his own strength and determination, but your small act of sympathy that night may well have taken on totemic significance in his mind, a bright spot to fix on as he fought his personal demons."

"So he got clean just so he could go supervillain?"

"And there we turn back to the Big Book. Between the night of his arrest by you and January 1st, the last date on which the Teatime Anarchist retrieved any future-histories, all of Eric's contingent futures were substantially positive. Therefore, whatever has turned Eric from that path happened after January 1st. Occam's razor dictates that it is related to whatever has boosted him from B Class to at least A Class, and since we are already dealing with power-boosted breakthroughs with Temblor and possibly the Green Man, I find his change of status significant.

"But although this is all very important to know, we should also not lose sight of the fact that you may also have tremendous leverage with Eric, even now. If you should encounter him again in the field, I want you to keep that in mind. Can you?"

Wondering how I'd react if I fought Eric again kept me entertained all the way to my rendezvous with Detective Fisher.

Since Max had the superhuman beat (not so much *had* as held on to it with both hands and threatened to quit when they tried to promote him after the Villains Inc. mess), most of his assignments were heater cases — crimes kept on the front-burner because of all the media attention. For *this* one, though, his team was keeping a low profile. When I flew down, they were waiting for me, hidden in a stakeout van around the corner from Mr. Ludlow's.

Max opened the back of the van when I knocked, looking his usual rumpled self. "Astra. Glad you could make it." Officer Wyatt was with him, and a woman I didn't know. Phelps was gone, of course; so was Max's superior, Garfield, and the investigations and hearings that removed them went right up the chain of command. Max had a new boss and the city had a new Superintendent of Police.

I climbed in and he closed the door. "Hi, Jimmy." I held out my hand to the new girl. "Hi, I'm Astra."

She grinned with a dimple. "Jenny. Jennifer Stole."

"From the lab!" Jenny nodded. She wore narrow, wire-rim librarian's glasses and kept her hay-blonde hair pulled back in a tight ponytail. Max smiled around the unlit cigarette between his lips.

"Tell the kid what we've got."

She flushed at being put on the spot, but rallied.

"We haven't wanted to exercise the physical search warrant yet, but we have subpoenaed Mr. Ludlow's financial, phone, and Internet records. We've also tapped his landline. We have the house under thermal drone and remote observation and even teleport detectors in place — "

"How did you do that without going inside?"

"Laser sensors targeting his windows. Any teleporter popping in will raise the interior air pressure for a microsecond, which will be felt by the windows and measured by the lasers."

"That's very clever. Sorry."

She waved it away. "We hoped he'd come home — we'd have had you guys down on him in a second."

I wanted to talk to him, too. I imagined facing him down on his porch again, a replay of last year. *This* time... How strong *was* he now? How had he leveled up so much? I could still hope it wasn't really him.

"So, now you're here, we go in," Max said simply. "Ready?"

He lit up and blew a cloud the instant he was out of the van. We made a tidy procession, down the street and around the corner, and Fisher actually knocked — pure formality since the house was empty. He stubbed out his smoke beside a stack of empty flowerpots, nodded to me, and I took hold of the knob and popped the door, breaking the lock. Listening with all my super-duper might just in case, I heard no sounds in the house. We moved in off the porch, me in front with Fisher's team stacked up behind me.

When a quick room-to-room showed the house was clear, they holstered their guns. Fisher handed me some gloves and I snapped them on. I was really only here in case Things Happened, but the odds of Mr. Ludlow crashing through the wall were pretty long. I mostly stayed out of the way and watched them; Jenny made a beeline for the study desktop, leaving Jimmy to sort through the mail and check the phone while Max wandered through and just took it in.

The place was *tidy*. Even the piles of paperbacks by the couch were stacked neatly and had been regularly dusted. His entertainment center — with the newest Playcube and high stacks of game boxes — was just as orderly. Curiosity took me into the kitchen to check the fridge.

"It looks like rehab was successful," Max said behind me.

"No alcohol, not anywhere."

He nodded. "And the books and games. Private entertainment to distract him, keep him from going out and being sociable where there might be temptation. I spoke to Timothy Curran, the Crew's manager. Eric has been mostly going right from work to home since rehab. He's been clean since last year."

I looked around and it all made me feel worse. He'd come home from war with issues, hit bottom, pulled himself back up and gotten it together — why had he gone supervillain? What had *happened*?

I found myself whispering. "Does he have family? A girlfriend?" I'd never thought to ask.

"Parents dead — this was their home. No siblings, no girlfriend after the war."

"Did he owe money?"

Fisher flicked me a *look.* "Stop it, kid — don't go getting jammed up over this. It's nothing you could have seen when he was on the job." He shrugged. "It could be something from his old life. He had to have some point of contact with the others, maybe they were Army buddies. We'll find out."

I wondered what Fisher would think of Blackstone's obvious theory: that the hypothetical teleporter, Drop, had been the "hostage." If Blackstone wasn't sharing, it had to be because he thought the CPD might still be compromised. The problem was, *Drop* might be Mr. Ludlow's point of contact.

Wandering back into the living room, I naturally drifted over to his bookshelves. Mostly cheap paperbacks, a surprising number of them superhero fiction, but there were exceptions. I frowned, looked at the neat stacks by the couch.

"Fisher?"

"Yeah, kid?"

"Can I take a look at these?"

He looked around, nodded. "Leave it as you find it, but go ahead." Carefully laying each pile down so I could pull books and put them back, I started flipping through titles.

The fiction books were seriously worn, the bigger ones with broken backs. Almost all of them had used bookstore stamps inside their covers. But there was another set of books, all in their own pile. These were worn too, but carefully. No stamps, lots of dog-eared pages along with pages marked by colored stickies. Thumbing through the books showed a lot of highlighted pages, too.

"What have you got?" Looking up, I found Fisher standing behind me.

"I don't know." I held up one, a copy of *The Sleeper Must Awaken*. "It's mostly action and adventure novels except for these — have you ever heard of the Foundation of Awakened Theosophy?"

"FAT?" Officer Wyatt asked from across the room. "He has a couple of junk-mail letters from them." Fisher squatted beside me, hand out. I passed it over and he read the back cover and inside page.

"Jenny?" he called without looking up from the book. "Check his computer history for anything to do with FAT. And let's look at his bank account's transaction history again."

"Um, boss? You should — "

"*Hope!*" Shelly rattled my ear. "*The 1st Precinct's been hit!*

Not many people can take a flight with only my grip between them and a fall to messy death without screaming — Shelly loved my rides, but even a terminal-velocity fall wouldn't crack the titanium shell around her "brain." Fisher insisted I give him a lift, brave man (if I dropped *him*, he'd splat and get better — but it would probably be a bit obvious). I flew fast as I safely could, but by the time we got there it was all over but the shouting.

The precinct building on the corner of 18th and State looked fine — if you ignored the big hole in the north wall. Chicago's finest swarmed like a kicked beehive with no one to sting where the wall had been blown outward. The breakout had thrown bricks into the nicely trimmed trees and against the low iron fence separating the sidewalk from the precinct grounds. It wasn't a huge hole, just something an A Class Ajax-type might make punching through it on his way out. My gut clenched.

Dozer, Eric.

Riptide and Rush stood in the street watching the chaos. Riptide grinned when he saw us land.

"Hey, *chica*. Somebody knocked over the cop-shop, put down the *pajero* that tried to pop our new boy. Nice."

The guy who took a shot at Mal in the café? In everything happening, I'd completely forgotten about him.

Fisher lit up and watched the scene. "How did you get here so quickly?"

Riptide shrugged. "Greek restaurant fire five blocks south. Rush got me there and I gave it a bath until the fire trucks arrived. We were just leaving when the call came."

"See anything?"

Rush shook his head. "A big hole, body in the holding cell inside. Looks like the same MO — they broke the dude's neck. No collateral damage this time and it happened fast. We got the call only after the bad guys let the station have its phones and computer system back."

"Thanks, guys." Fisher gave them a nod, turned away. "Astra?"

I skipped to catch up. "Sorry about Riptide — "

He threw me his default twisty smile. "He'll never love cops, kid — it's not worth getting pissy over. Do you see the obvious?" Another of his little tests.

"Besides the bricks in trees?" I followed him over the low fence. "Not really, unless you mean they busted their way out this time instead of in."

A nod. "So, not quite the same MO. We find out why, it'll tell us something about them."

I wondered how much this was telling Shelly. This time their hacker had circumvented a *police station's* security with everyone outside noticing zip. *So* not good.

Nobody questioned my being there with Fisher, and when he ground out his smoke in the grass and climbed through the hole, I floated after him. Rush had been right: one large holding cell, one body. Nobody else, but if they'd been sharing they'd probably have left, too. I didn't look too close at the sad body; I'd seen plenty of death, and couldn't tell Fisher anything the forensics people wouldn't.

Nobody else was in the cell yet, obviously waiting for the crime-scene guys. Either they'd emptied out the holding cells to either side or it was a slow day, and the cops outside the cells watched us but didn't interfere. After a quick look at the victim's neck, Fisher ignored the body.

"Do you smell anything?" he asked quietly.

I took a breath, shook my head. "Not really. Brick dust, cleaning bleach, people who don't bathe. Him."

He grimaced. "I hoped their teleporter might leave a signature."

"Detective Fisher."

The new Superintendent of Police stood in the holding block hallway. Sean Redmond wore a suit with a vest, and loomed large as he surveyed the mess, hands in his pockets. Age and worry had put jowls in his cheeks and set his lips in a determined frown below his thick mustache, but his eyes were sharp and focused. Blackstone had told us all about him; they called him Big Red and The Fixer because the CPD had sent him wherever a precinct had broken down internally. After the events of the spring, the mayor had appointed him to the top seat to clean house, and from what I'd heard from Fisher, he'd been doing exactly that.

Captain Verres stood beside and slightly behind his boss. I'd met Verres before at the Fortress riot last spring. Bull-necked, bald, and even bigger than Redmond, he radiated competence. I liked him, and he liked me too — seeing me eat an anti-tank missile and walk away had impressed the heck out of him.

"And Astra," Redmond added politely, nodding to me. "I'm sorry we haven't met previously. Detective? I'm assuming this is one of yours?"

"Looks that way, sir. The MO mostly matches the Daley Building hit so far."

"Be about it, then. You'll have every department's assistance. Captain Verres will coordinate with you and the DSA. Verres has just been informing me that our would-be-shooter's Paladin connection was more than hypothetical." Another nod and he was gone.

I exhaled. "He's..." Blunt? Focused?

"Yeah. Most cops go their whole careers without shooting someone or taking a bullet. He did both and he's the guy that broke the Nickelmen, our own in-house crime family. C'mon, kid."

We exited back through the hole. After another quick chat with Rush and Riptide, Fisher let us go; he'd called his team back from Mr. Ludlow's, and my part was done.

The afternoon wore on. Back at the Dome, I filled Blackstone in on what I'd seen and thought. He thanked me nicely enough, but didn't return the favor. Shelly was out, so I worked out my frustration by trying to beat Watchman down, *with* Malleus this time. He still won, but only by two falls out of three.

Watching Mal work out against Variforce's fields was even more satisfying, and I actually managed to get some studying done (I was only keeping my grades up by taking the minimum class load this year) before Shell got back after dinner with her mom — Mrs. H was blowing every vacation day she'd accumulated in the past three years. She bounced on my bed, bright-eyed and ready to share.

I closed my eyes. Instead of sharing what Blackstone had told me, I'd been a coward. Had anyone explained that the best Mrs. H could hope for was visiting rights? If they hadn't, now was the time — we were off the watch roster again tonight and the evening looked ready to become Sleepover II.

My phone chirped and I looked at the name displayed. Julie? I hit the button.

"Hi, Julie. I — "

"*Hope, God, turn on CEN, now!*" she said the instant I picked up. "*You've been outed!*"

Chapter Fifteen: Astra

Secret identities are a staple of superhero fiction but are less common in real life. Many superheroes only wear masks to ensure that they are not easily recognized out of costume, and although they may use codenames in public, their true names are known. With the release of a viral video file today, Astra, celebrated by many as one of Chicago's greatest daughters, joins the ranks of heroes whose names are known.

CEN News clip.

I wanted to scream and vomit from horror. They had my *face*. The CEN commentator showed a split screenshot, me in my half-mask and wig opposite my high school senior yearbook picture. Shelly'd gone statue-still, looking at nothing, and now her eyes were wide. "It's on Powernet, too — they pulled it off a Viewtube video file that went up an hour ago. I can — "

"No, you can't," I croaked. I'd covered my mouth to keep the scream in, but even my frozen brain realized where she was going. "You can't hack Viewtube *and* Powernet *and* CEN, *and* thousands of people who've downloaded it. And you can't wipe their memories."

"*Hope?*" Oh. I'd dropped my cell. I picked it up.

"It's okay, Julie. Thanks."

"*What are we going to do?*"

Lie. Like *that* would work. Anyone falsely accused of being an active superhero could disprove it pretty easily by pointing to a zillion alibis, but when it was *true* — There was no way to hide once enough people were looking at you.

Closing my eyes, I couldn't stop seeing my double mug shot. I settled for staring at my toes. They were close; without thinking, I'd slid down to sit against the foot of my bed, legs tucked up, to hug my bare knees. I felt *naked*.

But her simple question got my brain moving again.

"The Bees can't do anything, Julie. Thanks, but I've got a list." *Throw up, scream, cry, keep Shell from seizing control of the Internet to protect me.* "I'll call you?"

"But — Sure. Promise?" My eyes prickled, but despite everything that was about to happen I couldn't help smiling a little. Julie always wanted to fix things and I loved her for it. I had wonderful friends.

"Promise." I hung up and stared at my cell.

"Shell? Could you let Bob know? He should..." He should do a security review of my family.

"I'm already calling *everybody*. Including Legal Eagle."

"Thanks." I took a steadying breath, wiped my eyes. "I'll call Mom and Dad."

I hadn't made plans for this — I'd avoided even *thinking* about it — but it turned out Mom had. Of *course* she had; Dad had been a reservist cape for ten years. As Iron Jack, he hardly ever went into the field and nobody recognized him when he did (even his voice changed), so there wasn't much chance he'd ever be outed — but there's an important difference between *not much* and *no chance*. Dad's response was *completely* predictable, and I hung up knowing Legal Eagle was getting a second call tonight.

After that I dressed. A sleep-top and shorts didn't go with a war council.

Blackstone and Quin waited for me in Blackstone's office — I was getting pretty familiar with the place now. Both were dressed for an evening out, which meant this had ruined everyone else's night, too. Quin looked like a homicide waiting to happen. Blackstone looked...concerned.

"Are you all right, my dear?"

No. Never again. And I was a selfish monster.

I wasn't even that worried about my family, really; after last spring's scare when we found out somebody in the Chicago mob knew my private identity, Blackstone had talked me down from near-screaming panic. The truth was that secret identities weren't that secret; *somebody* outside your circle always knew. Need-to-know people in state and federal agencies had always known who I was, *organized crime bosses* knew who I was, a handful of people who knew me had guessed. Mrs. H was just another one I'd found out about.

Having a secret identity had meant the *public* didn't know. It had meant I could still be a normal — normal*ish* — college student, could hang out with the Bees, have a life outside of the Sentinels. It had meant that nobody outside of my social circle knew who *Hope* was or gave two thoughts about her.

And it had meant that if it ever got too much, I could quit, take off the cape and walk away and disappear back into plain Hope Corrigan. I hadn't realized how much that mattered.

And now that was gone.

I wasn't scared of supervillain nemesi coming at me through my family (like I *had* any except on the new season of *Sentinels*), or even attacking me on the U of C campus; that kind of thing never happened now. I was terrified because *I* couldn't hide anymore. How selfish was that?

"Hope? Hope?"

I blinked. "Yes. I'm fine. What do we do?"

"Post-outing interview," Quin put in quickly. "I'm thinking Terry Reinhold — he's practically become our team's imbedded journalist. You assure the public that while you're upset at the invasion of privacy, you're still a dedicated Sentinel."

I nodded, laced my fingers over my knee and squared my shoulders. "And then?"

"Get seen a *lot*, but keep the mask on. Lay low as Hope for a while. Your picture will eventually drop out of the news cycle — mainstream news stations won't use it after the original story runs its course. We'll have to worry about paparazzi — they'll come after you anywhere for new shots to sell to the tabloids. We can handle them by setting you up with some Vulcan-improved anti-camera nodes; they're sensor and laser packages that detect camera lenses and use the laser to block pictures with lens flare and blooming. We'll do the same for your parent's home to discourage snoops going for 'background.'"

"That doesn't sound so bad."

"What you don't get back is any realistic expectation of public privacy, and your parents, your brothers will be — maybe not hounded — but at least sought for human-interest video bites for a while."

I actually started to relax a little bit. Mom and Dad could deal with that easy enough; they'd been interviewed plenty because of the foundation and were used to being well-known faces in Chicago. Aaron and Josh lived in different cities. Toby ... would hate the attention since it wasn't about *him*, but he'd deal. He'd probably learn to use it.

I'd call my professors — all two of them this fall — to apologize and let them know I wouldn't be back to class. *Maybe* I could set foot back on campus next semester. I hoped so; was lunch in the student commons or coffee and cupcakes in Calvert House with the Bees too much to ask? Media celebrities went to school, right? It could be fine.

And that's what's called denial. Someone had dropped another bridge on me; all I could do now was live with the damage.

I'd been quiet long enough that Blackstone cleared his throat.

"On the bright side, my dear, you'll finally be able to show your birth certificate." The brief smile wrinkled his eyes. "As to how this happened, it appears to be a political attack. The video file originated from Representative Shankman's Chicago offices, under a dummy account. That is what Shelly tells us, and since outing a superhero's secret identity is a serious civil tort, we will be able to demand that Viewtube take the video down and sue for the records needed to prove its origin. That said, individual responsibility for uploading the file may never be proven."

"What about CEN? Powernet?"

"They didn't out you — they are merely reporting the story. As will every other media outlet before this is over." He sighed.

"Hope, I've seen this before. We may be able to exact a pound of flesh from Shankman's office over this. If we're extremely fortunate, the person who made the video file will have made enough mistakes to be caught, and we'll be able to sue him or her for every penny he'll ever make as an example to others. But now that it's out, freedom of the press covers anyone who runs with the story."

I nodded again. I knew all that, really. He leaned back and tapped his desk.

"Meanwhile, I think it's a good idea to expedite our plans for the cadet team. It will give the media something else to talk about. And," he sighed again, "give you something else to think about. And who knows? Perhaps Rush will make the news again soon by dating two models or some such thing — he's been amazingly low-key of late and it's not in character."

He rubbed his eyes, conjured a smile for me.

"Fisher has also requested that I assign you permanently to his investigation of the Wreckers. He believes it may take him places where some superhero backup will be appropriate. Watchman says you can handle just about anything in this town, and the rest you can beat on until backup arrives. Can you do it?"

Translation: With everything, are you up to going out in public now?

No. I nodded. I'd keep nodding. "Yes. I'll call him tonight."

Chapter Sixteen: Megaton

The Paladins, Humanity First, all those groups are dedicated to the proposition if power corrupts then superhuman powers corrupt absolutely. Personally I don't get it, even if there are enough supervillains out there to support their point. The way I see it, superpowers are like money — they allow people to act and act big. If superhumans want to help, great. If they want to get what they want or rule their corner of the world, not so great. It doesn't get any more complicated than that.

Malcolm Scott, aka Megaton.

"Wahoooo! Yeeah!" The ear protectors in my new helmet let me hear my own voice as I roared into the sky.

"*Everything okay, there?*" Astra laughed on the Dispatch channel, sounding clear through the muted blast.

Andrew had finished my costume over the weekend, and he and Astra brought it to me this morning, then took me down to The Pit for my helmet. Vulcan was a skinny dude in a lab coat with a serious case of bed-hair — the kind you get when you sleep on a couch in your lab. Just looking at him I could hear his inside-voice cackling maniacally, and he'd practically jammed the helmet on my head and shouted in my earhole.

"Ear protectors and speakers," he'd said happily. "The pick-ups in the helmet will screen out most of your blast volume while letting you hear everything else. And of course it's wired for full Dispatch connectivity, heads-up-display on the visor, and it'll stop a bullet. Your costume's got a layer of my impact-weave, too. Good luck."

And just like that, he forgot about me, going back to a disassembled whatever-it-was. Astra had said goodbye to a weirdly polite Galatea robot who stood around holding his tools, then taken me up to the load bay. I'd been wondering about leaving blast-marks with my takeoff, but she'd wrapped her arms around my waist and launched us. A couple thousand feet over Lake Michigan, she'd let go and I lit off, climbing on my own roaring column of flaring light.

"Yeah! Yeah! Yeah!" The roar vibrated my bones as the gees pushed back along the vector of my blast. Saturday and Sunday had been full of careful tests measuring my blast strength and control against Variforce's fields. Cool enough, but *this —*

"That's a yes?"

"Yes! It's — " I made the mistake of turning too far and flipped *hard.* The world turned into a spinning roaring confusion as I flailed around with no idea where the ground was.

"Cut it! Stop blasting!"

I pulled the heat in. The roar stuttered, died, and then I was just falling. *And this is* so *much better. Shit shit shit shit shit!*

Astra flew close and fell beside me. She smiled brightly, ignoring the fact that we were plummeting headfirst towards the lake.

"Okay, ignore the bright sparkly water, we've got plenty of room until we hit. So, feet down, arms in, look up. Ready? Go."

I lit off again, starting low and ramping it up as I felt the push dig in. It was like — it *was —* balancing on top of a rocket as it thrust; all the force in one direction and small changes in position making big changes in attitude while fighting angular momentum.

"Got it. I've got it."

"So, what have we learned?"

"Don't rubberneck? Stay away from the ground?"

"Those are good. Now keep up." She poured on the speed and turned us out and away from the city.

"How far are we going?"

"At least to Canada! Watchman says to stay up until you run out of juice or get hungry!"

We didn't make it to lunch or Canada, but only because we didn't fly a straight line. Astra pushed me into corkscrews, reverse burns, climbs, drop-and-pops, and every other tight trick she could think to have me try. We scared lots of birds, I spun out a *lot*, and she showed me one cool thing that just about made everything worth it. Unassisted skydiving.

Free-falling from high enough I almost needed oxygen.

"Yeeeah!"

"I know, right?" She fell beside me, arms wide like she wanted to embrace the world. *"I finally get why people jump out of airplanes for fun! Makes you wonder, doesn't it? You'd think as a species we'd be genetically programmed to absolutely hate having miles of air below us! It's like our brains evolved for flying but our bodies had other plans."*

"I could stay up here forever!"

"I know. But there's lunch and Willis' sandwiches. And the news cameras that tracked our outbound flight. Sure you've got the hovering down? Ready to meet the public?"

"I won't go down in a flaming ball of fail. Maybe."

She turned us back towards the city. *"So, truth or dare?"*

"Um, dare."

"Call your parents. Shelly tells me you haven't talked since the first day."

"I can't."

"C'mon. You must *honor the Dare — if you don't then Shell and I will play horrible horrible tricks on you until you're afraid to open a door or even use the bathroom. You'll be hiding in bushes and your life will be a living hell. Breaking the Dare is baaad."*

When I didn't laugh, she sighed.

"Okay, here's why. I know all about contingent futures and stuff like that. Anything, **anything,** *can happen, and someday your dad's going to stroke out doing an all-nighter at the office. Tax*

attorneying is high-stress stuff. Or your mom's going to catch a nasty bacteria from all that raw natural food she eats, and you're going to be standing at their grave hating yourself because you didn't forgive them. Or it'll be the other way around and we'll be wearing black and handing them a folded flag — since Sentinels are state militia members, you'll rate one — and they'll be devastated because they never made up with you, told you how much they were sorry. Or you'll take a chance years and years from now, you'll talk, all will be forgiven, and you'll kick yourself for not doing it a zillion years ago. Or — "

"Stop. I'll call them, just — Just leave it alone." All the fun was gone, and I swallowed around the block in my throat.

"My parents are Humanity First activists." In my peripheral vision, I saw her *look* at me. "Not really — they just go to their meetings and read their stuff and donate — but they believe all that crap. They think I'm freaking dangerous, and they want me out of the house and away from my sister."

That shut her up, and I got a quiet minute with only the roar and wind. Not that it was anybody's freaking business, but I could live through another shouting fight with Dad. And maybe he'd reconsider. Maybe the Pope wasn't Catholic.

"So, my turn. Truth or dare."

"...truth." I could practically hear the flaming mortification in her voice, but she didn't take it back or try and apologize, which kicked her up a notch in my book. *"Last time I said 'dare' I was ten and Shelly made me decorate my hair with wet gourmet lollypops and take a picture."*

"Seriously?"

"Seriously. I was almost crying for the awful waste. I loved those, especially the strawberry and cream ones. So, truth" — she paused, touched her earbug — *"and you'll get a while to think about it."* She cranked up the speed. *"I've got a call to go see some Paladins."*

Chicago came in sight over the flat, sparkling plane of the lake and she took us lower, closer to the water so we flashed over the tops of late-season sailboats and yachts as the still-early sun threw our shadows ahead of us. I managed to come to a credible hover over the load bay, but panicked and cut off when my blast column started to singe the floor, barely missing Galatea. I dropped the last ten feet, awkwardly, but Astra didn't laugh as she helped me up. Neither did Galatea. She looked locked and loaded with enough boom to fight a war.

"We'll have to work on that. Takeoffs might need an acrobatic toss to get you high enough for safe ignition."

"A what?"

"Later. Gotta fly!" She grabbed her maul and Galatea's harness handle and was back out through the bay doors. I just stood there. What did I do now?

"*Mr. Scott,*" Blackstone said in my ear through the Dispatch link. "*If you would be so good as to join me in the City Room.*"

This time only Blackstone remained with the Dispatch staff to watch the screens.

"Did you have a good morning, Mr. Scott? And have you chosen a codename yet? You should hurry."

"Huh? I mean, sure,. Andrew had one, I think..."

He nodded, eyes on the screens. "Megaton. His instincts are good. Do you like it?"

I shrugged. "Sure. What's going on?" The main board showed a drone's-eye view of a building in a business park, surrounded by glowing icons.

"Detective Fisher is leading a joint CPD-DSA team to serve warrants for the arrest of the president of the local Paladins chapter and four of his associates. The warrants arise from a discovered link between the Artist's Café shooter and the chapter, with strong evidence that someone there passed him information and ordered the attempted hit on you.

"Since the suspects are not superhumans and are not likely to employ superhumans, Detective Fisher would normally not require our help. However, we are talking about the Paladins, and one of their rogue action-arms struck Astra with an anti-tank missile last spring. The good detective doesn't want to take chances and we need to get them into police custody quickly, specifically, into the protection of the closest CPD hardcells."

"Why?"

"Because, Mr. Scott, the press has already speculated on a Paladin link to the café shooter, and a police standoff at their offices will only confirm it. Need I remind you that the last two people with a high public profile for directly attacking superhumans are now dead?"

"Oh. That's not good."

"Indeed. Galatea may get to try out her new teleport-interdiction module."

Astra

I'd never wanted to be a time-traveler so badly in my *life*, and it had to be a sin how happy I was for the possibly bad situation going down with the Paladins.

Watchman could have taken Mal flying as easily — should have, but he and Riptide, Seven, Rush, and Variforce were out of town dealing with a major tanker-truck spill and fire, and Blackstone was already looking ahead to my leadership position with the cadet team. The Hillwood picks would be here tonight.

And I've started so well.

Mal had been a surprisingly fun break from obsessing about my own problems (I'd missed Sunday Mass for the first time in months because I was scared to show my face at Saint Chris). Fun right up to the moment I jumped in where it wasn't my business.

I filled Shelly in as we flew, since otherwise she'd be back on him about it as soon as she got over the distraction of trying to track down whoever had outed me so we could wreak hot, hot vengeance — her words.

Guessing from the emptiness of its parking lots, pre-lunchtime on a Monday, the business park the Paladins leased their building from had seen better days. Detective Fisher and his joint team timed their approach so that they pulled into the lot outside the office as we landed.

"The CPD thermal drone shows five occupants in the building," Shelly whispered in my ear as we dropped to join Fisher's team and the ten Platoons the DSA had sent. Platoon wore dark-visored helmets so you couldn't tell at a glance that all ten were the same person, but if you knew a Bob or a Tom long enough, you could tell. Were they part of the same Platoon team that had helped us in the spring?

I put on my game-face and gave everyone a nod. "Fisher, Jenny, Wyatt, Bobs. Galatea says five in the building. How are we going to play it?"

"Agents Robbins?" Fisher waved the Platoons ahead. Armored like a SWAT team expecting to dance, five peeled away and the rest stepped around me as we walked so I found myself behind their wall as we advanced on the door. One opened and the other four moved in behind, still paired to keep me out of line of sight of any cameras.

The front lobby was a secure room — no inside windows or easy access to the rest of the office, just a thick door, waiting chairs, and a phone. One Bob blocked the camera in the corner with his badge while another picked up the phone and punched the receptionist button.

"Ma'am," he said to whoever answered. "This is Agent Robbins and Detective Fisher of the DSA and the Chicago Police Department. We have warrants to search these premises and detain members of your organization. You have ten seconds to open the inside door or we will make a breach." He hung up, looked at me, and counted down curling his fingers into a fist.

Right. At "ten" I gripped the doorknob and *pushed.* The heavy lock snapped with a loud pop and the agents went through ahead of everyone, guns up and yelling "Down, down, down!" Nobody was taking chances with the Paladins deciding their war with superhumans extended to the government.

The hall on the other side of the door opened into offices and a large bare meeting room, folding chairs set up for maybe fifty. The place was all threadbare carpets and water-stained ceiling tiles. Framed posters lined the walls, anti-cape stuff mixed in with motivational posters — which was just weird, like finding a cute cat picture at an Aryan Brotherhood hangout.

"'Catch on fire with enthusiasm and people will come for miles to watch you burn.'" Shelly read. "Now that's *seriously* wrong."

I laughed, but at least the accompanying picture was just a rock-musician waling on his axe, not any of a half-dozen absolutely awful images my Shelly-corrupted sense of humor conjured up.

"Storm troopers! You have no right!"

"*Debra Gardner*," Shelly whispered through my earbug. "*Office administrator and agitprop writer.*"

Aaand there went the fun.

A Bob talked the hysterical lady down and his team pulled our catch together in the meeting room. I set up five folding chairs so they could at least have their backs to a wall and see each other while we waited, all the Bobs facing outward and Agent Robbins talking on his earbug to the outside team. Detective Fisher's team pulled the hard drives from the office computers, dumped their phone logs, looked for anything stupidly incriminating to take with us on the first sweep.

I watched our suspects, trusting the Bobs to alert me to anything incoming like the Wreckers. And they watched me. Ms. Gardner looked like she wanted to spit.

"The great Astra." The handcuffs made her lean forward, but she kept her back straight, ignoring Galatea. "So now you don't even *pretend* you're not the government's bitch."

I rested Malleus on my shoulder. "Funny. Go on and poke me some more — nothing can hurt as much as a missile. You *do* know that if superhumans ever take over the government and put all of you *patriots* in camps, I and my friends will be dead, right? Because they'll have to go *through* us to do it."

She actually managed a sneer, more than any of the rest seemed up to. "So you believe their lies."

And just like that I was tired of it. Last year, Ajax had tried to give me some historical context for the anti-superhuman groups, and I thought I understood them, but the lens of the Paladin worldview would never let her see me as anything but the enemy.

And am I any different?

"I know all about acting as your conscience requires, Ms. Gardner. And I'm not here *for* you — Galatea and I are here in case somebody tries to *kill* you. So you do what you do, and we'll do what we do, and we'll trust God to sort us out. Can I get anyone a drink of water?"

Fisher's team moved *fast*, and we were only there for fifteen minutes. We used the DSA vans to transport the Paladin staff downtown to the CPD hardcells, the cells normally used for keeping superhuman detainees *in*. Vulcan met us there with cases of gear and he and Shelly got to work making the cells even tougher.

I followed Fisher out to where he could light up. "What are you going to do now?"

"We're done, here." He took a deep drag. "We've got closers to handle the interrogations, and my team doesn't do normal-on-superhuman cases, which is what this is; their only connection to our case is someone in their office conspiring with the shooter."

He looked back at the doors. "If they're smart, they'll throw us the guilty one. He's the only one we want and the only one we need to protect — if the Wreckers were just going after anyone with a loud hate on for superhumans, they'd be wading in blood already."

Ugh. An image I *so* didn't need. "Think they're that smart?"

"No, but we're good. Don't worry, we'll nail the bastard who sicced the café shooter on your friend, maybe more than one. So we file everything, get back to working on the Wreckers. I'm going to want you with us in the next couple of days; we need to pay a call on the Foundation of Awakened Theosophy — we're just waiting for the warrants."

What? I'd completely forgotten about our search of Mr. Ludlow's place and it took me a moment to figure out what he was talking about.

"You think this foundation is part of it?"

A shrug. "No idea. More likely Ludlow met fellow travelers there — which means we want to see membership records, that kind of thing. It might be nothing, but that's detective work; pull on every string until something pulls back."

He stubbed out his cig. "Kid? FYI?"

"Hmm?"

"Sorry about your getting outed. I thought you should know, bright-eyed and bushy-tailed story chasers are already interviewing your old schoolmates going back to preschool." He shrugged. "They know about your friend's origin-chaser 'suicide' and it's going to be in every background piece on you along with her memorial portrait. The footage from the café shooting isn't public, but you might want to tell Galatea to be more careful in the future."

Chapter Seventeen: Astra

Celebrity superheroes are like Hollywood stars: we have entourages, agents, image and publicity people, legions of fans, and we get into trouble any time we don't speak from a script.

Astra, *Notes From a Life.*

My life had become an after-school special, and any moment now people were going to break into *song*. The whole Best Friend Dies Origin-Chasing and You Got the Breakthrough story had filled the Internet with a collective "Aaaaw!" Quin was fielding multimillion-dollar offers for the rights to my biography, and letting Shell take over the Internet was sounding better and better. Together we could bring down civilization and they would *stop talking about me*.

Nobody was talking *to* me — Quin wasn't letting me near any newsies after Sunday's interesting session with Terry. It hadn't gone *badly*, exactly, but only because Terry was cool — his first question, off the record, had been what I'd like to do to the person who'd outed me, assuming we ever found out who.

The Bees were texting me messages of support, which was nice even if Annabeth's included bloodcurdling suggestions I could have used to answer Terry's question. She'd become my most vocal advocate; according to Julie, she almost made one opportunistic journalist eat his recorder. Megan just insulted the guy in ways he only vaguely understood.

I finished my one patrol of the day before returning to the Dome, ignoring the crowd of protesters outside as I flew in. This morning they mostly looked like Shankman's partisans — word of the investigation into his office had got out and his pet-newsies were spinning it as persecution.

They needed *something*; their attempts to blame us for his taking a bullet weren't gaining any traction, and since he'd come through surgery fine and would be out of the hospital in days, that story was going to go away too.

Since Willis had prepared rooms for tonight's new arrivals and I was off-duty, I changed into civvies, put my hair in a tail, and decided to take my mind off the media frenzy and my pending responsibilities by studying up on the Foundation of Awakened Theosophy. Everything — and I meant *everything* — really had conspired to drive it out of my mind. But Fisher was right; the Paladins were a sideshow. We needed to know what had changed things for Mr. Ludlow, and if Fisher was looking at the FAT (Shelly'd gotten a kick out of the acronym), then I needed to learn all about it.

Five minutes after opening my epad and looking up *The Sleeper Must Awake*, I wanted some good swear words. Blackstone should have learned about this last *week*.

The Foundation of Awakened Theosophy was a *cult*.

"Yes, my dear?"

Blackstone's eyebrows rose when I made a slashing motion across my throat. His always-open door closed, and I handed him my epad.

"Have you seen this?"

He scanned the page, looked up. "I am aware of the Foundation. It's a two-year-old fad among origin-chasers. Has it become important?"

I nodded. "Mr. Ludlow may be a member, and it's about more than breakthroughs."

"I think you had better sit down and tell me about it."

I sat, took a breath and opened my mouth, thought again. *Organize.*

"Last weekend, before I went with Fisher to exercise the warrant, you suggested that whatever had turned Mr. Ludlow happened after January."

"Yes."

"Eric's been reading FAT books and I just called Jenny and she says that they won't know until they get a look at the Foundation's membership records but from his emails it looks like he's been a member since early February." *Breathe, Hope, breathe.* "A serious one."

Blackstone sat back, rubbed his nose. "Indeed. That *is* interesting."

I'd never heard of it, but it didn't surprise me that Blackstone knew about the Foundation. He tapped his desk phone. "Chakra, please."

"*Dear to my heart?*" It was late morning but she sounded like she'd crawled out of bed to answer the phone, and wanted to crawl right back *in.*

My expression made Blackstone smile. "Good morning, my dear. I am with Astra right now and wondered if you might join us?" Chakra responded with an easy laugh and an entendre-filled promise to be quick while I tried to pretend I hadn't been there to hear *anything.* My ears were red, but I wasn't stupid — she did it because I made it fun, and Seven had been right; when I wasn't blushing, I was laughing. I wasn't judgy, really, just mortified.

And I really needed to grow up. Last night Chakra had found me to talk about my feelings about Eric going to the dark side, even apologized for not being able to warn me of all the drama she'd seen coming with her precognitive gift. She'd been nice and *not embarrassing.*

Blackstone made small talk until she swept in, dressed like a gypsy dancer. One look at our faces and she sat and adjusted her skirts, back poker-straight. Blackstone always dressed ready for the stage, so I was the only one not in "uniform."

"Yes?" No archness, no play, just *what's going on?*

"The Foundation of Awakened Theosophy. Our Mr. Ludlow may be a member. What can you tell us about it?"

It was like she'd slipped on invisible schoolteacher glasses.

"It's one of the newer breakthrough-trigger fads, based on the theosophical enlightenment movement. After the Event, a lot of people started claiming they knew how to reliably trigger breakthroughs. Statistically, their results have varied, but never very far from the baseline of random incidents of extreme physical or mental stress."

"That is what I understood," Blackstone concurred. "The government has always been extremely interested in discovering a reliable breakthrough-generator to address our national superhuman deficit."

I blinked. "Our what?"

"Breakthroughs are caused by trauma, my dear, and despite our own supervillains, here in the U.S. we have less of that than the Chinese states, for example. Or the Middle East. Fewer mass-deaths. Fewer disasters. Certainly no civil wars. The downside of peace and prosperity is fewer events which tend to create superhumans." He was back to rubbing his nose. "We make up for that by better mobilization and support and by attracting superhuman immigration — Lei Zi being the perfect example. She was twenty when she brought her family here from Beijing at the start of the China War."

"She's an immigrant? I didn't know." She'd come on the team during the bad months right after Atlas' death, when I hadn't been paying attention to much of anything. Now she was just *there*, solid, professional, distant in a leaderly way.

He raised an eyebrow at that. "She comes from a diplomatic Communist Party family, and probably learned English while counting blocks in the nursery. Apparently they were considered less than reliable by the party leadership when the purges began. But we're wandering afield now."

I had a sudden burning desire to know *that* story, but I nodded. Chakra's eyes were focused on something else, and she hummed thoughtfully.

"Actually, I think I can see the attraction of the FAT for Eric." She made sure she had our attention, smiled. "As I said, it's based on the theosophical enlightenment, particularly on the version of theosophy preached by Helena Blavatsky. It builds on three propositions: the universe as we experience it is an illusion surrounding an unchanging Truth she called the Absolute; outside of the Absolute, everything is in flux, forever uncreated and recreated; all souls are monads, units of individual consciousness which are discrete parts of the universal oversoul, the part of the Absolute that is conscious of itself. Monads are eternal, but also constantly in flux with the rest of the universe."

She stopped to let us catch up and I ran it through my poor little brain.

"So...reincarnation? Nirvana?"

"Oh, yes, Blavatsky's theosophy was strongly influenced by Buddhist philosophy. More important, the Foundation of Awakened Theosophy has updated her system to explain breakthroughs. According to the FAT, Monads also experience spiritual evolution — the Event was caused by the first Awakened Soul, which recreated the world. The Foundation doesn't say who that blessed soul is, but it strongly hints he is its founder, Doctor Simon Pellegrini."

"I see." Blackstone considered for a moment. "And Mr. Ludlow?"

Chakra shrugged. "The Foundation teaches a system of study, meditation, and initiation that is supposed to 'awaken' a disciple who becomes sufficiently spiritually advanced, which is what makes it attractive to origin-chasers who don't want to risk injury or death to achieve a breakthrough. But it also claims it is able to strengthen breakthroughs — a draw for weak breakthroughs whose powers are at or below D Class."

"Wow." I thought of how easily Shelly might have been sucked into that if it had been around four years ago. Or maybe not — Shelly liked *quick* solutions. "But Eric is a *B Class* Ajax-type."

Blackstone shook his head. "But not the strongest, my dear. Perhaps his war experiences convinced him that he needed to be stronger. Which is not necessarily his motive now..."

"Could he have met the other Wreckers through the FAT?"

"Or been introduced to the FAT by a Wrecker. The Crew mixed with a lot of CAI and support teams during the cleanup in California." He nodded significantly without elaborating. Chakra wasn't part of the charmed circle with the need-to-know scoop on the Teatime Anarchist or the Big Book.

I needed to call Jenny back, suggest they look into the Crew's California adventure.

Chakra filled us in on more about the FAT than I'd absorbed before I'd run to Blackstone, but by the time I got back in my rooms I realized I couldn't tell Jenny anything. Or ask her anything else that might make her wonder. Asking whether Mr. Ludlow had joined FAT had probably been okay — since I'd been there, it was natural enough to ask about if I was at all interested in the case. But I was a cape, not a cop; investigation was *their* job, and if I started displaying a deep interest in a specific part of their investigation, they'd wonder *why*, which would be bad for The Secret.

Which sucked; Fisher had his own secrets, which he knew I knew, but that wouldn't keep him from coming after *my* secrets if he thought they might be important to Solving the Case. I trusted Fisher, but that wasn't the point; when Shell and I had given Blackstone the Big Book — till then he hadn't known how *big* it was or that I was its "guardian" — he'd sat us down to find out who else knew about it (Dr. Cornelius and Orb, who knew about the Big Book but didn't know what it was, and Jacky, who could keep secrets like nobody's business). Then he'd explained the secret to successful conspiracies: they remained *secret*. The ideal number of conspirators was two (one just wasn't a conspiracy), and each conspirator above that number increased the chance of the secret being blown.

Betrayal, carelessness, bad luck, it didn't matter: it could just be a conspirator acting out of character and tipping someone else to the fact that *something* wasn't as it seemed. Once someone knew something was up, the conspiracy was half-blown; with a conspiracy of secrecy like ours, if someone else figured out even part of it then the best-case outcome was we'd bring them into the conspiracy. Which meant one *more* member, *more* chances of someone else noticing, etc.

So it stayed a circle of four: Shell, me, Blackstone, and Mystery Member — the one on the government side Blackstone had turned *his* vetted files over to. He wouldn't tell us who that was (my money was on Veritas) or how he'd done it; it might have been by untraceable drop so Mystery Member didn't know *him*. Knowing Blackstone, probably.

Which really meant there were two cells of the conspiracy: ours, and whoever the one on the government side shared knowledge of the files with. Yes, Blackstone had *definitely* done an untraceable drop. Unless he needed a way for Mystery Member to touch him back...

Trying to think like Blackstone made my head hurt.

Then it became the *last* thing on my mind. *"Hope?"* Shelly whispered in my ear. She hadn't gotten back from working with Vulcan yet.

"Shell?"

"Toby is going to be okay, *but you need to get to Cook County Hospital. Right* now.*"*

The security guy at the door didn't blink when I landed outside CCH's emergency rooms — they got superhumans arriving from above all the time even if they usually arrived in costume — and I dashed inside.

"Hope Corrigan," I blurted to the duty-nurse behind the counter. "My brother is here? Toby Corrigan?"

Shell beat him to it. *"He's in the ICU, stable condition so stop freaking out!"* I thanked him — he must have thought I was crazy — and forced myself to follow the red line at a responsible walk. *Fast* walk, but one foot on the floor at all times.

"Hope," Blackstone broke in through Dispatch. *"Shelly has filled me in. Seven is on his way, and please try not to be too visible. We are securing the situation."*

I nodded, choked a laugh. "Understood. Mom and Dad — "

They were there, on the other side of the glass doors, and I almost broke them going through.

Dad looked up. "Hope?" And I knew Toby was okay. Then I was in his arms and he held on tight and the panic squeezing my heart finally loosened. I could breathe.

He sighed into my hair. "We were waiting to call you."

"What — What happened?"

Mom's eyes were bright with unshed tears.

"The hospital called us half an hour ago, when Toby woke up. He was found last night and admitted. They — Someone attacked and beat him. He was found on the street, unconscious..."

"They couldn't identify him until he woke up," Dad finished for her. "Whoever attacked him stole his wallet and phone."

"How could anyone have gotten to him?"

"He wasn't wearing his Argus Security watch, didn't tell them where he was going, so he wasn't under the Sentinels' security umbrella."

"W-why? How — " I shut up. It was *so* Toby, and I wanted him better so I could give him a kicking.

"Broken ribs, bruised kidneys, stuff," Shelly recited off a list. *"Biggest problem is cranial fracture, cerebral contusion, subdural hematoma."* Obviously she'd hacked the hospital system and I didn't care. *"Subdural bleeding stopped; now that he's awake, the initial prognosis looks real good — CCH is one of the best hospitals for head injuries."*

Dad hugged me again. "They don't know what happened yet."

He meant well, but I'd been to plenty of trauma scenes. "Someone beat him half to death, Dad. Shell just read me the list. It's my fault."

"Stop." Mom wasn't having it. "This is the city, Hope." Dad nodded agreement and we just stood there.

We moved to chairs, and after a bit a doctor came out and talked about short-term memory loss — unslurred speech and good visual tracking and reflexes let the doctor hedge on the side of optimism — and then Seven arrived.

I looked up when he slipped in to sit down beside me. He squeezed my hand and flashed a smile warm with sympathy, and I realized I hadn't thought about The Kiss since returning it to him Friday night. Not even Saturday before my world had blown up again.

My return smile must have been blinding. He blinked, then tossed an easy smile back. I just sighed and rested my head against Dad's shoulder. I wasn't crushing on Seven — I'd been obsessing over the possibility of yummy, yummy Seven and wondering if he was crushing on *me*. That he hadn't chased me down after Friday night answered that. Whatever the kiss on Omega night had been about, it hadn't been an "I really *like* you kiss." And that was a *good* thing; life was complicated enough right now.

Beautiful as Seven was, friends was good.

Now, trying to ignore the sick-inducing hospital smell and sounds my super-duper senses couldn't block out, I looked at Seven's pants-covered legs next to my bare ones, thought about the picture I'd presented flying here, and groaned. I was dressed for hanging out in the Dome, in one of my Astra shirts (*good* cotton, $39.99 in the gift shop) and a pleated athletic skirt. I'd never been so glad that my wardrobe choices now included the kind of bottoms cheerleaders had no problem showing to a stadium full of sports fans. Not that I'd thought about the up-skirt view *at all*, flying here.

And gee, Hope, boys and clothes now? *Can you be more shallow?*

Close to another hour passed before they let us in to see Toby, and by then he was out again — the doctor promised it was a natural sleep this time. A neck brace held his head straight, bandages mummified his left hand, and tubes came out of him everywhere. Between the mummy-wrap completely hiding his hair and the swelling, purpling flesh that disfigured his face, I didn't recognize him at all. Unbelievably, it looked like they hadn't broken his nose.

Looking at him lying there, my head felt hot and stuffy, chills and fever together, and I fought the gut-sick urge to find someone and make them *pay*. If I could blame someone else, it wouldn't be my fault.

Mom called Aaron and Josh now that we knew he was going to be okay, and I called the Bees. Major hospitals almost always had at least one newsie hanging around to watch for capes, or someone that tipped them off for a little extra income; they might have missed my entrance, but *Seven*... The fan sites were sure to go crazy the instant word of the attack got out and Annabeth, at least, religiously followed them.

I also called Blackstone to let him know I didn't plan on being back in the Dome to meet our new teammates; he told me in no uncertain terms that if I showed my face before tomorrow we were going to have *words*. They'd put us in a more private waiting room just off of the ICU, and I split my time between Mom and Dad; they were too old for curling up with stuffed animals, but they could always hold onto me. Our family had seen more than its share of hospital time. There'd been Faith, of course, and then my childhood cancer, but Corrigan boys had broken bones and racked up lots of sports injuries and Stupid Stuff — me too, for that matter — and I *hated* hospitals even if I wasn't afraid of them anymore.

Father Nolan arrived without ceremony, round face solemn, and quietly led us in praying the Rosary. Dad and Mom took him into Toby's room so that he could perform a blessing of the sick, but I couldn't make myself go back in with them.

Instead I stepped out into the hallway, where Seven stood talking to a couple of Bobs.

He gave me a quick look, relaxed. "How's your family?"

"Stoic. We're real good at that."

That brought a thin smile. "I've been talking to Shelly. There weren't any witnesses and the detectives have barely talked to his roommates. Has Toby said anything?"

I shook my head. "The doctors said he doesn't remember most of yesterday, but short-term memory loss is pretty common with his kind of injury."

"Well, we've got a full security ring now, and..." He stopped, tilting his head and listening to his earbug. "And we've got an all-hands mobilization."

"I didn't — " Stupid, I wasn't in the Dispatch loop now. I tapped my earbug. "Shel — Galatea!"

"Geez, you're stood down!"

"What's happening?"

"The Green Man's hit O'Hare!" Seven was already *sprinting* away as I stood frozen — Rush would for sure meet him at the doors. This so wasn't happening...

"I'm not — Tell Blackstone I'm on the board!" I ran.

Chapter Eighteen: Grendel

"In the beginning, Queen Lurline tied the magic of Oz into the fairy blood of the royal family. Although usurpers can take the Emerald Throne, as the Nome King and Mombi have done, should the royal line of Oz be ended then Oz will no longer be a fairy land. I am alive and in exile because I was an only child."

Ozma, *DSA Interview 54.291*

"What's the point of making the A-list if they don't treat you like a star?"

Reese had been bitching almost since we went wheels-up. He'd been impressed enough with the corporate jet the Sentinels had sent to deliver us to our new home, even if it was obviously from a rental fleet — no big "S" on the side or anything else. Then he'd tried to charm the flight attendant into opening the in-flight bar. Reese probably didn't hear *no* very often, but he heard it five times in five minutes.

Then he told her he could get her into the Mile High Club without using a plane.

He probably would have laughed off her "Sit down and shut up," but at that point Ozma had looked up from her magazine. Reese might be so full of it that if I poked him with a claw he'd explode and cover the cabin in brown, but he didn't have shit for brains; he sat down and shut up.

For five minutes, but at least he wasn't hitting on the staff. And at least the leather couches were comfortable; I didn't fit in the lounge chairs, but the nice attendant had assured me that the furniture would take my weight.

"I mean, where are the *girls*?"

I showed a mouthful of fangs. "I can twist your head off. They'll really like you then."

Ozma opened her third magazine. "Boys. I *will* stop this plane."

Reese slouched, kicking his feet. "You'll what, blow us to Oz?"

She smiled without looking up again. "In due time."

"And they should have given us *costumes*."

I growled. "So we could what? Step out onto a red carpet? We're not heroes yet."

"Hey, we — "

"*We will be descending to make our approach to O'Hare in a few minutes. Please fasten your seat belts and make sure all drinks are in their holders.*"

"What drinks? The stupid stuck-up stewardess wouldn't *serve* us any — " The plane heeled hard. There hadn't been a bump of turbulence until now.

Frowning, Ozma snapped open a compact, studied it. "Hmmm."

"What?" Reese practically whined. "Like now's a good time to fix your — "

"Hat." She snapped the compact closed. "I didn't bring a *hat*. Are you done?" She ignored him to turn to the attendant. "Would you please instruct the pilot to take us over the tower? Any altitude is fine."

The attendant had been listening to her headset. "Miss, we've been instructed to turn away from O'Hare. We'll be getting new instructions in a moment."

"I'm sure. However, we are needed on the ground now. The Green Man has attacked the airport, and every hand will count." A snap of her fingers and her scepter-wand appeared out of nowhere. It was like hearing a rifle chamber a round, and the cabin felt a lot smaller.

"Brian? Be ready to open the door and step out. Reese?"

He bounced out of his seat. "Oh *yeah*, now it's happening. Just watch out!"

"Just — just hold on." The attendant made pushing motions like she could make us sit back down, and retreated to the cockpit. One hand on the door latch, I looked at Ozma. She gave me a real smile, looked past me as the attendant returned.

"We're going to directly overfly O'Hare at eight thousand feet. He'll tell me when."

Ozma extended the smile to her. "Thank you. You will see that our luggage is delivered?"

A wide-eyed nod. "Good luck."

Reese groaned. "Enough chit-chat. Let's move!"

I unbolted the door, holding onto the latch and frame as the cabin lost pressure. Holding onto the cockpit hatch with one hand as the plane banked around, the attendant held up the other while listening to her head set. One minute, two, and she made a fist, mouthing "Go!" over the wind. I threw myself through the door and into the open sky.

What a great way to see Chicago.

Astra

"Out of the way! Coming through! Make a hole!"

I had only gotten a few steps before realizing the blindingly obvious — then I'd turned around and pushed through the door to Toby's room. Father Nolan had barely finished donning his stole when my announcement that the Green Man was attacking O'Hare stopped the proceedings. Dad and Mom shared one of their telepathic looks, then Dad was at the door and we *both* ran.

If you're going to run in the hall, a hospital is a good place to do it: they're used to staff moving at less than sedate speeds at times and they gave us room — a good thing since Dad wasn't as maneuverable as me and took up a lot more space. Bursting through the lobby doors, I locked forearm-holds with Dad and got into the air. He changed as we lifted above the hospital wing, popping buttons, shredding seams, and gaining a few hundred pounds as he changed to the living metal that was Iron Jack. I adjusted my grip and flew *fast*.

Every flier in the city was in the air, lots of them carrying passengers like me and I spotted Safire carrying Jack Frost, and Blue Fire flew with Wisteria. All of us converging on O'Hare.

"Lei Zi, Watchman, Variforce, Riptide, and Megaton are right behind you!" Shelly reported.

"Megaton?"

"Mal! I'm stuck at the precinct, but I'll co-pilot him, no sweat!" Great — a flying cannon guided by a teen robot who didn't want to be left out of the action.

"Shell..."

"Hey, I recorded all his testing sessions — I know what he can do within a millimeter! I won't let him toast anybody!"

I shut up and focused on getting us there.

O'Hare is *big*. It's the fifth-busiest international airport in North America, with tens of thousands of travelers a day, and even with every speedster and flyer on deck there was no possible way to clear everyone out of the way. Like last time, the green wave had started at a water source; this time Lake O'Hare, a concrete-sided lake that was really just a rainwater basin. The green included trees, but mostly looked like some kind of creeping vine, growing and moving nearly as fast as a person could sprint on open runway.

"Drop me!" Dad yelled from where he dangled below me. "Get the planes!"

Right. Below us the spread flowed north, toward the main terminals, and between the green and the buildings a half-dozen airbuses waited along the runway approaches to take off. I looked around. Above us, the closed airspace looked clear except for one big jet that had been making its final approach and was red-lining its turbines and clawing back into the sky. I dropped Dad. In his Iron Jack form, Dad was as tough as an A Class Ajax-type — he bounced and rolled to his feet, headed for the planes. The day of the Event, Atlas had flown up from O'Hare to catch planes dropping out of the sky, or really to help them to dead-stick landings. I wasn't *that* strong, but I yelled for Safire.

"Hey, girl! You want to double up?"

"Front and back?"

"Absolutely! Love the casual look!"

She dropped Jack Frost off and landed in front of me. *And for today's crisis, Safire will be kinkily fashionable in a pink-and-purple flamed latex catsuit...* We dove under the first plane in line, looking for the hardpoints. She put her shoulders under the forward fuselage, right behind the landing gear, and I did the same between the middle gear. It says a lot about our world that they highlight the flight-assist hardpoints with yellow squares now. She lifted first and I followed, taking most of the weight as we flew the airbus across the field to the west side., A ground security guy there was already opening gates in the perimeter fencing to let passengers debark by emergency ramp and escape onto York Street.

And let emergency vehicles in.

The racing creepers got to the third plane before we did, but Dad ripped ropes of tangling super-kudzu runners away from the landing gear as we lifted. Jack Frost flash-froze wide sweeps of the stuff that tried to get past him while tarmac cracked and heaved around new trees climbing for the sun. Watchman flew the other planes to safety while the others attacked the green flowing towards the terminals. Megaton blew apart new trees and cleared whole strips of green, but this time the tide front stretched around us, throwing new arms of advance between our defenses even as more capes arrived. There was no Dispatch chatter, no strategy as we dug in. I grabbed a service truck and pushed it across the runways at the edge of the green, scrapping new growth away, but it came back faster.

"Reinforcements!" Shell sang out. *"Sort of."*

Grendel

Since I could pretty much fall from orbit and walk out of the crater, I'd drilled in free-falling at Hillwood; now I spun so I could see the jet as Ozma jumped after me. Reese jumped last — actually stepping out to close and latch the door behind him before flying after us.

Golden hair whipping around her face, Ozma was *laughing,* so at least she was having fun. I angled belly down for maximum air resistance and decided our pilot was pretty good; he'd really put us right over the airport and the green wave attacking it. No need to angle our descent — a rock would have hit the top of the tower.

Reese caught me and Ozma in twin updrafts before we free-fell too far, and took us in. I was impressed — he had to be twisting air into tornado speeds to even slow me down. I shifted into armor mode, skin thickening and knotting into plates. I knew Reese — he'd drop me from as high as he thought he could just for kicks as soon as he had me over a spot where I wasn't going to happen to any capes or bystanders.

And he did, maybe five hundred feet above the tarmac and naturally *over* the green. I smacked down into a runway, not that it wasn't already cracked into pieces and buried under green — new trees and what looked like mutant kudzu, kudzu that *crawled* faster than I could run when I wasn't configured for speed.

Thanks, Reese. Absorbing my armor to run faster and extruding longer claws, I headed north for the terminal — the only landmark I could see above the trees — ripping up vines that tried to eat my feet with each step.

A fresh-faced blonde kid missing her cape landed beside me. "Glad you could make it, but can I give you a lift? Seriously, we don't have time to for you to cut your way out!" Standing there ignoring the vines, she had to lean back to see higher than my pecs.

"Sure — hey!" Grabbing my right wrist in both hands — they barely got all the way around — she lifted off hard and threw us straight at the tower.

Past the tower, close enough I could have reached out and given it a swipe as we arced over the main building and down to the screaming, stampeding crowd.

"We can't help them empty the connected planes and concourses faster," she explained as we flew. "But we need to clear the bottlenecks outside! Keep anyone from trying to drive out of here! Push any stopped cars out of the road so people can get away to the north!"

She dropped me on top of my first job — an abandoned airport shuttle stuck in a jam of taxies so wide people were crawling over them. Normally I scare people if I happen to them suddenly, but nobody paid me a second glance as I scrambled down off the shuttle. My biggest problem was where to move it to that wouldn't put people under it, and finally I just tipped it off the road, crushing parking meters. Then I started sliding and stacking taxies, clearing openings for people to run through, trying to get a feel for the place.

The terminal building was *huge*. It stretched around a massive multi-level parking lot, and had a hotel smack in the middle. Escapees from the terminal building had to flee along the stacked arrival and departure roads. Finished with the bottleneck, I started dissuading drivers actually trying to *drive* out of the airport through the crowd — reaching through windows and ripping keys out as necessary, then shoving them off to the side. Chicago taxi drivers are tough, and *stupid*. One of them turned out to be carrying and shot me in the face, but that just meant I wasn't polite and squeezed his pistol into a paperweight before moving on.

I didn't wonder what was happening to the others — I had my own little corner of screaming chaos.

Megaton

"*Left! Fifteen degrees!*"

I couldn't see around my blasts as they scraped advancing trees and vine away from the tarmac, couldn't hear shouted directions over the roar, so Galatea guided me using other capes' mask-cams.

"*Walk it left five degrees!*"

Were we winning? I had no idea. We'd kept my part clear, kept the planes parked and hooked up to the nearest concourse from getting buried in green and pushed over by upthrusting trees, and on my right some guy had dropped out of the sky to literally blow away aggressive green with tornado-speed winds.

"*And how are we doing, Megaton?*" Blackstone queried. Unbelievably, I was actually getting tired — a really weird feeling, not muscle fatigue, more like I'd been running too hard and not getting enough oxygen to my brain.

"I'm not sure, sir, but I may be getting down to fumes!"

"*Your suit telemetry does indicate some levels of distress,*" he returned. "*Lei Zi has tasked Rush with your extraction should you be unable to continue or break contact.*"

"Check, roger, acknowledged, whatever I should freaking say, sir."

"*Traditionally, a 'Copy, Rush tasked with extraction' is appropriate, but we're a little loose here, my boy. Hold as long as you feel you can, then call for relief.*"

"Good to know!" I tried deep breathing, couldn't tell if it helped, but the choice was *easy*. Stand your ground until you can't stand. *You owe a life, so save a life.* If this was my down payment, then Rush was going to have to *carry* me out of here.

Astra

We weren't going to make it.

Dispatch and airport security reported that the concourses were mostly clear, but there was always *somebody* — lost and panicked kids, injured passengers, some of them possibly trampled, and others not so mobile. And the terminals were full of choke-points: escalators, stairways, gates, any narrow pass, with thousands trying to push through like their lives depended on it. Even with all the capes not holding the line pouring into the buildings, it would take time we didn't *have*.

I dropped another battered bystander by the aid station getting set up around the O'Hare Airport Rescue building. A scratch-team of workers was getting the big runway-scraping bulldozers into gear; they were built for pushing heavy snow, but their drivers were going to try and back up the capes. Another team was laying a berm of foam as a perimeter; when the green broke past us, they were going to use it to channel a lit up fuel-spill for a firewall. Maybe it would work.

"*Astra, status?*" Lei Zi broke in. Without my mask-cam, I was a wandering wildcard even if Dispatch could track my location by my earbug.

"Dropping passengers, going back into the terminal!"

"*Scratch that — retrieve Ozma at my position and get her to Blue Fire!*"

What? What? "Retrieve Ozma and deliver her to Blue Fire, got it. Galatea?"

"*They're south of the west concourses, Blue Fire is in the middle on Megaton's right!*" She hardly had to tell me; flying back over the terminals, I spotted Lei Zi by the cracking, jumping field of supercharged Saint Elmo's Fire that danced along the edge of green in front of her as she drew from the nearby power station to fight her arc of the front.

Ozma stood by Lei Zi, watching with interest. For a teenager with a wand, she was the furthest thing from a Magical Girl I could imagine, dressed in casual Lands' End pants, buttoned blouse, even a *scarf*. The wide white and sparkling belt was interesting, and of course the wand was the princess's signature scepter — maybe twenty inches of achingly artistic etched gold that forked into a smooth Y towards the end. The cradle of the Y framed her classic Z-inside-an-O, the crest of her royal house.

She smiled a perfect smile when I landed. "You're my ride?" If it hadn't been for four years exposed to Annabeth, I'd have cried from sheer physical envy. She thrust her wand through her belt, held out her hands like she'd done this before. I smooth-lifted and then we were over the green starting to break through Variforce' waning fields and Megaton's blasted zone to Blue Fire's end of the fight.

Blue Fire *ruled* her zone, her cold blue flames licking out in auric spikes to freeze the attacking green and turn it to dust. She shivered, swaying with fatigue, but nothing made it past her searching flames. Ozma didn't blink at Blue's blue-tattooed skin and brief outfit. I wasn't sure what to say — what was *planned* — but they were both ready.

"How big a flare do you need?" Blue gasped, already clued in.

Ozma pulled her wand. "Can you put a ring around me?" I scooted out of the way, fast, as Blue threw a flare of aura out to twist around her.

"Perfect!" Ozma laughed and began chanting in Latin. It sounded almost like a *limerick*, and she reached out at the end of each line to touch her wand to the dancing flames.

"*OMG*," Shelly whispered in my ear — she had to be watching from Blue's mask-cam. Every touch of Ozma's wand broke a tongue of blue flame free from the fire ring to dance around her. Each dancing flame grew, stretched, went from blue fire to a burning blue fire*man* complete with flaming axe. She kept chanting as more and more burning firemen sprang free to dance the widening circle, once twice, three times and then spin away to race up and down the front of the green tide.

"*OMG*," Shell repeated. I nodded, pretty stunned myself. Blue looked ready to die of shock, aura stuttering before she got it back under control. I lost count of burning firemen somewhere after thirty but they kept coming, reminding me of Mickey Mouse's broom army in *The Sorcerer's Apprentice*. I could almost hear the music as they rushed away to hack and freeze vines and trees — literally — in their tracks.

"*Thoughts?*" Blackstone gently broke in to ask.

I found myself laughing helplessly. "I'm glad she's ours?" *Please, let her be ours.*

"*Indeed, one hopes so.*"

Episode Three

Chapter Nineteen: Grendel

"It is an eternal experience that every man who has power is drawn to abuse it; he proceeds until he finds the limits."

Montesquieu.

"There are always breakthroughs who believe they can do anything. We're here to prove them wrong."

John Chandler, aka Atlas.

They gave us our own *annex*.

"Mr. Lucas?" The English butler (c'mon, *really?*) hadn't looked twice at my fangs or claws as he led us through the underground Hilton. A Hilton with doors that were too hip to go swoosh because that would be a cheap sound effect, but should have.

"Your rooms are the first on the left of the common room. Your Highness, yours are the second on the right. Mr. Lasila, you are next down from Mr. Lucas. The pantry is through the door on the end. The others will be joining you when they have time to move their things."

"Right..." Reese looked impressed by the "common room." Ozma didn't, but probably nothing would impress her short of Buckingham Palace.

She nodded smartly. "Thank you, Willis." Of course she remembered his name. "This is lovely, and I'm sure we will be quite comfortable. When will I be able to see my lab?"

He practically clicked his heels. "Your boxes are being delivered, Your Highness, and I will take you down presently if no one else makes themselves available."

"Then we will be fine for now. Thank you."

"Your Highness. Sirs. Call if anything is needed."

"Should we tip?" Reese snarked when Willis disappeared through the door. "Is he off to polish the silver?"

Ozma just smiled. "Since our bags are already here, I suggest we unpack and clean up." She yawned behind her hand, suggesting that sleep might come before serious unpacking. She and Reese were covered in ash even after he'd blown them off. I hadn't been on the right side of the airport to see the slash-and-burn fight, but apparently Her Highness had ended the Green Man's attack pretty decisively. No surprise there, but she actually looked a little wilted.

The big burnoff had thrown up enough smoke to give me shade as I'd worked clearing the road for emergency vehicles to get into the airport. Chicago's capes had still been doing cleanup when we left, including the tiny cheerful blonde who'd given me the lift; last I'd seen her, she'd been proving she could fly for a family of kids.

Finally figuring out how to make the door panel work, I stepped into "my" room and had to take a minute.

Willis had meant what he said: *rooms*. Bedroom, dressing room, bathroom, and everything in my size, which was quite a trick. Even the shower (a separate tiled *room*, not a stall) gave me plenty of space, and the bathtub was big enough to host a flock of migrating ducks. Welcome to the big leagues.

I called Aunt Donna to let her and Uncle Carl know I'd arrived, found out we were on TV, and turned on my big-screen (yep, the remote had been sized for my clawed hands).

Holy shit.

Chicago's news crews had to be crazy freaking daredevils to get the kind of footage they had, and the screen panned over the line of attacking green. I spotted Ozma and the blonde standing with some barely dressed blue-flaming chick and a freaking flaming chorus line of *dancing blue firemen*. Burning blue firemen, complete with fire axes and fire hats, long fire coats, and a pretty good sense of rhythm. Crazy girl had style.

I showered and worked on the hair.

Willis called to let us know that our new comrades would be down to meet us, so I dressed and stepped out in costume to meet everyone; it's always best to get it over with. Reese and Ozma didn't have costumes yet — the school had the uniform and variations on it — but my needs had gotten me one. It was just a pair of very heavy duty reinforced and stretchable black bike shorts and an armored belt I could store fragile stuff in. The whole thing could accommodate my changing clothing sizes and held up pretty well in a fight.

Everyone else was waiting for me. Ozma had changed into a party dress for the occasion, but Reese just slouched in jeans. The others were all in costume.

"Wow," the blue and silver robot girl said. The girl I'd met at the airport nudged her. *Astra*. I should have realized — how many tiny blonde teen Atlas-types were there? She'd dressed for the party in a skirted costume instead of her normal battle gear and minus her mask. Crash and a guy in a red and black leather costume I didn't recognize flanked them on the couch, but I didn't pay attention to them.

"Wow?" she teased the robot. "Apologize." She aimed her grin at me as robot-girl rolled her eyes. "Shell just likes big muscles. Is the Mr. Universe build your default look?" She laughed, smiling like we hadn't all been in a desperate fight with nature just hours ago.

"Um, yeah." *Shell?*

"We brought offerings. Truthfully, Willis made them."

They'd piled the table in the middle of the dropped area high with food: toasted sliders, chips and dip, wrapped mini-sandwiches and fancier things on toothpicks, and bottles of everything. The smell of the hamburger sliders made my mouth water and my fangs started growing. I dialed them back, but not before Astra saw and her eyes widened. *Shit.*

She looked away, transferring her smile to Ozma.

"Willis told me your...assistants?...have taken over the lab Vulcan equipped for you. Should we invite them up?"

Ozma shook her head, hands busy piling a plate full of sliders. Everyone else had already dug in. "They don't eat. Nox would threaten somebody and Nix is shy, but thank you." She handed me the plate and a bottle like she was serving tea and cakes, and Astra's eyes followed the plate back to me before she looked away again, smile still up. She sat legs crossed and back straight, mirroring Ozma, and I almost choked when I realized what they were doing; it was high tea at Buckingham Palace and they were seriously trying to out-princess each other.

You have got *to be kidding me.*

Astra — what was her real name? Hope? The cheerful girl sitting there drinking a Coke with her pinky-finger extended like she was holding a teacup, dressed like a superhero cheerleader, had killed Seif-al-Din, the supervillain who killed *Atlas.* She'd dropped a godzilla pretty much on her own, and taken down a demonically possessed A Class Atlas-type if the Sentinels fansites weren't just making it up.

And she couldn't look at me. Shit.

Astra

Boys could be so *stupid.*

First he came walking out like he was ready to flex for the judges — he might as well have oiled up first — then he got all...*sensitive* because I was surprised to see his teeth growing.

I'd read his files, I just didn't think he morphed to *eat.*

And now he couldn't look at me. I suppressed a sigh and kept smiling, but of course he shut up. Which was too bad; Shelly said I had a "thing" for deep male voices, and while Seven was easy to look at, I could listen to Brian's voice all day long. It started at a solid bass and worked its way down from there, like the growl of a downshifting Harley Davidson, and I was *really* tired if I was waxing specifically poetic about voices.

Since he wouldn't engage and Reese wanted to engage way too much, I passed the time bouncing witty and-how-are-you-enjoying-Chicago back and forth off of Ozma. It was better than stewing in mortification because I'd reduced possibly the strongest boy in the *world* to a twitching pile of silent embarrassment.

I mean, how could you *apologize*? Sorry, your growing fangs startled me? Now go right ahead and chow down? Yeah, that would work.

Ozma knew what I was doing and played along, but I bailed out. Five minutes into a discussion of the merits of Hillwood, I cocked my head to the side like I was listening to my earbug, and *lied*. Duty called. Or Blackstone. Maybe Fisher, but *somebody*. I left the honors to Shell, maybe she could blow the party up worse. And anyway, we'd all be seeing each other at tomorrow's newbie orientation.

Mom's hostess lessons let me retreat with grace — she knew how to exit a party at high speeds without offending anyone or even looking rushed — but tired as I was, I didn't know what to do with myself. I couldn't go back to the hospital. After our part of the O'Hare cleanup, Dad had suggested I stay away from the hospital for now; the doctors had drugged Toby again to discourage any movement less necessary than breathing, and my presence would just attract more newsies. He had hugged me when he said it, but stay away still meant *stay away*.

So I went upstairs to the chapel to talk to Quan Yin.

Standing in front of the crypt shrine, I lit my normal votive candles for Atlas, Ajax, and Nimbus with a prayer for each. Then I added three more, one for each death at O'Hare: a businessman from Germany who got pushed over a balcony in the panic, a tourist crushed against another car by a driver trying to bulldoze his way out of the departure lane jam, and an airport worker who got caught under the sweep of vines and asphyxiated before anyone could find him.

I lit one more with a prayer of thanks that there hadn't been more — dozens of panic and trampling injuries, but not the hundreds who would have died if we hadn't stopped the green.

And I lit one for Toby. The jerk. What had he been *doing*? As always, Quan Yin's luminous white jade face seemed to smile peacefully and I felt better. A little.

Behind me, Father Nolan chuckled. "And why did I know I'd find you here?"

"A little birdy told you?" I turned to see his smile.

"Certainly not. Well, perhaps Mary of the Pagans." He briefly transferred his smile to Quan Yin, refocused on me. "I would be remiss in my chaplain's duties if I didn't come by and see how you are doing." He sank into a pew, sighed. "And how are you doing, Hope?"

I sat beside him with a sigh of my own, sniffed. Father Nolan handed me his handkerchief and I used it.

"Better than Toby, Father. Dad kept his secret from us since the day of the Event. Mine didn't last a year."

"Did you believe it would last? Most high-profile superheroes don't, unless they go to extremes to hide or alter their appearances entirely. Most don't even try. Will you dispense with the mask?"

"No. There aren't that many pictures of me without it. And nobody looks at Hope."

"Now there, you are inarguably wrong, but in the interest of amity I will let it pass. Hope, you are not responsible for what has happened to Toby." His mouth set into stern lines. "Do not tell yourself otherwise. Perhaps if you had covered yourself head to toe in concealing body armor, disguised your voice with a device, you could have kept your secret. Perhaps. But you are not responsible for all that may befall your family because you are now a publicly known superhero. Please allow others their agency and moral culpability."

"I *know*." I wiped my wet cheeks. "I just can't make myself *believe* it. Toby — "

"Toby will recover, and if it is learned that his attackers were motivated by your good works, that will be on their heads. Do the police know anything yet?"

"No. It's not his investigation, but Fisher promised he'd keep me in the loop. There weren't any witnesses and — They may never find out unless Toby suddenly recovers his memory."

"Then you will have to forgive unknown strangers. And forgive yourself." He waited until he got a nod from me, and rose with a groan. "And I am not getting any younger. We will be observing a Mass for the fallen Sunday at St. Christopher, for today's dead and those in recent days to this latest outbreak of violence. Will you come?"

I nodded. "Thank you, Father — "

"*Ozma has left for her lab,*" Shell broke in quietly.

" — and I have to go now, too."

"*Going to tell me what's going on?*" Shelly asked when I punched the button for the maintenance level. We'd put Ozma's lab down with the armory and the wards.

"A private conversation. Leadership stuff." Private meant exactly that, and she wouldn't be able to override the Dome's protocols to listen in. It wasn't a conversation *I* wanted to have right now, either, but given everything happening and how fast it could all go real bad... "I won't be long, and then we can dish. Promise."

Nothing else was going to happen until tomorrow, anyway; Blackstone had decided to give the new guys the day to settle before getting down to business, and he was deep into situation analysis with all of the information from the new Green Man attack.

"*Okay.*" Shell pouted audibly, but couldn't make herself sound down. "*Crash and Reese have got a Dance Dance Revolution face-off going on the Common Room game system, anyway. I don't think Reese is very smart.*"

I swallowed a giggle and agreed. Challenge a speedster to a dance off? *Yeah, good luck with that.* And with her computer-precision, Shell would totally own them both. If she joined in, she could download new moves off the Internet between steps.

The doors opened and I stepped out. The maintenance level was just like the others but without the starship-meets-Hilton trim, and even more secure. Willis, not usually a font of information, once told me the original designers had intended the level to include hard-cells for holding superhumans, but Atlas and the others had flatly refused to include detainment as a duty of the Sentinels charter. There would have been no way to keep us independent of the government *at all*. We'd just be supercops.

They'd given Ozma the space right across the hall from the armory (Willis had lettered the door in *green*) and she had already figured out the vocal latch; when I touched the door screen, it slid open at her "Come in!"

An oak cabinet stood in one corner and shipping boxes lay open beside the lab tables. Another corner had been turned into a temporary greenhouse. Megan would have said there were enough plant lights to grow a serious indoor marijuana crop, but I had no idea what the climbing vines and flowers were. Which was weird; Mom had a serious flower hobby and I'd helped dress lots of events so I could recognize breeds of poppy, lily, and tea rose, but I didn't know any of these. Ozma knelt examining the plants. She still wore her party dress, and she dusted the soil off her hands as she stood to greet me. Beside her, two dolls watched me warily.

Dolls. A tiny goth punk, with long raven hair and a look that said he'd cut me if I messed with his princess, sat on a stack of books. The other doll, crouched in the plants, was dressed in silk leaves and sported fairy wings. She smiled uncertainly, like she hoped we'd get along

"Hello," I said carefully. I couldn't stop staring. I didn't get a whiff off of them, confirmation that I'd finally stopped being able to "smell" magic. I'd stopped smelling the wards long ago, but wondered if I'd just gotten used to them.

Ozma smiled. "Those are interesting magic wards you have. They shield the Dome from all outside magic?"

"Doctor Cornelius set them up for us."

"He did a very good job. Not my magic tradition, but a potent one." She followed my eyes, smiled. "Would you like to meet Nox and Nix?"

I flushed. "I'm sorry! It's just that magic ... gives me the wiggins. I know there's really no difference between magic and Verne-tech superscience, but — Sorry."

"And yet, here I am. With you to thank, too. Thank you. And why?"

I opened my mouth, closed it, huffed helplessly. *Oh well, in for a penny...*

"How true are they?"

"I'm sorry?"

"The stories about Oz?" Mom had grown up with Grandma's childhood collection of Baum's Oz books and Dad had read them to me for bedtime stories. Which had made the Future Files on Ozma *really* disturbing — and sent me back to them to confirm what I'd remembered.

Ozma pointed us to a pair of lab stools, waiting for me to take one before seating herself. Her pictures really hadn't done Baum's description justice; she was perfect, a jewel of a human being, and though she looked *maybe* sixteen she carried herself with a sense of easy confidence in her worth and position that went down to her bones. She might as well have been wearing a t-shirt that said "I'm the Princess of Oz. Who are you?" — but the question would be absolutely unironic, asked with a cheerful, friendly smile that reminded me of Annabeth of all people.

She let me settle myself and adjust my costume skirt while she thought about it. Nix flew herself and Nox up onto the table beside us to watch.

"Baum and the rest were storytellers first, chroniclers second," she said finally. "None of them were particularly enamored of factuality when it got in the way of telling children's stories, so some of it is true, some isn't quite, some of it is entirely fanciful, and it's all cleaned up for bedtime reading. Perhaps if you told me what you want to be true?"

"I — can you make someone who is alive human again?"

Her perfect eyebrows rose. Obviously *not* what she had been expecting.

"For example?"

"Well, say that the Tin Woodsman wanted to be human again? Could you?"

"What an interesting question." She gave it some thought. "Nick Chopper's meat parts were replaced piecemeal, of course, but he was so proud of his untiring tin body that he never wanted anything of it back. Other than a heart. Is your living but not human friend enchanted?"

I was wound so tight my hands were trying to shake, and I fisted them against my thighs. "No. She's a copy? A..." I had no *idea* how to explain quantum-ghosts. "She's a cybernetic twin."

"So she has no physical connection with her original body?" She frowned pensively when I shook my head. My heart sank.

"Only her mind, but — There is the story of Peg Amy, and I know you have Glegg's Box of Mixed Magic..."

"So how much of that story is real? Yes, Glegg turned Peg Amy into a tree, and yes, she was chopped down, a branch later carved into a doll, the doll brought to life by Glegg's Re-Animating Rays, and she was finally restored to human form when Glegg's original enchantment was broken in more or less the traditional fairy tale way..." She tapped her perfect chin.

"Certainly at one point she was completely dead, but the dead piece of wood was still an enchanted bit of her body. People get turned into things all the time in Oz and the lands around it — I once spent a few hours as a knickknack in the Nome King's hall. I assume we are talking about Galatea? Shelly? Does she want to be human again?"

"I doubt she's even given it much thought." *As in zero.* "I'm sure she hasn't realized why you're here — she wasn't into the Oz stories like I was..." I swallowed, took a breath to get the quaver out of my voice. The shaking in my hands had turned into alarming tremors in my gut. "She's so proud of what she can do now, but — "

Ozma kept quiet, waiting for me to finish.

"But she's not *safe*. Not if she scares the wrong people. They could take her away and... I can't — I can't..."

"You can't protect her."

"I'd do *anything* for her."

Now she smiled wide, a shared smile, like we knew the same secret. "Nothing truly bad, I'm sure," she contradicted. "But then, I am not the best judge of how much badness is in a person." She bit her lip thoughtfully — the first inelegant mannerism I'd seen out of her. It made her look a lot younger.

"Before my father's reign, all rulers of Oz had been witches or wizards, not simply dependent on them. I decided after taking the Emerald Throne that the stability of the monarchy required me to become at least as good a witch as my grandmother was, so I studied with Glinda for years and years and collected a great many magical treasures." She waved at the boxes around us, smile fading, and sat straighter if that was possible.

"When Mombi and Ruggiddo bound Glinda and the Wizard, I knew I couldn't win against them on my own. I scattered the royal treasures, the Magic Belt, the Box, all the rest, throughout the mortal world before they trapped me and erased me again and sent me into exile. The Magic Belt found me and woke my memories, and now I search for the rest of my treasures and build my magical strength. There may be something I can do for Shelly. But."

Her eyes glistened, bright with sadness deep enough to drown in. "I miss my beautiful emerald city, but I weep for my brave Gillikans, my fine Quadlings, my happy Munchkins and Winkies suffering under the tyranny of those two, and every weapon I have or can make is bent to their freedom. I will drop a house on Mombi and feed Ruggiddo scrambled eggs for breakfast and sit on the Emerald Throne again."

Nix looked sad and Nox determined as they both nodded their agreement.

"I — " I had nothing. What could I possibly say to that? I looked down at my fists, opened them. "Then, a trade? Certainly you will need more than magic. Please."

Her eyes widened. I'd managed to surprise her again. "An alliance?"

I nodded convulsively. "I know about war. My father fought to end the war in China."

Her smile wandered back, this time with a touch of whimsy. "And you will fight for people you don't even believe in?" I realized what I'd said, and flushed a hot, hot red. She'd been so *convincing*. Was insanity contagious? She laughed at my expression, and crazy or not even *that* sounded graceful, nearly musical.

"But I accept, even if you won't believe it until you see it. I know a word keeper when I see one." She cocked her head. "So the mighty Army of Oz is two now. Brian will be happy. And one of my treasures ... I have not yet retrieved it, and it may not do what you want of it for Shelly, but will you accept my promise in coin?"

"Yes, but..." Giddy with triumph, I forced myself to stop and take a breath. *She can do it, she can —* "I can't, not unconditionally."

Her gaze didn't waver. "What are your conditions?"

"I won't..." *I won't help you steal Kansas, not even for Shelly.* How could I say that without telling her I knew plans she might not even *have* yet.... "I won't do anything *truly* bad."

She nodded in perfect understanding.

"And only you can be the judge of your badness. Done. I accept your word and your judgment." Her lips quirked. "I feel that I should dub you Lady Knight or something. And I shall, but until that day, I am yours to command, apparently." She laughed again, delighted at getting her turn to shock me. "Blackstone informed me that you would be our fearless leader. I don't think the others know."

Okey dokey... I stood up, felt like melting. I was *so* done. "Two questions?"

"Of course."

"How old are you, really?"

"Sixteen. But I have been sixteen for a very long time."

"And what did you promise Brian?"

Her clear diamond eyes were dark. "A small and a great thing. Only justice for his murdered family."

Chapter Twenty: Megaton

Although superheroes are popularly portrayed in the media as crime-fighters and even vigilantes, they are more often engaged in rescue work. For example, the charters used by Crisis Aid and Intervention teams (CAIs) list their mission as 1.) Civilian rescue, 2.) Disaster prevention/mitigation, and, 3.) Superhuman containment and safety. Note that none of these three missions covers non-superhuman law enforcement.

Barlow's Guide to Superhumans.

Not that we don't mind nailing bad guys when we catch them in the act.

Hope Corrigan, aka Astra.

Shouldn't there have been some kind of, I don't know, welcome ceremony? Maybe the Dance Dance Revolution face-off was it. Reese came in last, and was a good sport about it. Shelly won on points, but Brian was the surprise winner on style — he dropped at least fifty pounds of muscle to get streamlined and took the mat to display locks and pops that could have gone into a hip-hop music video.

The boy had serious skills.

I left the common room to Shelly, Jamal, and Reese. Astra — Hope — and Ozma had cut out fairly early and Brian had disappeared not long after his win. Shelly was a blast when she wasn't pushing, and Jamal was cool (since he lived and trained somewhere else I hadn't had much chance to get to know him, but just by hanging he seemed to calm Shelly down). Reese was a player, but not nasty about it. I knew guys like him on the team. *Had known*, past tense. Not my team anymore.

Maybe that's why I was done: these guys weren't my crowd yet and it sucked remembering impromptu road-parties crammed into connected hotel rooms or weekend jams in a teammate's basement. Or not. I stared at my cellphone for maybe the hundredth time today. I'd thought, *maybe*, after my big debut today, after half of the Green Man Attack coverage seemed to be about the new kids, after I'd helped *save the freaking day...*

The door chimed.

"Come in."

Shelly bounced in. The kid had missed out on fighting the Green Man in person today, but being able to order me around had kept her from being too disappointed. Her artificial eyes lit up at the sight of my cellphone and I winced. She was still flying high on her mom being back — convinced, despite everything I'd told her about *my* parents, that one phone call, a face-to-face, and all would be well.

"So, are you going to?"

Screw it. I owe Astra the dare anyway. My thumb hit "1."

Four rings and it picked up. "*Mal?*" Sydney's breathless voice. She was old enough to read the caller ID.

"Hey, Squirt. How you doing?"

"*Great!*" I could practically hear her wide gap-toothed grin. "*Where are you? When are you coming home? Why are Mom and Dad —* " I heard a faint "*Hey!*" as someone took the phone away from her.

"*Hello?*" It was Mom.

"Hey Mom, it's Mal." Dumb opening, and now I had too many words to start again. She didn't start at all for way too many breaths.

"*Mal — I'm sorry, your father — I can't talk to you.*" Click.

That was it. Shelly's eyes got big — obviously she'd dialed up her hearing — but I kept the phone to my ear in case the dead silence was a transient reception break. If I didn't hit "End," it wasn't over.

"Did she just — "

"Yup." I closed the phone. Shelly's face cycled through expressions and settled on *pissed*. Not that I cared. "Out. Now."

"But — "

"Now!" She went. I put my phone down and found my helmet. Jamming it on, I got out, down the hall to the emergency shaft up to the launch bay, and lit off hard as soon as the bay doors cracked wide enough to let me through without scraping any leather off.

Clear of the Dome, I banked left and poured on the speed. Sound-baffling helmet or not, all I heard was the roar as I lit out over Lake Michigan and *away*.

Grendel

"Brian?" Nix's soft call woke me up faster than an alarm clock. I pulled my pillow over my head. "Brian?" Getting a growl back that time, she giggled. Nix doesn't take me seriously.

Tossing the pillow aside, I glared at the shadows. "I know there aren't any loose vents in here, and the locks are personalized. How did you get in?"

"The mirror in your bathroom, silly."

I jerked up so fast my dreads whipped me in the face.

"Mirror — she can't... arrrghhhh!" Yeah, like Ozma would play peeping Tom. *Nix* might — the little doll had a thing for me I couldn't understand — but the full-body flush the darkness hid was really flashback to the impromptu welcoming party.

I'd been used to girls liking what they saw, before the day of the stadium attack and my breakthrough. *Really* liking; my thing for high-impact dance had given me seriously ripped muscles and female appreciation had given me a wink and a smile that said it all and then some. At Hillwood, being a toothy, clawed manimal hadn't really had a downside; there were students a lot freakier and nobody stronger. I'd been too busy training to be as bad as I could be, and all the girls loved the hair.

So why do you care if the blonde doesn't like your teeth? Get a grip.

"What does Her Highness want tonight?"

Nix flew over to perch on my knee. "She's located a treasure and wants us to fetch it."

"Which one?"

"The Wishing Pill."

Okay... She had to have a serious need if she was going after that one; in the stories, the Wishing Pills had been handy and harmless — in her telling, not so much. More handy, less harmless. Lots less. What does it tell you that a pill guaranteed to grant you one immediate and present wish still hasn't been used after one hundred years? And now she wanted the Army of Oz to collect it.

Ours not to reason why... I flipped Nix laughing into the air with a twitch of my knee and rolled out of bed. Five minutes later I was all ninja'd up except for the hood. Ninja Beast; you've got to love it.

Seeing me ready, Nix landed on my shoulder, opened her bag of Travel Dust, counted "Three, two, one!" and dumped it on us. The tornado grabbed us up, tossed us, spun us, generally had its fun, and dropped us into a dark back-alley where I nearly tossed my cookies. I *hate* Travel Dust. (Someday I'm going to ask Glinda how that convenient tornado really got Dorothy to Oz, but *I* think the fix was in.)

So, where were we? Since it was still night, we couldn't be halfway round the world. The alley smelled like an alley, old oil and piss, and was crowded by a couple of big trash bins and an ancient car that looked like the only way it would ever move again was on top of a truck. The bin beside us didn't reek of spoiled food, so not a restaurant, but I smelled *something* that made me think of Mom's kitchen before everything had happened. I carefully opened a pocket and the carry case inside, extracting the Seeing Specs. Slipping the gold-rimmed bifocals on, I whispered "Magic."

Not a glimmer. The building had no magic protections, always good to know — a couple of items we'd retrieved had already been found by Merlin-types. Those trips had been interesting.

"It's inside," Nix whispered.

"You're sure?"

She nodded and darted upward, to come back down hugging the wall. A camera covered the steel alley door, and she dusted it with Thieves' Powder. I sometimes teased the princess about the names she gave the stuff she made — no more imagination than Gleg — but she was a firm believer in Truth In Advertising. Nix did the same to the lock, and through the specs the camera and lock sparkled. She waited only long enough for me to pad up to the door and crack it open with a single hard snap before darting inside.

I stayed outside and sweated. No, it wasn't a warm night.

The existence of superhumans gave security specialists fits, but technology adapted. Someone can teleport into any locked room? Use a sensor to detect sudden changes in air pressure. A thief can ghost through walls? Build in sensors that react to fast temperature drops. Invisible intruders? Pressure plates in the floor, and of course motion sensors still work for just about anybody. These days, a lot of those options are pretty low cost and standard for businesses with high-value inventory, but they're all vulnerable to Nix's direct attack on the security systems. Her soft call came minutes later and I went through the door.

And just about gagged. A single breath started the sneezing fit, finally killed by holding my nose. My eyes watered.

The place was a *spice shop*.

Carved wooden shelves and cabinets full of tiny drawers lined the walls. Boxes, fancy labeled bags, tins, even little cloth sacks, filled every nook and cranny. The place also sold tea and oils. How the hell were we going to find a little silver pill in all this? Nix turned helplessly in the air. I breathed shallowly and tried to think.

Ozma's royal treasures always looked weird enough before she got them and fully re-infused them with the magic of Oz, but they always found themselves in settings that echoed their stories — they couldn't simply be buried or lost at sea or something. So, why here? A pill wasn't a spice. The Three Wishing Pills had shown up in Baum's second book, *The Marvelous Land of Oz*. I was pretty sure that only one had been used then, the others lost, but obviously

Ozma had sent an expedition to recover them. Pills came in boxes, bottles —

"Nix. We're looking for a spice tin. It'll be tube-shaped with a screw top. It's got a false bottom that screws off, too."

She looked around and almost wailed. There were hundreds of tins of all shapes and sizes, lots of them tubular, and we didn't have all night. *But Ozma scattered her royal treasures years ago — if the Wishing Pill had been hidden in something intended for sale, it wouldn't still be here.*

"Look in the high shelves, the stuff meant for decoration."

Nix found it, an antique *pepper* tin and I should have remembered that). Stored high in the back of a shelf, it twisted open to reveal a burnished silver pill wrapped in silk in the hidden compartment. The pill had been etched in almost microscopic detail, and the Seeing Specs magnified the patterns into fancy lettering I couldn't read.

Found: one Wishing Pill. One *unused* Wishing Pill. Nix thought it was pretty. I wondered just how dangerous it was.

We left a square-cut emerald by the cash register to pay for the lock.

Astra

Ever been so tired that thinking feels like trying to write your name in syrup? Not with syrup, *in* syrup; between the family crisis, the Green Man attack and cleanup, and talking with Ozma, I'd been smashed flat. And I still had no idea if I'd done the right thing. But guess what being a team leader means? More homework. I found the file waiting on my epad when I got back to my rooms, and curled up with it after brushing my teeth and climbing into my sleep shorts and tee.

Blackstone was still hip deep in Green Man data from the first two attacks, but we got a *lot* more on the second attack from ready and watching drones (you can bet the DSA staked out all the airports as likely targets) and he'd sent me a preliminary report. Not for analysis — I wasn't going to spot anything his twisty brain might miss — but because he firmly believed in making sure all potential decision-makers had as much information as he did. Which meant Lei Zi was probably reading in bed, too.

"*Hope?*" Shelly queried through Dispatch.

"Hmm?"

"*Mal's gone on a night flight.*"

I closed my eyes. "I don't think anyone's set a curfew yet, so why am I concerned?" That had always been one of Mom's favorite leading questions. *You say you took your bike out riding? Why am I concerned?* I *so* wasn't ready to be Mom.

"*He called his folks first. Want to hear it?*"

I put the pad down, covered my eyes. I *really* couldn't do this now.

"*No.* Shell — What do I have to do to get you to *listen* to me on this? And hacking his phone? Forget the trouble you could get into — that's just *wrong!*"

She didn't answer.

"Shell?"

"*I was there when he called.*"

My heart sank. "Oh. Well, I wasn't invited and I don't want to hear it." More silence, which was just great. I was right and *I* felt guilty. *Focus on the important thing, Hope. You can talk it out later.*

"It didn't go well?"

"*... His sister sounds nice, but his mom hung up on him.*"

My stomach joined my heart's quest for a lower elevation and I leaned forward to rest my head on my knees, so tired I could cry. That stupid, stupid dare. Straightening, I let out a shaky breath. *Okay, Hope, you've made a mess. Now, you deal.*

"If Dispatch worries, tell them I'm on it. Where is he going?" Skinning out of my bedclothes and pulling on my workout shorts and athletic tee, I wondered if Blackstone needed to know. No. What he didn't know, he couldn't be responsible for.

Tonight, Chicago's famous skyline met the sky to disappear into a blanket of cloud that put a dropped ceiling on the world. The GPS in Mal's helmet put him out over Lake Michigan and heading north along the eastern shore. I flew to intercept, following a red targeting icon painted on my contacts, vanishing dots below the glowing pointer indicating closing distance.

There. Flying low over the lake, between clouds and water, Mal lit the night with his flaring rocket-tail as I curved in behind him and moved up to slide into his peripheral vision. I knew when he saw me; he started and corkscrewed out of control — nearly smacking into Lake Michigan before he straightened out.

"Shit!" he broadcast wide-channel. *"You just about killed me!"*

I crossed all my mental fingers, tried to channel Megan at her snarky best.

"That was my plan, death by stupidity. You know you're not that floaty, right? And we still don't know how deep your gas tank goes." I could practically *hear* him thinking about that.

"I'm not going back yet."

"No worries — I just don't want to have to fish you out of the lake. Want to see something cool?"

"...okay."

I put myself in front and turned us back towards Chicago, then piled on the speed. The kind of boy who couldn't let a girl show him up, Mal stoked his fire to catch up and pull ahead. Naturally I gave it more, too, and we flew into the city at a respectable if sub-sonic speed. I took us up Jackson Boulevard and then *up* through cloud to land on the east edge of the Sears Building. Mal did his awkward landing thing, where he cut off his blast about eight feet off the roof to avoid scorching it and landed with a light grunt.

"You're getting better at that. How are your takeoffs?"

He shrugged. "Fine on fireproof surfaces. So what — whoa. Wow."

"Oh yeah." I dropped to sit on the edge and swing my bare feet over Franklin Street. I'd checked the cloud ceiling before leaving the Dome to make sure, and tonight the view was my favorite kind. The Sears Building and a reef of other skyscrapers thrust upward out of a luminous sea, light-speckled pillars of glass and steel over clouds lit by the city below.

"That's just...wow." He carefully lowered himself to sit beside me and I tried not to smile. He hadn't been flying long enough to be completely blasé about heights yet.

I nudged his shoulder. "This was Atlas' favorite hangout. You know the safest way for you to get down from here is to jump and *then* light up, right? So, to use a Shellyism, are you still feeling all angsty?"

He gave it a minute, which was good. The magic of Chicago will work on anybody.

"I'll get over it. I heard about your brother. Sorry. If it was Sydney..."

My turn? A guy, or a girl trying to be one of the guys, would say "S'okay," and "He'll be alright." Empathy expressed, accepted, done deal. I bit my lip hard.

He shifted when I didn't say anything. "Hey. I didn't mean—"

"S'okay. He'll be alright. Want to hear a story?" I put a bright smile behind it, and when he didn't say no I took a deep breath. "Now that the news about me is out, lots of people are saying how privileged I am. Chicago blue blood, society debutante, *you* know. But you've heard about Shelly's story?"

He shook his head. Well, he was probably avoiding reading the news too.

"It's my Big Tragedy, the hook they're using to really *sell* me as a human-interest story." I sighed. "Has she told you exactly how she became Galatea?"

"Just that she died."

I looked for the pearly white halo of the Dome, but the cloud sea was a little too thick to be sure.

"We met in grade school and were closer than sisters. Joined at the hip. I was a — I was pretty shy as a kid, scared of a lot of things, and she was fun and fearless. I worshipped her. She was the leader in all our adventures, and — She jumped off a building origin-chasing when we were fifteen, and gravity doesn't give you second chances."

I kept looking for the Dome, listening in case he moved.

"My family is great, but it had been just Shelly and me forever and I felt like half of me, the stronger, braver half, was *gone*. I was so *mad* at her and just...just lost. That's when the Bees pretty much kidnapped me."

"The what?"

"The Bees. Julie Brennan, Annabeth Bauman, and Megan Brock. The Bees."

I swallowed around the lump in my throat. "They were the It Girls of my class, and Julie was the queen bee. Julie and I knew each other 'cause we were in the same parish, did catechism class together."

Hah. The clouds had thinned a bit and there was the Dome, shining bright. I sighed.

"Julie dragged me into their circle, made sure I sat at their lunch table, and if I went my own way, one of them would chase me down. Usually Annabeth, since nobody can ever get mad at her. I couldn't be a *Bee*, of course — wrong initials — but eventually it was Hope and the Bees. Look."

I pointed out the glowing halo of cloud that marked the Dome. He shifted beside me.

"So what's your point?"

Finally looking at him, I gave him my brightest smile. "No point. Just that it sucks now but you've got a bunch of annoying new friends who won't let you do something stupid like run out of juice over the lake." I floated off the edge to hang by the building. "Coming?"

"Yeah. Sure."

Boys. So eloquent.

And who cared? It was *way* past my bedtime, and I needed every minute of sleep I could get if I was going to apologize *and* have it out with Shelly tomorrow.

Chapter Twenty One: Astra

*Shelly and I had a drinking game (soda shots — we weren't old
enough to drink yet). We'd put on an episode of* Sentinels *or* The
Guardians *and take a drink for every cheesy line of fight dialogue. In
a real life fight, dialogue mostly consists of orders, swearing, and
one-syllable words like "Stop!" and "Give up!" when it's not just
grunts and screaming.*

From the journal of Hope Corrigan.

A jarring buzz pulled me out of dreamless sleep, rising in pitch until
my fogged head couldn't ignore it anymore. Forcing sticky eyes
open, I looked at my clock: one-thirty. It had read twelve-something
when I closed my eyes, and since I obviously hadn't slept more than
twelve hours, somebody was going to die. I'd explain the error of
their ways and then kill them as a warning to others.

"*Hope?*" Blackstone's voice replaced the buzzing. Rats. I
couldn't kill Blackstone.

"I'm awake."

"*My apologies. Detective Fisher has called; they have
discovered Mr. Ludlow's location, and we are to proceed with an
arrest.*"

I flailed my way out of bed. "Five minutes! Who else is
coming?"

"Watchman, Rush, The Harlequin, and Variforce. Galatea is engaged with Vulcan working on counter-Green Man ordnance. Take ten minutes, my dear."

Ten. I could do ten. My bedclothes went on the floor *again* as I scrambled into full armor gear. *Does this count as a new day, or did someone decide to reopen the old one?*

Willis was the God of Coffee.

Caffeine swept the veils of thwarted sleep away enough for me to notice an odd, minty taste in his offering. "Red ginseng," he reported, pouring for Variforce. "And other natural stimulants, my own secret recipe. Side effects include sleeplessness followed by a brief coma. Be sure you're somewhere comfortable."

I reconsidered my cup, but took another gulp. Nobody else gave it any thought. I'd been the last of the picked team to arrive in the Assembly Room, all of us in costume, even Lei Zi and Blackstone. *How long does it take to climb into a tux, complete with waistcoat and bowtie? Did Chakra help?* I squeaked, almost a hiccup, and put down Willis' evil brew. I was definitely feeling warm, and the stuff should be illegal.

Blackstone's stage-magic powers didn't include mind-reading tricks, thank God, but he took the lowering of my cup as a signal to begin.

"Two hours ago, a patrolman stopping for coffee recognized Eric Ludlow from a police BOLO. Our Mr. Ludlow apparently has a taste for red satin and cream cheese cupcakes. The patrolman got his own coffee and then called it in, and a thermal drone was able to get eyes on our suspect when he left — a happy result of having so many eyes in the air watching for the Green Man."

He brought up an aerial shot of a Chicago neighborhood and zoomed in.

"Mr. Ludlow took his cupcakes to a closed business on South Anthony and 94th Street." A red X highlighted the building. "That is the good news; his hideout is part of a small and isolated row of business buildings, with only a handful of homes and a nice open business lot separating them.

"The bad news is that thermal imaging shows us that Mr. Ludlow is alone. Detective Fisher wants to wait to move in, in hopes of catching the rest of the Wreckers. Superintendent Redmond, however, disagrees; the presence of a teleporter on the team means we could lose Mr. Ludlow at any time. The superintendent has authorized his immediate arrest."

Lei Zi nodded and took over. She expanded the image Blackstone had dialed up.

"Hopefully, the fight will remain contained within the strip of businesses. However, should the battlefield widen, you must remain aware of our first responsibility, preventing civilian casualties. As you can see, to the west across Escanaba Avenue, we have dense residential neighborhoods. To the east and south, we have more open ground — at worst, you might tear up the Chicago Skyway. Police will be standing by to close the toll road when the fight begins. They will also move in with vans to fast-evacuate the apartments on either end of the business row."

She stopped, looking around the table.

"They will not begin evacuating until we commence our assault. This is not procedure. Again, Superintendent Redmond feels that the risk of alerting our target — and possibly losing him — is too great. I have expressed my disagreement, but it is his call to make. Rush and The Harlequin will assist the evacuation, and Variforce will stand by and deploy his fields to keep Mr. Ludlow and any launched debris away from civilians and police. Any questions?"

The question wasn't rhetorical; she fully expected that any uncertainties be ironed out before we deployed. When no one spoke up, she continued.

"Watchman, Astra, the two of you are tasked with bringing Mr. Ludlow down. Options?"

My stomach tightened and I flexed my hands on the table. The report from the precinct attack had mirrored the Daily Center attack. Eric, Dozer, had fought in the China War, he could kill, but both times it had been Twist, the telekinetic with the steel cables, who had killed their target.

"I want to talk to him," I said before I could change my mind. Beside her, Blackstone smiled thinly.

Lei Zi didn't smile. "That would concede the element of surprise, Astra, and give him a chance to escape the civilian-free zone he is in." She wasn't disagreeing, just stating obstacles.

"Watchman can stand by ready for a hard drop if he runs. Or attacks. Tactical surprise is as good as strategic surprise. And if he's focused on me, Watchman gets a good first shot."

"You have seen our strength estimate. Mr. Ludlow is now at least an A-Class Ajax-type. He was strong enough at the Daily Center to keep Watchman off of him, and his helmet broke before he did. Allowing him to come to grips with you would be suboptimal."

"No, I mean, I understand. But — " I swallowed, forced my voice level. "He's a veteran, he — he lost more than he should have for his country. Sometimes, we get frustrated, we even feel it might be best to go straight to the killing. It's not right, ma'am, and he's *guilty*, but — We owe him." *Atlas believed in him.*

I didn't look around. Lei Zi didn't look away.

"Watchman, you may wait for Astra's call, or not, at your discretion. Understood?"

"Yes, ma'am."

That ended our planning. Rush and The Harlequin left first, to be in position with the police units mobilized for the operation. Watchman towed Variforce in a force-field harness while I flew hands-free except for Malleus.

"*Astra?*" Lei Zi called through Dispatch. "*The drone places Mr. Ludlow closest to the loading bay door facing South Anthony. You will enter there and proceed as seems best.*"

My stomach twisted tighter. "Enter through the loading bay door, understood." The line remained open for a breath, but she didn't add anything. I focused on flying, and we arrived over our target in minutes.

The police had been prepositioning themselves while we were briefed. Looking down, I could see the orange glows of hot engines, more than a dozen police cars and vans on the perimeter and more on the toll road waiting. Captain Verres introduced himself as the head of the mission's CPD side as we came in, but it was our operation tonight and he didn't start barking orders. Lei Zi passed field control to me to keep clarity of command, and if Verres was surprised at all, it didn't show in his voice.

It was a formality anyway; I had only one real order to give.

Watchman stayed up-top and Variforce went into glider mode to drop down and join the police beside the closest apartments. As soon as he was down, I dropped to the front of the parking lot.

And stood there for a long moment, staring at the loading door and listening to the solitary growl of trucks on the Tollway behind me, rumbling north and south, into the city or away while everyone slept. Did I knock? Did I call inside?

Let's go reintroduce ourselves. Atlas' voice, and *not* the attitude I needed for this, but it helped.

I flew up to the dock, gripped the rolling steel door with one hand, popped its bolts, and pulled up. The door rose and I stepped through into the dark, finding the light switch before Eric had time to roll off of his camp cot, shirtless and barefoot.

My heart thundered in my chest. "Hello, Mr. Ludlow. I'm sorry, but you're under arrest." *Not* the strongest opening and somewhere Atlas was laughing, but Eric hunched, face pasty-white, like I'd already hit him.

Then he pulled himself straight. "No, I'm not. Sorry, Ms. Astra."

"I don't want to hurt you, Mr. Ludlow, and you know I'm not alone. Let me — "

He charged. Ajax-types move *fast* — their own body mass is negligible compared to their strength and big as he was, Eric closed in the blink of an eye. I spun away on my outside foot and my vision still flashed at the impact that threw us both back outside. We missed the door but the wall didn't stop us. I lost Malleus.

I slid across the parking lot, pulling air into shocked lungs. "Eric, stop!"

He leaped to his feet. "I can't! You don't under — " then Watchman landed on him. The hit drove him into the ground, throwing up shattered concrete as I scrambled for Malleus. My left shoulder felt on fire; he'd hit like a *train*.

I found Malleus, swung around, and ducked a spray of concrete as Mr. Ludlow rose to throw Watchman down, breaking his attempted hold. He bent to pick Watchman up and I hit him, form perfect behind my flying swing. He reflexively twisted, Malleus catching him on his upper arm — which *didn't* break. He still screamed as I followed the force of my swing to spin around him and my second hit took him in his lower back. He went down hard, away from Watchman, but rolled and came up, this time backhanding the recovered Watchman as he came on again.

The *crack* sounded like steel plates coming together and Watchman tumbled but I came down on him again, dropping with an overhand swing that hit the same upraised arm. Which pushed aside the force of my hit as he grabbed me.

"No!" was all I had time for before he slammed me *hard* through the pavement into the packed earth beneath and I lost Malleus again.

"Stay down!" Watchman shouted, and then Mr. Ludlow disappeared as Watchman hit, flying them both across the parking lot, the avenue, and into the concrete wall that rose to the toll road.

At least we're moving away from the houses. I grabbed Malleus and flew after them.

Worst fight of my *life*. Before the end, I was swinging through a grey haze. When Watchman finally dropped him with a hammering rabbit-punch to the base of his skull, I fell to my knees and dry-heaved.

"Are you okay?" he gasped, bent over himself. It hadn't been any fun for him, either.

"Is *he*?"

"He'll heal — Ajax-types are good at that." He staggered over, rolled Mr. Ludlow onto his stomach, and got him into the alloyed titanium thumb-cuffs that had miraculously stayed on his belt. If Eric tried to break them, he'd rip out his thumbs first.

I slid back to sit, looked around. We'd ripped into the roadway's southbound lanes. At one point, Watchman had decked Eric with a concrete slab. The left side of my face felt hot and numb from a back-swing hit and I'd lost my mask somewhere. He'd even managed to knock my earbug out — which beat having it hammered into my ear canal. I'd lost my cape somewhere and a dent in my armor wasn't letting me breathe deep.

"The wagon is back down the hill," Watchman said. "Grab an arm?" Balancing him between us, we flew him down to the waiting police. They'd formed two lines from the buildings to the Tollway embankment. Rush, Variforce, and The Harlequin waited for us, along with a smoking Fisher

"Nice fight, A," Rush said, stepping out of the way.

I huffed. It hurt to giggle. "Yeah, the scriptwriters will fix the lame dialogue..." Endorphins make me stupid and I should never open my mouth right after a hard fight.

And I saw him. Against all reason, not all the apartment residents had taken the offered vans and a crowd had gathered beyond the police line. One pale face I *knew* — the business suit from the Daily Building fight, the "hostage" who'd disappeared, the one Blackstone thought was our teleporter.

"Down!" I shouted, launching myself through the police line. And I *got* him — my half-dead but empty left hand wrapped in his jacket collar, and then we were down on the ground and I barely kept myself from smacking him — he wasn't Eric and it'd kill him — he gaped up at me, face shocked white, and we —

Chapter Twenty Two: Grendel

In psychology class, I read about a government-funded study that proved that men were more helpful to beautiful women and that good-looking guys did better on job interviews. No kidding. The study didn't ask if people are more polite to the physically intimidating. The answer is yes. Except when they're not.

Brian Lucas, aka Grendel.

The alarm snarling by my bed died horribly, so Galatea took over my entertainment center's speakers.

"*Get your big grey ass out of bed!*" The subwoofers shook the room. "*Suit up or I'm gonna come down there and kick your ugly butt!*"

"I can twist your head off."

"*Oh, like I can't get a new one. They haven't had time to smack you with the training manual yet, but you just killed a Def-1 alarm and You're. Not. Moving!*" She kept cranking the volume but by the end she was lying; I was up and pulling on my uniform (best thing about it, two easy steps).

"What's going on?"

"*Talk less, move faster, Assembly Room now!*"

I got out into the common room before Ozma, who emerged buckling the Magic Belt on over a silk green and white robe. Reese staggered out, pulling on sweats, and we trailed in Ozma's wake. Mal joined us in the hall outside the elevator, looking pale. Jamal caught up with us outside the Assembly Room; obviously he'd made good time coming across town.

Blackstone, Riptide, Galatea, and Seven waited for us. The screens opposite the doors had all been turned on and displayed overhead and up-close views of some kind of police action. Helicopter spotlights and area lights mounted on police vans lit up the scene, and open line chatter from cops and our guys filled the room.

Someone had trashed the place. One building had a big hole in it, and it looked like someone had bombed the crap out of an empty parking lot and stretch of road. Police surrounded the battlefield, but nothing was going on. Mal pointed to icons along the side of the main screen; Watchman, Rush, Variforce, and The Harlequin were on the scene.

"Please be seated, everyone," Blackstone said — for our benefit, the others already were. Nobody was talking, Galatea stared, wild-eyed, at something somewhere else, and the tension I could *taste* was making my claws grow.

"Less than five minutes ago," Blackstone began once we'd settled, "an unidentified superhuman we have named Drop removed Astra from the scene of a Sentinels-CPD action. She had lost her earbug earlier, and as we have also lost telemetry from the Dispatch links to her mask-cam, her current condition and location are unknown. We are reviewing footage, and do not yet know if this was a trap. Procedure dictates that in an attack on a Sentinel, the full team complement be put on alert until we are certain it is not the opening move of a general attack.

"We are securing the Dome, and will be pulling the field team back once Eric Ludlow, the target of tonight's action, is deposited in the CPD's hard-cells."

Mal cleared his throat. "What are we doing to find Astra?" None of the others said anything, and Galatea wasn't hearing anyone in the room.

"Everything we can," Blackstone said finally, mouth tight. *We're doing everything we can*: what adults said when they had no idea.

When everything they could do was being done by someone else and probably wasn't worth shit.

"So the Wreckers have got her?" Mal asked. "We got one of theirs and they got one of ours? Why? For leverage? And we can't *do* anything? That's crap!"

Blackstone winced.

"The CPD investigation of the Crew is ongoing, and they are following several promising leads. We are assisting, and our first priority is to learn what we can from Dozer. In the meantime, Galatea will coordinate with you as we remain on alert. You are to consider her instruction as coming from Lei Zi or myself. Are we clear, Mr. Scott?"

"Sure. Sir, I owe her — "

"We all do, young man. And we will get her back."

We crowded back into our common room, and Reese found the sodas in the mini-kitchen. "Shit, nothing like this ever happens in Saint Paul!" he crowed.

Jamal, who'd been a pretty laid-back kid at the party, looked ready to smack him. *I* couldn't; if I hit anybody, it counted as seriously excessive force. Ozma heard my growl and sat beside me with a sigh.

"He's a gooch, the provokingest boy I've ever met and his heart isn't true." She cocked her head. "But things that aren't can be made to are, with practice and attention."

Galatea sat alone, still in her silver-and-blue chrome form, ignoring the whole room. She could have been a movie prop. Mal watched her but wasn't getting bothered by it, and Ozma took to sipping a mini-soda and humming to herself. It sounded like a limerick.

Great start to a new team. If this was a *Sentinels* episode, we'd be tracking some clue the bad guys had left behind and getting ready to bust through the wall to their secret headquarters. Unless it was close to the end of the season, in which case Astra would stay kidnapped into the break as a cliffhanger. But nothing bad ever happens to the determinedly perky ingénue, right? *Yeah, and they kill major characters in this series.*

Finishing her drink, Ozma set it down and capped it, whispered, "I am retiring to the lab to see if our new captain is findable. Don't let anyone hurt Reese."

Sure, give me the hard job.

Astra

I woke from a falling nightmare because I couldn't breathe. I couldn't sit up, couldn't see *anything*. No, blinking hard and trying to get a full breath, I could see shapes in the dark...barely. My face ached and, when I tried to touch it, weights held my arms down.

A whimper escaped before I could stop it — I was back in the Dark Anarchist's cell and if I started I wouldn't stop screaming. *Don't panic. Don't panic.* Whatever was constricting my chest was keeping me from hyperventilating, and I took a few minutes to not panic.

Okay. What would Atlas do? Kick ass. Not an option. What would Blackstone do? Gather information. Okay. I was lying on a mattress. Sheets? Pretty good ones, smooth under my hands, not hotel-rough. I tried moving again, pulled my working right arm in until it *clinked* against my side. *Oh.* My bracers were holding my arms down, feeling like they weighed tons. Why? Breathing mystery solved anyway — it was my dented cuirass keeping me from getting all the air I wanted. But — Why couldn't I move? Why was everything so *heavy*?

Move now, think later. Don't panic again, just, don't, *Shelly will laugh.*

I *really* wanted to hear her laugh.

I dragged my right arm over my chest, found the clasps with my half-numb left hand. I'd barely been able to lift Mr. Ludlow with it after the fight, and tears ran down into my hair before the last clasp finally popped open. Right arm free, my left bracer went faster even though the clasps were shut hard. They hadn't been damaged tonight, but my fingers still felt bruised from fighting with them.

All my moving around hadn't brought anybody, and I took a few minutes to stop gasping, letting the spots clear from my sight. Every shift made my left arm throb from my shoulder to my hand, and it should have been feeling better by now.

Okay. Exploration told me the clasps on my cuirass hadn't been bent out of shape fighting Eric, and aching fingers finally popped them. I pulled the *heavy* front piece away and it slid off onto the floor with a loud thud. Sitting up, I wanted to scream, and I sat and gasped through clenched teeth until my left arm settled down to throbbing agony. At least I'd left the back piece on the bed; an eternity later, my legs were free of their impossibly heavy armor and more tears fell as I painfully swung my legs off the bed. Everything hurt too *much.*

I can move, that's progress. What happened? I couldn't remember. Grabbing Drop, incredible, head-spinning nauseating pain, an...old man? Shouting, surprised. He'd touched me. Then, just nothing. Nothing until I'd dreamed of falling.

And now everything was too much. Too heavy, too painful, I couldn't *see* right... *Oh no. No no no no no.* Hand over my mouth, I kept the scream down to a whimpering, breathy whine.

I'd been *de-powered.*

Don't panic don't panic don't panic. The perfect mantra for mind-blowing panic, and the giggling helped, too. Crying was even better, but made my aching face throb.

Of *course* I hurt — I wasn't healing anymore.

It took a while to think of anything else. I didn't think I was dying, but it might be hard to tell.

Way back last year, Ajax had given me a series of lectures on how *fragile* normal people were. It had amazed him how fast super-strong breakthroughs forgot. Not just bones and stuff, *insides,* and they didn't heal like I was used to doing now. His lectures had given me nightmares. Accidentally hugging one of the Bees too hard...

Watchman had probably seriously concussed me just last week, head-slamming me into a steel-plated floor. The hypothetical concussion, which meant *bleeding into the brain*, went away with no symptoms beyond transient dizziness; if I'd been normal, it would have continued until alarming symptoms like blown pupils, vomiting, and death made me pay attention. The rabbit-punch Watchman had used to end the fight tonight (if it was still tonight), used by a normal person on another normal person, could easily cripple or kill; it was a hit to the medulla oblongata, the brain stem, which did *not* normally regenerate.

Playing field hockey in school had cured me of any fear of aches and pains, and the fight-club beatings Ajax, now Watchman, administered had gotten me past worrying about serious injury because I *healed*. Fast. Now, I was shivering. I might have been concussed *tonight*, my head certainly hurt enough, and who knew what kind of internal bruising I'd sustained?

I made myself cough, didn't feel anything sharp and jabby, and didn't taste blood. Okay. I'd had a *little* time for Bad Stuff to heal a bit before getting snatched away; maybe I wouldn't pass out or stop breathing. My armor had protected my guts and ribs, and poking around there didn't make me scream. Not like my left arm.

Sniffling, whining experimentation with the arm told me it wasn't *broken*, though I might have bruised bones, and maybe pinched nerves the way my hand felt half asleep and had zero strength. I couldn't lift it far from my waist without serious weeping. I finally pulled together the courage to stand — falling would *hurt* — and almost cried again just because nothing seemed wrong with my legs.

Okay. Okay. I needed light. Though I really wasn't sure I *wanted* it; focusing on my pain was keeping me from freaking about where I was. I slid my feet, carefully avoiding pieces of armor, and found the source of the little bit of light in the room; a friendly moon-glow nightlight plugged into a socket on the other end of the bed. Giggling hurt my arm. The nightlight showed me the gleam of a doorknob — locked, but with a light switch beside it. I took a breath, flipped it on.

The horror. Mom would never combine oranges and tans like that. I was in a hotel room. No, no windows. And hotel doors didn't lock from the outside. And the bed wasn't a queen, more like a single like you had at camp. Nothing bigger would have fit; it wasn't a closet but barely qualified as a room. A bed, a small dresser, that was it. And a bathroom door. I flipped on the bright, bright bathroom light and almost jumped to see myself in the mirror. No mask (I'd forgotten I'd lost it, not that *that* was a problem anymore), and the right side of my face, the part that felt all hot and tight, was swelling.

My cape had come off with my cuirass. I opened my collar, carefully washed my face and neck, checked my pupils for dilation (nope), and used the glass by the sink to take a drink. Then I went back and sat down on the bed. I was *so* tired, tears of denied sleep made me blink.

But what was going *on*? I'd been captured by supervillains; I was supposed to wake up strapped to a table. Or something. Compared to my first experience — not that I *ever* wanted to repeat January, the occasional memory-nightmare was bad enough — this was surreal. I almost broke into giggles again when I realized that they'd locked me in by installing a right-hand doorknob in a left-hand door; if I had the key I could have unlocked it from the inside. Someone had improvised just for broken little me.

Long minutes staring at the door failed to make it dramatically open, and I finally decided that nobody was going to appear to drag me off and Do Things to me any time soon. It was probably still night and they were sleeping, which sounded like a really, really good plan. Sleep now, dramatic interrogation later. No. I needed to stay up, check for dilation, be ready when someone opened the door.

I kept my eyes on the shiny new doorknob, started counting by threes, and got to twenty-one before my eyes closed and I slumped forward off the bed. Landing on my shoulder woke me hard. You can't scream when you can't breathe, and by the time I got some air, I was only crying.

Stop being a baby. Shelly's heartless voice. *You've hurt worse.*

Not fair — then all I'd been expected to do was lie there and get better.

So do that. Duh.

Okay, fine. The dresser was heavy wood, but the bed frame wasn't and I dragged the bed painfully across the carpet and up against the door. It wouldn't keep anyone out, but pushing it back would wake me up. Probably. *Happy now?* Anyway, it was my best shot at being awake and aware when they came through the door. And maybe I'd be rescued before morning. Please. I wiped my eyes and nose, climbed onto the bed, and carefully lay on my right side, curling up to take as small a space on the bed as possible.

I didn't make it to twenty-one.

Chapter Twenty Three: Megaton

"There are two kinds of asymmetrical warfare: terrorism and guerilla war. Guerilla war is aimed directly at the political, military, and supporting apparatus of a state, while terrorism is aimed at the citizens of a state. The Heroic Age has tremendously weakened the ability of states to defend against both; superhuman guerillas and terrorists often cannot be detected until they strike — they do not need to acquire or build weapons and bombs.

Prof. Charles Gibbons, *The New Heroic Age.*

Blackstone let everyone sleep in, but that only meant we were awake enough to take more hits the next day. He delivered the hits in the morning briefing, opening with a news clip to let a fresh-faced, improbably chipper newslady incapable of frowning deliver the old news.

"O'Hare airport remains closed today. Flights are being diverted to Chicago Midway and even Bolinbrooke's Clow. Some airliners are refusing to risk their planes in Chicago, and tourism and business has been severely impacted. Many Chicagoans who can afford to take a vacation are doing so. The full impact of the Green Man's campaign has yet to be determined, and will entirely depend upon how quickly and definitively he can be neutralized as a threat to this city.

He froze the image, and from her smile, you'd have thought she was talking about the unseasonal but nice warm spell.

Supervillain terrorist strikes again, economy impacted, when are the heroes going to do something about it? Blackstone, at least, looked like he hadn't slept in a week trying to answer that question. Deep lines carved his face and shadowed his eyes, but the look he swept around the table burned. I found myself sitting straighter.

"Beginning with yesterday morning, congratulations to everyone here, especially our newest members. Without Megaton and Tsuris' help holding the line — " he gave us a stiff nod " — the attack would certainly have reached the terminals. Grendel also performed well without any backup, and of course Ozma played a key role in shutting down the attack. Which we will return to later."

A click brought up a new scene, this one a riot outside an office front.

"With the Green Man attack dominating the news cycle, the first story about Astra's brother, Toby Corrigan, didn't hit the media until yesterday evening. Unfortunately, it got out on social networks a good deal earlier. A flash-protest by Astra fans outside the Honorable Representative Shankman's campaign office started around four, and one or more of Mr. Shankman's campaign security detail got rough with the protesters. Although the police are still sorting out who stepped over the line first, the protest turned into a riot that broke all the office windows and sent several participants to the hospital. None of Shankman's campaign staff were injured."

Click. Sign-wavers outside a construction business.

"On the topic of protests, news has gotten out that Dozer is indeed Eric Ludlow, Gantry, a member of the Crew. Indeed, after last night's fight and arrest, it was inevitable. Only police protection is keeping Humanity First protesters from picketing the Tollway repair site where the Crew is working to reopen the road as quickly as possible. They are settling for picketing the Crew's business property."

"So," Rush quipped, "half the city's protesting and the other half is leaving town?"

"It would seem so. And of course, with much of the CPD's manpower being reserved for the next Green Man attack, goon vs. villain activity is spiking. And now, Astra."

Click. The room darkened for better viewing, and a drone's eye-view image of last night's battlefield came up, a digital clock in the lower corner counting up. The side of one of the buildings exploded outward, camera tracking on Astra and Dozer as they skidded across the parking lot. I wasn't the only one who winced. Watchman came down on Dozer, and from there the footage was a series of fast-motion hits and screen freezes with digital notations; an analyst's godlike after-action dissection of the brutal fight. It ended with a frozen shot of a prone Dozer.

"Astra and Watchman successfully completed their part of the operation," Blackstone reported needlessly. "Then Astra saw this man in the crowd."

The picture switched to a white, staring face caught in what looked like a mask-cam shot. The image split to show the same guy, the clearer image a shot of the hostage taken by Twist in the Daley Center attack.

Reese and Brian looked blank, Ozma thoughtful, but everyone else...Rush whistled. Seven started swearing.

"Detective Fisher has been studying our hypothetical teleporter's MO. Based on the methods of entry and exit used in the courtroom and precinct attacks, he has concluded that Drop must be touching his targets, and may only teleport himself and others away — he cannot bring targets to him.

"Thus, in the Daley Center attack, he teleported himself and the Wreckers to the hall behind the courtroom, then went around and inserted himself in the audience section before the attack commenced. Attacking the precinct, it now appears likely that he teleported the Wreckers from a van on the street into the cell, and they returned to the van for their getaway.

"Last night, Astra spotted him and made a grievous tactical error. She tried to capture him, knowing that he could teleport others besides himself. The image on the left is a shot of her target from Rush's helmet-cam in the moment before Astra grabbed him. Quite obviously, Astra was not able to handle what she found at the other end."

Astra couldn't handle — She'd buried Seif-al-Din, taken down a *godzilla*, we'd just watched her and Watchman finish a far from one-sided beat-down on an absolute combat-monster.

"Do we know anything, yet?" Watchman asked. He hadn't said a word until now, and kept flexing his fists like he wanted to meet whatever Astra couldn't handle. Everyone looked at Blackstone, but I looked at Shelly.

The robot-girl was starting to seriously worry me. I knew her unfocused stare meant she was tapping the Internet plus every accessible or hackable signal source around — the way she'd hit every security camera on Michigan Avenue the day I'd been shot at. But she'd only taken a second, then; now she'd just sat through the entire show without blinking or responding to anyone around her.

She'd explained to me that she had completely downloaded herself into her current "prosthetic body," that she wasn't piloting it remotely because she didn't live somewhere else or online — her brain was in there, protected inside a titanium-alloy sphere in her skull — but she was *wired*. Now all she'd say was she was "searching," and she stayed that way until the rest of the team returned to base and we all went back to bed. She stayed that way now.

Blackstone looked her way too, shook his head.

"No. We do know now that it wasn't a planned grab, but what this means from their side remains pure conjecture. We don't know our enemy or their motives, and so can only guess at their methods or what they will do with her now that they have her.

"Eric Ludlow, Dozer, has invoked his Miranda Rights and is not giving us anything. Ozma," he acknowledged the sun-haired goddess listening politely, "has reported that she cannot locate Astra using her mirrors. As I said last night, we are doing everything we can. We do have leads. Astra personally turned my attention to a group that may be behind the Wreckers, or at least a potential link to them. We are calling in *all* our resources, including some that we cannot field officially. That is *my* responsibility, however. The focus of this *team* must be elsewhere."

Ignoring the round of protests, he brought up the Green Man's leaf-face icon.

"The city may be coming apart, but the Guardian teams can handle the goon-on-villain action and, if need be, support the CPD in the case of further riots. This team must be ready for the next attack. Again, regarding yesterday," he nodded to The Harlequin, "Quin believes that our new members couldn't have made a better entrance, publicity-wise. Now when we make the formal announcement, the public will have already seen all of you in action.

"But although yesterday's action can only be considered a success in the sense that we managed to prevent a high number of casualties, the attack has yielded us a great deal of information. We now have a much better understanding of our enemy."

You could have heard a pin drop as the Green Man symbol changed to a drone's-eye view of O'Hare.

"The first and most obvious commonality between the two attacks is the source: both attacks originated from a contained body of water: Potowatomi Lake and Lake O'Hare. Also, both attacks were aimed at transport centers — and ecologically, air transport is the most fuel-intensive and therefore most polluting method of transport there is. The second observation gives us a good idea of the Green Man's targeting priorities, but we will not assume that he intends to restrict himself to such targets. The first observation provided our entry-point into understanding his nature."

The picture changed again, this time to a thermal imaging shot of the airport. The clock in the corner of the frame unfroze and began fast-forwarding.

"This footage was recorded by a patrol drone that caught the start of the attack. You will observe the bottom right corner of the picture."

The spot marked Lake O'Hare looked indistinguishably blue against the surrounding field, then a point of green appeared and spread to cover the lake. The green shifted to yellow, to orange, and finally to red before exploding outward, red at the edges, orange to yellow to green towards the center, but the lake stayed angry red. The red front of the attack met high energy opposition around the terminals (tagged for the heroes, including me), and we all watched as the lines stabilized, fluctuated, began to break towards the terminals and then died in a line spreading from the position marked by tags for Blue Fire and Ozma. Finally, the red heat-signature of the lake dropped to orange and continued to move back down the scale.

Blackstone froze the picture.

"The thermal recording of the attack confirms Chakra's observations. She was able to psychically monitor the attack almost from its beginning. Chakra?"

She smiled back at him, turned her head to look at us. "The attack is not directed by the Green Man," she said softly. "The attack *is* the Green Man. It is best to think of the trees and plants he grows and controls as the cells of his body. The lake at the center, which investigators have found choked into a steaming soup of algae and water plants afterwards, is his heart, the source of his power."

Nobody said "What the hell?" or "You're kidding." They didn't even blink. Riptide actually laughed.

"So next time we drop a load of Agent Orange in the water and that's it?"

"Possibly a more thermal attack," Blackstone corrected. "Although conclusions are preliminary, DSA researchers believe that chemical attacks would be ineffective against such robust growth. And of course we don't want to poison the ground we're fighting on."

There were nods and suggestions around the table, a group of costumed people considering ways and means of attacking a plant-mind, which was just *weird*. Jamal saw my expression and flashed a quick *welcome to the game* smile.

"Hopefully," Blackstone concluded, "we have a little while to prepare before the Green Man forces us to test conclusions again. In the meantime — "

"Wait," Reese popped up. "Aren't we just going to use Ozma's blue fireguys again?"

Blackstone frowned, rubbing his eyes. "Forgive me. I should have mentioned that Blue Fire's experience yesterday was terribly debilitating. She is now being treated for extreme exhaustion, and there is no guarantee that she will be available for Ozma to work with next time. It is unwise to base a strategy upon a unique resource in any case, so we consider means that can be carried forward by more than one superhero on the spot."

More nods from the older capes, and Reese slumped in his seat muttering, "Whatever." Ozma gave him a look and Grendel thumped him.

The briefing went for another half-hour, updating the patrolling capes (Watchman, Variforce, and even Riptide in the current crisis) on known and possible threats, and bringing everyone up to speed on the other investigations associated with the team: the ongoing investigation of who fronted the guy who shot at me, and zero leads on whoever attacked Astra's older brother. On that last one, The Harlequin stepped in to caution everyone.

"Accusations are flying everywhere, people. The loudest noise, what set off yesterday's riot, is that some of Shankman's partisans, or thugs from Humanity First, decided to send a message. So for everyone here who hasn't lived through a media-storm yet, the sacred words of holy truth are 'No Comment.' Variations like 'I Can't Comment On An Active Investigation' are allowed, but be safe; if *anyone* outside this circle asks, your opinion is 'No Comment.'"

Her look promised she was dead serious and that any of us unwise enough not to take her seriously would be dead or wish he was, and nobody laughed at the rubber girl in the spandex clown costume. *Okay...*

Blackstone cleared his throat.

"People, we are on post from now until the Green Man matter is settled. If he does not attack again soon, hopefully the DSA will have time to track him — that's their job and they're very good at it. Since he's capable of uploading videofiles onto the net, either he is not a disembodied nature spirit all the time, or he has helpers — either way, the government is pouring hundreds of agency man-hours into figuring out where he came from and finding him."

He sighed, shoulders rounding before he pulled himself straight.

"Everybody. I — all of us — want to focus on getting our teammate back. Please be aware that agency profilers suggest that in the Green Man we face a serious risk. Eco-terrorists such as the Green Man traditionally avoid inflicting casualties. However, his attacks are escalating. Three people have died, and City Hall is not responding to his demands. The experts judge it entirely possible that he may decide that the time for restraint is past if he is to achieve his objectives. If he does not draw back at the prospect of more killing, our next engagement may be far more desperate."

The meeting broke up with that, but Blackstone wasn't finished with all of us; he tasked Brian and Watchman with the job of helping the CPD transfer Eric Ludlow to the Detroit Supermax — apparently an over-the-top A Class Ajax-type couldn't be held safely in Chicago — and he kept me, Jamal, and Seven behind. While everyone else was doing busy stuff, we were to go to the hospital and watch over Astra's brother and parents for the day, and then go to the airport to pick up one of the resources Blackstone had talked about calling in. She was arriving after sunset.

She?

Chapter Twenty Four: Astra

By three methods we may learn wisdom: First, by reflection, which is noblest; second, by imitation, which is easiest; and third by experience, which is the bitterest.

Confucius

Just because you can do something, that doesn't make it a good idea.

Hope Corrigan, aka Astra

The bed shook, pitching me out of shallow sleep. Chakra had been calling me in my dreams but couldn't hear my answer, and I didn't remember why she would be looking for me until the bed's push across the carpet brought me painfully awake.

At least some plans go right; I was awake and the thick carpet made the bed dig in and gave whoever wanted in a hard, swearing time. My slight weight wasn't stopping them so I slid off the bed and wobbled to my feet. Biting off a hiss as my shoulder screamed, I managed to be standing upright and facing the door when they got it open. We stared at each other. They couldn't hear my racing heart or know I was working hard not to hyperventilate. I had no idea what they saw, but what I saw wasn't *that* intimidating; just two guys, my business-bland teleporter and a dark-haired guy who looked like a fast food middle-manager. They couldn't be as bad as Ripper. Could they?

Middle Manager's right eye twitched and my entire body fell asleep, numbed. I didn't collapse into a heap because someone else was driving, and they wanted me to stay where I was. *He* winced sharply and pulled his left arm in to his side.

He made me step further back and they moved quick, pushing the bed out of the way, then bringing in a linen-covered cart. Middle Manager gave me one last hard look, face clenched in pain, and they were gone. *Suck it, tough guy.* Not a nice thought, and a weepy part of me wanted him back when the door closed and the numbness left with him, but if someone else was going to drive my body, they were going to have to live with it, too.

The thought kept my wailing panic at bay. A neuralkinetic — at least B-Class. *Barlow's Guide* listed them as rare. What else? My poor little brain remembered the detail, obviously true, that neuralkinetics got their target's own sensations as feedback. Which meant he also knew how hurt and — admit it — freaking terrified I was, too. My eyes prickled.

I couldn't hide anything. *So* not good.

I sniffed, took a breath, and pulled the cover off the cart.

Plate covers, and under them breakfast. Eggs, bacon, sausage, hash browns, toast, jam, orange juice, milk. *What? Just... What?* Dropping to the bed, I put my head on my knees until I got my breathing under control. Then I ate everything, wiping my eyes with the linen napkin.

Finished, I pushed the bed back up against the door and cleaned up. Fortunately, the costume design meant I could reach all parts of me without having to remove the bodysuit top; I washed without showering — no way was I getting naked *here*. Pulling the top down far enough to clean my pits and look at my shoulder involved more hissing and crying. It was *black*. My face was purpling, too, but that didn't scare me. By the time I finished cleaning up I was shivering almost too hard to stand, but I got back to the bed okay.

And it was time to think. I didn't want to.

What did I *know*? Since nobody had come to my rescue in the night, wherever I was couldn't be found, and if my dream was real then the place was shielded against magic and psychic detection. Which didn't mean they *wouldn't* find me, and telling myself that helped me breathe. Fisher had leads, and hideouts had to be built, which meant paper-trails somewhere. And this place was weird.

It wasn't a hotel or home, but the little room I was in wasn't a cell (a careful look even found a phone-jack behind the tiny dresser). It only had space for the single narrow bed, and the doorway to the bathroom didn't have a door in it; privacy was preserved by closing the bedroom door, which had obviously been lockable from the inside once upon a time.

Climbing back to my feet, I confirmed that the bare walls couldn't hide a camera anywhere, even in the light fixture. No way to prove I wasn't being listened to (and Blackstone would be ashamed of me for taking this long to even think of any of that), but tapping proved the walls were interior drywall. Reinforced by something, but not concrete or brick, and the heavy door was just wood. Again, not a cell, and I had *no* idea what that meant, beyond the hopeful thought that whoever was in charge had never contemplated holding prisoners.

Which didn't mean they wouldn't want to play, and just the thought of what Manager Man might want to do with his powers nearly made me lose my breakfast. I pushed that one down by focusing on *plans* — which in the end amounted to stealing the breakfast knife and hiding it under the mattress; if they didn't miss it, I could use it to carve a message into the wallpaper behind the dresser or something. I couldn't get more proactive than that, and I lay back down to rest my aching arm.

Please, guys, get here soon. Please.

Megaton

Seven posted Jamal and me outside Toby Corrigan's hospital room, two helmeted boy-wonders. It was easy to see Astra's family had money; it was a nice room and so was the public lounge outside it. The place was its own little wing, four patient rooms watched by one nurse's station with only one door into the place, which might be why they'd moved him up here.

I tried to understand what Blackstone was thinking and came up blank, but even the CPD was worried enough to put two more cops outside the lounge. If they were cops; they looked suspiciously like Bob.

Seven alternated between pacing and talking to Astra's parents. Galatea's — Shelly's — mom had joined them after we got here. Shelly's mom looked just like her, which would have meant great things for her if she'd grown up, but Astra's parents not so much; Mrs. Corrigan was taller by at least a head and her dark pulled-back hair gave her tired face a witchy look. Mr. Corrigan was sandy haired and nearly as big as Brian. Then he smiled at something Seven said, and I saw where she got everything from. I looked away. Why were we here? I jumped when Galatea spoke in my ear.

"*Hey Mal, having fun guarding the Monster?*" She sounded almost her normal annoying self, and I put a hand to my helmet so nobody would wonder if I was talking to thin air.

"The who?"

"*The Monster. He and Hope are only a couple of years apart — he used to pull all sorts of tricks on us. I did a* lot *of supervillain sketches of him. By the way, there's someone outside to see you...*"

Seven looked up and gave me a nod. Jamal shrugged. *Okay...* So the girl was a computer; I didn't think I'd ever get used to the way she could talk to different people at the same freaking time.

Beyond the doors everything was normal hospital, and Galatea directed me down the hall to another public lounge, this one looking a lot more like a waiting room. Not that I paid attention; Tiffany was waiting for me — she spun around when I came through the door. Dad stood behind her.

"Son," he said. I almost walked out. Tiffany looked tragic, like she wanted to say something, but she looked at Dad and got out of the way. Dad took a step, stopped.

"Your friend came by to see us this morning. She wanted to thank you. Someone named Shelly called and said you'd be here."

I was going to kill her. No, I was going to tell her I thought her mom was *hot*. "So you're here why?"

"To see that you're all right." He looked at the door, still open behind me. "Son, can we sit down?" Tiffany said something and slipped by me into the hall. I let go of the door handle, let it close, then felt stupid standing there and took a seat.

"Okay, Dad. Sitting. So, what?"

He looked at his hands, took a breath. "When I got home last night, Sydney told me you called. She wouldn't stop crying, said your mother wouldn't let you talk to her."

"Mom said *you* — "

"I wasn't there, Son. Your mother and I have been...fighting." He clenched his hands on his thighs, looked me in the eye.

"Son, I didn't want you wrestling. Your mind will last longer than your body, and I hated seeing you dropping science. You've got — But that's all done." He shifted uncomfortably. I got my size and weight from him. "Your mother left this morning. She's taken Sydney and gone to her sister's in Oregon. 'Where it's safe,' she says."

"You're lying." I was heating up.

"No, I'm not. I want you to call her when you — when you can. Son — " He ran fingers through his short gray hair. "Your mother has always wanted to leave the city, ever since the Event. Most of the Humanity First stuff in our house was hers — though I supported her views on a lot of it. I won't apologize for that. We both wanted you and Sydney growing up in a safe environment. Now she thinks you're ... she worries about Sydney."

"And why are you still here, Dad? You gave me to the *Sentinels*." I felt like I was glowing, but he shook his head.

"We gave them custodial rights. We — we didn't know what to do. But I'm not going anywhere, Son. I realize that might not be what you want to hear, right now — I'm sorry. I'm sorry. We didn't take any of this well, and I hope someday you'll forgive us."

I was back on my feet, and he stood, too.

"Dad, you can't just — *Shit!*" Everything I'd wanted to say since the first day came up in my throat, blocked it all. He gave me an awkward man-hug and I squeezed my eyes shut.

"So." He pulled us apart. "Are you going to introduce me to the young lady who's so worried about you?"

I introduced Dad and Tiffany to everyone. She liked Jamal, but Seven made her forget how to talk. All the parentals looked like they were going to start a Superhero Parent Support Group on the spot. There would probably be bumper stickers: *Proud Progenitors of a Chicago Sentinel* or something. I finally figured out why Blackstone sent us, at least part of the reason; Seven was here to provide his luck to Astra's family, Jamal and me because of our mobility if something happened somewhere else.

When the sun went down, Seven sent Jamal and me to meet our mysterious resource. They'd actually managed to reopen a couple of runways at the Chicago Executive Airport, and Jamal took us to the terminal. Riding through the streets in hypertime on Jamal's bike (a clone of Rush's) was a freaky experience, like the whole world was one big 3D stop-motion shot. We found Bob — *How many of this guy were there?* — waiting with a car in the parking lot.

"Crash. Megaton," he acknowledged.

Jamal kicked down his bike-stand as I peeled myself off the back. "Have they landed yet?"

"They have." He pointed out to the field, where a twin-engine business jet was taxiing toward the terminal. Crash took his helmet off and played with his cornrows.

"Right. Right. Dude... Just, be cool, okay?"

"Be what?"

"Seriously. She's not as scary as she seems. Well, she is but — " He shrugged helplessly. What the hell was I missing?

The plane coasted to a stop and the cabin door opened, steps swinging down. Reese had told me they'd rated a deluxe cabin with a flight attendant, but this one had to be smaller; the pilot got off first, then helped someone else hand down their luggage. Then two more people stepped down and headed our way.

One of them was a bouncy blonde, seriously pale but dressed for summer, almost dancing on the tarmac as she pulled her luggage. The other walked at a fast clip, not in a hurry, just moving along. Her midnight-black hair was pulled into a tight tail and her pale skin stood out against all the black. Black leather jacket, black jeans, black boots, black carry-on — the only luggage she had — and absolutely zero smile.

Over the curb and crossing the parking lot, she stopped in front of us and handed Bob her bag.

"Bob, this is Acacia. She's on a liquid diet."

"Good evening, Artemis. It's good to have you home."

"Not yet. But it will be."

Chapter Twenty Five: Astra

A breakthrough is nothing more than an awakened soul, a monad that has deepened its connection with the universal oversoul. The ancients used to think of the night sky as a black dome and stars as holes through which the light of Heaven shown; so it is with each incarnate soul, and breakthroughs shine the most brightly of all. Each of us has it in himself and herself to awaken, to make that connection and burn with the light of Heaven.

Dr. Simon Pellegrini, *The Sleeper Must Awaken*.

It had to be the most surreal day of my life. After careful consideration, I dubbed the neuralkinetic Puppetman. Puppeteer was already taken, and Geppetto sounded too clever. It was an important decision; if he wasn't already a known supervillain and I reported him first, I got naming rights. That out of the way, I actually fell asleep again — amazing, I know, but if I didn't move it didn't hurt *too* bad, and in the absence of terror my poor abused body wanted to sleep and heal; I could have used some serious painkillers, but the Sandman was willing to work without them.

They didn't come back until lunch, so I missed a beautiful opportunity to carve the Gettysburg Address in the wall. We repeated the scene; they pushed on the door, I woke up, got up. Puppetman didn't take his eyes off me as they replaced the cart, but he didn't freeze me in place either. He probably didn't want to share my pain again.

As soon as they left, I retrieved the knife and, careful of my arm, pulled out the dresser and carved as fast as I could while keeping it readable. *Astra Depowered Old Whitehair Guy/ Drop/ Neuralkinetic.* Not great, but the best I could think of. If they moved me and if the team ever tracked me this far, then at least it was *something*.

After eating the sandwiches they'd brought this time (Willis's sandwiches were *much* better but these looked professionally cut and served, which had to be A Clue), I checked my arm again. It didn't feel *worse* anywhere, and my left hand had more feeling in it, but I was sniffling and tearing by the time I pulled my collar closed. I pushed the bed back against the door and got horizontal again.

I wasn't trying to be all plucky and fearless — it was just that nobody was *threatening* me. The room, the food, the fact they didn't talk (Drop hadn't even made *eye contact*), it was all very unvillainous. I mean, sure they obviously hadn't planned to capture me, but they had me and were acting like they didn't *want* me. Like I'd come along and spoiled their plans. Shelly would have been banging on the door and demanding to know what was going on, and it said something about me that I didn't even try and listen at the door. I really didn't want to know. If I didn't think about it, I wasn't back *there*, in the Dark Anarchist's cell. And these guys definitely weren't Ripper, which didn't mean I was safe but was still a lot.

Which left me time to obsess on the rest of my situation. Now that my head was clearer, I knew the old man from last night — I'd seen him in the author's picture on the back cover of Eric's books. Doctor Simon Pellegrini, and it was no wonder they were ignoring me now; he'd killed Astra with a touch and I was just little Hope Corrigan again, no threat to anybody. And since I wasn't wearing Blacklock's finest titanium accessories right now, they obviously didn't expect my powers to come flooding back any time soon.

Was it permanent? Did I *want* it to be? I couldn't begin to wrap my head around the possibility. If the team busted through the wall and rescued me, then what? Surgery and physical therapy for my arm and then... Back to school? A normal life? All I had to do was get through this last adventure and eventually the public would forget about Astra. No more training, no more fights, no more bad accident scenes or disasters to clean up after. No more nightmare-fuel. Would one less cape make a difference?

I tried to picture living with the Bees in Palevsky Commons. Pledging, hanging out, having a *life* again. Would that be wrong?

And, making it not all about *me*, what did it mean?

It seemed like a hundred years ago Blackstone had been talking about the California quake, the Green Man attacks, and Mr. Ludlow, and wondering if there was a process for boosting breakthrough powers. Well, duh, if Dr. Pellegrini could steal my powers then I was willing to bet a lot of money he could *boost* powers too. Were all the Wreckers boosted? It would explain a lot.

But if Dr. Pellegrini could reliably boost powers, then why wasn't he busy making himself obscenely rich the legal and easy way? Forget about his cult; national governments would pay billions for him to boost their supersoldiers like he'd done Eric. And was it a stretch to jump from Eric to linking the man to Temblor and Green Man? If he *was* behind everything, what was he trying to do? What did the California quake *and* the Green Man attacks *and* killing goons and Paladins have in common?

My mind went round and round it all, like a kitten chasing its own tail until it fell over from vertigo.

The third time they pushed the door open, they were cartless and had Twist with them, wearing his armor so I couldn't see his face. My heart sank and turned into a lump of ice in my gut; obviously the Pollyanna part of my brain that had silently hoped my benign neglect would continue was wrong.

Twist led the way and the others followed behind me. I managed to walk straight and not shiver as they took me down a long hall of doors just like mine but with locks on the outside and most of them open, through a pair of doors into an empty dining room. A *big* dining room, with the look of a place used for conventions or seminars. One wall was all bay windows so I could see it was night outside, and three big chandeliers hung ready to light the place. Only one was dimly lit. Years of working for Mom made it easy to recognize the function of the place, and if it wasn't for the weird bedrooms I'd have thought I was in a big hotel. Some big abandoned hotel.

And they were making use of the space, too; the room had been cleared of tables to leave space for a steel platform with a raised chair in the middle of it. A bunch of boxes had been stacked on the platform, like they used it to move stuff, but I didn't see any wheels.

Trying to soak in all the clues I could, it took me a moment to realize the room wasn't completely cleared; a table by the windows had been set with covered plates, and Dr. Pellegrini waited for me there.

Twist took me straight to him.

"Good evening, Miss Corrigan." He stood and removed the dish covers as I carefully sat and waited for the spots in front of my eyes to clear. Puppetman actually pushed my chair in for me, and my trio of keepers retreated across the room to take up stations at what I assumed was the kitchen doors.

I arranged the dinner napkin in my lap, took the opportunity to examine him as he filled our water glasses.

Except for his eyes, he could have been one of my university professors — he even had the regulation tweed blazer with leather elbow patches, and he sounded and looked like the kind of older professor whose father or grandfather had made a big pile of money so he could ignore it in pursuit of higher knowledge. But there was nothing absentminded or preoccupied in his silver-gray eyes, and he looked at me like I was his next fascinating thesis subject.

He sat and arranged his own napkin, and only Mom's social training let me pick up my soup spoon and taste the basil-sprinkled cream of tomato. He carried the small talk while we ate our way through the soup and salad courses, let silence rule the fish course,

215

and got more personal with the dinner and dessert courses. He inquired after Toby's condition and apologized for not letting my arm heal a little before "suppressing my gift."

The boggling weirdness of the whole thing had me nearly seeing double. Laying his dessert fork beside the remains of his cheesecake, he finally laughed.

"Miss Corrigan, you should see your face. I am sorry; this isn't supposed to be how it goes, is it?" He smiled, putting his hand over his heart. "When a supervillain mastermind captures a brave and beautiful young superhero, certain things are expected, aren't they? Threats, bondage, tedious monologuing. Well, I thought we should make you comfortable while we could."

"They won't trade Mr. Ludlow for me, you know." My right hand joined my left in my lap so he couldn't see it was shaking.

"Of course not, and I am more than happy with the way things fell out last night. Even if you have forced a degree of improvisation on our plans."

"So are you going to kill me?"

He actually looked shocked. "Perish the thought! I would never snuff out a light as bright as yours."

"A — What?"

"Have you read my books? No? They are often poetic, but less than metaphorical. When I close my eyes, you are one of the brightest lights I see, shining with all the power of the Oversoul. Beautiful. With all that I do to awaken more souls, ending your light would be the blackest crime."

"But my powers are — "

"Occluded, Miss Corrigan, merely occluded. They will return in time. Again, I apologize for the physical discomfort it leaves you in now but, considering my plans, it is entirely likely that our paths will cross again and so for me it has been a fortuitous opportunity to meet you. 'Know your enemy,' as Sun Tsu said. The Teatime Anarchist quite failed to do so, didn't he?"

My face felt like ice and I wondered if I was going to faint. My inside voice decided it was time to start screaming and crying incoherently, but I didn't give it a vote. The fight in Reno was classified big-time, and even the *government* didn't know what really happened.

"Yes, he did," I managed. "Were you allies?"

"Allies? No." He shook his head. "The man was too obsessed with politics. But we were both useful to each other — indeed he advanced my research by at least a decade. I will always wonder how he knew what he knew."

He refilled my water glass, giving me a moment. His aesthetic hands had age spots on their knuckles.

"So. I know the official story is that a DSA team tracked the Teatime Anarchist to Reno and deputized an Army supersoldier team to take him out, but I know that he had acquired you, and I don't believe he could have been taken that way. Will you satisfy an old man's curiosity?"

I swallowed. "He killed himself."

He raised an eyebrow, studying me. "I see. Well. I am sure it must be an upsetting topic for you, and I assure you that there will be none of that here. Are you quite finished? Is there anything you would like?"

We dipped into the end-of-night conversation prescribed for winding up a social engagement — something I could do on autopilot while keeping the panicked babbling inside my head. When my escort trio took me back to my room and locked me in, I pushed the bed back against the door and threw up in the toilet.

Grendel

Ozma disappeared back into her lab after the morning briefing, but Blackstone gave Watchman and me the job of riding along with the DSA team transporting Dozer from his Chicago PD hardcell to Detroit Supermax.

The DSA marshals gave me as much room as the transport plane's bay allowed, but I was used to that; Dozer — Gantry, Eric Ludlow, whatever — was trussed up in what amounted to a titanium straitjacket for the trip, but I'd morphed into my heaviest strong form and looked so much more like something they should be worried about. The scruffy-looking, chain-smoking cop along for the ride — he'd introduced himself as Detective Max Fisher — split his attention between the marshals and Dozer. Watchman ignored the marshals completely after making sure that they stayed clear of the compartment hatch; he'd told me if Dozer tried anything, he intended to throw him off the plane and deal with him on the way down. Planes are fragile.

Detroit Supermax — not actually in Detroit but close — had its own airfield, so we didn't have to offload prisoners like Dozer and drive him through "civilian" areas. Why didn't Watchman just fly him from Chicago to Detroit himself? According to the handbook I'd finally started reading: Rules. We weren't feds or cops, and couldn't take charge of prisoners and transport them between jurisdictions. But we could "escort" as contractors. Dumb, I know, and with all the precautions we didn't fly out of Chicago until the afternoon. We made the trip without Dozer so much as twitching, but he didn't act beaten down, just like he wasn't ready to fight. I could have slept through the flight, and when the ramp dropped, we paraded off onto the tarmac.

Detroit was a city with no luck. Every city got hammered by the Event, but even before then Detroit had been in decline, an industrial town losing its jobs. And Detroit hadn't had an Atlas or Ajax stepping up to help, so the place had had a really hard time. With its anti-superhuman sentiment, the city hadn't had a lot of success attracting superheroes for its two Guardian teams either; in Hillwood, we learned about it as a law enforcement Worst Case Scenario.

So the city diversified; it built Detroit Supermax to hold the superpowered prison populations of twelve states, and even contracted with the federal government for some of their prisoners. It was a big business; the place held virtually every supervillain the Sentinels had ever taken down and dozens more. Watchman caught me looking around, and chuckled.

"Doesn't look like one of the most secure prisons in the world, does it?"

It didn't. The airport sat outside the prison, and there wasn't a barbed wire-crowned fence anywhere. No tall guard towers either — just a two-story brick wall with weird metal cones spaced along the top. We loaded Dozer into a waiting open-topped van, and it took us through a gate that deposited us in an elevator. It didn't feel like we went down far, but when the elevator-gate rose we drove out into a space bigger than a decent-sized athletic stadium. It curved, stretching away in both directions, and the wall directly across from us had only one entrance I could see, another big gate.

"The outside ring circles the prison, it's the only way up and out," Watchman said. "It's full of switchable mines, laser sensors, remotely manned weapons, you name it. It's never been breached, and forget about digging out through the ceiling or floor. Let's just say they're hostile environments. The Army puts its convicted supersoldiers here."

Yeah, now this was more like it. Half an hour later, we'd dropped Dozer off and were on our way out.

"Truth is," Detective Fisher said once we were back out under open sky, "most of what we walked through down there is just the last line of containment; they have ways of controlling the inmates, keeping a breakout from becoming general. The Pit is built to keep people *out* as much as it is to keep them in." He lit up again. "You okay, kid?"

"Hell, no." I shook myself, feeling like I'd just climbed out of a bottomless hole. The DSA agents gave me room — a couple of them twitched, half-hefting their autorifles without realizing it.

Most people's reactions to me are pretty predictable; my size, claws, fangs scream *Danger! Danger!* to the piece of the human hindbrain tasked with instinctual threat-assessment, so even when they're not scared, normal people dance around me like I might accidentally eat someone. Fisher didn't. He smirked, chuckled dryly. "Yeah, I get that. Let's go home."

Watchman flew wingman outside the plane for the flight back. Detective Fisher used the time to tell us Astra stories featuring her police liaison job. Half the stories involved dead bodies; cops have a strange sense of humor.

We touched down after dark and Watchman gave me a lift back to the Dome. With nothing going on, I went and found Ozma's new lab.

Open boxes sat on every table and had been stacked in corners. They'd certainly provided her enough glassware, even a sealed clean room for mixing the really interesting stuff (that made me feel a lot better). Her Witchy Highness sat perched on a lab stool, poring over a notebook. Someone had decided labs required lab coats and she'd turned hers green.

Beside her, Nix stood in front of one of Ozma's smaller mirrors, behind a camera set up on a stack of books. She waved at me then went back to watching the mirror. The goth girl standing *behind* the watchful doll looked away from the mirror long enough to check me out, and holy shit, it was Artemis, the Sentinels' mysterious vampire-vigilante. Midnight-black hair and cold eyes to match, in a face pale enough to make you believe she never saw daylight. Just a *look* from Spooky Girl, and my body started bulking up for a fight.

I shook it off. "Princess."

Ozma held up a hand, made a notation in her notebook, then leaned over to whisper something to the mirror. "Yes!" cried Nix, and I heard the camera *click-click-click-click* as she captured whatever was there. Then the mirror cracked all the way across, spiderwebbing from edge to edge. Ozma sighed, dropping her head to rest her chin on folded arms.

"Hello Brian. I hope you had a boring day?"

"Better than yours?"

A pointed finger directed my attention to a stack of broken mirrors propped against the wall. "Watch out for glass, I swept three mirrors ago." I felt the crunch of glass slivers underfoot.

Right ... how many years bad luck? "What are you doing?"

"Watching our Astra. Wherever she is has good magic or psychic wards and I've only been able to catch her in one mirror, and we can't go through it to get her or make her see us."

"But she's okay?" She hadn't mentioned any of this in the morning briefing.

"She is alone and injured, poor child, but fiercely, fiercely brave. Look." Sitting up, she tapped the laptop beside her and brought up a screenful of picture files. Now I understood what the camera was all about; since she obviously couldn't *keep* a mirror on Astra, Ozma was opening a view and snapping as many shots as she could before the connection was literally broken.

The viewing wheel showed dozens of shots. It looked like we were seeing through a bathroom mirror into a small bedroom. We might not have been able to see her except she'd pushed the bed she was lying on up against the opposite door. In the earliest ones the lights were out so there was nothing at all to see beyond dark shapes, and in most of the rest she was asleep, but a series of eight shots had caught her looking in the mirror. She'd had her costume top open, poking her shoulder as tears ran down her face. Half her face was purple, her shoulder and arm purple and black, and her lips were pressed tight over her teeth. My throat closed up.

Ozma sighed. "I've met our team doctor and he believes, based on the time since the fight, that she isn't healing." She patted my arm. "Someone has stolen our hero's power, but we will have her back."

Nix nodded solemnly.

Spooky Girl hadn't said a word, or moved, and I jumped when she said "Send the pictures."

"One moment." Ozma pulled the flash drive out of the camera and plugged it into the laptop. Another short stream of pictures dropped onto the screen and she forwarded them to the epad I hadn't seen in Spooky Girl's hand. In the new shots, Astra stood with her back to the open bedroom door, like she'd just come back in. Behind her the camera had caught the faces of two men I didn't recognize, part of a third. Ozma laughed delightedly and Nix cheered. I didn't.

She's scared. Freaking terrified. I couldn't say why I knew, it didn't show on Astra's face, but I felt my claws growing. My body was weirdly psychoreactive tonight.

"Nice timing," I said, almost growling. Spooky Girl looked up from her pad and gave me a predator's smile.

"Timing, yes," Ozma agreed, turning her head to frown at me. She knew what it meant when my voice got deeper. "Since it takes too long between pictures, I have been attempting a sortilege formula to choose informative moments. None of the pictures tell us where she is, that would be too gracious a gift, and I can't find other mirrors around her. Artemis?"

Spooky Girl's spooky smile widened. "Got another one. The third guy's Redback, a street villain with the Sanguinary Boys — one of the few left outside Detroit Supermax after the Sentinels rolled them up last year. He can paralyze you with a look — maybe more than that now, if Blackstone's right — but I made him a snack the couple of times we met. Shelly? Have you narrowed down the location?"

"*Do vamps sleep in the daytime? Yes they do, and is one of fifty rooms narrow enough? Hi, Brian!*"

I almost felt sorry for the guys holding Astra. With a magical princess, a vampire vigilante, and a techno-ghost hunting them, they didn't have a chance. But only almost; I wanted to *talk* to them and "fifty rooms" sounded real promising.

Ozma patted my arm again. "Stop bulking up, Brian. They are not hurting her, and I believe your strength will be required presently." Her lips quirked. "So go. Eat. Fuel up and be prepared to ride to the rescue. Shoo."

"Don't go too far, pretty boy," Artemis said without looking up from her epad. "I'm going to need you to break stuff soon."

The promise of violence in Spooky Girl's voice started my fangs growing again and, with one last look at the screen, I let Ozma push me away. The princess was good about her promises, too; if she didn't think it would be long, it probably wouldn't be, and my looming wouldn't help.

But I needed to find out where the workout rooms were so I could seriously attack something.

I got my fight-fuel; Willis — the Dome's majordomo and wasn't that a weird title — had made sure the kitchen got my dietary requirements. Protein, lots of it. But I didn't get my workout; as usual, Ozma nailed it and I hadn't even finished gorging on the tower of rare prime rib cuts the cooking staff had prepared for me when my earbug sparked with an excited *"Move it, people! Assembly room now! Follow the lights if you're lost, newbies!"*

A cheeky light flashed over the dining room door. Robot-girl was going to be seriously annoying.

Even the Sentinels' weird Verne-type, Vulcan, sat for *this* meeting, and with the addition of the detective and a beefy DSA agent (whose dark glasses made him look just like Bob in shades), we filled the seats. Nox and Nix sat on the table in front of Ozma, and Nox couldn't take his eyes off Artemis (I could understand why; Nox liked *dark*, and with her black body armor, hooded Death's-head, and guns, the vampire looked like a freaking goth assassin).

"Hey — " Reese started. The eyes in the black skull half-mask focused on him and he shut up. A smile flickered across her lips before she returned her attention to Blackstone.

"Thank you, everyone," Blackstone said once we'd all sat down. The old magician looked better than he had last night. "We have found Astra, and we are going to get her. Detective Fisher?"

The rumpled detective got to his feet and took control of the screens. We gave him our complete attention.

"My team is tasked with the Wreckers investigation. Eric Ludlow, Dozer, had cleared his email history and his phone records were unhelpful. However, bank records showed us that he joined this organization — " the symbol of an eye in a radiating triangle backing the words *The Foundation of Awakened Theosophy* came up on the screens " — last January. We were unable to get a warrant to do any digging until a search of the Crew's records from the California Quake put him together with *this* man." The image changed to a shot of a guy, brown hair, brown eyes, average everything.

"This is Steven Kellough. A C Class teleporter, he was employed in rescue and recovery operations in the weeks after the quake, where he met Eric. He is a longstanding member of the Foundation of Awakened Theosophy and is now Drop, the Wreckers' A Class teleporter." The screen split to show his shocked face caught on mask-cam last night.

"This was enough for us to get a silent warrant for all Foundation records. Artemis — " he nodded to the dark angel at the table " — began consulting with us en-route, and she and Galatea have given us this." The screen widened, changing to an aerial view of what looked like a resort.

"The Foundation owns several properties in and around Chicago, including this country 'retreat' used by higher-level initiates. It's rented out for conferences when not in use by the Foundation, and with pictures Ozma obtained for us, we were able to match the room in which Astra is being kept to the blueprints for the main lodge." The overhead shot turned into a schematic of the building, zeroed in on a wing of narrow single-occupant bedrooms. "Although according to their schedules, the retreat is not in use — the Foundation paid a pretty big penalty to cancel a corporate retreat scheduled for this week — based on current power-usage, the place is not empty. Using Ozma's pictures and Artemis' and Galatea's findings, we have obtained a no-knock warrant which the Sentinels will exercise tonight."

Rush slapped the table. "So what are we waiting for? Let's go get A back!"

"Agreed," Lei Zi said. The Chinese superhero had always sounded coldly precise the few times I'd seen her on TV, and tonight wasn't any different. She stood and took the control wand from Detective Fisher.

"First, some tactical realities. We believe that Astra has been depowered — " She had to wait for the shocked dismay around the table to die. "From the pictures secured by Ozma, her injuries from the previous night do not appear to be healing. Just as significant, she does not appear to be restrained by anything more than a locked door. This dictates our tactics; we are not going in like a hammer to retrieve an egg.

"Additionally, we do not know the numbers and powers we will face; only three Wreckers are definitively known: Twist, Balz, and Drop. Ozma's pictures netted us another ID, Redback. Dispatch will provide his relevant stats, but be aware he may be much more than he was. There may be more unknowns, and again we are dealing with someone who can enhance or take away breakthrough powers. The place is also protected by powerful shields. Magic wards or psionic shields can always be purchased, expensively, but to borrow one of Atlas's favorite phrases, 'Assume any unknown breakthrough can deal with you.'"

"So what's the plan, boss?" Riptide asked.

"Tonight's op has two goals: recovering Astra and capturing the Wreckers. Fortunately, we now have two teams. The rescue team will be our new Young Sentinels, supplemented by Artemis and The Harlequin. They will move in to secure the bedroom wing and extract Astra. Once the rescue team has extracted Astra, the capture team will move in to sweep up as many of the Wreckers as we can. Hopefully we can net all of them, but the rescue is our first priority and we are assuming complete communication blackout once we go in. So here is how we will proceed..."

Chapter Twenty Six: Astra

I am one of the strongest breakthroughs in the U.S., and I'm a damsel in distress. One of my action figures comes with Blacklock restraints, which makes Chakra laugh uncontrollably. I so don't want to know.

Hope Corrigan's journal.

I gave myself a few minutes to just not think — not that I could do much until I stopped wanting to gag and could stand up. I rinsed, splashed water on my face, and leaned on the sink until I was steady, then went back into the bedroom and pushed the dresser away from the wall to add *Pellegrini/DA* to my scratched message. Blackstone and Shelly would figure it out. Pushing the dresser back, I lay down again and looked at the ceiling. The walls were too thick, but the air vents were in the ceiling; if I climbed on the bathroom sink, could I knock a hole through the plaster and paneling? The thought of trying to pull myself up into the overhead one-armed made me cringe, but if they were done with me for the night, it was worth a shot. Right?

And I *had* to get out. Dr. Pellegrini wanted *breakthroughs*, and if he'd helped the Teatime Anarchist's evil twin set off the California Quake, then he was willing to kill a thousand "sleepers" to awaken a single soul. Had he been behind other mass-casualty attacks? My gut churned and I curled up, hand on my stomach, not breathing until I could lie out straight again.

Time to try the ceiling.

I moved *slow*, careful of my arm and listening for the door. The rod holding up the shower curtain came down pretty easy, and the toilet and the sink were set close enough together that I could step from one to the other.

I could slip, too.

I lost the rod, but the bathroom was tiny enough I didn't fall straight to the floor — instead I hit the wall, slid down to and off the toilet, and nearly passed out when I hit the tiles. I lost all my air, locked in my first gasping breath.

Don't scream don't scream don't scream don't scream. The walls were thick, but someone might be standing guard outside my door.

Rapid blinking eventually cleared my eyes and I let go, took another breath, and curled up on the cool tiles to cup my burning, throbbing arm. Whimpering was undignified. So was sniffling and wanting my dad. For that matter, lying on the bathroom floor lacked gravitas, too; my fans would be disappointed.

Then the lights went out.

Get up! Get up get up get up! My foot found the shower rod and I jackknifed painfully to grab it. Back to a wall, I pulled myself up. Whimpering *was* undignified, but moving fast gave me a good excuse. Even the bedroom nightlight was out; I might as well have been in a cave somewhere. Using the rod, I found the bed, then the dresser, then the wall opposite. I hugged the wall; the shower rod was pretty heavy, and in the pitch black I could swing at whatever came through the door before they knew where I was.

Yeah, right. I closed my eyes, and opening them made no difference. *They'll probably laugh.* Maybe, but if they came to take me away, they'd have to earn it. I wished I'd had time to write everything I wanted to say to everybody on the wall.

A crash made me jump halfway to the ceiling, whimper some more. Then a freight train stomped by my door. A second crash and then a roar like a hurricane. The door opened and wind rushed in, I swung, connected — "Ouch!" — and dropped the rod from nerveless fingers as I wobbled.

A hulking shape I'd only met yesterday loomed in the dim light from the hallway.

"Astra?"

The lights came back on to reveal a fanged, gray-skinned monster with dreadlocks flying in the wind. *My* monster and the most beautiful thing I'd ever seen. He staggered when I wrapped my good arm around his neck and pulled myself up to plant my lips on that beautiful, toothy mouth.

Grendel

The Sentinels liked opening with kinetic strikes, and Watchman released me on Galatea's "*Mark!*" I dropped without a word to free-fall towards my target, morphing into the densest, toughest-skinned form I could manage as the air whistled by me.

Below me wasn't much to see; mostly dark, lit only by walkway and grounds lights, the resort looked asleep. Then it didn't look like anything at all — Galatea's hack of the local station cut the power and dropped the building into deep shadow, leaving only a single point of light.

Lei Zi's plan was less a plan than a series of conditional intentions. Artemis was to infiltrate the target and signal once she knew Astra's precise location; that was the high-powered LED flashlight I was falling towards. With that signal, the rest of our part unrolled as a choreographed entrance — Lei Zi and Blackstone had drilled us on it until we could repeat our parts and go-no go cues.

Hitting the turf outside the end of the bedroom wing felt like landing on thick sponge, and I had to scramble fast out of the dirt crater. I had to dial up my eyes' light-gathering abilities before I saw Artemis, shadow in shadow where she waited by the door at the end of the bedroom wing. She pointed up as I started for the door.

Right — my turn. I popped the carry-pack off my belt, pulled out my flashlight, stuck it into the grass with the lawn-spike Vulcan had glued onto it, and flipped it on. The green-tinted cellophane taped over the end gave the *rest* of the team's go-sign. *Then* I charged the door.

Artemis didn't move out of my way — just turned into mist before I charged through where she'd been. I smashed the door aside and powered down the hall without slowing. The door at the end was a fire door, but it didn't put up any more fight than the outside door had and Artemis came out of the mist behind me.

"Duck," she said, tapping my back, and I did as the swarm of micro-missiles shot over our heads to explode in the pitch-black dining room beyond and pump it full of tear gas. Before the gas could reach us, Tsuris turned the hallway into a raging wind-tunnel to blow the stinging cloud further into the resort.

"Go." Artemis tapped my back again as she started shooting. *Bang bang bang. Bang bang bang.* "Third left, stay down." Turning myself around and crawling up the hall, I felt the hot wash of Galatea's freaking rocket-boots on my back as she roared past to join Artemis in delivering the bang and boom. I rose to a crouch, kept moving; anyone getting past those two would to have to dig into the carpet and *crawl* up the hall unless he weighed as much as me — Balz certainly wasn't getting any of his tricky spheres into play.

Easy so far, so why was my heart racing and breath coming like I'd been punching through stone? Leaning into the wind, I and counted doors: one, two, *three*. I popped the door, took a step and flinched from surprise as something bounced off the side of my head with a yelped "Ouch!"

"Astra?"

The lights came back on and I found myself staring down into wide blue eyes. *Yes!* Then she grabbed me, one arm around my neck, and before I could move she pulled herself up and kissed me hard.

I almost fell back into the hall, but managed to grab onto her as she went boneless. Somewhere in my head I heard someone *laughing,* smelled jasmine, and remembered what Lei Zi had said about Chakra tagging along. *Laugh it up, lady.*

The girl who'd just blown my world weighed as much as a kitten and I carefully tucked her up so she curled in against me. Headed up the hall, I had to lean nearly halfway to the floor against Tsuris' indoor hurricane as she clung like a limpet, giggling into my chest. Over the wind I could hear the banging of Artemis' pistols behind me, deeper roars as Galatea flushed racks of tiny brilliant-missiles. Back outside and past Tsuris and Megaton — last line of discouragement for anyone who could fight Tsuris' wind — I lowered Astra to the grass as Crash and The Harlequin came from nowhere.

"Astra?" The Harlequin whispered, and sighed when she nodded. "This is going to hurt, honey. Sorry." It might have taken three seconds for her to slip an inflatable brace around Astra's arm and strap it to her chest — all Astra did was suck in her breath. She had to ask three times if Astra could hold on before the girl nodded again, then she and Crash lifted her onto Crash's bike and the two of them disappeared in a blur of speed.

The Harlequin broke radio silence. "Team Two, we have secured the package — go to town. Team One, withdraw." The roof of the dining hall blew off as Galatea thoughtfully made a hole for Team Two to come in hot. The Sentinels *really* liked kinetic strikes: Watchman's landing shook the building.

Episode Four

Chapter Twenty Seven: Astra

Police, especially big-city police, think of themselves as the Thin Blue Line, the protectors that stand between the law-abiding and the lawless. And this is absolutely true, but the public also thinks of police as the enforcers of the will of the State — not a positive association in even the most liberal democracies. This is why, despite appointed action-review boards and civil liaisons, Crisis Aid and Intervention teams try to avoid any appearance of law enforcement — or even of uniforms. Which doesn't mean they don't help enforce the law.

Dr. Alice Mendel, *Superhumans and Society.*

It really is possible to be *deliriously* happy, and I'm pretty sure I was laughing when Brian took me out of there. I also remember Quin almost crying when she asked me if I could hold on and they threw me on Crash's bike so he could *slowly* take us out of there in hypertime. Just a couple miles down the road he dropped us into realtime in the middle of a bunch of paramedics where the police were waiting to move in, and they laid me out on a stretcher.

   Doctors poked me sometime later (one of them might have been Dr. Beth), and Chakra was there (that's when the pain disappeared) and Blackstone asked questions (lots, over and over), and then I got to dream and spend some time in one of my favorite places: at Atlas's cabin, in his arms watching the stars. Sometime in the night they turned into Brian's, and that was okay, they were still wonderfully strong arms.

Eventually, a tickling nose pulled me awake. Opening my eyes, I didn't recognize the ceiling, but smelled that unmistakable hospital smell. Where was I? Monitoring equipment made noises by my bed — had I been hurt bad enough to hook up to alarms? I was feeling almost no pain, a huge change from yesterday.

"Hey, little Miss Sunshine. I thought you were going to sleep all day."

I knew that voice. Carefully turning my head, I couldn't keep the grin off my face. Yup, Jacky sat in a chair by the window where she could see the whole room. Not quite as pale as she used to be, but she'd still put kids off of Disney princesses for life.

"I disappear for a day and they drag *you* back?"

She smiled. Well, a smile for her (hey, *I* can see them even if nobody else does). "Blackstone asked for off-the-books help but I could have done that from the Gulf. I came back to get in on the ass-kicking."

"Really? Did you get to shoot anybody?"

"Only a little. Mostly skeet-shooting and they bugged out before the heavy artillery arrived. Hardly worth the trip, so I'm going to stick around for a bit, do some hunting."

"Great. Don't scare the new kids." Who was I kidding? God knew how much I'd missed Jacky.

"Awww, are we all done bonding?" Shelly bounced into the room followed by the Bees, making me blink and look around again. This had to be a hospital, because Annabeth had bought out the gift-shop for the cloud of *Get well soon!* balloons floating behind her. Was I in the same building as Toby?

Julie laughed, Annabeth cried, Megan snarked at Jacky, and everything was right for a while, until my brain began working again and I started asking questions.

The good news was Toby was doing better; the professionally pessimistic doctors were expecting him to make a complete recovery, though he probably never would remember that night. I *wasn't* in the same hospital; they'd brought me into Northwestern Memorial, isolated and under serious guard. X-rays had shown no broken bones or concussion, and experts in fight trauma had confirmed stuff I'd guessed at: severe impact and wrenching, pinched nerves, but I'd be fine with time and careful exercise.

That was the *only* good news. Last night's raid had been aimed at extracting me first, so they hadn't netted any more Wreckers despite giving it a strong try once I was out of there (nobody had said so, but I could reconstruct the op).

Dr. Beth didn't see any sign of my powers returning yet. Pellegrini had said they would come back — and now that I had time to think, ambivalent didn't *begin* to describe how I felt about that — but Beth didn't know if they'd creep back or come back in a rush (which explained why I had half a dozen sensors on me — he wanted to know the exact moment it happened). Shelly solemnly informed me that Dr. Beth had researchers at Detroit Supermax monitoring Mr. Ludlow to see if it worked the same in the other direction, but Eric wasn't getting weaker yet either.

And the city was going crazy. Protesters picketing The Crew. Protesters picketing Shankman. A morning *riot* outside the Dome between Humanity First protesters and a few hundred of my *fans* (someone in the CPD leaked the story of my injury and rescue last night). Goon vs. supervillain violence, supervillain vs. goon megaviolence, and a serious exodus of Chicagoans who could get out of town for a while, straining the airlines still serving the city and sparking, oh yeah, *more* fighting at bus terminals and even gas stations. Only Atlas-types like Watchman and Safire were keeping the freeways from turning into parking lots, the Chicago Police Department was getting pushed to the wall, and every Guardian team in the city was out in the streets, despite what Blackstone thought of using superheroes for normal law-and-order stuff.

And the DSA was no closer to finding the Green Man.

Then everyone was gone, even Jacky and Shell (who left a new earbug so she was as close as a whisper). I caught sight of Seven and Variforce in the room beyond before the door closed, keeping out the world.

I wiggled around a bit; strange beds always have an uncomfortable spot. The ceiling looked really interesting — I could count the little refracting squares in it if I got bored — but I didn't expect to be alone for long; I might have answered questions last night, but Blackstone was sure to arrive at any moment to debrief me within an inch of my life.

Since I could *walk*, they had to let me out soon, right? I closed my eyes. Smiling made my face hurt, from a hit that shouldn't have left even a bruise after twenty-four hours. I'd seen extreme sports-injuries before, and even with Chakra's wonderful magic I knew recovery was going to take a while. Until my breakthrough powers came back, at least.

And I *wanted* them back; listening to Jacky and Shell explain what had happened while I was gone, what was happening *right now*, I'd said goodbye to eating lunch in the student commons with Julie and Annabeth and Megan. So now the thought that Pellegrini might have been lying made me swallow rising panic. What if I wasn't *Astra* anymore? If anyone walked in now I could blame my wet eyes and sniffling on pain.

I blinked my eyes clear. "Shell?"

"What? Do you need anything? Are you hurting?"

"Nope. Could you come back? There's something we need to talk about."

"You — You — I can't — Aaagh!"

Shell incandescently speechless was a sight to treasure and I tried hard to not laugh; it *wasn't* funny. I did hold it down to painful giggles while my BFF's mouth opened and shut.

"I can't believe you *did* that! Or even thought of it!"

Okay, speechlessness over now. I rolled my eyes.

"You're kidding, right? *Galatea*? You're codenamed for Pygmalion's statue that the gods turned into a human woman for him? It's the original Pinocchio-myth! I couldn't find the Blue Fairy, and I wanted you to be safe! Sorry!"

"But, *Ozma*? You signed on with Crazy to invade La-La Land if she'd make me a Real Girl again? And why didn't you *tell* me?" Grabbing fistfuls of her synthetic red hair, she looked pretty demented herself.

"Asks the girl who told Tommy Archer I liked him."

"Hey, you'd never have said anything and you melted into a puddle if he just *looked* at you! I'm not broken! You don't need to *fix* me!"

"And when the DSA seizes you as a threat to national security? They don't even need an arrest warrant — they can seize you as property! Vulcan's property!"

"I don't belong to Vulcan!"

"Yes, yes you do! All except the software between your ears and *that* belonged to the Anarchist! And if they knew what you carry around in there they'd come and get you *yesterday*!"

"Blackstone would never — "

"Blackstone couldn't stop them! Shell!"

She closed her mouth, heaved a completely unnecessary breath while I glared at her, breathing hard myself. Yelling *hurt*.

"Shell," I tried again. "You were safe while you were hiding somewhere far away in TA's super-secret lair, a voice in my head and a ghost in cyberspace. Now...please Shell, *please* be more careful."

Her shoulders hunched, but she folded her arms and glared back. "So why are you telling me? Why don't you just do whatever Ozma comes up with if it's for my own good?"

Using my good arm, I levered myself up and back into a more sitting position.

"Because it was stupid, Shell. Because you're Power Chick now. Robotica, anyway. The city's coming apart out there, and I can't do anything because I'm just Hope again."

Ever since the day of my breakthrough I'd told myself that, if I'd ever had a choice, if I could have just given my powers back, I'd have walked away. Not all the time; just when I was tired or scared, or wishing for more normal in my day — nothing but the whining of someone who wanted it easier — and now I was so scared I might not get it back I could hardly think straight. Really, could I have *been* more stupid? More self-centered and shallow?

I picked at the blanket. It was *soft*, like a piece of cloud. Chakra had told me what Mal's choice had been, and all this just drove the lesson home with a big old cosmic hammer. *Yes, I can be taught.*

"I want it all *back*, Shell," I whispered to the blanket, made myself look up. "And if I want it back for me, I can't, I can't take it all away from you, make you just Shelly again. Sorry."

She tried to hold the glare, gave it up with a sigh and unfolded her arms. "Dummy. I'm going with you."

"Um, what?"

"If you're going to invade a fictional fairyland, I'm coming with you."

"It would be all manner of shocking if you didn't," Ozma said from the doorway. Brian loomed behind her.

"Private, duh, do you mind?" Shelly huffed.

"It is private now. I have informed the door we will not be receiving." She wore casual slacks and a loose silk tee and of course the wide, white jeweled belt that went with everything. She was going to start a new fashion trend, I could just tell. "And I petitioned Blackstone for the privilege of seeing you first. The dear man feels he is in my debt."

And is he? Was she going to collect him for her Army of Oz, too? Not a wizard but a magician? What, exactly, had I done?

Grendel

Never mix into a girl-fight, even if it looks like it's winding down. Her serene Highness ignored Galatea's laser glare as I did my best looming monster impression. I loom, therefore I am. Astra — Hope, and didn't the name just freaking fit her right down to her cheerfully hopeful default expression — went from scowl to smile in the time it took her to turn her head. That left the job of carrying the chill to Galatea, and the robot-girl tried hard.

It didn't work real well against Ozma's super-imperturbability.

Hope's eyes slid past Ozma to focus on me, got wider. So did her smile, and she mouthed a *Thank you* before looking back at the princess. Every muscle in my body twitched and started bulking up like a fight was coming. Yeah, right — like she could threaten me on a *good* day.

"I am glad to find you well," Ozma went on while I tried to figure out why the girl made me so twitchy, "and I have come bearing gifts. Brian?" I handed her the pepper tin, and she deposited it in Hope's good hand with the kind of flourish that would look silly from anyone else.

The girl obviously had no idea. "Thank you? I suppose you can never have enough pepper..."

Ozma laughed. "May I?" Taking it back, she unscrewed the bottom compartment and held it out.

Holy shit. Holy freaking shit.

Now the little silver pill inside glowed softly, slowly pulsing dim and bright. It looked like a piece of the Moon — not a moon rock like the astronauts brought back but a piece of the Moon like you saw it on an icy clear night, sailing in its own halo.

"Baum always went light on description," Ozma observed.

Gosh, do you think? After the retrieval, I'd gone back and reread the pill parts of the story; "silver pills" didn't exactly cover it. Hope couldn't take her eyes off it — perfectly understandable since the pretty little thing was practically singing a subliminal siren song. She swallowed.

"What does it do?" she whispered softly. "How do you use it?"

Ozma laughed again. "It's a little big, so *I* would take it with water. It's the last of the Wishing Pills. In the story, you had to gulp it down and then count to seven by twos and wish for what you want to have happen. Baum threw the silly riddle in to make it look harder, but it's really that simple; the hard part is what happens next."

"Next?" That came out as almost a squeak.

"Next." The princess wasn't laughing anymore. "The bigger the wish, the harder the test. The Wishing Pill turns by degrees into the worst pain you have ever imagined, ratcheting up until the wish is granted or until you change your wish to 'I wish I'd never swallowed the pill!' Wish for that, and you won't have. The pill will be back in your hand, unswallowed."

Hope bit her lip, looking pale under the purple bruising. "I've taken things that have disagreed with me before."

"Never like this, I promise you. You need to keep true to your wish in the face of unbearable pain. I couldn't, not even to save myself and my friends. When it was me, I wished it out again." She closed the tin, cutting off the calling moon-glow. "And there are limits. The wish must be for something immediate, concrete, and present. You can wish for Shelly to be human again, or for a chest full of diamonds, or for a total physical makeover, but not for peace on Earth."

Hope and Shelly traded a look that meant absolutely nothing to me, but I was beginning to wonder if Oz was lots darker than Ozma let on. Seriously? A torture-test to see if you were worthy of having your wish granted?

But when you thought about it, the stories had lots of bad things happening: a king who sold his wife and kids to an evil gnome in return for immortality, a lady with a collection of heads she liked to swap to match her clothes. Hell, *Ozma* had been robbed of her memories, turned into a boy, and raised by an abusive witch — not exactly bedtime story stuff when you thought about the details.

Watching the girls, Ozma nodded. "I will keep the tin in my magic cabinet. When you *wish* to use the Wishing Pill, simply call on me — or on Nix if I am not present — to deliver it to you."

The princess got us out of there as smoothly as she got us in, barely nodding to Variforce and Seven. Variforce waved us on; Seven was too busy giving signatures to a pair of nurses who looked ready to drag him into the nearest supply closet. She followed me close as I broke a path for us to the lobby and out, and I got my usual stares and starts from the civilians, but I was really too bothered to notice.

"So what was all that about, princess?" We had a moment while our driver, who Galatea called New Tom for some reason, pulled the van around to meet us.

Ozma looked up, distracted. "Hmm?"

"I get that Astra — Hope — made a deal with you, but why the big production now?" She'd practically rushed us here, stopped at the door long enough to hear the two BFs' bonding moment (it had gotten kind of loud), timed her grand *Ta-dah!* entrance.

"Oh, that. The Question Box."

"Huh?"

She patted my arm. "The Question Box surprised me this morning with an uncharacteristically unambiguous instruction to tell Hope about the Wishing Pill. ASAP was involved."

I growled. "You used it again?"

"No, it got my attention. And it was certainly right; I have acquired two recruits for the price of one."

She left it at that and I didn't push it, but I couldn't say I was happy. I didn't trust the Question Box. Sure it had been one of Ozma's royal treasures for most of a century, but it had been made by an evil sorcerer who hadn't got much good from it and it certainly hadn't warned the princess of the *coup d'état* that turfed her off the Emerald Throne. And these days it didn't wait for questions — it answered questions you didn't know you *had*.

New Tom got us back to the Dome, where we found The Harlequin waiting for us in our common room with Vulcan and a guy named Andrew, with something to make me forget all about the Question Box: costume designs.

They couldn't be serious.

Chapter Twenty Eight: Grendel

"The worst thing about being outed is losing my sense of safety. And not just my *safety — people around me are at risk now, too. A few months ago, I got shot with a shoulder-launched missile by Paladin fanatics while doing my job — now that they know who I am, they or anyone else can attack me anywhere, which means it's statistically more dangerous to stand next to me and I have to be* alert *all the time. Do you understand? Standing in line at Starbucks, I'm putting other people at risk. Compared to that, the loss of privacy is just really, really annoying.*

Astra, excerpt from the Citywatch "outing" interview.

They were serious.

And they were crazy.

With all the footage of our "arrival" in Chicago to fight the Green Man, the Sentinels' PR guys had as much chance of keeping us under wraps for a full, publicized introduction as they did of keeping Rush's tabloid-selling sexcapades out of the news (my favorite was his bet with the Chicago Bears cheerleaders). So Chandler Communications — the PR firm run by Atlas' big brother — went the other direction; they dropped our codenames and power-sets on the Sentinels' website and solicited costume ideas.

Yeah, really.

"C'mon! Just wear it once. Please?" Nix darted around my head, a hyper hummingbird.

Andrew, a guy who looked more like an Olympic triathlon athlete than a fashion designer, had brought each of us *three* costumes based on the "best" fan submissions that he expected us to model, with near-poster sized computer renditions of each so we could get a good look. The Green Man could attack any minute, and we were doing a freaking fashion show.

Every one of Reese's costumes incorporated a helmet and body armor — fliers are great targets — and one included a huge cape. A bunch of people had gone back to the source for Ozma's costumes; hers were art-deco and fluttery things, but since she wasn't going to be a first responder superhero that was okay. Mine...

"Pleeeease?"

I grew fangs and growled at her while Ozma laughed. Reese knew better and just smirked silently. Andrew and The Harlequin wisely stayed out of it.

Armor wasn't really on the menu for me — completely redundant and hard to adapt to my changing measurements anyway — but one fan had sent in a fantasy-medieval dragon armor design of plates held together by cross-webbing straps that could stretch to accommodate. It came with the biggest, most bad-ass sword I'd ever seen — seriously, the thing was as tall as I was and the blade had to weigh at least a hundred pounds. Vulcan claimed he could make it tough enough for me to swing more than once.

I was supposed to be a knight under a curse.

The second "costume" went with heavy black spandex shorts, which showed they'd at least researched the Academy's gym uniforms, but added Celtic or Maori tribal tats all over my chest, arms, neck and shoulders, and even my face. I had to admit, the black-on-gray look was pretty cool and ratcheted the intimidation factor — which I was already naturally good at — even higher.

The third costume had gone ... the other way.

"Pleeeease?"

I was going to swat a fairy.

Costume number three was black dress pants, a snow-white shirt, black tie, and black vest with a fancy scrollworked 'G' for Grendel on the breast pocket. The tie hung loose as a noose, the shirt was untucked with sleeves rolled halfway up, and the vest was open, but still, what? What was it, prep-school grunge?

Andrew solemnly assured me he'd made it with materials that could expand as far as I could, like he thought that helped.

"Pleeeeeeeeeeeeeeease?"

"Nix," Ozma admonished the doll. "Please don't be tiresome." She gave me a look. "You do realize she will wear you down." *Translation: I want to see it, too.*

"Fans have way too much time on their hands."

"You could always be *my* knight ..."

"Yeah, no."

"And I do not believe you want to be any scarier."

I growled at her and she laughed, completely unimpressed.

Five minutes later, I had the freaking tie on. Andrew nodded and Ozma and The Harlequin smiled while Nix squealed, and Reese stopped smirking.

What?

Megaton

Variforce smacked me out of the sky again, but I managed to get my feet under me and blast before I splashed into the lake. Again. *And what have we learned? I can blast just fine underwater.*

The whole exercise was The Harlequin's fault; she'd insisted that I needed more public exposure, and since the Green Man wasn't attacking (yet) and my powers didn't support a patrol function, she'd convinced Watchman and Variforce to move my training outside. Five hundred feet over Lake Michigan.

I blasted my way back up to decent altitude, tracking Variforce high above me in his cloud of supporting fields. The mission was simple, I just needed to get past him to "tag" Watchman. Naturally, we had an audience; telescoping cameras pointed our way from boats and the shore and cape-watchers with binoculars followed my bright blast-column as I climbed toward the afternoon sun.

Maybe Dad was watching.

"*One more time, Megaton,*" Watchman warned me, "*and we're done. Since we could be going into action any time, we don't want to run you out of juice first. So put it all in.*"

He didn't sound a bit worried by the possibility that my "all in" might actually *reach* him. At least my "all in" didn't include an Astra-style death ride, but what could I put "all in" that I hadn't?

Doctor Beth had spent hours and hours breaking down what my explosive blasts were actually *doing*, and he'd found out a few interesting things that made *no* sense. First, my blasts didn't really come from inside me. Instead they drew from some internal source but they erupted fully in thickening waves *outside* the point of my body projecting them; which explained why I could keep my gloves on when I "shot" explosive bolts from my hands — there was a still zone between my skin and the eruption point. Same for my legs and feet when I rocketed.

Second, there were at least three factors to the energy blast I projected: heat, light, and "pure kinetic force." What the hell was pure kinetic force? Dr. Beth didn't know. He called it a "force without a material component outside its source," like magnetism or gravity, and he suggested I should visualize my kinetic blasts as explosions of *invisible pellets* that "dissipated when they encountered a solid object to which they could transfer their kinetic energy." According to his fancy toys, kinetic force was normally the main component of my blast; the heat and light, and the bang and roar, was just wastage from the main reaction (though I could dial it up to where heat and light was the main component, like I had when facing the green).

So how could I use what I had? Variforce's fields could dissipate heat and refract light easy, so "all in" had to be the kinetic kick — but the concentrated fireworks that came with them made my blasts easy to track; he just thickened his fields at the point of impact, dissipating the hit all through his cloud of fields. It was like punching a sack of gym balls.

But he had to focus on the point of impact. If I could spread his focus and close the distance... *Okay then, maybe "all in" does mean a death-ride this time.*

I poured on the roar, picking up speed and targeting Variforce squarely in my helmet sights, visualized a tight stream of invisible pellets, as organized as photons in a laser, aimed, and erupted.

The blast looked dim in the afternoon light, at least by my standards, but Variforce's fields went almost opaque where he braced them for the hit as I twitched, fired, twitched, fired, twitched, fired, blasting as fast as I could at different angles while still closing on him. Separation disappeared as his field cloud seemed to leap at me, and then I gave it everything I had, almost straight into him, kicking my rocket-column up another notch and blasting hard.

The fields tore, shredded, and I was past him and *through*, clear sky between me and Watchman. I didn't even think, just fired one more time, tagged him before he could blink — and couldn't believe what I'd done. It didn't even rock him, fast-shot weak as it was, but it was a *hit*.

"*And that's game,*" came Watchman's dry voice. "*Congratulations, Megaton. Variforce?*"

What? I looked back and down. Variforce's field cloud churned, closing the hole I'd blasted through it. I'd probably roared through within a few inches of the guy.

"*I'm good,*" Variforce confirmed. "*And, kid? Good hit. You'll make a decent opposition force with more training.*"

Watchman dropped lower, letting Variforce anchor an outlying thrust of field to him for faster flying, and we headed in. "*How do you feel?*" He asked as the shore got closer.

"Okay, I guess. A little tired, like I've been running laps. I've got a lot more — I just have to let it build before I let it go. Kind of like charging a capacitor." One bright spot to all this was I could let my inner science-geek come out.

"*Good to know. Once the whole Green Man thing is behind us, we're going to have to take you somewhere and see just how much you can build up. You may be one of the most powerful energy projectors we've seen until now.*"

"I could have a nuclear option?"

"Maybe. If you do, let's wait to use it until we know the size of the hole you'll make. Got it?"

Caution rang in Watchman's voice; he wasn't my coach, he was my firing range instructor. *Don't play with your guns until we can test-fire them somewhere safe — the life you save may be your own.* He hadn't had to tell me twice. I knew what "Let's see what this does" experiments led to: evacuating the school, if you were *lucky*, and we didn't want to accidentally blow anyone else up, did we?

Flying over the line of cameras on the shore, I still felt pretty good.

Astra

Everything was *heavy*. My muscles hadn't atrophied or anything, but when I'd gained my powers, I'd lost my sense of the weight and solidity of things. I'd had to learn to touch the world lightly. Even when I'd been hurting, put back together by surgeons after breaking nearly every bone in my body and traumatizing every organ, just standing up, making myself move, hadn't made me hurt worse. Now, dressing to leave the hospital left me wiped and shaking, remembering how much fighting pain took out of a normal person and grateful again for Chakra's magic hands.

They took me out through a side exit, where fans and paparazzi couldn't see me and spot which car I got into. New Tom held the door while Seven kept his hands free. Rush had replaced Variforce before they let me check out (he could carry me out of any bad situation before it had time to *get* bad, I supposed), and he helped me into the car. The armored sedan's tinted windows meant I didn't have to wear shades Hollywood celebrity style, though I could have used a pair to help hide the bruising. New Tom drove carefully, like I was fragile, but got us to the hidden parking entrance to the Dome without incident.

Seven stayed with me, and Blackstone and Jacky were waiting for me in the Assembly Room. Blackstone stood when I came through the door. He took my good hand and kissed it.

"How are you, my dear?"

A lump rose in my. "I'm okay. I — I'm okay."

"Good. We won't keep you long, but we really must debrief you, understand everything you went through yesterday. Are you up to it?"

This time I just nodded, and he pulled out a chair. Seven sat with me and Willis appeared from nowhere with coffee, obviously Jacky creations this time. It felt so normal I could have cried as I sipped from my mug. I cupped it for the warmth and started at the beginning. "Teleporting with Drop leaves you disoriented..."

Blackstone's usual procedure meant recording and listening to the full story, beginning to end any way you wanted to tell it, then going back and digging into moments of interest, looking for details. He let me talk, and not talk when I needed a minute to collect myself for the hard stuff, nodding to show his attention. Jacky stayed quiet, sitting statue-still through most of it.

He didn't ask for descriptions of anyone, but he focused on the dining room, the platform I'd seen, and every remembered detail of my dinner conversation with Dr. Pellegrini while I wilted under the effort of not forgetting anything.

I still didn't know what to think of yesterday. I'd been captured and held prisoner *again* (the second time in one year, which at least gave our television writers plenty of "real" peril to use), but this time, once the terror of helplessness wore off, I really had felt more like a nuisance — except to Dr. Pellegrini, who'd been *delighted*. And Pellegrini had sounded more like a scholar and humanitarian than a mass-murderer.

Blackstone picked up on my confusion, but was too professional to offer any perspectives; he'd call them guesses and they might have biased my reporting. He'd listen to the recordings of the session later, pick my statements apart for meaning and nuance and pull out more solid extrapolations than I ever could, but even I knew there was something there I should *see*. There was *something* I wasn't getting but couldn't forget. It was like staring at one of those computer-generated pictures that looked like a flat surface of dense black-and-white squiggles that transformed into a 3-D silhouette when you squinted just right: you knew it held meaning, you just couldn't see it.

Head pounding, I gave up before he did, but he let me go before my voice started shaking with fatigue. Jacky followed me out. Silly me, I thought she was just taking me to my new rooms.

The staff had finished moving my rooms, along with Shelly's and Jamal's, to the "new" wing set aside for the cadet team, and extreme fatigue kept me from really noticing the big gold 'YS' covering the common room's double doors. The applause that burst out when they opened startled me, but Jacky kept me moving.

Everyone was waiting for me and in uniform, even Jamal who wasn't spending much time here yet. I almost didn't spot all the parentals (and a blonde civilian I didn't recognize) behind all the color; the room had turned into a serious fashion show for our newbies, and I stared.

Reese looked superhero-standard in a *good* way in a gray and white leather armor-stiffened bodysuit and helmet, and Ozma looked royal and ethereal in a strapless white catsuit and Magic Belt under a gauzy open-front overdress. It was gathered at her breasts by a huge jade Z-inside-an-O brooch and floated around her like an under-the-arms cloak, with long white opera gloves to match. *Brian* looked like Frankenstein's monster gone GQ. *Casually* GQ, hulking muscles, tight dreadlock mane, fangs, and all. It was like looking at a Siberian tiger — he still looked like he could eat you, but he was beautiful.

Galatea, Crash, Megaton, Tsuris, Grendel, Ozma — *my* team, and I realized only now, the team that had come to get me last night.

So of course I cried, and thanked everybody, and got hugs from Shelly and the parentals including Shelly's mom. There was *cake,* and a happy flying fairy, and eventually Jacky got me through the room with last hugs and into my new bedroom and into bed.

And sometime in the night Atlas sat down for dinner with Dr. Pellegrini and me to point out the obvious: we'd captured Eric and outed the Foundation. And Pellegrini didn't care.

Chapter Twenty Nine: Astra

"There is a reason why you train all the time, solo and as a team; you've got to know what you can do, what the others can do, and what you can do together. Most supervillain 'teams' are not a serious threat to most CAI teams because, whatever the power imbalance might be, CAI teams train."

Blackstone, 9th annual Crisis Aid and Intervention Conference address.

Jacky was the worst correspondent in the *world* and still hadn't told me everything about her first New Orleans trip, so we had serious catching up to do.

The blonde from last night was Acacia, and Jacky had brought her along to keep her out of trouble. She was also the nicest vampire I'd ever met (admittedly out of two, and I only got minutes to meet her before she went to sleep with the dawn, but Jacky had described lots of others), and she matched every blonde joke I'd ever *heard*. Hanging with the Bees, I'd heard a lot.

Not that she was a ditz, but she made it hard to tell; she was a *fan*. From what Jacky said while whipping up some Jacky Creations (I'd seriously missed her coffee, too), the girl had grown up in a one-church Louisiana town and had somehow become a goth and a fang fan in a community that didn't consider *black* an appropriate color except at funerals. Trying to picture her as a goth hurt my brain, but apparently she'd found a sick monster in New Orleans who thought it worked for her. He'd drunk her blood, tortured her, brainwashed her, and triggered a vampire breakthrough somehow (and Jacky couldn't talk about that except to say he hadn't been like Psycho-Vlad).

Jacky told me the story over breakfast, after I'd called my parents to check up on Toby. She didn't say *exactly* what happened to Acacia's sire — apparently the whole thing was serious, deep, cut-your-throat classified — but I guessed that decapitation and fire was involved. Jacky'd used her evil vampiric mind-enslaving powers to make Acacia forget all the bad stuff that had happened to her, but the girl had sworn off goth. *Now* she embraced a wardrobe of bright colors, frills, skirts, and lace. Bows and even silk flowers were involved; it was like a florist's shop had exploded.

But she was still a fan, just a Jacky-fan and by extension a superhero fan. All this had happened during Jacky's *first* trip to New Orleans, and now the two of them were — and here I couldn't stop laughing — living together in a haunted French Quarter property Jacky was converting into a coffee shop and *detective agency*! Apparently decapitating a few vampires bought you respect, and she was working with her voodoo queen grandmother, a too-good-looking-to-be-real lawyer, a werewolf police detective, and a vampire godfather to police the Big Easy's supernatural community.

Oh. My. God.

"You're getting too much fun out of this," Jacky said as I giggled helplessly into my hand (I'd already spit my morning coffee across the breakfast table). I shook my head desperately, tears streaming. It would never do for the Young Sentinels' new fearless leader to laugh until she fell out of her chair. Mal and Brian looked our way between bites of Willis-served omelet (in Brian's case, a *stack*). Reese stayed focused on his epad.

"Please please *please* tell me you're making this up," I finally gasped, snorting with complete inelegance. "I can't — I can't, believe this. So is she your new sidekick?"

"*No.*" That came out with her Voice of Doom, which *I* could never manage without sounding ridiculous, the voice that said *We shall not speak of this again.* She sighed. "Seriously, I brought her along because she's pretty helpless for a vampire. She panics when she's alone."

Still traumatized. Suddenly it wasn't funny anymore. I reached over and squeezed Jacky's hand. "She couldn't have a better friend. So, when are you going back?" She looked at her mug and I was instantly suspicious — Jacky didn't *deflect.*

She shrugged. "I've got some hunting to do, and I want to show Acacia a couple of my Chicago safehouses just in case New Orleans ever turns vampire-hostile. And your mom has invited me to Friday dinner." Her lips twitched. "Demanded I show up, actually."

"Yes! You need to meet Shelly's mom, she'll probably still be in town. And we need to — "

"*ALL SENTINELS! ALL SENTINELS! REPORT IMMEDIATELY TO THE LAUNCH BAY! ALL SENTINELS! ALL SENTINELS! — "*

My earbug practically vibrated, but they weren't taking chances — the alert came through every speaker in the room too — and the reflexes of endless drilling pulled me out of my chair. Mal half-stood, wide eyed, Brian started to bulk up but wasn't sure either, and Reese didn't move.

"Move it, guys!" I shouted on the run. "Young Sentinels means Sentinels! Shelly! Get everybody!" When I wobbled off-balance with my brace, Jacky grabbed my good elbow to help me go faster.

In the starship-base that is the Dome, even our elevators are wicked smart; they opened when we got to them and snapped closed the instant sensors told them there was nobody immediately behind us in the hallway. Brian made it a tight squeeze for the rest of us and the emergency speed of our ride almost threw us to the ceiling at the end, but we didn't beat everyone — Blackstone and Quin had probably come from Dispatch. All the rest except Shelly and Vulcan arrived within a minute, even Chakra.

"Breakout at Detroit Supermax," Blackstone said once the last of the older heroes arrived. "All duty-listed Sentinels are going; all Young Sentinels remain on base and on call. Watchman — "

"Take Grendel," Ozma said — an instruction, not a suggestion. Blackstone looked at me and I froze up before nodding.

"And Grendel. Watchman will be towing the floater, no time to catch a jet. Astra, the Dome is yours. Move, people!"

Only superheroes would accessorize an aircraft with outside grips. Watchman showed Grendel a pair on top to hold on to as the floater lifted, Variforce shaping his fields for a ride-along as the sleek flyer rose through the bay doors and out of sight. Streamlined for high speed, the floater couldn't go faster than a helicopter without an Atlas-type assist; Watchman would get them there faster than anything non-military could fly.

Tsuris shrugged. "Guess we're not Sentinels after all, huh?" Ozma raised an eyebrow, looked over at me, and the question unstuck my frozen brain. I took a breath.

"Section One of your Operations and Procedures Manual? Superhumans under eighteen may not be knowingly deployed into military or police operations?" Not the complete story; Shelly hadn't gone either, hadn't even come to the bay, which meant Blackstone considered her job with Vulcan too important to take her away.

"So why *Brian*?"

Why? I opened my mouth, but Ozma answered first. "Few in that prison can hurt or stop Brian, and fewer can kill him."

It's still going to make a mess. I didn't say it. We were down one heavy because of me, and maybe we could get away with it. Last night's operation had been legally iffy — Blackstone had explained that they hadn't sent the under-eighteens into direct contact with the Wreckers, so they'd probably get a pass on it. But it was a terrible risk — the legal fallout of fielding Brian in a *prison break* could kill the Young Sentinels before we really started, and Blackstone had to be seriously worried to chance it. I hugged myself, cold. The Brotherhood and the Sanguinary Boys we'd put away were there. The survivors of *Villains Inc.* were there. What were they flying into?

And why was I trying to remember a dream... Oh, *no*.

"Shelly! I need to talk to Blackstone. Now!"

Grendel

A guy could get used to this. I held on as Watchman towed our little wagon train, Variforce trailing behind on his glowing force-field tethers.

"Grendel," Blackstone said in my ear. *"How are you doing?"*

"It's a nice day out. Sir."

"Good. Attention, everyone. Less than five minutes ago, Detroit Supermax went silent. Fortunately, the installation security system includes an outside trigger which trips in just such cases. This brought its independent and shielded secondary DSA system online, and we are getting some information.

"The separate cell blocks appear to have switched into isolation mode, which is good. We're not getting feed from inside several of them, which is bad. The Detroit Guardians are going in before us along with the local DSA response unit to secure the situation, and it may all be over before we arrive. However, given the nature of Detroit Supermax's guests, we will not be counting on this."

He went silent, came back.

"Also, be apprised that it is Astra's opinion, and I concur, that we may be facing the Wreckers — Dozer's capture may very well have been a Trojan Horse gambit. If this is the case, we may be facing the known Wreckers as well as Redback, a psi apparently now capable of seizing control of your body, and Dr. Pellegrini, whom we believe capable of boosting and suppressing breakthrough powers. You all read this morning's tactical summaries. Lei Zi?"

Lei Zi took over.

"We form three groups and will make our entry to the prison through one of the emergency entry shafts and attempt to link up with the Detroit Guardians. Watchman and Grendel will take point and secure the bottom of the shaft. I, Seven, Rush, Artemis, Variforce, and Riptide will descend second as the reaction team. Blackstone and Chakra will remain upstairs in support. Questions?"

"What's our objective?" Rush asked.

*"That will depend on what we find downstairs. The entry shaft will put us on the edge of the dark zone. Whatever we find, our job is to throw them out of Beta Block if they're there and to secure its cells. There is a good chance they are there after **Temblor**. And yes, he is still alive. People, we will not be down there alone. The prison garrison is already present, and more CAI teams are coming in. Regardless, we may find ourselves dropping into a complete Charlie Foxtrot."*

So, no pressure...just dropping blind into a pit full of superhumans with criminal tendencies, who might be free-range already. I felt my fangs growing and was glad nobody could see my smile.

"Do not let go, monster," Nox whispered in my ear.

I almost lost my grip on the floater, which would have been as embarrassing as hell. I couldn't *see* him.

"What are you *doing*?" Now that I knew to pay attention, I could feel the psychotic little doll's grip on my tie under my prep-school collar.

"Her Highness used her Magic Belt to render me invisible for a time," he hissed. "I must accompany you, for she has given me a magic compass and a mission."

"A mission? What does she want *there*?"

"It is for *you*, monster. The Question Box has spoken again — 'Today a monster will meet its maker.' The compass will tell me who he is. The princess fulfills her oath to you today."

Astra

The quick pass-along conversation with Shelly and Blackstone helped, and I managed to keep the bubbling panic out of my voice. Reminding everyone we were on alert, I directed them to check their epads for schedules (I knew Willis had been tasked to walk the newbies through in-Dome security procedures today, and they could do it in costume) and got out of the launch bay with no more sarcasm from Reese.

Back in my rooms I scrambled out of my fancy brace and into my uniform — the easier skirted formal costume, not my field costume — then back into the brace. Even being careful, I caught a few eye-watering ouches; Chakra's pain-suppression magic wasn't saving me from the consequences of straining my healing arm. Not that I was going anywhere, but Blackstone's departure left me "in charge." Five minutes after fly-out I walked into Dispatch.

David had a full line of Sentinel bobble-heads up, and he'd left his drawer open. Did he expect *more* action? And what was Blackstone *thinking*? "Astra. Congratulations." David pointed to the top corner of the main screen. A little box with my symbol in it showed I was the Sentinel On Watch. Blackstone had left a sidelined nineteen year-old college sophomore in command of Chicago's superhero assets — which was *insane* — and the little glowing box looked cheerfully innocent of intimations of doom.

The cloud view on the main screen had to be from Watchman's cam, and it displayed their airspeed: nearly seven hundred miles per hour. He could have flown a lot faster alone, but with over two hundred miles to fly, he'd still get them there in a little under twenty minutes.

Twenty minutes for anything to happen.

"What do you think?" I whispered. Everyone else stayed focused on their stations, but that didn't mean they weren't listening.

David shrugged. "I think this is worse than the Daley Center. If all of the dark blocks are breached, they're not going be able to hold the prison."

"What can't we see?"

He threw a basic map of the prison up on the screens. Maybe a third of the blocks were black.

"Alpha through Delta blocks are dark. That includes the juvenile detention wing, but mainly the hardest cells and the isolation cells — the cells for superhumans too dangerous for direct human contact. But more than fifty percent of superhumans are D Class, and the spread for supervillains is about the same, so it's a question of cells, not blocks. There are a handful of prisoners, if they get out of their cells, the prison isn't holding them. The rest... We'll see."

I nodded unhappily. Time was against us, and what David wasn't saying was that it all depended on the capabilities and goals of whoever was making the jailbreak happen. I tried to think like Blackstone. If they'd gone in with a shopping list, then we might be all right. If they'd gone in to crack Detroit Supermax wide open...

If it *was* the Wreckers, what did they want? Dozer, obviously, but who else and why? *NOJ — not our job.* It had been one of Atlas' favorite expressions when anyone had brought up politics or police business. Blackstone reserved it for questions outside the current mission, and it was currently outside of mine. *My* job was what could happen in Chicago now, and I was two days out of the loop.

"Shelly?"

"*Hope? Kinda busy here.*" Down in the pit helping Vulcan with his force-to-heat tests, whatever those were, she'd barely poked her virtual head up long enough for me to run my Wreckers theory by her and get it to Blackstone before I cringed my way through dressing. She could multitask like the most advanced computers around, but could only do her *serious* thinking on one thing at a time (plus, I knew from long experience she was still just a bit mad at me for making plans for her behind her back).

"I know." I ignored David's raised eyebrow. "Can you give me a summation of everything current on the Green Man and Blackstone's notes? I *really* need to catch up."

"*Oh, right.*" The chill thawed a bit. "*Would you like the DSA file, too? You're cleared.*"

"Yes, please. David? I'll be in the guest office upstairs?"

He threw me a mock-salute. "No worries. Everything going on out there is Guardians work right now, anyway, and you can stand your watch from anywhere in the Dome. It's gotten better since yesterday, fewer incidents since everyone easily panicked has gotten out of town or hunkered down."

I sucked in a breath; I'd completely forgotten about the ongoing state of badness in the city outside, even though it was *right there on the screen* in the orange borders. Was it *that* easy to lose track of the small stuff in the face of looming danger? Still.

Don't panic, Hope. So the field team is on a field trip — what is the worst *thing that could happen while they are gone?*

That question really answered itself; my goal changed from not panicking to keeping it out of my voice again. I was getting good at that.

"Does everybody know *we're* mostly out of town?"

"A bunch of cape-watchers and newsies saw everyone fly out, but we're not required to notify anyone official... Crap."

I nodded. "Do me a favor? Could you get Superintendent Sean Redmond on the phone? Stay on the line, I'll talk to him upstairs."

"Got it, boss."

I ran, wincing, up the stairs to the office level. Just the one flight of steps winded me. Closing the door on the guest office, the one Chakra used when she needed to go into meditate-mode and didn't have time to retreat to her rooms, I caught my breath, made sure my mask and hair were straight, and sat behind the desk.

The desk's flatscreen computer monitor lit up with the team icon. *"Astra, I've got the superintendent's office on video conference, and they're getting their boss."*

"Okay. Thanks." I sat straight, breathed deep, smiled for the video feed, and Superintendent Redmond's stern jowly features filled the screen.

"Superintendent," I opened. "Good morning, and I apologize for calling you away from your — your morning." *Darn it, that could have been smoother. Breathe, Hope, breathe.*

His lips did something under his mustache that might have been a smile. Or not. *"I'm sure this isn't for anything trivial, Astra. What can I do for you?"*

"I thought you should know, sir, that an emergency has called away all of the field team and support team, with the exception of myself, Galatea, and Vulcan, and I'm still on the injured list. Given the current state of alert..."

What might have been a polite smile turned into a definite frown. The lines of his face deepened, but he looked away and gave himself a couple of breaths before looking back at me.

"That's unfortunate. May I ask why?"

"I — " I didn't know how much of it was classified. How much would the Proper Authorities want kept out of the news? His frown deepened, and I decided. "They are responding to a possible jailbreak at Detroit Supermax. Please don't — "

"Damn. Sorry. And of course I will keep that to myself. What CAI resources do you have?"

"I'm going to ask our Head of Dispatch to give you a rundown of all available capes, sir. I know that Dispatch makes the response decisions anyway, but with the alert — "

"You thought it was a good idea for me to know my people wouldn't be able to count on the big guns for a while."

"Yes, sir."

"Good call. And thank you. So, you are the officer of the day?"

"I — yes. Sir? There is one more thing."

"Go on."

"The Green Man investigation is ongoing, and mostly under DSA jurisdiction. However, Blackstone — Blackstone had reason to believe that the Green Man might be connected to the person backing the Wreckers, and the Wreckers may be involved in the jailbreak, may have planned all this before we caught up with Dozer."

The superintendent's expression didn't change. "Do you believe that the Green Man may be primed to use this opportunity?"

I nodded. "I do. We stopped him at O'Hare, and with our heavies gone..."

"The perfect window, yes. Thank you, Astra. I hope you're wrong, but best prepared and all that." He breathed deep, sighed. "If we're being alarmists, the drill will be good. Good luck to you, young lady, and I had best be about it."

He cut the connection with a brisk nod and I melted in my seat. *That went well, didn't it?*

"David?"

"*I heard. I'll get right on our end.*" And he was gone, too. I let out my breath.

Pulling up the file Shelly had sent me, I tried to forget everything outside. How was Grendel doing? He'd seen action the day of his breakthrough, had strength and fight-training at Hillwood, but — *Stop that. Ozma said it, almost nothing in Detroit Supermax has a chance to kill him. So focus.* Focus seemed to be my mantra.

Focusing on what *might* happen here would help me forget the team was flying blind into what could be the biggest superhuman jailbreak in *history*. Really. What could go wrong?

Grendel

Broiling sun over the drum line, head buzzing as the beat of the base drums hammers my ears and pushes my blood. The wave of screams strips away my in-the-zone focus and rips our final dance routine apart. At the edge of the field, Mister Carplin takes three deep breaths, face purpling, and attacks Misty. He pulls out chunks of her bottle-blonde hair before she bites a finger off. All up and down the drum and band and dance lines, they're trying to run away or kill each other, but I'm running for the stands, my family. I see the first whacked-out breakthrough erupt into a mass of shrieking bloody razor ribbons and start killing. Half the crowd ignores him, too busy tearing into each other like ferrets on PCP... My scream drops two octaves into a bone-shaking roar.

I worked on my fighting form all the way there: claws that cut steel, frame stripped for speed, muscle bulk for strength — basic assault form plus the extra horrors I'd pulled out of my drugged and rage-crazed brain the day of my change. My neck swelled until my skull sat on a broad cone of muscle over my shoulders and I couldn't turn my head more than forty-five degrees, my back hunched as my spine thickened, and short bone spurs pushed themselves through the skin over my wrists. Changing everything so fast left bones and muscles aching, but my hot blood rose anyway.

If I was going to meet the Ascendant, I had to look my best.

Watchman got us there fast — I was still changing when I felt us slow down and then we dropped *hard*. The roof of the prison was a huge lawn inside the surrounding walls, buildings no bigger than maintenance sheds. Watchman brought us all down beside one of the smallest, its door marked by a flashing green light. The floater roof popped open, everyone exiting into the bright sunshine as Variforce, Watchman, and I kept an eye on everything.

The place looked like a treeless park, like there should be running kids and dogs and picnic blankets, and Artemis just looked *wrong*, holding a pistol in each hand, sweeping around to cover half the floater's circumference. But then, *I* didn't match the setting, either.

"We are now in a dead zone," Blackstone said like he was observing the weather. "Which makes it more likely that the Wreckers are indeed behind this, and means we will not be able to communicate with each other or Dispatch. Chakra will do her best to keep track of you, but be careful."

Lei Zi nodded sharply, pointed at the nearest building with two fingers, and Watchman and I stepped up. Watchman opened the door under the flashing green light, and the hatch buried in the floor of the single room inside cracked inward. Lights came up to show a deep shaft.

I expected Watchman to drop into the open shaft. Instead he grabbed my shoulder, leaned in.

"I've read the action report on the LO Stadium attack," he said. "And I know you sparred at Hillwood. But you've had *no* serious fight training yet, so listen: heavies like you and me go against other heavies, but that's just half our job — we also take the first hits, block, move forward to break up attacks so our teammates can respond to what we meet. And since we have no idea what we'll find down there, we're the point of the spear, the head of the hammer, and if the others catch up to us, we're not doing our job. Got it?"

I nodded.

"Good. Follow me." He stepped off into the air and dropped.

Open shaft, bad guys of unknown power and nastiness at the bottom, and the promise of payback...*I've seen this movie, and I like how it ends.*

I dropped after him.

The shaft couldn't have been deeper than four or five stories, and Watchman slowed himself down so gravity could catch me up and we hit the bottom together. And kept going — the shaft floor didn't give way, it *exploded* and we fell through into the space below. The smoke and dust cleared to show a big empty room with a hatch in one wall.

"Nice back door," I coughed, waving dust away from my face. So much for my clean college-prep look. Above us, the shaft filled with Variforce's golden fields as he brought the rest down after us.

Watchman chuckled.

"Trust me, if anyone tries to open it in the other direction, bad stuff happens. The choke point we need to control first is through that hatch and two intersections away. If anybody's out there, we need to push them back past that. Assume anyone not in a guard uniform or superhero costume is an inmate — orange jumpsuits are a clue."

When he threw the lever by the hatch, the light over it turned flashing red and a voice started counting down: ninety nine, ninety eight, ninety seven ... At last, the hatch unsealed.

"Ready?"

I nodded, made sure Nox still clung like a limpet on my back beneath my vest, and followed Watchman. Out through the hatch, he turned us left.

The place had no cross corridors, just T-intersections with recessed doors opposite the off-halls. It was all white walls painted red by silently strobing emergency lights, seriously secure-looking doors. Every thirty feet or so, we stepped through hatches that should have been sealing each corridor section.

But there was no sound. This was a prison in the middle of a breakout? I could hear my blood singing in my ears and not much else. That changed when we hit the first T.

Aaaaarhkrhkrhkrhkrhkrhkrhk! The grinding shriek went beyond sound and threw Watchman back as barely less painful echoes bounced off the walls. Behind us, Variforce pulled up a field to block off the corridor between us and everyone else — good call, the shriek was shredding paint, vibrating the walls like drumheads. Watchman climbed to his feet, dazed and bleeding from his ears.

"Sonic attack. Beta Block is that way — go get him."

I gathered myself, stepped out into the off-corridor, and *charged.*

Aaaaarhkrhkrhkrhkrhkrhkrhk!

A thousand hammers pounded me, sound solid as falling anvils as I sprinted down the hall, but even bulked up I could move faster than an Olympic runner. The screamer's eyes went wide in the same moment I recognized *her*: Cocytus, the wailing river, named for one of the rivers in mythical Hades. Three years ago, she'd used her sonic-projection breakthrough to kill a couple dozen of her classmates at a team pep-rally and two of the capes who came to stop her. Her scream climbed, but my ears had already shut themselves down and my eardrums would regrow.

She turned to run and I roared, reached, captured a skinny arm to pull her back around, and dug the bone spur in my other wrist into her neck. Her eyes went wider, face white, and she collapsed in a twisted wreck of spastically locking muscles.

Spinning in a crouching circle while my hearing came back, I looked for targets but she'd been alone in the corridor except for the bodies of two guards in shattered armor. Watchman ghosted up beside me and then ahead to the next T-junction. Rush appeared beside me, squatting beside Cocytus.

"Jesus H. Christ, what did you hit her with?" His voice sounded tinny and hollow.

I grinned through my fangs. "Venom. Locks up every muscle in her body. She can barely breathe and *forget* about shrieking."

"Okay..." He checked her pulse, pulled back an orange jumpsuit sleeve, put some kind of patch on her arm and she went limp. Safety first — I was already moving up again.

Halfway to Watchman's position, the ceiling came down on me.

Chapter Thirty: Astra

It's funny that canes made a comeback as an executive status-marker. Blackstone carried a cane and made it look good, so was it his fault? Fashion is set by the popular and powerful. I heard somewhere that President Kennedy killed men's hats — before he was president, gentlemen wore hats outside, but he didn't like them. So now it's a rule; the boss gets a cane. It says you're rich enough to eat in places that check your coat and cane so you don't have to prop it against your chair at the table, or something. At least capes never came back as street fashion.

Astra, *Notes From a Life.*

Reading Blackstone's Threat Summary made me want to go back to bed and pull the sheets over my head. The Green Man was a "life force or nature spirit?" The DSA still had no idea who he *was* — Deep Green disclaimed any knowledge of his activities and their known membership was all accounted for — and his attacks were evolving; The Potowatomi Woods attack had just used local fauna, but the O'Hare attack had been *seeded* for that extra nastiness with the mutant kudzu and thorns.

And it looked like all the Green Man needed was a still body of water. Like, oh, *Lake Michigan*. A notation of Blackstone's suggested that small bodies of water might be required, but since both targets had been pretty far from the lake to begin with there was no way to know.

There was no commonality in attack duration, and Blackstone and the DSA experts agreed that the attacks had both continued until they accomplished their goal or were stopped; the Green Man hadn't run out of juice, so we had no idea how long an attack could continue or how far one could spread.

I put down my epad and leaned back to stare at the ceiling. My shoulder was starting to throb dully, and David had called up five minutes ago to tell me that the team was now out of radio-contact — more evidence the Wreckers were behind the prison break, if that was what it was.

So, we really didn't know where the next Green Man attack would come from or how far it would go if we couldn't stop it. And the DSA was no closer to figuring out who the Green Man was, hadn't been able to follow his Viewtube-broadcast ultimatums back to a useful source. The villain was a counterterrorism task force's worst nightmare.

I was surprised *any* civilians were left in Chicago.

"Shelly? Tell me you and Vulcan have something we can use on the Green Man?"

"How optimistic do you feel today?"

"Shell..."

"We're fitting a rack of incendiary missiles — magnesium fuel, other hot-burning alloys and accelerants. Vulcan thinks he can use The Stuff as a catalyzer to get a microsecond flash of superheated burn, and his numbers look good."

"When can we test it?"

"We can't — not without EPA approval."

"You're jok — Really?"

"Yep. No joke."

"Then how can we use it?"

"You don't want to know."

"Yes, I do."

"No, you don't."

"Shell!"

She wasn't laughing, but I could hear it in her voice anyway.

"Illinois law allows the governor to 'waive environmental and safety regulations applying to Verne technology when significant danger to civilian life is present.' He's extended that to a blanket waiver for emergency situations."

"Seriously? We can only *test* a new superheat-bomb when people are already in danger?"

"Adults, right?"

I covered my eyes. "We'll just have to hope the Green Man waits until everyone's back and we have more options."

"Um, we can hope..."

Outside the office, the lights in Dispatch went red and alarms began wailing. My insides turned to ice.

"The Green Man's heat-signature just showed up, didn't it?"

"Uh-huh."

The alarm didn't sound any better from the Dispatch floor. The big screen showed an aerial view of Monroe Harbor just off Queen's Landing with a thermal imaging overlay. Inside the harbor walls the water was heating up and turning into green *soup*.

Riptide. We could have dropped Riptide out there to tear apart any concentration of "Green Man" that formed — watch it try and regenerate from that. The missed opportunity made me want to cry.

"David, go to evacuation protocols. From the lake to the river." This time, the Green Man was coming for the *city*; through Grant Park and the Dome, across Michigan Avenue, right into the heart of the Loop. If we let it get that far. "And would you please get me the superintendent?"

"On it, boss."

"Thank you." I keyed the general Dispatch line while the chapters and sections of procedures Blackstone had been drilling me on marched through my mind like a troop of origami soldiers. "Mobilize all CAI teams and reserves. Sifu to join Crash and Sprints in clearing the park, pull all bystanders between us and the lake into the Dome. Tsuris to clear the water over and around the Green Man of morning sailors. Galatea to arm up and stand by. Megaton to report to the east doors and prepare to repel incoming green. CAI teams and reserves to assist in evacuation of the city and the defense of designated hold points."

I closed the line. "Shelly, from the previous attack, how long have we got before the attack begins? And is Blue Fire available?"

"She's still on the injured list and couldn't light a match right now, and we have less than five minutes, more than three — this is a wider green plume, so maybe five."

So no easy fix, but we had enough time to clear the park, maybe not all the boats. "Dispatch line for Safire, Red Robin, all other close fliers. First priority, join Tsuris and insure Monroe Harbor is cleared of bystanders. Get them to whatever Vulcan calls a safe distance."

The screen in front of me scrolled the visual confirmation of my order, tagged each flier's response. One, two, three, four, five close enough to be useful in the time we had. The town had a lot of flyers.

"I've got the superintendent," David said.

"Thank you. Screen here, please. Hello again, sir."

He didn't look any happier than earlier. "Hello again, Astra. I've seen the feed. Do you know the Green Man's target?"

"If we're lucky, sir, it's the Dome. But I don't think so."

He chewed his mustache, scowling ferociously. "Agreed. Do what you can to slow it down, and we are prepared to try and stop it east of Michigan Avenue."

I felt stupid; of *course* the CPD would have been working with the DSA to develop its own countermeasures.

"Understood, sir. Thank you."

"Thank *you*, and good luck." He cleared his screen and I took a long breath. Time to stop panicking instead of thinking.

"David, reroute all CAI heroes with green-effective powers to Grant Park. We need to hold the line here as long as we can."

"On it, boss."

How many more mistakes was I going to make?

Grendel

The concrete slabs breaking themselves on my back felt like styrofoam movie-set pieces — but now I had to decide: forward or back?

Back, a voice like wind-blown petals whispered in my head. Chakra? *Back, they are being attacked!*

I heaved my way out of the pile and into a nightmare — the Sentinels were fighting *shadows*, black holes in human shape. Too many moving too fast to count, they squeezed out of seams in the walls and threw themselves at the circled team.

"They're projections!" Lei Zi shouted when I pulled myself out of the rubble. "No restraint!"

They certainly weren't using any. The emergency lights dimmed as Lei Zi drew power and blew swarming shadow-figures apart with bright sparking explosions, Riptide pulled water from somewhere to *saw* pieces off them, and Seven and Artemis tapped them with syncopated center-of-mass shots while Variforce kept them back. Worked for me; I waded into the freezing, inky swirl of dancing, screaming phantoms and they were solid enough. Rush staggered by me in a blur, Cocytus over his shoulders in a fireman's carry and shadows hanging off them.

The things were so light they bounced away when I punched at them, so I flailed, grabbed, tore my way through the screaming, gibbering tide — not that the other guys needed much help; they made a ring of death around themselves and the shadows broke on it. I fought my way into the ring behind Rush and we moved back together, away from the blocking deadfall and back down the junction.

The shadows bled away before we'd retreated to the end, leaving the two dead guards, bone-white and frozen solid by the shadows. Watching the frost melting in their hair and from Cocytus, I realized I was growling, fangs growing; it was the stadium all over again — twisted breakthroughs tearing at each other, at everyone, no sides, no reason, just out-of-their-minds rage and killing.

Empty clips chimed on the floor as Artemis swapped in full clips, and she looked up at me, eyes shining from the skull-shaped half mask she wore. Most people at least got *careful* when my eyes went red and my fangs got so long I couldn't talk. The vampire didn't flinch.

"Easy, big guy. Remember: You're still human. It's a choice."

"Watchman is waiting," Lei Zi said. "Artemis, go see and report."

She holstered her guns and vanished into mist, flying ahead to disappear into the deadfall.

Lei Zi nodded, looked at me. "Grendel, can you clear the way? Watchman is engaged up there, or he would have come back."

I looked at the rubble. It wasn't quite floor-to-ceiling, which meant that it wasn't a complete structural collapse with all the tons of earth on top of it; moving it wasn't likely to bring the place down.

"Yes," I growled and turned away. Back up the corridor, I threw myself into the pile to toss concrete chunks aside and rip fallen support beams away. Artemis blew by me before I'd gone far, wet chilled fog in the air. Her transformation from sweeping mist to solid black-clad vamp was one of the weirdest things I'd ever seen, even after two years at Hillwood. "Watchman is engaging prisoners in some kind of equipment bay, and there's plenty of room to join in!" She disappeared again, and this time Riptide went with her in a spout of water.

"Nox?" I whispered.

"Her Highness directed that we be within fifty feet for the compass to scent our quarry. We are not yet."

I dug faster.

Megaton

I remembered closet-geek Tony telling me once that when the City of Chicago first sponsored the Sentinels, city planners wanted to build a tall shiny headquarters in one of the cratered and burned out properties in Miracle Mile. Blackstone, an ex-Marine, had *words* with them and instead we got the Dome — a low-slung bunker of a building in the middle of an open park away from other structures, with lots of open firing lines and avenues for fast civilian evacuation.

Except the civilians weren't evacuating, and I stopped at the east doors. I'd seen lots of crowds at games and rallies, and there had to be at least a couple hundred sign-waving protesters crowding the Columbus Drive side of the grounds. Mostly Humanity Firsters, they weren't staying off the grass and were doing a fist-pumping organized chant over the wailing alarms. I tapped my helmet, still uncomfortable with the whole earbug and Dispatch thing. With the helmet-cam, it was like having an invisible coach riding my shoulder.

"Dispatch, the crowd isn't moving. Some dude with a megaphone is trying to out-shout the sirens." He was doing a pretty good job too — something about masked thugs of the criminal state, and it even rhymed.

I got a long pause, then *Astra* responded. *"Confirmed, Megaton. Do not engage with the crowd in any way. You're getting backup."* Great. I could always get above the crowd, but didn't want to waste juice flying — it could be a long day, and the last Green Man fight had nearly tapped me out before we won. And what was Astra doing in the captain's chair? Wasn't that like Ensign Chekov commanding the *Enterprise*?

She was a nice kid, real nice, but we were so hosed.

Boots thumping in step broke the crowd noise and six black-armored and seriously armed security guards formed a line behind me in the door, assault rifles held to their chests and pointed down.

"Megaton?" Helmet One said (really, he had a big white '1' on his black helmet). "John Sikes. The lady tells us we're to keep you clear." They split, three to each side and I followed without thinking as they trooped out. The chant broke, the protest leader standing frozen at the sight of my faceless Stormtroopers of the Evil Empire, and Sikes stepped aside to snag his megaphone.

"Attention, citizens of Chicago. This area has been declared in a state of civil emergency, and in accordance with city ordinance you are required to vacate the area for your safety. Failure to do so may result in prosecution for interfering with city safety personnel, and the city and its employed contractors will not be liable for injury or loss of life. Have a nice day."

He tossed the megaphone back to the still-frozen dude and we moved out, pushing forward through the stunned crowd to the edge where I could see across Columbus Drive. I looked towards the fountain, but couldn't see it through the trees. My palms were slick inside my gloves and I tried to breathe evenly.

"This isn't your first dance, kid," Sikes said without looking at me. "You'll be fine." The others bracketed me in a box formation, facing out to the crowd.

I swallowed. "I didn't have time to think about it, before."

"Yup, that's the sucky part. Relax, you'll meet your dance partner soon enough."

Astra

"The crowd is not dispersing, ma'am."

The screens confirmed Sikes' assessment; the crowd was rhythmically working itself up again, nervously ignoring Megaton and his team. I'd completely forgotten about the protesters, *stupid* since there was always at least a dozen out there on any given morning.

I kept my voice steady. "Thank you, John, and they're not your problem. We're keeping the doors open, and when the green reaches Columbia Drive, you are to fall back into the Dome with any protesters who decide to take cover. You are not to try to herd the crowd but may assist at your discretion. Understood?"

"Fall back, no civilian direction, yes, ma'am."

I closed my eyes and breathed through my nose, counting. The headset David had handed me carried every open team link, dialed down to background conversation, and I felt like Megaton; I wanted to be out there, *doing*, so bad that I realized I was trying to fly — and wasn't even feeling any lighter.

"Park evacuation?" I asked David.

"Nearly complete, our speedsters are good."

"Harbor?"

"There aren't a lot of boaters this late in the year. Tsuris blew most of the boats up against the harbor walls and the other fliers have cleared almost everyone."

Clear faster. I didn't say it.

"David, please ask Ozma to proceed to the atrium and be ready to take our protesters in hand. Shelly — Galatea —are you ready to go?"

"I'm in the launch bay, locked and loaded." Despite everything, I had to smile. For once, she sounded serious, like this wasn't an adventure. On the screen, Green Man's heat signature edged into red. Any second now...

"Here he comes!" Shelly announced redundantly as the red wave exploded out of the harbor.

Chapter Thirty One: Grendel

"At 8:00 this morning, Detroit Supermax went silent. Director Kayle is mobilizing all local DSA assets to the prison, and residents of the surrounding neighborhoods are evacuating. The Detroit Guardians have entered the prison, as have the Chicago Sentinels. Detroit's deputy mayor has issued a statement calling for calm. 'We do not know anything about the situation inside, but at this time the Mayor has called for the mobilization of the DPD's SWAT units to the prison and authorized the use of deadly force to contain any breakouts.' All citizens are advised to remain off the streets and indoors."

MCTV public broadcast.

I was *supposed* to be the point of the freaking spear. I pushed us through the collapsed section in less than a minute, Variforce propping up the junk I left behind me, and then I ran, feet pounding the floor. Rush blurred ahead of me.

More guards were down in the equipment bay, blast-holes, *targets* — Dozer mixing it with Watchman, Riptide and Artemis dueling it out with Balz' whirling sphere cloud, Rush whipping through a crowd of laughing identical skinheads armed from some busted-open armory, more orange suits, some up, some down. Nearly all of them stopped to look at me.

Okay boys and girls, let's get acquainted.

I crouched, pulled up a wall-shaking roar that dropped into infrasound depths to shake their nerves and share that feeling of existential dread that unheard sound beats can give, pounded the floor with my fists, and *charged*. It's all in your presentation — some Hillwood students refused to spar against me at *all* after I opened with that, but I could deliver, too.

A few spheres smashed off me on my way through, and I hit Dozer like a train. Bonus, the wall behind the big guy was reinforced — concrete flew but the inner web of supporting bars held. His breath whistled out of him.

"Behind him!" Nox shrilled in my ear, shaken about but still on target. "The door! The door!" I grabbed Dozer's belt and the fancy blinking restraining collar that obviously wasn't doing its job and used him to batter down the closed hatch behind him. I had to swing him twice, but he didn't make it hard.

This *is the guy that beat on Astra?*

I followed Dozer through the buckled hatch, tossed him across the room at Twist. The Wrecker caught him in his snaking cables, dropped him while I whipped my head around as far as I could, checking the smaller space.

The room was a *lot* smaller than the equipment bay, with lower ceilings, and it was full of a railed steel platform with a steel chair in the middle. Twist wasn't alone. Behind him were two more armored Wreckers, one sitting in the chair, along with an old man — Dr. Pellegrini — and a bunch of orange-suited juvies. What the hell?

"Him!" Nox whispered harshly. He couldn't point, but I'd sort it out later. I roared again, shaking the room, charged — and froze, feeling like my whole body had gone to sleep.

What the *hell*?

Astra

"Rate of advance?" My mouth had gone completely dry, but it still worked.

David looked up. "The Green Man will reach the Dome in under two minutes."

"Is everyone in the park and harbor out of the hot zone?" Or what we *thought* was the hot zone, anyway.

"No. Maybe three minutes." I had no idea how he got *that*, but he'd been watching the screens for years — he'd probably tracked so many superhuman fights and emergencies he could feel the flow before reading a single stat.

I cleared my throat. "Dispatch, Mr. Sikes. Mr. Sikes, time to invite everyone in, we close the doors in two minutes. Dispatch, Megaton. Megaton, you're going to need to hold the green back from the Dome for at least one minute. Understood?"

"One minute, got it."

"Thank you. Shelly?"

"Yes, oh fearless leader?"

"Time to get in position, Shell. Good luck."

"Here we come to save the day, right?"

"Always." I hope.

On the main screen, her icon separated from the Dome, arcing towards the bay. I looked down at the screen in front of me; David had dedicated half of it to a display of the CPD's mobilization and bystander evacuation.

After spring's godzilla attack, the city had fast-tracked a review of its emergency procedures; this time was a *lot* different.

Superintendent Redmond had designated everything from Randolph to Roosevelt and from the lake to the Chicago River an evacuation zone. All traffic lights in the zone went to "exit" mode to stop all unauthorized incoming traffic and expedite outgoing traffic, and lights in the surrounding buffer zone redirected traffic away. Sirens on all street corners alerted pedestrians and announced the size of the zone. Radio, TV, even automatic cell-texts did the same as the emergency system seized control of the communications grid.

It wouldn't empty the Loop. Five minutes was hardly enough

time for that and not everyone *could* leave, but thousands would get out safe or get into shelters and the CPD would have more room to move.

"Look at that," David said, almost reverently.

The superintendent had obviously been thinking hard about the other Green Man attacks and Lake Michigan. David traced what looked like a pre-positioned string of chemical tanks, running along the entrenched train tracks that ran north to south just west of the Dome. The sunken tracks separated Michigan Avenue from Grant Park, and we could see they'd opened the tanks.

"They're going to — "

"Yep." David nodded approval as the tanks lit off and the spilling stuff turned the deep track bed into a burning *moat*. "And look." Where David tapped the screen I could see tanker trucks standing by on all the street overpasses, Jackson, Congress, Balboa, further out, with hoses ready. I crossed myself while David chuckled.

"Smart man," he said approvingly. "It might work. At least long enough. We need one minute, if we've got it."

One minute, and I couldn't do anything. And I shouldn't, I wouldn't... "Dispatch, Mrs. Corrigan please."

Since Mom wasn't part of the Dispatch circuit, I got a dial tone and two rings first, then "Hope? Where are you? How are you?"

I closed my eyes. "In the Dome, safe." Maybe. "Cook County Hospital is — Are you going to be able to move Toby?"

"Your father is carrying him out with me now," she said over the background chaos. I exhaled; they were on the other side of the river, they had plenty of time. I pictured Dad, gone Iron Jack and carrying Toby through the halls, bed and all. He would if he had to.

"Thanks, Mom." I glanced at David; he was intensely fascinated by whatever he saw on his screens. "Give everyone my love, I've got to go."

"I know, sweetheart. Be safe now."

On the main screen, the wave of green hit Columbus.

Megaton

I heard it before I saw it, a rolling storm of cracking, popping bangs louder than gunshots as the Green Man ripped across the park walks and through Buckingham Fountain. When the wall of green hit the yellowing trees across Columbus the screaming started. Stiles had pulled back, and *now* the protesters who'd decided we were bluffing panicked as erupting trees and vines threw concrete into the air like leaves in front of a blower. I made sure they were all behind me, pulled the heat up through my bones, and waited as pressure built under my skin.

"Astra?"

"Yes?"

"So, what's the downside to being a superhero?"

"Fanfic." I'd never heard her swear, but the way she said it sounded filthy. I laughed and let it all go, roaring out of me in a wide fan of heat and boiling light and sound.

Grendel

Freaking hell. One of the anonymous Wreckers had tightened up, almost mimicking my stance; I'd forgotten about Redback, but it looked like the Wreckers had brought him. Pellegrini'd gone white when I came through the hatch — at least I'd scared the son of a bitch — and now he relaxed, smiling.

"Step lively, everyone," he said to the kids with them. Juvies? He'd broken into Detroit Supermax to get a bunch of *kids*?

They scrambled onto the platform, watching me, and I couldn't *move*. There was no resistance — there wasn't *anything*. Pellegrini watched me with interest, like I was an experiment he found fascinating. He was the Ascendant, the LO Stadium Killer, he *had* to be, and I. Couldn't. *Move.*

"Thank you for returning Eric," Pellegrini said as Twist deposited the big guy on the platform. The old man smiled almost regretfully. "And I'm sorry we can't take you with us; certainly, you are one my grandest achievements. It's a pity your brothers and sisters proved so unstable — "

Nox launched himself from my shoulder, a blur in the air turning into solid and pissed-off doll. Pellegrini had time to reflexively flinch before Nox was on him, swarming up his suit-front. I felt a warm, fragrant wind that could only be Chakra pass through me from head to toe, driving out the numbness as she set me free.

Redback's eyes widened as I leaped, and then my claws were around his neck and I threw him to the floor, bounced him twice, heaved him at Twist, and lunged for the platform.

"Get us out of here!" Twist shouted while Pellegrini screamed and clutched at Nox as the doll went for his face. Silver light flared and Nox dropped to the platform, Pellegrini kicked him away as Twist wrapped his cables around Redback and then the room went *weird*, like I was looking at a funhouse infinity illusion. The platform rocketed away without moving an inch, and then it was gone like it had never been there at all.

Astra

"Sikes is keeping the doors open," David observed.

"I shouldn't have told him when to close up." Another mistake, and I made myself not cringe; a Platoon, John Sikes had been to hundreds more of these dances than I had. "Give Galatea permission to launch the instant the hot zone is clear, and please get me Superintendent Redmond." David had seen more dances, too, and I was trying to micromanage.

"Galatea launches at discretion, get Big Red. On it, boss."

I watched the screens. Megaton was holding the green on

Columbia and away from the Dome, and with such a wide arc of advance, the tide sweeping around the edges of his defense was flowing slowly enough that it looked like all the supporting capes would be able to get the last of the civilians out of the park as long as they had somewhere to run *to.*

"I've got the superintendent, boss. No video this time."

"Thank you. Hello, sir. We are going to attempt a solution to the Green Man momentarily. However, the park is still being evacuated; will you be able to keep the overpasses open?"

"We have designated escape lanes, Astra, but will close them when the Green Man reaches the tracks. The CAI teams are standing by in support."

I nodded, remembered he couldn't see me. "Thank you. We'll — " The thermal overlay on the main screen went white. The Dome sat on stabilizers and we *still* felt the shock. "Goodbye!" *Seriously? Goodbye?*

Around me, the background noise of a dozen exchanges cut as we all watched the screens. The images came back, but a white cloud completely obscured the aerial view of the harbor. The Dome view showed the wall of green had frozen all along the arc of Megaton's burn and the grounds west of us.

"Shelly?"

"Still here, dropped the full load on him. We'll know in a ... oh come on*!"*

The green tide stirred into motion again, and I felt dizzy as my skin went cold. Failed. We'd failed.

Okay, we blew it. So deal.

"Dispatch, Ozma. Ozma, please assist Sikes and Tom to lead all guests downstairs. David, please send all nonessential personnel below as well." The whole Dome was tough, but the lower levels could be sealed to ride out a nuclear strike. I tuned out the scraping and shuffling as half of the dispatchers handed off their tasks to CPD counterparts downtown and left their stations. My mind spun through useless options while my mouth switched to autopilot.

"Dispatch, all fliers to continue clearing the park and assist surrounding evac. Dispatch, Megaton. Megaton, how long can you hold the Green Man off the Dome?"

What could we do that we weren't doing? Could the CPD hold the line? What was I *missing*?

Megaton sounded like he'd been doing sprints. *"I have no freaking idea. What happened?"* David reconfigured the screen in front of me.

"The blast wasn't hot enough," I said, voice steady. "Heat density fell just short of the threshold needed to cook the soup."

"We've got nothing else? How much heat do you need? I think I can bring it."

I blinked.

Chapter Thirty Two: Megaton

A lot of people have asked "How could you do that?" Well, I was pissed off and it seemed like a good idea at the time.

Malcolm Scott, aka Megaton.

You'd think I'd started speaking in Martian. Astra made me repeat myself — and I didn't sound less crazy the second time — then told me to stand by. Yeah, like I was going anywhere; I felt like one big high-pressure hose, drawing whatever it was from wherever it came from to turn the ground in front of me into Hell's furnace. Tuning it hotter meant I wasn't just blasting the freaking mutant green wave back, I was throwing its burning bits into the green behind the front as I tracked my blasts up and down the line.

But I was already starting to feel hollowed out, whatever that meant.

"*Megaton,*" Astra finally came back. "*Galatea says your tests haven't found your limits yet but the numbers look good. But —* "

"But I can't get myself there while I'm pulling up the juice, and it's going to have to be one big bang. You'll have to drop me on it."

"*Yes. You don't have to do this.*"

"This is *our* freaking town — I'm sick of the Green Man's shit and he doesn't get to play here anymore."

"*... Galatea will deliver you to the target, Megaton, and drop on your word. Good luck.*"

My helmet ear-guards and my own blasting kept me from hearing Galatea until she was right on top of me. She cut her boot jets, landing like a cat (and I really had to learn how to do that).

"*Ready?*" she shouted, hands out. I looked back at the Dome to check the doors were sealed, stopped blasting, and we locked arms. She launched, and I found myself flying *backwards* over the waves of green as she took us to the harbor.

"*You know that you're completely insane, right?*"

"Really?" I worked on not letting go — my gloves helped me grip her silver chrome arms — and started pulling juice. How much could I pull and store? "I'd be in class right now except for this green freak, so just drop me when I say when and bug out."

As we swung out over the harbor I remembered the bus, the sick feeling that made me want to beat my head against a wall to stop the memories, to do anything to make it not happen. Mom hanging up on me, leaving Dad and me because I might hurt Sydney. The Green Man had wrecked my family and I poured on the hate, feeling the hot pressure build until it burned like nuclear fire under my skin and I clenched my teeth with the strain of holding it in. *More.*

Below us the boats against the harbor wall were tilted crazy angles beneath strangling green climbers, blackened and scarred by Galatea's attempt, and the still steaming water rolled with thick slime. The green screaming *face* looking up at me had to be my imagination, but it worked for me. Galatea brought us in low, which was a mistake — a vine shot up to grab my ankle and she almost torched me when our sudden stop jerked her around. *Now* it was paying attention to us? *Too late, sucker.*

"Get out now!" I yelled, and now she was the crazy one — she held on.

"*When you're ready, unless you can breathe pea soup!*"

The climbing vine thickened, squeezing like a python. Now? Now? The vine wrapped around my waist, pulling us down while Galatea tried to cook it with her rocket exhaust without flaming me. It started burning, but instead of letting go it twisted upward, climbing my arms, and locked us together.

Oh, shit.

She looked down at me, a smile quirking her shiny blue robot face. *"Now?"*

"Now. Payback's a bitch."

She cut her rockets and we dropped into the soup.

Astra

"Shelly!" I screamed when they fell. In the thinning steam cloud, she'd placed them perfectly; they dropped into the middle of the bay, the center of the Green Man's cauldron of life.

Megaton *exploded*, a flash that lit the room and whited out the screens. I blinked repeatedly, eyes full of after-image. *This* time the green went berserk, thrashing against the Dome.

"The doors are buckling," Sykes reported from the atrium.

"The CPD has fired the overpasses," David said without looking up from his screen.

"Is the park clear?" I whispered.

"Crash says yes."

"Dispatch, Safire. Safire, we are feeding you GPS tracking on Megaton's helmet. Please retrieve Megaton from Monroe Bay soonest, he may need medical attention."

"Get Megaton, on it. Astra, what the hell was that?"

"Megaton. Hurry, please. David? Green Man status? Expansion rate?"

"Zero."

"What?"

"Zero. That last crush was it. It didn't cross the tracks or break across the overpasses. Big Red's fire wall held."

"Thermal on the harbor?"

"Cooling fast — half the water in the harbor got turned to steam and it's getting refilled with cold Lake Michigan water." He wasn't exaggerating; the cleared screens showed half the harbor wall was just *gone*. What bits of boat I could see were on fire, and rising smoke and steam was obscuring drone visuals completely. And all the thermals were headed down as heat dissipated.

I blinked, sat down before I fell. "Is this a win?"

"This is a win. I'm sending Crash for Galatea. She has an internal GPS unit and transmitter in her skull, and we're pinging it. Location only, no response. Would you believe she's in the middle of Buckingham Fountain?"

"Wait — "

"Hey,A,I'vegotShellyandshe'samess. Vulcanshowedmehowto detachherhead inanemergency andI'mbringingherin."

I couldn't breathe, like someone had kicked me in the gut. Not Shell, not Shelly too. God couldn't be that unfair.

"Affirmative, Crash," I heard David say. "Vulcan will be waiting for you." He took off his headset, swiveled to face me. "Astra, everybody's where they should be and doing what they should be doing if the Green Man wakes up, but looking at the crater Megaton left, I'd say he's compost. And I can reach you in the Pit."

"But — "

"Quote: 'The Sentinel on watch may, on discretion, maintain oversight from anywhere in the Dome.' End damn quote."

I stared back at him, dizzy with the need to get to Shelly.

"Get out of here, Hope. We've got this."

I swallowed. "Please give Superintendent Redmond my compliments."

And I ran.

I hated the Pit, just being down there made my skin crawl, but I skidded through the door and into Vulcan's main lab. Crash had come and gone before I got there, and only Vulcan and Galatea 1.0 stood at his bench, examining a sphere with bits of skull-plate sticking to it.

She's modular. She's modular. As long as her brain is fine, she'll live.

"Vulcan?" He looked up. He always looked like he'd forgotten to feed himself, and now his thin face was pinched.

"Astra. It's all over? Crash didn't say."

"Yes. Shelly?"

"Her sphere is intact, but damaged." He shook his head, disgustedly shoving away a bundle of cable leads. "She's on independent power right now, her internal battery, but all of her input/output and power connections are gone, a combination of heat and feedback. With all sensory input cut ... she doesn't know what happened or what's happening."

"You can replace the connections, right?"

"Not in time. Not soon enough to recharge the damaged battery. The polymorphic neural net that supports Shelly's mind isn't just a collection of molecule-sized physical circuits — it's a carefully balanced field, really. The power that feeds the neural net has to be uninterrupted and modulated down to micro-current levels to sustain the field balance. When the battery dies..."

"Can't you get her out of there?"

He ran long fingers through his nest of flyaway hair.

"Download a copy of her current field configuration? No. Not without cracking the sphere open completely, which will collapse the field. Her neural net will return to a blank slate. Once I fix her battery and bring back power, we can restore her from her sleeping quantum-mirror self copy, but since she can't mirror her neural-net the way she did her original meat-brain, she hasn't been able to do 'backups.' She'll be the Shelly of last spring, when she first transferred herself into Galatea."

I wiped my cheeks, nodded. "Okay. Okay. Thank you. I'll need the lab to myself for a bit. Please."

"Okay," he echoed me. He wasn't good with *human* stuff, and his face twitched through a couple of aborted replies. "I'll leave Gal," he finally said. I waited for the doors to seal behind him before I sank to the floor by the bench.

"Are you well?" Galatea 1.0 asked politely.

I nodded; if I didn't, she'd call Dr. Beth. "She's dying."

"Vulcan is correct: she can be rebuilt."

But she won't remember our fight with Villains Inc. Or Annabeth's and Dane's engagement party, or her friendly crush on

Jamal, or her reunion with her mom. Or today. She'll be Shelly 3.0, not the Shell who just saved the city.

That Shell would be dead.

No. Not again. I pulled myself to my feet.

"Dispatch, Ozma's lab please. Nix? I'm down in the Pit, and I need you to bring me the Wishing Pill now."

"Really? Are you sure?"

"Yes."

While I waited, I carefully cleaned the scorched bits of wreck from Shelly's sphere. Was she dreaming in there? Waiting patiently in the silent black for input leads to restore her senses? Counting against an internal clock and watching her power die? She couldn't know I had to wipe tears off her chromed shell.

The doors slid open and Nix buzzed in. She clutched the marble-sized silver pill in her tiny hands, and flying close she dropped it in my open palm.

"Thank you."

She nodded, wide eyed, and flew back to perch on a free-standing drill or scope or widget that couldn't do anything useful right now.

The bigger the wish, the bigger the test, Ozma had said. Fixing a broken bone? Not much. Moving from one place to another? Probably even less. A chest full of gold? More, but probably manageable. Restoring a shattered, scattered body? Who knew? Ozma couldn't do it.

She didn't have Shell.

I swallowed the pill.

As big as it was, I almost choked but managed to force it down and it sat, cold in my stomach. I closed my eyes. Shelly alive. Shelly kicking the playground bully for me. Shelly laughing after skinning her knee doing a stupid somersault off a tree. Shelly planning our evening excursion to The Fortress to see the superheroes party. Shelly poring over superhero costume sketches, playing with Gray, yelling at Toby for being a jerk. I wished for Shelly as the cold pill in my stomach warmed, heated, turned to fire, turned to lightning, turned to boiling fusion that radiated up through my chest, out through my arms and legs. I wished for Shelly as my eyeballs boiled and my skin caught fire. I wished for Shelly as I screamed. I wished for Shelly.

"Hope? Hope, stop it!" Someone shook me, and I opened eyes I couldn't believe I still had. My throat burned, absolutely raw, and I wanted to vomit endlessly.

Nix crouched on my chest, crying, the widget she'd perched on a smashed wreck against the far wall. Except for my throat, the unbelievable pain was gone like a nightmare — I'd shattered my cast, but my shoulder felt like my fight with Dozer had happened weeks ago. Vulcan stared down at me. *Of course, he wouldn't have left the Pit.* He didn't let go until my frozen lungs unlocked and my stomach unclenched so I could inhale. I couldn't believe he'd had the nerve to come back in and grab me; strength back, I could have taken his head off without realizing it thrashing around.

I wanted to cry with Nix. My powers were back, but it hadn't worked. I hadn't been strong enough. Shelly was —

"Hope?"

Vulcan yelped as I sat up so fast I knocked him on his ass. Nix tumbled into my lap.

Shelly sat on the edge of the work table, wearing a blue denim miniskirt and white t-shirt with sparkly blue print that read *I killed myself origin chasing and all I got was this stupid t-shirt.* She swiped strands of wild red hair away from her face, stopped, grabbed her left hand in her right and squeezed her palm, eyes widening. Her head twisted around as if she was searching for something invisible, whipped back to me.

"Hope? Oh my God, Hope, what did you *do?*"

Chapter Thirty Three: Megaton

The moment of empowerment instantiated by a breakthrough presents the new superhuman with an immediate existential crisis, and this crisis remains long after the purely physical crisis which triggered the breakthrough is past. Granted life by her gift, small or great, how will she use what she has been given? Why does she have it? This "Why?" is a theological question for some, but atheists face it as well — indeed, the question is simply a more urgent form of the defining human question.

Dr. Alice Mendel, *Breakthroughs and the Crisis of Being*.

It's a good thing I'm more rugged and durable than I used to be — as it is I pretty much violated any warranty that might have been issued with my powers. *Don't boil water you're swimming in* had to be at the top of any list of Things Not To Do, but my natural heat resistance plus what Andrew built into my costume kept me from cooking; so instead I almost drowned before Safire fished me out.

My explosion hadn't been all heat; I'd thrown out enough concussive force to turn the boats left in Monroe Harbor into toothpicks *and* light them on fire. Safire flew me back to the Dome over the overgrown wreckage of Grant Park, and I didn't see any green moving — good thing since I was so emptied out I probably couldn't have pulled up a fart, forget about blastworthy action. The Green Man hadn't got past the CPD's fireline to Michigan Avenue, but everything from the lake shore to the line lay buried in green trees and vines — they'd climbed halfway up the Dome and the Atlas Memorial was just *gone*.

"Cleanup will be a complete bitch," Safire laughed, looking down. She held me in her arms like a baby and the woman did not wear push-ups; I felt like I was being smothered in latex-packed marshmallows.

Say something, you moron.

"Not my job, really."

"Nope," she agreed cheerfully. "It's the Crew's, and I can help, and Watchman and Astra — when her powers come back, poor kid. Lake Shore and Columbus are forestland now, but this is nothing like the Big One last January...there we go!" The roof opened over the Dome's launch bay and she dropped us in, through the bay, and down the shaft to Dispatch. We popped out onto the Dispatch floor under the big screens, and she swung me to my feet.

"Here you go, sugar! Gotta go clear some traffic, it's nuts. And congrats."

"Huh?" Real smart, but I was talking to myself — she was already gone, leaving me dripping on the carpet. So, what now? *Congrats?* That's when the clapping started. David stood up from behind his console and put his hands together hard as I stared around, and one by one every dispatcher, at every station, rose until the whole room had joined his applause.

What?

Grendel

How can you tell if a doll is *dead*? Lack of a pulse? I tucked Nox back under my vest and turned myself around, but the fight was over out in the equipment bay. Groaning orange suits lay all around and there were no spheres left in the air. The place smelled of ozone, probably from Lei Zi; the rest of the team had to have hit the scrum like an avalanche after I bulldozed through.

Lei Zi didn't even ask what was behind door number one, or wasn't anymore; Chakra had to be whispering into her brain like she had with me. She just tasked me with looming while they zip-tied or

Sandman-drugged or otherwise restrained all the orange suits still moving. Moving *carefully*; I growled a few times, flying on frustrated adrenaline and ready to play, but nobody in orange moved too energetically. A few minutes into the cleanup at least half the orange suits, the skinny bald clones, freaking *disappeared* and nobody else blinked. I wasn't going to open my mouth to ask.

Then the red flashing lights died and our Dispatch connections came back.

"We can stand down, everyone," Blackstone reported. *"The DSA team has been able to wrest control of the prison security system from Phreak, and between ourselves and the Detroit Guardians, we hold the prison. Good job, everybody."*

I dialed my fangs back as hatches opened and guards who'd been locked out of the blocks by the hijacked system flooded in. *Good job, my ass.* The Bad Guys had been bugging out when we got here — if I'd gone right for Drop first... But I hadn't seen him, had I?

And what did Pellegrini want with *kids*? At least Nox had tagged the son of a bitch — there'd been blood all over the little razor he'd pulled, and I hoped he'd scarred the mass-murdering bastard. I'd consider it a promise of things to come, monster to maker, and if Nox woke up I was going to buy him a harem of dolls. Or not, but I owed the little psycho a debt, and —

Across the room, Lei Zi clapped her hands for everyone's attention. Three words, *The Green Man*, and we were headed out as fast as we came in.

Astra

I'd never seen Dr. Beth *not* smiling before, even if it was only the "everything will be fine" smile the best doctors kept for scared patients. He wasn't smiling now.

Shelly kept closing her eyes, blinking, biting and licking her lips, feeling her arms and shifting her position on the examination table. Tremors shook her body every few minutes. Dr. Beth had cleared everyone else out of the infirmary, but for all she noticed me I might as well not have been there. Her hand was cold when I took it, and she jumped when he gently peeled a sensor from her shoulder.

"Well, Shelly, Hope has continued her custom of bringing me people who are suddenly breathing." He watched her like she was the deepest mystery he'd ever seen. She probably was.

"Twice isn't a custom," I protested weakly when Shell didn't say anything. I was starting to get scared.

"Perhaps, but I eagerly await the next occasion. Shelly, you are a perfectly healthy sixteen-year-old girl. I take it this is not welcome?"

"I can't *see*," she whispered, blinking. "I can't hear anything."

"That's not — " I started, but Dr. Beth snapped his fingers beside her head. She flinched.

"I imagine you feel you can't," he said kindly. "Your robot eyes could see into the infrared spectrum, like Hope's. And you could hear into the ultrasonic range. And all your links are gone, yes?" He tapped his forehead.

She nodded.

"And the rest?"

She slipped her hand from mine to hug herself. "I'm *naked*. I feel *everything*." A tear tracked down her face. "I'm stuck and I — " A convulsive breath brought another tremor. Dr. Beth nodded.

"Your world is suddenly very small and you feel every point where it touches you."

"Yes!" She swallowed. "I can taste my *mouth*."

"Everyone can, you've simply forgotten how to ignore it. But you'll remember. I prescribe rest, for now, and a quiet place with not much happening. Hope?"

I nodded and took her elbow. She slid off the table and came with me easily enough, and I wanted to scream.

I turned the indirect lighting in my rooms up as bright as I could as Shelly stretched out on my bed and tried not to move. She didn't react when I carefully sank down to sit on the end by her feet. I counted heartbeats, the most beautiful sound in the world, and remembered the day I first heard Jacky's. Father Nolan would draw some interesting observation from my having witnessed two resurrections. Except in both cases they hadn't been *dead* — just differently alive.

"You used the Wishing Pill, didn't you?" Shell whispered.

I nodded.

"Why couldn't you have just wished me *fixed*?"

I shook my head but kept my mouth shut.

"Why?"

"Because you can't wish for something you don't want. Not a true wish." She looked away, but since I'd started I had to finish. "I wished for you, Shell. Not you in a robot body or in my head or in a secret future computer CPU somewhere. I wished for you. I'm so, so sorry."

She wiped her eyes, sniffed. "My *nose* is running. God, I hate this." Sobs convulsed her like hiccups, and she folded in on herself. When I touched her ankle, she rolled over to my side and I pulled her into my arms.

"SuperPooh's around here somewhere if you want him," I whispered into her hair, and she laughed wetly.

"Cheater. That's not fair."

"Really?" the Shelly standing at the foot of the bed asked. "'Cause I could use him right now."

I screamed and almost crushed Shelly. "Sorry! Sorry!" I loosened my grip.

"What?" Shelly gasped.

I stared at the new Shelly. "You can't see her?"

"See *who*?"

"You! How — Oh. *Oh*." I wanted to laugh and cry at the same time.

"What? *What*?"

I glared at virtual Shelly. "Your quantum-mirror backup just arrived."

She nodded. "Woke up in the Teatime Anarchist's computer as soon as the signal from Galatea was completely lost. Well, it took me a little while to really wake up. Then I had to catch up on everything since last spring. Good to know the neural link in your head is still working. Hold on." She disappeared and the TV behind her turned on to show her grinning face. *Now* Shelly got it.

"Better?" New Shelly asked from the TV. "Hey, me."

I nodded, still trying to breathe right, but Shelly almost shrieked.

"Better? Seriously? *Seriously?*"

"Hey! No harm no foul! Remember the bio-seed we sent Hope to give to Mom and then chickened out on? Gulp it down, give it a few months to wind itself into your new meat-brain and bang! We're connected again."

My mouth dropped open so far Mom would have objected. Then the giggles started and I couldn't stop.

"Hope? Hope?" Eyes closed, I wasn't sure which Shelly was talking.

I'd made *two of them*.

Chapter Thirty Four: Astra

"Personally, I'd rather leave other people alone. But when someone comes round and bothers your neighbors, you've got to put your boots on."

John Chandler, *Atlas: The Last Interview.*

"Could anyone be more of a cowboy?"

Hope Corrigan, *Notes from A Life.*

The team got back three hours after they left, flying in over the ruined and wild forest that had been Grant Park. The Green Man had gone south almost as far as Roosevelt, trying to get around Superintendent Redmond's fire line and into the Loop, but focusing on the Dome had kept him from crossing Jackson north of us. All the heroes in Chicago couldn't have stopped him, but the CPD had held him long enough.

I handed Dispatch duty back to Blackstone the second I could, left Shelly to fight with herself (Chakra could referee), and flew out to help find and deliver everyone hurt to the designated aid stations. There'd been a few traffic accidents in the evacuation, mostly fender-benders, and injuries, people falling or being accidentally pushed down in stairwells and other tight spaces, but most people had helped each other.

I felt *great*; I'd forgotten how fast my powers let me bounce back from physical trauma. After flying hurt citizens around, I joined Watchman and Variforce to help clear around the Dome — the green had come within an inch of breaking through into the atrium before Megaton went off — until Blackstone sent me to represent the team at the press-conference staged by the mayor's office just before sunset.

I got to stand beside Superintendent Redmond and behind the mayor at the podium hastily set up on Congress Plaza. The frozen tide of green half-covering the battered Atlas Memorial just across the Congress Parkway bridges made a dramatic backdrop as the mayor thanked the CPD and all the heroes for saving the city; no details yet, just getting word out that the Green Man was dead (at least we hoped so and the city was willing to take our word for it so things could get back to normal). *"Hope?"* Shelly — which one? — whispered in my ear after the mayor read his short speech and started taking questions. *"Blackstone would like to see you in his office as soon as you can get away."*

My stomach sank, but I kept the smile on and shook hands with Big Red and the mayor (the newsies got some nice shots) before flying away.

Blackstone sat reading reports and watching a narrow-brimmed fedora sitting on the corner of his desk next to a megaphone. He smiled when I stepped through the open door.

"Astra," he greeted me cheerfully. "Good job today, my dear. We're going into an after-action meeting before we stand down tonight — not in depth, just catching everybody up — and I want you on my left at the table. It's a leadership thing, and we need to — "

"I — no."

I *never* interrupt, and he stopped, looked at me. He frowned. "And you need to sit down. Careful of the hat."

"What?" I sat and tucked up my costume skirt, wondering what he was talking about. He gave me a tired smile.

"Ozma assures me that tomorrow at sunrise it is going to turn back into a rather obnoxious protest leader, but I can't help feeling that if I bump it... You would think I'd be used to magic by now, but neither mine nor Chakra's is quite so *physically* spectacular. Do you have a problem with sitting at the front, my dear?"

"*Why?* After I screwed up so bad? You left me on watch and — The Green Man — I was all over the place! And Shelly..."

"I've watched the recordings, and you appeared to be quite on top of it."

"I didn't do anything but follow the book! If it wasn't for Megaton, the Green Man would have eaten the city!"

Blackstone put his hands together and regarded me over steepled fingers.

"Rule number one of winning, my dear, is to avoid fighting a stronger enemy. Rule number two is, when you *do* fight, avoid losing so badly that there won't be a rematch. The Green Man always picked the time, place, and objective, and if the entire team had been on hand this time, we *might* have been able to contain him again. I am convinced that he coordinated with the Wreckers to insure that we could *not* be here today.

"Perhaps I should not have gone to Detroit, today, but like you I believed that the Wreckers were involved, which meant we would likely face another communications blackout, which meant Chakra and I needed to be on the spot."

I slumped. "So I didn't even help you there, either — you already knew."

"I'd already seen the possibility, but that *is* my job. And I considered the possibility that the Green Man would attack while we were absent, because that's also my job. I'm afraid you are going to have to live with having been the Sentinel in charge of the successful defense of the city. I'm sure the blow to your reputation will be considerable."

"But — "

"Haven't you wondered, my dear, why I've been loading you down with studies, why I brought Watchman on the team, why Watchman doesn't split police-liaison duties with you now, why I've succumbed to Quin's blandishments and allowed a junior team, why I let you choose our new Young Sentinels?"

I shook my head, stopped. What had Seven said? *Thinking five steps ahead is his job, and I'm pretty sure he's always up to something.* The little hairs on the back of my neck felt electric, and my seat creaked before I loosened my grip.

"Why — What are you doing?"

He sighed, stood up. "Walk with me, Hope?"

He took me down to the Assembly Room, to the "trophy" wall with all its framed news clippings, magazine covers, publicity shots. He stopped in front of the oldest news photo of Atlas, in his cheesy first costume, the one that looked like Elvis Presley in a cape.

"You know," Blackstone said quietly. "John was only a few months younger than you were when he had his own breakthrough. You're not like him. John wandered up here from Texas, and Alex did what older brothers do — he knew a guy who knew a guy, and he got John a tryout job slinging bags around at the airport. Fresh from slinging hay bales on the ranch, he was all wiry muscle, restless energy, no idea what he wanted to do with his life besides see more of the world than Texas. But the Event — when he leaped into the sky and caught that plane — he knew what he was supposed to do with what he got, and *there* you're exactly alike."

He chuckled, surprising me.

"Took him a while to figure out *how*, though, and he thought the whole mask-and-cape thing was pretty ridiculous — especially since everyone knew who he was already. You've heard him talk about that, but it was Alex, the marketing and public relations expert, who convinced him that people would be less scared and the government would have a harder time locking up and experimenting on *superheroes* who had the public behind them. He still said he felt damned silly wearing the cape and answering to *Atlas*. But."

Blackstone always looked a little sad when he talked about John, but when he turned away from the wall there was a twinkle in his eye. A ghost of a smile played on his lips.

"This morning, you were just Hope Corrigan, no powers, on the injured list. When I left you in charge, the first thing you did was change into costume, mask and all. Why? Everyone knows who you are now, and you weren't flying off to save the day."

"I — " I had no idea. Why had I wasted time changing?

He nodded.

"The same thing happened to John. It became who he was, like a policeman's badge or a soldier's uniform. He became Atlas, and you've become Astra. It's not just a name you wear, anymore, and your mask doesn't hide you — it shows who you are. Your powers are back, and that is a very *good* thing. Chicago has its Astra back." He turned back to the wall and tapped a glossy picture of me flying over the city, taken last fall. It had been shot from the ground looking up and it caught me against the sky, laughing as I flew, Atlas alert and watchful, higher in the sky above me.

"But powers aren't enough, my dear, and strong as you are, you know you're hardly invulnerable. Even if you were, you can't be everywhere. You're just one more Atlas-type. But so was Atlas, and we need you to *be* Atlas."

Now I was *completely* lost. Virtual Shelly popped into existence beside me.

"He's leveling you up, dummy," she said, eyes rolling. Blackstone chuckled, touching his earbug before I asked.

"Shelly is correct, Hope. I've gotten you the toughest A Class trainer I could steal, and I *am* sorry for the bumps and bruises. I've made you *the* face of the Sentinels with our city's law enforcement." He smiled. "And since you don't have the seniority or experience to be leading the team in the field yet, I've given you a starter team."

Wait, what?

What what whaaaaaaaat?

I dropped into a conference chair, covered my eyes and tried to breathe normally.

"But I haven't *done* anything, yet!"

Blackstone started *laughing*.

"Dear God, Hope." He wiped his eyes. "What *haven't* you done? Forgetting all the cape stuff, *I* am alive today because of you. I allow you to choose your team, and you give Shelly her life back! You have a way to go, but you are not the scared little girl I met last September, and even then you were stunningly brave."

The smile dropped but the twinkle stayed in his eye.

"But you don't have ten years to 'level up,' Hope. Shelly knows this. More Ultra-Class threats will appear, the political situation will get more precarious as the threat level rises, and we *need* Atlas. He was a national figure, the iconic cape, a symbol worth more political and public capital than all the rest of us combined. We don't have him anymore, but he can have *heirs*." He waved at the wall, all of it, first group shot to the Times Funeral Edition.

"The Sentinels are heirs. The Young Sentinels will be the next generation of heirs. And you are his principal heir. You can close your mouth; we've talked about legacies before. I'm not saying you've earned it, it just worked out that way.

"So go clean up, briefing in an hour. The Green Man may be gone, but there will be others. We need to find out what Dr. Pellegrini and the Wreckers want with a bunch of young supervillains. We've got to formally introduce the Young Sentinels to the city — not that they haven't had a hell of an introduction already. And we've got the biggest cleanup job Chicago has seen since the Event. If you hurry, you may have time to see your family first, so get moving."

"C'mon!" Shelly echoed, laughing. "Vulcan and I have worked up a new Galatea-shell I can telepilot for the meeting, too! Awesome Girl and Power Chick ride!" Blackstone's deadpan, determinedly *serious* expression was too much, and I lost it completely to dissolve into helpless giggles.

Here we come to save the day...

Chapter Thirty Five: Astra

"Everyone is the center of their own story, and thinks that they know what is going on and that they have some control over the plot. The truth is that everyone has plans for you or plans that don't involve you, and really all you can do is choose what to do with what happens next."

Hope Corrigan, *Notes from A Life.*

Believe it or not, I enjoyed cleanup. For Watchman and Riptide and Variforce and me it meant two solid days of non-stop clearing, uprooting the trees that had shattered and covered Lake Shore and Columbus so that the Crew could lay passable roadway. Till they finished, Michigan Avenue would be a bumper-to-bumper nightmare. For the rest, there was already talk of leaving the new primeval forest more or less intact except around the Dome, filling in Monroe Harbor (which was half-choked and half-wrecked now anyway), and rebuilding the landscaped park and fountain on the new land.

Virtual Shelly picked up for Shell without a hitch, though she had to settle for tele-operating an older Galatea model. *Shelly* left the Dome to stay at my place while Mrs. H got everything settled for her, which was all good as far as I was concerned. She wasn't acting mad, or sad, or *Shelly*. She was still scaring me, and Mom would know what to do.

Blackstone used the cleanup days to pull together a detailed after-action briefing of the Green Man Attack. He gave us huge props for the way we handled it — they were going to give Megaton a medal for sure, at least, I hoped so — and saved his comments on my misuse of Tsuris for a private conversation.

He was right; I'd misused Tsuris for civilian rescue when I should have put him on holding back the green as soon as the other flyers arrived. When Vulcan's heat-bomb didn't do the job, he'd ignored my instruction for all fliers to assist with evacuating the park. Instead he dropped to the south end of Grant Park and used his ground-stripping winds to keep the Green Man from outflanking the CPD's fire moat. From the reports of his officers on the spot, Big Red pretty much concluded that Tsuris stopped the Green Man from tearing into the Loop south of Roosevelt before Megaton and Galatea blew him up.

But Blackstone also said, "Hope, when Charlie dances the foxtrot, you bring your moves — you don't sit it out trying to think of the best moves."

And he used the briefing to finally share the preliminary DSA analysis of the Detroit Breakout. Redback (obviously boosted to A Class or higher) "hijacked" the body of a prison officer to get inside, used codes provided by Phreak to hack the security system, and released Dozer from his hard-cell confinement. With the cell blocks locked down, Dozer cleared the room for Drop to teleport everyone else in on his nifty platform. They had plenty of time to free exactly the prisoners they wanted before we even got there, but they focused mostly on juvenile breakthroughs. Blackstone had no idea why Dr. Pellegrini wanted a bunch of kids, at least nothing he'd share, but it couldn't be good.

Three days after the attack, we got our first Young Sentinels team picture on the I Love Me wall; Powers Magazine took the picture for their next cover, all of us standing in front of the wrecked Atlas Memorial; Galatea, Crash, Megaton, Tsuris, Ozma, Grendel, me, clean and shiny in our best costumes. Nox and Nix rode Grendel's shoulders for the picture, and everyone behaved at the magazine-sponsored photo party for us and the Guardian teams (well, almost everyone — Tsuris hit on Safire and Blue Fire before Ozma shut him down by miming a hat).

And then I took off, the old-school way by taking the backdoor and *driving* home. Our security reported a few die-hard paparazzi lurking on our street, but Ozma stopped me on the way out of the Dome and handed me a small case which turned out to hold a stylish pair of nonprescription glasses. She'd inscribed *Anonymity Spectacles* inside the case in gold; apparently, so long as I didn't do something startling like strip naked or, more realistically, start flying, even my own family wouldn't recognize me when I put them on...

Magic is just weird, and on any other day just thinking about using *glasses* as a disguise would have had me in a fit of giggles. Shelly would have found it totally mock-worthy. She wasn't mocking anything right now.

The leaves had started to turn, tints of yellow and orange hinting at Oak Park's extravagant explosion of color to come. I parked down the street, just in case watchers might know the make and model of my car. I'd kissed Seven and driven away less than a week ago, but it felt like forever. Dad waited for me at the door, and he knew exactly what I needed.

"Where's Shell?" I whispered, finally pulling out of the hug.

"Your room, where else? Come see me and your mother when you're finished."

Sunlight turned the wood floor into warm gold and sparked off school trophies and pictures. I found Shelly on my bed with Graymalkin stretched out on her lap, his tail flipping gently. For Gray, any lap was cat-heaven. Shell looked up when the door creaked. Her eyes and nose were red, and it took me a moment to look down and see what she'd spread out on the bedspread.

The Christmas tin. Our notes, pictures, plastic jewelry, and her funeral memorial program, black and silver-gray. *"In Loving Memory."*

She'd never asked to see it.

"Hey," I said. "Mrs. H. says you guys are leaving tomorrow."

She nodded. Blackstone had pulled strings, gotten her a legal new identity: Shelly Hardt, and the only lie about it was her age — it bumped her birthdate up to match her sixteen real years — and her hair color (and she was going to change that).

"Nervous about meeting your new dad?"

Mr. Hardt sounded like a keeper; apparently he'd called Shell as soon as Mrs. H. dropped the news on him, refused to stop talking until she believed a surprise teenage daughter was what he'd always wanted. I was prepared to love him unconditionally for that.

Shell ran her fingers over the stiff parchment program.

I swallowed, pushed a drift of pictures aside, and carefully perched on the bed.

"Can you still taste your own spit?" That got a chopped laugh out of her, but she didn't look up again.

I'm sorry. I couldn't say it — I wasn't, really, I couldn't be. Not ever. But I couldn't say *nothing.*

"I talked to Vulcan. He says he's been working with Virtual Shell and once you've got the neural receiver grown he can tie you in through her so you can tele-operate a Galatea like you did the first time, before you moved yourself in permanently. Virtual Shell's not going to do that again. She said she's decided that living inside a titanium head where someone can shoot at you isn't the smartest thing to do after all and she's going to stay where the Anarchist hid her — "

"Shut up."

"So you can patrol with me all the way from Springfield, and you'll be back here and on the team as soon as you graduate — "

She flipped around so fast her hair whipped her face.

"Shut up. Dummy."

I wouldn't cry. I wouldn't. "Shell, please..."

"Dummy." She sniffed, pulled a sleeve over her wrist to wipe her nose. "I messed up. *I* did. I left you and Mom and... For three years! We couldn't last a *weekend* without each other, had to do summer camp together."

"Springfield isn't far, I can fly — "

"Like you'll have time *ever*. That's not — I mean — I broke us up. Shelly and Hope. Power Chick and Awesome Girl." She held up the program, shook it. "I missed *everything*, I wasn't *there* — "

"Shell — "

"Shut up!" Tears dripped off her chin. "I didn't know, it wasn't three years for me! I was gone and then I was back and I said 'Sorry!' and you said 'Okay!' but it *wasn't*, I was *gone* and you were...you had to..."

I scooted over, feeling lighter than I had in days, and pulled her head down to my shoulder. She pushed back, punched at my arms until she didn't have room.

"Shell — "

"I'm *sorryyyyy*." Her wail trailed off into wet hiccups against my neck.

"You're the dummy." I laughed, light-headed, happy enough to sing. "I forgave you before the funeral. It took a while, but I learned how to last the weekend. You're just figuring this out now?"

"It'll be three years!"

I couldn't help the giggles. "It won't be the same. There's calling and texting and — again — you're going to be back piloting a Galatea, though Mrs. H will probably limit your hours during the week... She never let you play videogames that much!"

Finally she laughed, a real laugh this time even if it was a bit soggy. Gray protested, pulling himself out of her lap to stalk off with the offended air only cats can manage. I shook her gently.

"So, sleepover? You're not leaving till tomorrow, and you are *not* going back to the Dome tonight — Virtual You can't keep her mouth shut and both of you together would make heads explode. I'll bet we can get Mom to make funnel cake..."

"Deal. Game night?"

"Sure. And it's Shelly and Hope always, so no more tall buildings, right? Ever."

"Deal."

"Best friends forever."

Epilogue

Of course it never ends. You just sweep up and move on.

Toby got out of the hospital and came home to get better (I think Chakra had something to do with how fast he went from Critical Condition to healthy enough to release). Having him back home wasn't fun *but — shock — he didn't blame me for what had happened. Which didn't mean we were going to bond over it.*

Jacky stayed around and took Acacia "hunting," and three nights after the Green Man attack, the five goons who beat Toby half to death turned themselves in. According to Fisher, they gave full confessions and even provided enough physical evidence to make it an open and shut case. He said it had been a beating-of-opportunity; one of them had been at a bar popular with college students out slumming, heard Toby fight with his drinking buddies over the coolness that is me, and called up some friends when he stupidly decided to blow off his buddies and walk back to the dorms alone. The idiot.

The goons never said why they suddenly decided prison was safer than the streets, and I was never, ever, *going to ask Jacky about it.*

With the Green Man dealt with and the Wreckers out of our jurisdiction, we shifted to crime-fighter mode with the Guardian teams to get a lid on the goon and supervillain violence. It kept me busy, but Blackstone hadn't been kidding about moving me up —

team leader meant more than a token hat, and orienteering and training was another full-time job.

We managed to dodge the bullet with Grendel. The DSA had no interest in complicating things for us, and since the details of the Detroit Supermax Breakout were sealed — and almost completely unrecorded due to Phreak's blackout — we were able to suppress his part in the fight completely. Of course it wouldn't stick, but it would at least get us to Brian's eighteenth birthday.

And of course Shankman started making noises again as soon as he was strong enough to get in front of a microphone, calling for new laws restricting power use (like supervillains would pay attention to that). Humanity First endorsed his campaign, but at least Mal's dad was out of that. Mr. Scott joined the local Families with Breakthroughs organization along with Mom and Dad. Now that I was public, Mom could make the FWB a new favorite cause (she would probably make me show up at a meeting and talk).

And Sunday I went to St. Chris' memorial mass. It took everything I had not to hide behind the Anonymity Specs, but I sat with Mom and Dad and the Bees and remembered the names and prayed for their families as we all held candles. Sure I got a few stares (and I was going to be dealing with some almost hysterically excited kids after the mass), but I could feel the people who'd known me all my life closing ranks around me. Family. And as Father Nolan led the Prayer of the Faithful even Virtual Shelly joined in, a blythe and solemn spirit at the altar. Only I heard her echoing "Lord, hear our prayer."

Amen.

ABOUT THE AUTHOR

Marion G. Harmon (Marion for his great-grandfather, George for his father), is a former financial advisor and sometime bagpipe player living in Las Vegas. *Wearing the Cape* was his first novel, quickly followed by *Villains Inc.* and *Bite Me: Big Easy Nights*. *Young Sentinels* is his fourth book, and he thought his fifth book would be something completely different. Unfortunately, the idea for the next Astra adventure, *Girl's Night*, came to him before he could commit to something else.